高一同學的目標

1. 「用會話背7000字①」書+ CD 280元

以三個極短句為一組的方式，讓同學背了會話，同時快速增加單字。高一同學要從「國中常用2000字」挑戰「高中常用7000字」，加強單字是第一目標。

2. 「一分鐘背9個單字」書+ CD 280元

利用字首、字尾的排列，讓你快速增加單字。一次背9個比背1個字簡單。

3. rival

rival⁵ ('raɪvl̩) n. 對手
arrival³ (ə'raɪvl̩) n. 到達
festival² ('fɛstəvl̩) n. 節日；慶祝活動
} 都有 rival

revival⁶ (rɪ'vaɪvl̩) n. 復甦
survival³ (sə'vaɪvl̩) n. 生還
carnival⁶ ('kɑrnəvl̩) n. 嘉年華會
} 字人

carnation⁵ (kɑr'neʃən) n. 康乃馨
donation⁶ (do'neʃən) n. 捐贈
donate⁶ ('donet) v. 捐贈
} nation

3. 「一口氣考試英語」書+ CD 280元

把大學入學考試題目編成會話，背了以後，會說英語，又會考試。

例如：

What a nice surprise! (真令人驚喜！) 【常考】
I can't believe my eyes.
(我無法相信我的眼睛。)
Little did I dream of seeing you here.
(做夢也沒想到會在這裡看到你。)【駒澤大】

4.「一口氣背文法」書+ CD 280元

英文文法範圍無限大，規則無限多，誰背得完？
劉毅老師把文法整體的概念，編成216句，背完
了會做文法題、會說英語，也會寫作文。既是一
本文法書，也是一本會話書。

1. 現在簡單式的用法

I *get up* early every day.	我每天早起。
I *understand* this rule now.	我現在了解這條規定了。
Actions *speak* louder than words.	行動勝於言辭。

【二、三句強調實踐早起】

5.「高中英語聽力測驗①」書+ MP3 280元

6.「高中英語聽力測驗進階」書+ MP3 280元

高一月期考聽力佔20%，我們根據大考中心公布的
聽力題型編輯而成。

7.「高一月期考英文試題」書 280元

收集建中、北一女、師大附中、中山、成功、景
美女中等各校試題，並聘請各校名師編寫模擬試
題。

8.「高一英文克漏字測驗」書 180元

9.「高一英文閱讀測驗」書 180元

全部取材自高一月期考試題，英雄
所見略同，重複出現的機率很高。
附有翻譯及詳解，不必查字典，對
錯答案都有明確交待，做完題目，
一看就懂。

高二同學的目標——提早準備考大學

1. 「用會話背7000字①②」
   書+CD，每冊280元

「用會話背7000字」能夠解決所有學英文的困難。高二同學可先從第一冊開始背，第一冊和第二冊沒有程度上的差異，背得越多，單字量越多，在腦海中的短句越多。每一個極短句大多不超過5個字，1個字或2個字都可以成一個句子，如：「用會話背7000字①」p.184，每一句都2個字，好背得不得了，而且與生活息息相關，是每個人都必須知道的知識，例如：成功的祕訣是什麼？

11. What are the keys to success?

Be *ambitious*.	要有<u>雄心</u>。
Be *confident*.	要有<u>信心</u>。
Have *determination*.	要有<u>決心</u>。
Be *patient*.	要有<u>耐心</u>。
Be *persistent*.	要有<u>恆心</u>。
Show *sincerity*.	要有<u>誠心</u>。
Be *charitable*.	要有<u>愛心</u>。
Be *modest*.	要<u>虛心</u>。
Have *devotion*.	要<u>專心</u>。

當你背單字的時候，就要有「雄心」，要「決心」背好，對自己要有「信心」，一定要有「耐心」和「恆心」，背書時要「專心」。

背完後，腦中有2,160個句子，那不得了，無限多的排列組合，可以寫作文。有了單字，翻譯、閱讀測驗、克漏字都難不倒你了。高二的時候，要下定決心，把7000字背熟、背爛。雖然高中課本以7000字為範圍，編書者為了便宜行事，往往超出7000字，同學背了少用的單字，反倒忽略真正重要的單字。千萬記住，背就要背「高中常用7000字」，背完之後，天不怕、地不怕，任何考試都難不倒你。

2.「時速破百單字快速記憶」書 250元

字尾是 try，重音在倒數第三音節上

entry³ ('ɛntrɪ) n. 進入【No entry. 禁止進入。】
country¹ ('kʌntrɪ) n. 國家；鄉下【ou 讀 /ʌ/，為例外字】
ministry⁴ ('mɪnɪstrɪ) n. 部【mini = small】

chemistry⁴ ('kɛmɪstrɪ) n. 化學
geometry⁵ (dʒɪ'ɑmətrɪ) n. 幾何學【geo 土地，metry 測量】
industry² ('ɪndəstrɪ) n. 工業；勤勉【這個字重音常唸錯】

poetry¹ ('po·ɪtrɪ) n. 詩
poultry⁴ ('poltrɪ) n. 家禽 ｝字尾 y 表「集合名詞」
pastry⁵ ('pestrɪ) n. 糕餅

3.「高二英文克漏字測驗」書 180元

4.「高二英文閱讀測驗」書 180元
全部選自各校高二月期考試題精華，英雄所見略
同，再出現的機率很高。

5.「7000字學測試題詳解」書 250元
一般模考題為了便宜行事，往往超出7000字範圍
，無論做多少份試題，仍有大量生字，無法進
步。唯有鎖定7000字為範圍的試題，才會對準備
考試有幫助。每份試題都經「劉毅英文」同學實
際考過，效果奇佳。附有詳細解答，單字標明級
數，對錯答案都有明確交待，不需要再查字典，
做完題目，再看詳解，快樂無比。

6.「高中常用7000字解析【豪華版】」書 390元
按照「大考中心高中英文參考詞彙表」編輯而成
。難背的單字有「記憶技巧」、「同義字」及
「反義字」，關鍵的單字有「典型考題」。大學
入學考試核心單字，以紅色標記。

7.「高中7000字測驗題庫」書 180元
取材自大規模考試，解答詳盡，節省查字典的時間。

背了不忘記，才能累積！

背單字是學英文的第一步，背了會忘記，是增加單字量的最大障礙。利用「字根」背單字，能夠舉一反三，但是還是會忘記。

「一口氣背單字」以字根為核心，三字為一組，只要加快速度，就能變成直覺，終生不會忘記；唯有不忘記，才能累積，否則背到後面，前面的忘掉，就徒勞無功了。

背單字的時候，要連中文一起背。如：pose 擺姿勢，oppose 反對，suppose 猜想，中英文一起背，速度更快。只要會背字根為 pose 的 12 個單字，快到變成直覺，其它背起來就簡單了。

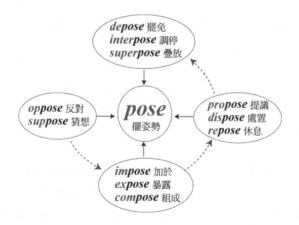

第一個目標，先背 12 個單字的中英文（**10 秒內背完**）；
第二個目標，背 72 個單字的中英文（**1 分 30 秒內背完**）；
第三個目標，背 20 組字根單字的中英文。

每一個英文單字，往往有很多個意思，例如：impose，字中的 im 表示 on，而 pose 等於 put，「放在上面」，一般人都知道作「加於」解，如果你背了這個字的衍生字 imposter〔ɪmˋpɑstə〕n. 騙子；冒充者，你才會知道，impose 還可當「欺騙」講。

　　這樣看起來，如果不把和字根 pose 有關的單字一次背完，英文單字永遠學不會，何況英文單字有 171,476 個，許多少用的單字，連美國本土人都不知道。

　　「一口氣背單字」還有一個優點，就是不需要背拼字，每個字以「字根」為主軸，一背一長串，字首、字尾都大同小異，換一個字根，就可能造出新的字。這是繼「一口氣英語會話」、「一口氣英語演講」後，又一大的發明。

　　本書的 CD，每個單字由美籍播音員先唸兩次，中文唸一次，目的是聽了英文就能直接想到中文；再以正常速度，每一回單字全部唸一遍，每三個字停頓一下；接著加快速度，每一回單字不間斷地唸一遍。讀者只要聽 CD，跟著背誦，很快就能夠變成直覺，終生不忘。

　　背單字是一項挑戰，編者研究英語教學 40 年，認為這絕對是全世界最有效的方法。背完之後，一定要把這個絕招與朋友共享，把這個方法傳出去，解決人類學英文的痛苦。

劉毅

爲什麼要改名爲「一口氣背單字」？

原先「一口氣英單字」出版後即暢銷，榮獲 2010 年 7 月 25 日「金石堂網路書店暢銷排行榜第一名」，讀者反應非常良好，大家都認爲這是一本背單字的好書。但是，我們研究發現，背誦方法要改變，要中英文一起背，才更有效果，因此我們將「一口氣英單字」改名爲「一口氣背單字」，讓讀者知道這個背單字方法的驚人發現。

背單字最大的困難，就是背了會忘。「一口氣背單字」第一個目標是背字根爲 pose 的 72 個單字，pose 這一組背完，其他字根就簡單了。「一口氣背單字」的最新方法，就是要連中文一起背。你可以：①背全部英文。②英文唸兩遍，中文唸一遍。③中文和英文一起背。

pose 擺姿勢	propose 提議
oppose 反對	dispose 處置
suppose 猜想	repose 休息
impose 加於	depose 罷免
expose 暴露	interpose 調停
compose 組成	superpose 疊放

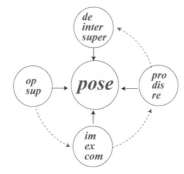

所有「一口氣背單字」的主軸，其他字根也類似。

背的時候，要背 pose 擺姿勢，oppose 反對…，目標是中英文能一起背下來，加快速度，變成直覺。背完之後，腦筋非常清楚。像 compose 是「組成」，背到後面，composer「作曲家」，composition「作文」，composure「鎮靜」，你就會發現，**compose** 除了「組成」以外，還有「作曲」、「寫作」和「使鎮靜」的意思。

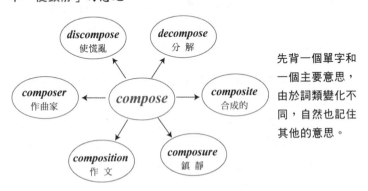

先背一個單字和一個主要意思，由於詞類變化不同，自然也記住其他的意思。

當你背到　de¦compose（分解），
　　　　　away¦　組成

　　　　　dis¦compose（使慌亂），
　　　　　not¦　使鎮靜

你便永遠不會忘記 compose 除了「組成」等意思之外，還有「使鎮靜」的意思。你對 compose 的了解，比一般字典還厲害。

　英文單字永遠背不完，但是背了字根為 pose 這一組單字後，再背其他的單字，就能舉一反三。只要熟背 20 組字根的單字，你的英文實力無人能比。背單字要下狠功夫，唯有背了不忘，才能累積。「一口氣背單字」不需要背拼字，直接背英文和中文，你試試看，絕對做得到。

劉　毅

「一口氣背單字」要連中文一起背

　　「一口氣背單字」以「字根」爲核心，經過特殊編排，押韻好記，易於背誦。依照下列的方式，並加快速度，便可終生不忘。

Step 1. 先背「字根」與「核心單字」

　　以字根爲核心，先將核心單字，分析理解，並以三字一組的方式反覆背誦，配合圖形增加印象，依照順序加強記憶，使核心單字進入大腦的長期記憶中。

字根 pose 的意思是 put「放置」

<u>pose</u> 〔 poz 〕 *v.* 擺姿勢

<u>op¦pose</u> 〔 ə'poz 〕 *v.* 反對
against¦put　【放在相反的位置，即是「反對」】

<u>sup¦pose</u> 〔 sə'poz 〕 *v.* 猜想；以爲
under¦put　【放在心裡面，即是「猜想；以爲」】

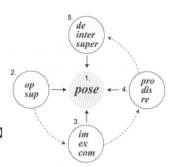

Step 2. 再背「字根本身的衍生字」

　　以字根爲主的衍生字，拆解字根與字尾，了解字義與詞性，並依照順序，三字一組，九字一段的方式背誦，配合圖形增加印象。

<u>post</u> 〔 post 〕 *n.* 郵政
　　【post 是 pose 的衍生字，
　　　從前郵局是重要的位置】

<u>post¦al</u> 〔'postl̩ 〕 *adj.* 郵政的
郵政¦*adj.*

<u>post¦age</u> 〔'postɪdʒ 〕 *n.* 郵資
郵政¦ *n.*

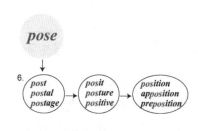

Step 3. 接著再背「核心單字的衍生字」

以核心單字為主的衍生字，拆解字首、字根與字尾，了解字義與詞性，經過特殊編排，配合背誦技巧，好唸好記，再配合圖形增加印象。

<u>op pos ition</u> *n.* 反對
against put *n.*

<u>op pos ition al</u> *adj.* 反對的
against put *n.* *adj.*

<u>op pos ite</u> *adj.* 相反的　*n.* 相反
against put *adj.,n.*

7.
opposition
oppositional
opposite

op
sup → pose

* 這三個字為 oppose「反對」的衍生字，故字義皆與「反對；相反」有關，並且三個字的字首 o，都讀 /ɑ/ 的音。

Step 4. 融會貫通

將所有單字依照順序反覆背誦，並配合圖形幫助記憶。書中每一個單元均附有「中英文背誦表」，可影印下來，隨身攜帶，利用零碎時間，將單字唸熟、記熟。

Step 5. 加快速度，終生不忘

將已背熟的單字，不斷地快速背誦 **100** 次，把短期記憶的單字變成直覺，不必想即可唸出，就變成長期記憶，終生不忘記。背完一回，你就自然想背下一回，不知不覺就會背好多回，越背越有成就感。

「一口氣背單字」背誦順序

本資料是精心編排，請一定要按照Group 1、Group 2 …
等的秩序背誦，先背每個字根的核心字，背到變成直
覺後，再背其他衍生字，不要急，會愈背愈快。

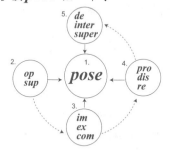

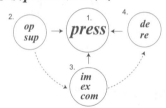

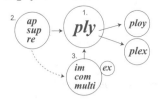

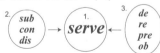

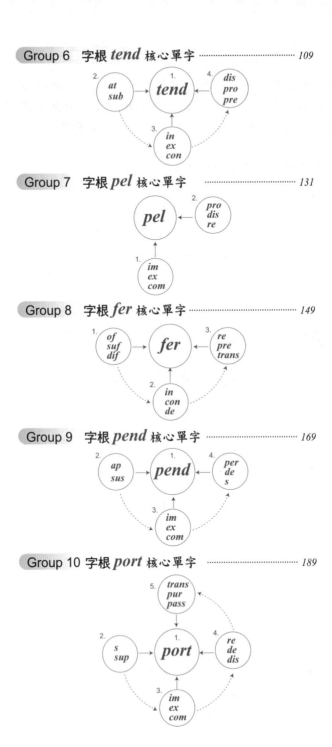

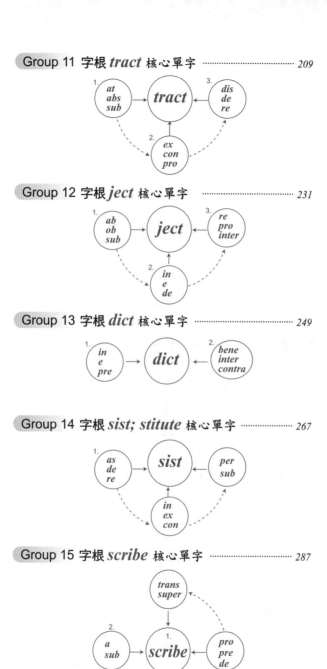

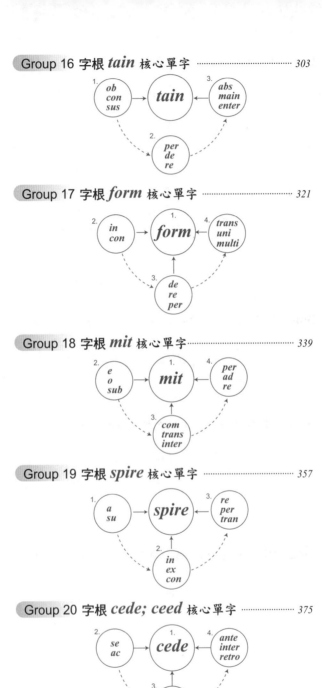

Group 1 字 根 *pose*

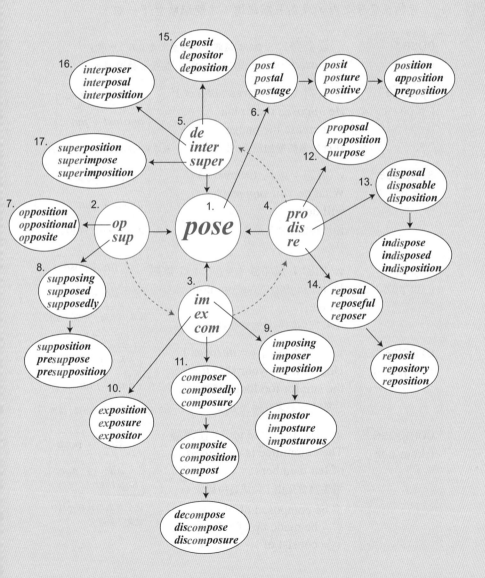

字根 pose

1. 字根 *pose* 核心單字

用手機掃瞄聽錄音

　　這 12 個單字，三個一組，一起背，可先背 6 個，再背 6 個，背熟至 7 秒之內，成為長期記憶，才能繼續背下一組。

pose[2]
〔 poz 〕

v. 擺姿勢　　pose 這個字根的意思是 put「放置」
He *posed* for the photograph. 他擺姿勢拍照。

oppose[4]
〔 ə'poz 〕

v. 反對（ = *disagree* ; *object* ）
He *opposed* their plan
to increase the budget.
他反對他們增加預算的計劃。

$$
\begin{array}{c}
\text{op} + \text{pose} \\
| \qquad | \\
against + put
\end{array}
$$

放在相反的位置，即是「反對」

suppose[3]
〔 sə'poz 〕

v. 猜想；以為（ = *guess* ）
What do you *suppose* he
will do?
你以為他會做什麼？

$$
\begin{array}{c}
\text{sup} + \text{pose} \\
| \qquad | \\
under + put
\end{array}
$$

放在心裡面，即是「猜想；以為」

impose[5]
〔 ɪm'poz 〕

v. 加於；強加於（ = *force* ）；欺騙
Don't *impose* your opinion
on me.
不要把你的意見強加在我身上。

$$
\begin{array}{c}
\text{im} + \text{pose} \\
| \qquad | \\
on + put
\end{array}
$$

放在…上面，即是「加於」
（ = *put…on* ）

expose[4]
〔 ɪk'spoz 〕

v. 暴露；揭露（ = *uncover* ）
Don't *expose* your skin to
the sun for too long. 不要把
你的皮膚暴露在陽光下太久。

$$
\begin{array}{c}
\text{ex} + \text{pose} \\
| \qquad | \\
out + put
\end{array}
$$

放在外面，即是「暴露；揭露」

compose[4]
〔 kəm'poz 〕

v. 組成（ = *make up* ）；使鎮靜
The committee is *composed*
of ten members.
這委員會是由十位成員所組成。

$$
\begin{array}{c}
\text{com} + \text{pose} \\
| \qquad | \\
all + put \\
together
\end{array}
$$

把全部東西放在一起，
就是「組成」

$$
\left\{
\begin{array}{l}
\text{be composed of　由…組成} \\
= \text{be made up of} \\
= \text{consist of}
\end{array}
\right.
$$

字根 pose

propose[2]
〔 prə'poz 〕

v. 提議 (= *put forward*)
David *proposed* a plan but
it was opposed by others.
大衛提出一項計劃，但受到其
他人反對。

```
pro    + pose
 |        |
forward + put
```
往前放，即是「提議」

dispose[5]
〔 dɪ'spoz 〕

v. 處置 (= *arrange*)
Be careful when you *dispose*
of broken glass.
當你處理破掉的玻璃時要小心。

```
dis    + pose
 |        |
apart + put
```
分開放，即是「處置」

repose
〔 rɪ'poz 〕

v. 休息 (= *rest*)
I will *repose* under that
tree.
我將在那棵樹下休息。

```
re    + pose
 |       |
back + put
```
放回去，就是「休息」

depose
〔 dɪ'poz 〕

v. 罷免 (= *remove from office*)
The king was *deposed* by the
revolution.
國王因革命被罷免。

```
de    + pose
 |       |
away + put
down
```
把你的職位拿走，叫你下台，
即是「罷免」

interpose
〔 ͵ɪntə'poz 〕

v. 插入；調停 (= *insert* ; *intervene*)
The father *interposed* in the
dispute of the brothers.
這位父親爲兄弟間的爭吵調停。

```
inter    + pose
  |         |
between + put
```
放在二者之間，即是「插入；調停」

superpose
〔 ͵supə'poz 〕

v. 疊放 (= *place on top of another*)
He used one hand to *superpose*
the other.
他將一隻手疊放在另一隻手上。

```
super   + pose
  |        |
above + put
```
放在～的上面，即是「疊放」

2. *post-postal-postage*

這一回有 18 個單字，分成二組來背，先背 9 個，再背 9 個，
必須背至 10 秒之內，變成直覺。

字根 pose

post²
〔 post 〕

n. 郵政 (= *mail*)
post 是由 pose 衍生出來的字，從前郵局是重要的位置。
He went to the *post* office to send a parcel.
他去郵局寄包裹。

postal
〔ˈpostḷ〕

adj. 郵政的 (= *relating to post*)
Mr. Smith works in the *postal*
service.
史密斯先生在郵政機關工作。

post + al
|　　　|
郵政 + *adj.*

postage³
〔ˈpostɪdʒ〕

n. 郵資 (= *postal charge*)
What is the *postage* for this
parcel?
這個包裹郵資多少錢？

post + age
|　　　|
郵政 + *n.*

posit
〔ˈpɑzɪt〕

v. 假定 (= *assume*)
Let's *posit* that everybody
already knows about it.
讓我們假定，每個人都已經
知道這件事。

posit 是 pose 的變體，
表示 put，放在某種狀
態，即是「假定」。

posture⁶
〔ˈpɑstʃɚ〕

n. 姿態 (= *body position*)
She posed for the portrait
in a sitting *posture*.
她擺出坐姿畫肖像。

post + ure
|　　　|
put + *n.*

把自己放在一種「姿態」上

positive²
〔ˈpɑzətɪv〕

adj. 肯定的 (= *sure* ; *certain*)
I'm *positive* about it.
這件事我很肯定。

posit + ive
|　　　|
put + *adj.*

position[1]
〔pəˈzɪʃən〕

n. 位置（= *location*）
Can you find our *position* on
the map? 你可以在地圖上找到
我們的位置嗎？

posit ＋ ion
｜　　　｜
put ＋ *n.*

「放」的地方即是「位置」

apposition
〔͵æpəˈzɪʃən〕

n.（文法）同位語
When I say "my friend Sue," my friend and
Sue are in *apposition.*
當我說「我的朋友蘇」，我的
朋友和蘇是同位語關係。

ap ＋ posit ＋ ion
｜　　　｜　　　｜
to ＋ *put* ＋ *n.*

把 A 並列在 B 旁邊，即爲「同位語」

preposition[4]
〔͵prɛpəˈzɪʃən〕

n. 介系詞
In the phrase "the window in the room," "in"
is a *preposition.*
在 "the window in the room"
這個片語中，"in" 是介系詞。

pre ＋ posit ＋ ion
｜　　　｜　　　｜
before ＋ *put* ＋ *n.*

「介系詞」要放在名詞之前

【背誦祕訣】

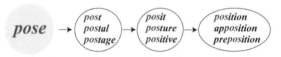

pose → post / postal / postage → posit / posture / positive → position / apposition / preposition

字根 pose 衍生出九個字，按照以下的背誦順序和要
訣，你馬上就背得起來。

{ post
  postal
  postage }　記住這三個字，都是 /o/ 的發音，背起來
　　　　　　就容易了。

{ posit
  posture
  positive }　記住這三個字，都是 /ɑ/ 的發音，背起來
　　　　　　就容易了。

{ position
  apposition
  preposition }　只要背了 position 的發音，背起來就容易了，要
　　　　　　　注意：apposition 中的 a，讀 /æ/，preposition
　　　　　　　中的 pre，唸成 /prɛ/，都是次重音。

字根 pose

opposition[6]
〔͵ɑpə′zɪʃən 〕

n. 反對 (= *disapproval*)
The plan met with strong *opposition*.
這個計劃遭到強烈反對。

op	+ pos	+ ition
against	+ *put*	+ *n.*

oppositional
〔͵ɑpə′zɪʃənḷ 〕

adj. 反對的 (= *opposing*)
The earth and the moon are kept from colliding by the *oppositional* force of gravity.
地球和月球因為有對抗的引力，而不會撞在一起。

opposite[3]
〔′ɑpəzɪt 〕

adj. 相反的　*n.* 相反 (= *contrary*)
The movie theater is on the *opposite* side of the road.
電影院在馬路的對面。
"Left" is the *opposite* of "right."
「左」是「右」的相反。

op	+ pos	+ ite
against	+ *put*	+ *adj., n.*

supposing[3]
〔 sə′pozɪŋ 〕

conj.　如果 (= *if*)
Supposing it were true, what would happen?
如果那是真的，會發生什麼事？

supposed[3]
〔 sə′pozd 〕

adj.　想像的 (= *imaginary*)
The *supposed* advantages of city life meant nothing to him.
都市生活想像中的好處對他而言沒什麼。

supposedly[3]
〔 sə′pozɪdlɪ 〕

adv. 據稱；根據猜測地 (= *as people believe*)
Mr. Williams is *supposedly* coming for a visit next month.　威廉斯先生據稱下個月要來訪問。

字根
pose

supposition

〔ˌsʌpə'zɪʃən 〕

n. 假定;推測 (= *guesswork*)

His theory is based on *supposition*.

他的理論以假定爲基礎。

presuppose

〔ˌprisə'poz 〕

v. 預先假定;以…爲前提

(= *suppose* ~ *in advance*)

You shouldn't *presuppose* that he is guilty.

你不應該預先假定他有罪。

```
 pre  +  suppose
  |         |
before + 假定;猜想
```

presupposition

〔ˌprisʌpə'zɪʃən 〕

n. 前提;預先假定 (= *assumption*)

His *presupposition* is that they can raise enough money for the plan.

他的前提是,他們能夠爲該計劃募到足夠的錢。

【背誦祕訣】

第一組 opposition-oppositional-opposite 三個字的字首 o 都讀 /ɑ/ 的音。

{ supposing (that)
{ = suppose (that)

{ providing (that)
{ = provided (that)
　 = if 如果

supposed 不要和連接詞 supposing 弄混,它是形容詞,作「想像的」解。

3. *imposing-imposer-imposition*

　　這一回也有 18 個字，分成二組，第一組是 impose 和 expose 的衍生，第二組源自 compose，快速背至 10 秒之內，就終身不忘。

imposing[6] 〔 ɪm'pozɪŋ 〕	*adj.* 壯觀的；宏偉的 　　(= *grand and impressive*) The castle is an *imposing* building. 這座城堡是非常宏偉的建築物。

> impos + ing
> ｜　　　｜
> 加於　+ *adj.*
>
> 能夠加諸印象在心中，
> 即是「壯觀的」

imposer 〔 ɪm'pozɚ 〕	*n.* 徵收者；課徵者；強制實行者 I would rather be imposed upon than be the *imposer*. 我寧可被徵收，也不要當徵收者。

> impos + er
> ｜　　　｜
> 強加　+ 人

imposition 〔 ͵ɪmpə'zɪʃən 〕	*n.* 徵收 (= *enforcement*) Everyone complains about the *imposition* of the new tax. 每個人都抱怨新稅的徵收。

> impos + ition
> ｜　　　｜
> 加於　+ *n.*

impostor 〔 ɪm'pastɚ 〕	*n.* (冒充他人的) 騙子 　　(= *deceiver* ; *pretender*) He turned out to be an *impostor*. 他結果是個騙子。

> im + post + or
> ｜　　 ｜　　｜
> on + put + 人
>
> 把別人身分加在自己身上的人，
> 即「冒充他人的騙子」

imposture 〔 ɪm'pastʃɚ 〕	*n.* 欺騙 (= *deception*) That is a thorough *imposture*. 那是徹頭徹尾的欺騙行為。

imposturous 〔 ɪm'pastʃərəs 〕	*adj.* 欺騙的 (= *deceiving*) The crowd never suspected his *imposturous* intentions.　群眾從未懷疑他有欺騙的意圖。

exposition

〔͵ɛkspə'zɪʃən 〕

n. 展覽會（= *exhibition*）；解說

The World *Exposition* was held in Tokyo last year.

世界博覽會去年在東京舉行。

ex + pos + ition
| | |
out + put + n.   把物品放在外面，即爲「展覽」

exposure[4]

〔 ɪk'spoʒɚ 〕

n. 暴露；揭露（= *disclosure*）

Long *exposure* to the sun may cause skin cancer.

長期曬太陽可能會導致皮膚癌。

ex + pos + ure
| | |
out + put + n.   放在外面，即爲「暴露」

expositor

〔 ɪk'spɑzɪtɚ 〕

n. 解說員（= *one who explains*）

People gathered to listen to the *expositor* in the museum.

在博物館裡，人們圍著聽解說員講解。

【背誦祕訣】

imposing-imposer-imposition 這三個字背的時候，要注意到前二個字重音節母音都是 /o/；impostor-imposture-imposturous 的重音節母音都讀 /ɑ/。

expose 有三個主要名詞，即 exposition，exposure 和 expositor，而 expositor 是在 exposition 中的「解說員」。

字根 pose

composer[4]
〔 kəm'pozə 〕

n. 作曲家（ = *one who composes music* ）
Mozart was famous as a *composer.*
莫札特是有名的作曲家。

compos	+	er
作曲	+	人

composedly[4]
〔 kəm'pozıdlı 〕

adv. 鎮靜地（ = *calmly* ）
He reacted *composedly* to the situation.
他對這個狀況的反應很鎮靜。

com	+	pos	+	ed	+	ly
all	+	*put*	+	*adj.*	+	*adv.*

全部的事都放下來了，
即為「鎮靜地」

composure
〔 kəm'poʒə 〕

n. 鎮靜（ = *calmness* ）
He reacted to the situation with *composure.* 他對這個狀況的反應很鎮靜。

compos	+	ure
使鎮靜	+	*n.*

composite
〔 kəm'pazıt 〕

adj. 混合的；合成的（ = *compound* ）
Police concluded that it is a *composite* photograph. 警方判定那是一張合成的照片。

com	+	pos	+	ite
together	+	*put*	+	*adj.*

放在一起的，就是「混合的」

composition[4]
〔 ͵kampə'zıʃən 〕

n. 組成；作文（ = *essay* ）
Students are asked to write a 300-word *composition.*
學生被要求寫一篇 300 字的作文。

compos	+	ition
作(文、曲)	+	*n.*

compost
〔 'kampost 〕

n. 堆肥（ = *fertilizer* ）
The farmer used *compost* to grow vegetables.
農夫利用堆肥來種植蔬菜。

com	+	post
all	+	*put*

所有有機物堆放一起，腐爛
即成「堆肥」

字根 pose

decompose
〔͵dikəmˋpoz 〕

v. 分解 (= *break down into pieces*)
The material will soon *decompose* by itself.
此物質很快就會自行分解。

de + compose
| |
away + 組成
apart

組成的東西分開，即「分解」

discompose
〔͵dɪskəmˋpoz 〕

v. 使慌亂；使不安 (= *make sb. uneasy*)
The speaker was *discomposed* by the noise of the crowd. 演講者因為群眾的噪音而感到慌亂。

dis + compose
| |
apart + 使鎮靜

與鎮靜分開，即「失去鎮靜」

discomposure
〔͵dɪskəmˋpoʒɚ 〕

n. 慌亂；不安 (= *uneasiness*)
The sudden blackout resulted in the *discomposure* of the audience. 突然停電造成觀眾的不安。

【背誦祕訣】

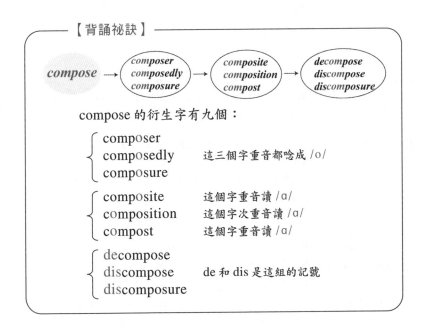

compose → composer / composedly / composure → composite / composition / compost → decompose / discompose / discomposure

compose 的衍生字有九個：

- composer
- composedly
- composure

這三個字重音都唸成 /o/

- composite 這個字重音讀 /ɑ/
- composition 這個字次重音讀 /ɑ/
- compost 這個字重音讀 /ɑ/

- decompose
- discompose
- discomposure

de 和 dis 是這組的記號

4. *proposal-proposition-purpose*

這一回共有 15 個字，先背前 9 個，propose 和 dispose 的變化，再背後 6 個，都是 repose「休息；安息」家族，須背熟至 8 秒內。

proposal[3]
〔 prə'pozl 〕

n. 提議；求婚 (= *offer*)
They put forward a *proposal* to reduce the time limit.
他們提出提議，要減少時間限制。

proposition
〔 ‚prɑpə'zɪʃən 〕

n. 提議；論點 (= *proposal* ; *statement*)
The students discussed the *proposition*
that all men are created equal.
學生們討論了一個論點：
人人生而平等。

```
propos + ition
  |        |
 提出  +   n.
```
提出來討論的，即是「論點」

purpose[1]
〔 'pɝpəs 〕

n. 目的 (= *aim* ; *intention*)
What is his *purpose* in
doing that?
他做那件事情目的何在？

```
pur    + pose
 |        |
forward + put
```
往前放讓別人看到，即是「目的」

disposal[6]
〔 dɪ'spozl 〕

n. 處理；處置 (= *removal*)
We should be very careful in the *disposal* of radio-
active waste. 我們對於放射性廢棄物的處理要很小心。

disposable[6]
〔 dɪ'spozəbl 〕

adj. 用完即丟的 (= *throwaway*)
To save the earth, we should
reduce the use of *disposable*
chopsticks. 為了拯救地球，
我們應該減少使用免洗筷。

```
dispos + able
  |        |
 處理  +  adj.
```
可以被處理掉，表示
「用完即丟的」

disposition
〔 ‚dɪspə'zɪʃən 〕

n. 性情；氣質 (= *nature*)
She has a sunny *disposition*.
她生性開朗。

```
dis  + pos + ition
 |      |      |
apart + put +  n.
```
將人的各方面分別放好，即是有「氣質」

indispose
〔͵ɪndɪˈspoz 〕

v. 使不願意 (= *make sb. unwilling*)
Low pay *indisposes* the workers to work hard.
薪水低使得員工不願意努力工作。

in + dis + pose
| | |
not + apart + put

沒有處置表示「不願意」

indisposed
〔͵ɪndɪˈspozd 〕

adj. 不願意的 (= *unwilling*)
He seems *indisposed* to answer the question.
他似乎不願意回答這個問題。

indisposition
〔͵ɪndɪspəˈzɪʃən 〕

n. 不願意 (= *unwillingness*)
He showed an *indisposition* to share the
information with us.
他表現出不願意和我們分享這個資訊的態度。

【背誦祕訣】

in + dis + pose
| | |
not + apart + put

dispose 的意思是「處置；
處理」，indispose 字根意
思是「沒有處理」，引申為
「使不願意；使不舒適」。

indisposed 也有「身體不適的」意思，等於 unwell。
同理，indisposition 也有「不願意；身體不適」之意。
爲了方便記憶起見，將 indispose-indisposed-
indisposition 都列爲「不願意」家族。

reposal
〔 rɪ'pozḷ 〕

n. 安息；休息（= *rest*）
After a long journey, we needed *reposal*.
在長途旅行之後，我們需要休息。

reposeful
〔 rɪ'pozfəl 〕

adj. 休息的；平靜的（= *restful*）
He had a leisurely and *reposeful*
Sunday in bed.
他在床上度過悠閒平靜的星期天。

repose + ful
休息 + *adj.*

reposer
〔 rɪ'pozɚ 〕

n. 安息者（= *one who rests*）
A funeral was held for the *reposer*.
有一場葬禮爲安息者而舉行。

reposit
〔 rɪ'pɑzɪt 〕

v. 儲藏；保存（= *store*）
The original copy of the
document is *reposited* in
the museum.
這份文件的原版保存在博物館中。

re + posit
back + *put*

放回去即是「保存」

repository
〔 rɪ'pɑzə,torɪ 〕

n. 儲藏室；寶庫；靈骨塔
（= *place for storage*）
All important papers are
stored in a secret *repository*.
所有重要的文件都儲存在一個
秘室裡。

reposit + ory
保存 + 地

repository

reposition
〔,ripə'zɪʃən 〕

n. 儲藏；保存　*v.* 放回（= *put back*）
The famous painting was *repositioned* in a
warehouse.
這幅名畫被放回倉庫。

5. *deposit-depositor-deposition*

第五回是最後 depose-interpose-superpose 的衍生，非常好背，你試試看。須背至 5 秒鐘內，變成直覺，才能終身不忘。

deposit[3]
〔 dɪˈpɑzɪt 〕

v. 存款；沈積 (= *store*)
John *deposits* part of his salary in the bank every month. 約翰每個月存部分薪水在銀行裡。

The flood receded, *depositing* mud in the street.
洪水消退後，街道上沈積著淤泥。

de	+	posit
down	+	put

depositor
〔 dɪˈpɑzɪtɚ 〕

n. 存款者 (= *saver*)
Because the bank was said to be in financial trouble, many *depositors* took their money out.
因為這家銀行據說陷入財務危機，許多存戶都把錢領出來。

deposition
〔 ˌdɛpəˈzɪʃən 〕

n. 罷免；免職 (= *ousting*)
Crowds celebrated the dictator's *deposition*.
群眾們慶祝這位獨裁者被罷免。

interposer
〔 ˌɪntɚˈpozɚ 〕

n. 插入者 (= *one who interposes*)
The stage barrier acts as an *interposer* between the audience and the performer.
舞台上的柵欄做為觀眾和表演者之間的屏障。

interposal
〔 ˌɪntɚˈpozḷ 〕

n. 插入；介入 (= *intervention*)
Children often learn the hard way that *interposal* is a bad idea. 孩子們常常需要痛苦的經驗，才能學會介入不是一件好事。

interposition
〔 ˌɪntɚpəˈzɪʃən 〕

n. 介入；仲裁 (= *intervention*)
The party was interrupted by police *interposition*. 這場舞會因為警方介入而被打斷。

superposition
〔͵supɚpəˈzɪʃən 〕

n. 疊放
The two waves were in *superposition*.
這兩個波浪重疊在一起。

superimpose
〔͵supɚɪmˈpoz 〕

v. 加於～之上;重疊 (= *overlay*)
The company logo is
superimposed on this
T-shirt.

super	+	impose
above	+	加於

該公司的商標被加在這件 T 恤上。

superimposition
〔͵supɚ͵ɪmpəˈzɪʃən 〕

n. 重疊
The *superimposition* of graph lines over
the image will make it easier to trace.
在這個圖案上重疊座標線,可以使這個圖更
容易描繪出來。

【劉毅老師的話】

pose 這個字根,我們背了 72 個字,以下還
有二個重要單字。

transpose *v.* 調換
〔 trænsˈpoz 〕

trans	+	pose
A→B	+	put

把 A 放到 B,即「調換」

juxtapose *v.* 並列
〔͵dʒʌkstəˈpoz 〕

juxta	+	pose
beside	+	put

放在旁邊,即「並列」

Exercise : Choose the correct answer. ⭐

1. Major airports usually have a(n) —————— for lost and found items.
   (A) proposal (B) expository
   (C) disposal (D) repository

2. Of all the classical ——————, Beethoven is my favorite.
   (A) interposers (B) expositors
   (C) composers (D) reposers

3. Police released a(n) —————— sketch of the burglary suspect.
   (A) reposit (B) deposit
   (C) composite (D) exposed

4. Golfing is one of those —————— "fun" things I hope I never have to do again.
   (A) supposedly (B) suppositionally
   (C) composedly (D) imposturously

5. The fire department urged residents to —————— of old Christmas trees in a proper manner.
   (A) oppose (B) dispose
   (C) propose (D) repose

6. I don't want to be an ——————, but would you mind if I stayed here for the night?
   (A) indisposition (B) imposition
   (C) interposition (D) imposer

7. The angry crowd called for the —————— of the president.
   (A) supposition (B) deposition
   (C) position (D) presupposition

8. I couldn't ＿＿＿＿＿＿ a reason for Sally's odd behavior.
   (A) discompose   (B) compost
   (C) post   (D) posit

9. Despite media reports of children being attacked, most
   pitbulls have a sweet and gentle ＿＿＿＿＿＿.
   (A) disposition   (B) exposure
   (C) posture   (D) purpose

10. It turned out the man claiming to be Elvis was a(n) ＿＿＿＿＿＿.
    (A) impostor   (B) depositor
    (C) postage   (D) pose

11. Many people will visit the ＿＿＿＿＿＿ of 19th century
    paintings.
    (A) composure   (B) interposal
    (C) exposition   (D) superposition

12. It will take 50 years for a plastic bag to ＿＿＿＿＿＿ in a landfill.
    (A) interpose   (B) depose
    (C) superpose   (D) decompose

13. Lyle is ＿＿＿＿＿＿ at the moment and can't take your call now.
    (A) supposed   (B) indisposed
    (C) positive   (D) disposable

14. Our new clients did not approve of the business ＿＿＿＿＿＿.
    (A) proposition   (B) reposal
    (C) composition   (D) imposture

15. There are two ＿＿＿＿＿＿ used in this sentence.
    (A) prepositions   (B) superimpositions
    (C) repositions   (D) oppositions

字彙測驗詳解

1. (**D**) 大型機場通常都有<u>儲藏室</u>，存放待招領的失物。

    (A) proposal〔 prə'pozl̩ 〕*n.* 提議；求婚

    (B) expository〔 ɪk'spɑzɪ,torɪ 〕*adj.* 說明的；解釋的

    (C) disposal〔 dɪ'spozl̩ 〕*n.* 處理；處置

    (D) *repository*〔 rɪ'pɑzə,torɪ 〕*n.* 儲藏室

    major〔 'medʒɚ 〕*adj.* 大型的   ***lost and found*** 失物招領處
    item〔 'aɪtəm 〕*n.* 物品

2. (**C**) 在所有古典<u>作曲家</u>當中，貝多芬是我的最愛。

    (A) interposer〔 ,ɪntɚ'pozɚ 〕*n.* 插入者

    (B) expositor〔 ɪk'spɑzɪtɚ 〕*n.* 解說者

    (C) *composer*〔 kəm'pozɚ 〕*n.* 作曲家

    (D) reposer〔 rɪ'pozɚ 〕*n.* 安息者

    classical〔 'klæsɪkl̩ 〕*adj.* 古典的
    Beethoven〔 'betovən 〕*n.* 貝多芬【1770-1827，德國作曲家】
    favorite〔 'fevrɪt 〕*n.* 最喜愛的人或物

3. (**C**) 警方公布了這起竊盜罪嫌疑犯的<u>合成</u>素描。

    (A) reposit〔 rɪ'pɑzɪt 〕*v.* 儲藏；保存

    (B) deposit〔 dɪ'pɑzɪt 〕*v.* 存放 *n.* 存款

    (C) *composite*〔 kəm'pɑzɪt 〕*adj.* 合成的

composite sketch

    (D) exposed〔 ɪk'spozd 〕*adj.* 暴露的；被揭露的

    release〔 rɪ'lis 〕*v.* 釋放；公布
    sketch〔 skɛtʃ 〕*n.* 素描
    burglary〔 'bɝglərɪ 〕*n.* 竊盜罪
    suspect〔 'sʌspɛkt 〕*n.* 嫌疑犯

4. (**A**) 打高爾夫球是那些<u>據稱</u>「很有趣」的事情當中，我希望我不必再去做的之一。
   - (A) *supposedly* 〔 səˈpozɪdlɪ 〕*adv.* 據稱
   - (B) suppositionally 〔ˌsʌpəˈzɪʃən̩lɪ 〕*adv.* 假定地
   - (C) composedly 〔 kəmˈpozɪdlɪ 〕*adv.* 鎮靜地
   - (D) imposturously 〔 ɪmˈpɑstʃərəslɪ 〕*adv.* 欺騙地

   golfing 〔ˈɡɑlfɪŋ 〕*n.* 打高爾夫球

5. (**B**) 消防隊極力勸告居民們，要以適當的方式來<u>處理</u>舊的聖誕樹。
   - (A) oppose 〔 əˈpoz 〕*v.* 反對
   - (B) *dispose* 〔 dɪˈspoz 〕*v.* 處置；處理　　*dispose of* 處理
   - (C) propose 〔 prəˈpoz 〕*v.* 提議
   - (D) repose 〔 rɪˈpoz 〕*v.* 休息

   fire department 消防隊　　urge 〔 ɝdʒ 〕*v.* 催促；力勸
   resident 〔ˈrɛzədənt 〕*n.* 居民　　proper 〔ˈprɑpɚ 〕*adj.* 適當的
   manner 〔ˈmænɚ 〕*n.* 方式；方法　　*in a ~ manner* 以~的方式

6. (**B**) 我不想<u>麻煩</u>你，但是如果我留在這裡過夜你介意嗎？
   - (A) indisposition 〔ˌɪndɪspəˈzɪʃən 〕*n.* 不舒服；不願意
   - (B) *imposition* 〔ˌɪmpəˈzɪʃən 〕*n.* 徵收；負擔
   - (C) interposition 〔ˌɪntɚpəˈzɪʃən 〕*n.* 插入；介入
   - (D) imposer 〔 ɪmˈpozɚ 〕*n.* 徵收者；強制執行者

   stay for the night 留下來過夜
   * (D) imposer 只用在徵稅和執行法律方面，在此不合句意。

7. (**B**) 憤怒的群眾要求<u>罷免</u>總統。
   - (A) supposition 〔ˌsʌpəˈzɪʃən 〕*n.* 假定
   - (B) *deposition* 〔ˌdɛpəˈzɪʃən 〕*n.* 罷免
   - (C) position 〔 pəˈzɪʃən 〕*n.* 位置
   - (D) presupposition 〔ˌprisʌpəˈzɪʃən 〕*n.* 前提

   call for 要求　　president 〔ˈprɛzədənt 〕*n.* 總統

8. (**D**) 我無法<u>斷定</u>莎莉行為如此奇怪的原因。

(A) discompose〔͵dɪskəm′poz〕*v.* 使慌亂

(B) compost〔′kɑmpost〕*n.* 堆肥

(C) post〔post〕*n.* 郵政

(D) *posit*〔′pɑzɪt〕*v.* 假定；斷定

reason〔′rizn̩〕*n.* 理由；原因　　Sally〔′sælɪ〕*n.* 莎莉【女子名】

odd〔ɑd〕*adj.* 奇怪的　　behavior〔bɪ′hevjɚ〕*n.* 行為

9. (**A**) 儘管有媒體報導小孩被攻擊，但大部分的鬥牛犬<u>性情</u>都很溫和。

(A) *disposition*〔͵dɪspə′zɪʃən〕*n.* 性情

(B) exposure〔ɪk′spoʒɚ〕*n.* 暴露；揭露

(C) posture〔′pɑstʃɚ〕*n.* 姿勢；姿態

(D) purpose〔′pɝpəs〕*n.* 目的

pitbull

despite〔dɪ′spaɪt〕*prep.* 儘管　　media〔′midɪə〕*n.* 媒體

pitbull〔′pɪt͵bʊl〕*n.* 鬥牛犬；比特犬　　gentle〔′dʒɛntḷ〕*adj.* 溫和的

10. (**A**) 宣稱自己是貓王的那個人，結果是個<u>騙子</u>。

(A) *impostor*〔ɪm′pɑstɚ〕*n.* 騙子

(B) depositor〔dɪ′pɑzɪtɚ〕*n.* 存放者

(C) postage〔′postɪdʒ〕*n.* 郵資

(D) pose〔poz〕*n.* 姿勢　*v.* 擺姿勢

Elvis

turn out 結果是　　claim〔klem〕*v.* 宣稱

Elvis Presley〔′ɛlvɪs′prɛslɪ〕*n.* 艾維斯‧普萊斯利【美國知名

搖滾樂歌手和演員，被歌迷們暱稱為「貓王」】

11. (**C**) 有很多人會去看那場十九世紀繪畫的<u>展覽會</u>。

(A) composure〔kəm′poʒɚ〕*n.* 鎮靜

(B) interposal〔͵ɪntɚ′pozḷ〕*n.* 插入；介入

(C) *exposition*〔͵ɛkspə′zɪʃən〕*n.* 展覽會

(D) superposition〔͵supɚpə′zɪʃən〕*n.* 重疊

12. (**D**) 在垃圾掩埋場裡，塑膠袋需要 50 年才能分解掉。

    (A) interpose〔,ɪntə'poz〕v. 插入；介入；調停

    (B) depose〔dɪ'poz〕v. 罷免

    (C) superpose〔,supə'poz〕v. 重疊

    (D) *decompose*〔,dikəm'poz〕v. 分解

    plastic〔'plæstɪk〕adj. 塑膠的　　***plastic bag*** 塑膠袋

    landfill〔'lænd,fɪl〕n. 垃圾掩埋場

13. (**B**) 萊爾現在不舒服，不能接你的電話。

    (A) supposed〔sə'pozd〕adj. 想像的；假定的

    (B) *indisposed*〔,ɪndɪ'spozd〕adj. 不舒服的；不願意的

    (C) positive〔'pazətɪv〕adj. 肯定的；明確的

    (D) disposable〔dɪ'spozəbl̩〕adj. 用完即丟的

    Lyle〔laɪl〕n. 萊爾【男子名】

    at the moment 此刻；現在

    take *one's* ***call*** 接某人的電話

14. (**A**) 我們新的客戶並不贊成這項商業提議。

    (A) *proposition*〔,prapə'zɪʃən〕n. 提議

    (B) reposal〔rɪ'pozl̩〕n. 休息

    (C) composition〔,kampə'zɪʃən〕n. 組成；作文

    (D) imposture〔ɪm'pastʃə〕n. 欺騙

    client〔'klaɪənt〕n. 客戶　　***approve of*** 贊成

15. (**A**) 這個句子裡使用兩個介系詞。

    (A) *preposition*〔,prɛpə'zɪʃən〕n. 介系詞

    (B) superimposition〔,supə,ɪmpə'zɪʃən〕n. 重疊

    (C) reposition〔,ripə'zɪʃən〕n., v. 放回

    (D) opposition〔,apə'zɪʃən〕n. 反對

字根 pose

 請連中文一起背，背至一分半鐘內，終生不忘。

1

pose	擺姿勢
oppose	反對
suppose	猜想
impose	加於
expose	暴露
compose	組成
propose	提議
dispose	處置
repose	休息
depose	罷免
interpose	調停
superpose	疊放

2

post	郵政
postal	郵政的
postage	郵資
posit	假定
posture	姿態
positive	肯定的
position	位置
apposition	同位語
preposition	介系詞

opposition	反對
oppositional	反對的
opposite	相反的
supposing	如果
supposed	想像的
supposedly	據稱
supposition	假定
presuppose	預先假定
presupposition	前提

3

imposing	壯觀的
imposer	徵收者
imposition	徵收
impostor	騙子
imposture	欺騙
imposturous	欺騙的
exposition	展覽會
exposure	暴露
expositor	解說員

字根 pose

composer	作曲家
composedly	鎮靜地
composure	鎮靜

composite	合成的
composition	作文
compost	堆肥

decompose	分解
discompose	使慌亂
discomposure	慌亂

reposal	安息
reposeful	平靜的
reposer	安息者

reposit	保存
repository	靈骨塔
reposition	儲藏

4

proposal	提議
proposition	論點
purpose	目的

disposal	處理
disposable	用完即丟的
disposition	性情

indispose	使不願意
indisposed	不願意的
indisposition	不願意

5

deposit	存款
depositor	存放者
deposition	罷免

interposer	插入者
interposal	介入
interposition	介入

superposition	疊放
superimpose	重疊
superimposition	重疊

這 72 個單字是精心排列的，先將第一組 12 個背熟到 7 秒鐘內，變成直覺後，再接著背第二組。背完這一回 72 個字，再背其他組字根，就輕鬆多了。

※ 本頁可影印後，隨身攜帶，方便背誦。

Group 2 字根 *press*

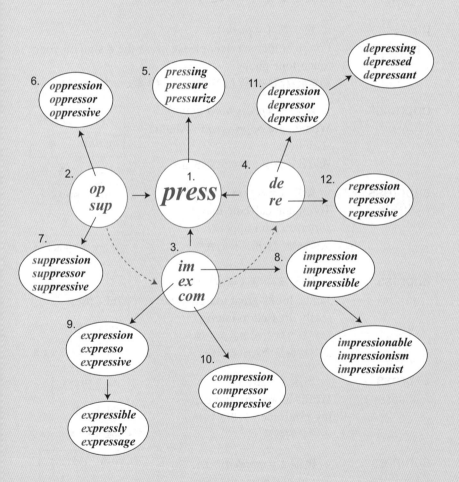

6. oppression
   oppressor
   oppressive

5. pressing
   pressure
   pressurize

11. depression
    depressor
    depressive

depressing
depressed
depressant

2. op
   sup

1. press

4. de
   re

12. repression
    repressor
    repressive

7. suppression
   suppressor
   suppressive

3. im
   ex
   com

8. impression
   impressive
   impressible

9. expression
   expresso
   expressive

10. compression
    compressor
    compressive

impressionable
impressionism
impressionist

expressible
expressly
expressage

1. 字根 *press* 核心單字

字根 press 的核心單字共有 8 個，前 6 個字排列順序
和 pose 一模一樣，你背了 pose 一組，press 一組就幾乎
背好了，這 8 個字要背到 4 秒之內，變成直覺。

press[2]
〔 prɛs 〕

v. 壓；按（ = *push* ）
For customer service, please *press* the # sign on your
touch-tone phone.
顧客服務請按電話上的 # 字鍵。（ "#" 英文唸 "pound" ）

oppress[6]
〔 əˈprɛs 〕

v. 壓迫（ = *press hard upon* ）
Women are *oppressed* in Islamic
societies.
在回教社會中，婦女受到壓迫。

op	+ press
against +	壓

有反抗的壓，即為「壓迫」

suppress[5]
〔 səˈprɛs 〕

v. 鎮壓（ = *repress* ; *subdue* ）
Too much caffeine may
suppress your appetite.
太多咖啡因會壓抑你的食慾。

sup	+ press
under +	壓

壓下去就是「鎮壓」

impress[3]
〔 ɪmˈprɛs 〕

v. 使印象深刻（ = *affect* ）
Janice looks great tonight; she
really dressed to *impress*.
珍妮絲今晚看起來真美；她
的打扮真是令人印象深刻。

im + press
in + 壓

壓進腦海裡，即「使印象深刻」

express[2]
〔 ɪkˈsprɛs 〕

v. 表達（ = *say* ）
Words alone will not *express*
my gratitude. 只用言語無法
表達我的感激。

ex + press
out + 壓

把想說的話壓出來，就是「表達」

compress
〔 kəmˈprɛs 〕

v. 壓縮（ = *condense* ）
Try to *compress* the story
into several brief sentences.
試著將這個故事壓縮成幾個短句。

com	+ press
all	壓
together	

全部一起壓，即是「壓縮」

depress[4]
〔dɪ'prɛs〕

v. 使沮喪 (= *discourage*)

Her leaving really *depressed* him.

她的離去使他十分沮喪。

```
de  + press
 |      |
down +  壓
```
把心情壓到谷底，就是「使沮喪」

字根 press

repress[6]
〔rɪ'prɛs〕

v. 鎮壓 (= *suppress*)

The police did their best to
repress the violent protest.

警方盡全力鎮壓這場激烈的抗議。

```
re  + press
 |      |
back +  壓
```
壓回去，即為「鎮壓」

【**oppress，suppress，repress 的區別**】

oppress，suppress，repress 意義接近，有時可以互用：

1. Most men ⎰ suppress ⎱ their emotions.
   ⎱ repress ⎰

   大部分男人都壓抑他們的情緒。

2. The Shiite people are a long ⎰ oppressed ⎱
   ⎱ repressed ⎰

   minority in the Middle East.

   什葉派教徒在中東是長期被壓迫的少數民族。

   oppress 有「壓迫；壓制；使煩惱；折磨」的意思；
   suppress 有「鎮壓；壓制；抑制；隱瞞」的意思；
   repress 有「鎮壓；抑制；壓制」的意思，我們只要
   背主要意思：oppress「壓迫」，suppress 和 repress
   「鎮壓」即可。

2. *pressing-pressure-pressurize*

這一回有 9 個單字，正是 press-oppress-suppress
的衍生字，必須背至 5 秒之內，變成直覺。

pressing[2]
（'prɛsɪŋ）

adj. 迫切的；緊急的（= *urgent*）
There is a *pressing* need for
renewable energy sources.
現在迫切需要可再生的能源來源。

press	+	ing
壓	+	*adj.*

pressure[3]
（'prɛʃɚ）

n. 壓力（= *stress*）
Reducing the number of
tests might relieve some
of the *pressure* on students.
減少考試的數量，可能可以減輕學生部分的壓力。

press	+	ure
壓	+	*n.*

pressurize
（'prɛʃə,raɪz）

v. 施壓；逼迫（= *use force to make sb. do sth.*）
The child was *pressurized*
into taking piano lessons.
這個小孩被迫上鋼琴課。

pressur	+	ize
壓力	+	*v.*

oppression[6]
（ə'prɛʃən）

n. 壓迫（= *stress*）
We must not tolerate the
oppression of minorities.
我們不可以容忍少數民族受到壓迫。

oppress	+	ion
壓迫	+	*n.*

oppressor
（ə'prɛsɚ）

n. 壓迫者（= *tyrant*）
The peasants revolted
against their *oppressors*.
佃農們群起反抗壓迫者。

oppress	+	or
壓迫	+	人, 物

oppressive
（ə'prɛsɪv）

adj. 壓迫的（= *cruel*）
Some people protested
against the *oppressive* laws.
有些人在抗議這幾條高壓的法律。

oppress	+	ive
壓迫	+	*adj.*

suppression
〔 səˋprɛʃən 〕

n. 鎮壓（= *conquest*）
The king charged his armies with the *suppression* of the uprising.
國王要他的軍隊負責鎮壓這場暴動。

suppressor
〔 səˋprɛsɚ 〕

n. 鎮壓者；抑制者；消音器
A *suppressor* will reduce the amount of noise from a fired weapon.
消音器可以減少武器發射時的噪音。

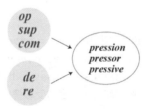

suppressor

suppressive
〔 səˋprɛsɪv 〕

adj. 鎮壓的；抑制的
The government took *suppressive* measures to stop the spread of the virus.
政府採取抑制措施，來阻止病毒的蔓延。

字根 press

【背誦祕訣】

oppression-oppressor-oppressive 是固定的變化形：

- op
- sup
- com

→ pression / pressor / pressive

- de
- re

→ pression / pressor / pressive

有兩組稍有不同：

- impression
- impressive
- impressible

背這一組的時候，把 impressible 代替 *impressor*（誤），因爲沒有這個字。

- expression
- expresso
- expressive

expressor「壓榨器」是醫學術語，一般少用，expresser「表達者」也少用，所以用 expresso 來代替。

3. impression-impressive-impressible

　　這一回共有 15 個單字，前 6 個是 impression 的
變化，後 9 個是 express 和 compress 的變化，要背
到 8 秒鐘之內，就終身難忘。

字根
press

impression[4] 〔 ɪm'prɛʃən 〕	*n.* 印象（ = *thought* ） I got the *impression* that Fiona wouldn't be attending the party. 我的印象是，費歐娜不會來參加舞會。
impressive[3] 〔 ɪm'prɛsɪv 〕	*adj.* 令人印象深刻的（ = *unforgettable* ） The singer's performance was *impressive*. 這位歌手的表演令人印象深刻。
impressible 〔 ɪm'prɛsəbḷ 〕	*adj.* 易受影響的（ = *easily affected* ） The Internet can be a dangerous place for *impressible* young minds. 網路對易受影響的年輕人而 言，可能是個危險的地方。

```
impress + ible
   |        |
使有印象 + 易…的
```

impressionable 〔 ɪm'prɛʃənəbḷ 〕	*adj.* 易受影響的（ = *impressible* ） Young Philip is very *impressionable*, so be careful what you say to him. 年輕的菲力普很容易受影響，所以你對他說的話很小心。
impressionism 〔 ɪm'prɛʃənˌɪzəm 〕	*n.* 印象主義 The term *impressionism* came from a painting by Claude Monet. 印象主義這 個名詞來自莫內的一幅畫。
impressionist 〔 ɪm'prɛʃənɪst 〕	*n.* 印象主義者 Henry claims his art is inspired by the French *Impressionists*. 亨利宣稱，他的藝術靈感來自法國印象派畫家。

```
impression + ism
     |         |
    印象      + 主義
```

expression[3]

〔 ɪk'sprɛʃən 〕

n. 表達（ = *communication* ）

These roses are an *expression* of my love for you.

這些玫瑰花表達我對你的愛。

expresso

〔 ɪk'sprɛso 〕

（ = espresso ）

〔 ɛs'prɛso 〕

n. 濃縮咖啡（用蒸汽加壓煮出）

I am in the habit of having an *expresso* for breakfast every morning.

我習慣每天早上早餐喝杯濃縮咖啡。

expresso

expressive[3]

〔 ɪk'sprɛsɪv 〕

adj. 表達的；表情豐富的（ = *expressing a lot* ）

Dorothy has an *expressive* face.

陶樂絲的臉部表情豐富。

> express 也有 expresser「表達者；表示者」，
> 但是較少用，所以沒有列出。

字根 press

expressible

〔 ɪk'sprɛsəbl̩ 〕

adj. 可表達的

The depth of my sadness is not *expressible* in words.

我的傷痛之深無法用言語表達。

expressly

〔 ɪk'sprɛslɪ 〕

adv. 明確地（ = *clearly* ）

I *expressly* forbade you to do that.

我很明確地禁止你那麼做。

> express　＋ ly
> ｜　　　　｜
> 快速的；明確的 ＋ *adv.*

expressage

〔 ɪk'spɛsɪdʒ 〕

n. 快遞費（ = *charge for express delivery* ）

What's the *expressage* for this package?

這個包裹快遞費要多少錢？

字根 press

compression
〔 kəmˈprɛʃən 〕

n. 壓縮
The surgery is supposed to relieve *compression* on pinched nerves.
這個手術是要將揪緊的神經舒壓。

compressor
〔 kəmˈprɛsɚ 〕

n. 壓縮機（ = *machine that compresses air or gas* ）
I borrowed my neighbor's air *compressor*
to inflate my bicycle tires.
我把鄰居的空氣壓縮機借來，
幫我的腳踏車輪胎充氣。

air compressor

compressive
〔 kəmˈprɛsɪv 〕

adj. 壓縮的
Concrete has a great deal of *compressive* strength.
混凝土有很大的壓縮力。

【背誦祕訣】

　　第一組都是 impress 的變化，要記住先背 impressive，再背 impressible，接續第二組，都是 impression 的變化。而 impressionable 正是 impressible 的同義字。

　　同樣的順序 expression-expresso-expressive，expressive 的後面也接 expressible，這樣就很好背了。

4. *depression-depressor-depressive*

最後這一回只有 9 個字，而且 pression-pressor-
pressive 的順序，你已經會了，背這一回就非常輕鬆
了。5 秒背 9 字，終生不忘記。

depression[4]
(dɪˈprɛʃən)

n. 沮喪；憂鬱 (= *dejection*)；不景氣 (= *recession*)
Bruce suffers from *depression*. 布魯斯患有憂鬱症。

depressor
(dɪˈprɛsɚ)

n. 壓抑者；壓板
The doctor used a tongue *depressor* to
inspect my sore throat.
醫生使用壓舌板來檢查我的喉嚨痛。

depressor

depressive
(dɪˈprɛsɪv)

adj. 憂鬱的；抑鬱的 (= *gloomy*)
Jeremy suffered from a *depressive* illness for most of
his life. 傑若米大半生都受抑鬱病之苦。

depressing[4]
(dɪˈprɛsɪŋ)

adj. 令人沮喪的 (= *sad*)
This movie is too *depressing*; let's watch something
else. 這部電影太令人沮喪了；我們看別的吧。

depressed[4]
(dɪˈprɛst)

adj. 沮喪的 (= *sad* ; *dejected*)
Patty has been feeling *depressed* lately.
派蒂最近一直覺得很沮喪。

depressant
(dɪˈprɛsənt)

n. 鎮靜劑 (= *calming drug*)
Alcohol is a very powerful *depressant*.
酒精是一種強有力的鎮靜劑。

比較：depressant *n.* 鎮靜劑
　　　【會減慢身體循環，使人放鬆、想睡】
　　　antidepressant *n.* 抗憂鬱藥
　　　【用於治療 depression「憂鬱症」】

字根 press

repression
〔 rɪ'prɛʃən 〕

n. 鎮壓 (= *control*)
America was founded by immigrants fleeing religious *repression* in Britain.
美國是由逃離英國宗教鎮壓的移民所建立的。

repressor
〔 rɪ'prɛsɚ 〕

n. 鎮壓者
Over time, some prisoners grow to sympathize with their *repressors*.
隨著時間過去，有些囚犯變得很同情他們的壓迫者。

repressive
〔 rɪ'prɛsɪv 〕

adj. 鎮壓的 (= *cruel*)
Dictators tend to be *repressive* of those under their rule. 獨裁者傾向於壓迫那些受他們統治的人。

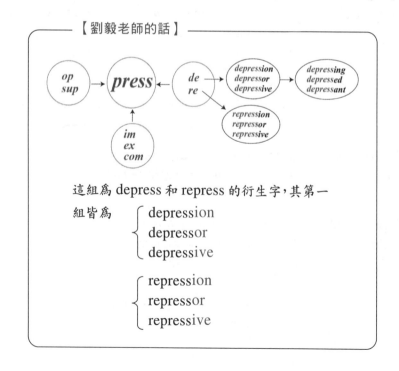

【劉毅老師的話】

這組為 depress 和 repress 的衍生字，其第一組皆為

- depression
- depressor
- depressive

- repression
- repressor
- repressive

Exercise : Choose the correct answer.

1. Doctors say regular exercise can help to prevent _____.
   (A) imposition　　　　　(B) depression
   (C) exposure　　　　　　(D) reposition

2. Some people perform better when they are under _____ to succeed.
   (A) posture　　　　　　(B) depressor
   (C) expresso　　　　　(D) pressure

3. The violence in this movie is suitable for adults, not for _____ youth.
   (A) impressionable　　(B) discomposed
   (C) oppositional　　　(D) impressionist

4. Norman apologized for being tired and said it had been a highly _____ week.
   (A) depressant　　　　(B) compressed
   (C) pressurized　　　(D) expressible

5. The only way to escape the _____ heat of summer is to stay indoors with the air conditioner on "high."
   (A) oppressive　　　　(B) depressive
   (C) compressive　　　(D) repressive

6. The _____ of childhood memories may lead to mental and emotional problems later in life.
   (A) supposition　　　(B) preposition
   (C) proposition　　　(D) repression

7. You never get a second chance to make a first _____.
   (A) expression　　　　(B) impression
   (C) suppression　　　(D) confession

8. After suffering years of brutal _____, the people of the Soviet Union finally won their freedom.
   - (A) opposition
   - (B) oppression
   - (C) expressage
   - (D) deposition

9. The on-going famine in Africa is a very _____ situation.
   - (A) depressing
   - (B) expressing
   - (C) compressing
   - (D) impressing

10. George cut his finger, so he applied _____ on the wound to stop the bleeding.
    - (A) purpose
    - (B) composure
    - (C) compression
    - (D) postage

11. Chloe has a(n) _____ collection of Barbie dolls.
    - (A) impressive
    - (B) repository
    - (C) impressible
    - (D) positive

12. These scissors are designed _____ for left-handed users.
    - (A) positively
    - (B) supposedly
    - (C) reposefully
    - (D) expressly

13. Something must really be bothering Jane; I've never seen her so _____.
    - (A) pressing
    - (B) pressed
    - (C) depressed
    - (D) impressed

14. Without realizing it, Tom's outward behavior was _____ of his inner thoughts.
    - (A) corrective
    - (B) indisposed
    - (C) compressive
    - (D) expressive

15. Scientists are studying the _____ effects of ginseng root on the common cold.
    - (A) interposal
    - (B) suggestive
    - (C) imposing
    - (D) suppressive

字彙測驗詳解

1. (**B**) 醫生說，定期運動可有助於預防憂鬱。
   - (A) imposition〔͵ɪmpə'zɪʃən〕*n.* 徵收
   - (B) *depression*〔dɪ'prɛʃən〕*n.* 沮喪；憂鬱
   - (C) exposure〔ɪk'spoʒɚ〕*n.* 暴露；接觸
   - (D) reposition〔͵ripə'zɪʃən〕*n.,v.* 放回

2. (**D**) 有些人在承受必須成功的壓力時，表現比較好。
   - (A) posture〔'pastʃɚ〕*n.* 姿勢；姿態
   - (B) depressor〔dɪ'prɛsɚ〕*n.* 壓抑者；壓板
   - (C) expresso〔ɪk'sprɛso〕*n.* 濃縮咖啡
   - (D) *pressure*〔'prɛʃɚ〕*n.* 壓力   *be under pressure* 承受壓力
   perform〔pɚ'fɔrm〕*v.* 執行；表現

3. (**A**) 這部電影中的暴力只適合成年人，不適合易受影響的年輕人。
   - (A) *impressionable*〔ɪm'prɛʃənəbl̩〕*adj.* 易受影響的
   - (B) discomposed〔͵dɪskəm'pozd〕*adj.* 慌亂的
   - (C) oppositional〔͵apə'zɪʃənl̩〕*adj.* 反對的
   - (D) impressionist〔ɪm'prɛʃənɪst〕*adj.* 印象主義的

4. (**C**) 諾曼因為感到很疲倦而道歉，他說他這一週壓力非常大。
   - (A) depressant〔dɪ'prɛsn̩t〕*adj.* 有鎮靜作用的；令人沮喪的
   - (B) compressed〔kəm'prɛst〕*adj.* 壓縮的
   - (C) *pressurized*〔'prɛʃə͵raɪzd〕*adj.* 加壓的；倍感壓力的
   - (D) expressible〔ɪk'sprɛsəbl̩〕*adj.* 可表達的

5. (**A**) 要逃離夏天的悶熱，唯一的方法是待在室內，冷氣機開「強冷」。
   - (A) *oppressive*〔ə'prɛsɪv〕*adj.* 壓迫的；悶熱的
   - (B) depressive〔dɪ'prɛsɪv〕*adj.* 憂鬱的
   - (C) compressive〔kəm'prɛsɪv〕*adj.* 壓縮的
   - (D) repressive〔rɪ'prɛsɪv〕*adj.* 鎮壓的
   on〔an〕*adv.* 開著   high〔haɪ〕*adj.* 強的

6. (**D**) 童年記憶中的<u>壓抑</u>，可能會導致日後生命中心理和情緒的問題。
(A) supposition〔ˌsʌpə'zɪʃən〕*n.* 假定
(B) preposition〔ˌprɛpə'zɪʃən〕*n.* 介系詞
(C) proposition〔ˌprɑpə'zɪʃən〕*n.* 提議；論點
(D) *repression*〔rɪ'prɛʃən〕*n.* 鎮壓；壓抑
memory〔'mɛmərɪ〕*n.* 記憶；回憶　　***lead to*** 導致；造成

7. (**B**) 要留給別人第一<u>印象</u>，你永遠沒有第二次機會。
(A) expression〔ɪk'sprɛʃən〕*n.* 表達；表情
(B) *impression*〔ɪm'prɛʃən〕*n.* 印象
(C) suppression〔sə'prɛʃən〕*n.* 鎮壓
(D) confession〔kən'fɛʃən〕*n.* 承認；自白

8. (**B**) 多年來遭受殘忍的<u>壓迫</u>之後，蘇聯人民終於贏得自由。
(A) opposition〔ˌɑpə'zɪʃən〕*n.* 反對
(B) *oppression*〔ə'prɛʃən〕*n.* 壓迫
(C) expressage〔ɪk'sprɛsɪdʒ〕*n.* 快遞費
(D) deposition〔ˌdɛpə'zɪʃən〕*n.* 罷免
brutal〔'brutl̩〕*adj.* 殘忍的　　***the Soviet Union*** 蘇聯

9. (**A**) 非洲持續的飢荒是一個非常<u>令人沮喪的</u>情況。
(A) *depressing*〔dɪ'prɛsɪŋ〕*adj.* 令人沮喪的
(B) express〔ɪk'sprɛs〕*v.* 表達
(C) compress〔kəm'prɛs〕*v.* 壓縮
(D) impress〔ɪm'prɛs〕*v.* 使印象深刻
on-going〔'ɑnˌgoɪŋ〕*adj.* 進行中的　　famine〔'fæmɪn〕*n.* 飢荒

10. (**C**) 喬治割傷了手指，所以他在傷口上加<u>壓</u>以止血。
(A) purpose〔'pɝpəs〕*n.* 目的
(B) composure〔kəm'poʒɚ〕*n.* 鎮靜；沈著
(C) *compression*〔kəm'prɛʃən〕*n.* 壓縮；壓緊
(D) postage〔'postɪdʒ〕*n.* 郵資
apply〔ə'plaɪ〕*v.* 應用；施加　　wound〔wund〕*n.* 傷口

11. (**A**) 克蘿伊的芭比娃娃收藏<u>令人印象深刻</u>。
    (A) *impressive* 〔 ɪm'prɛsɪv 〕 *adj.* 令人印象深刻的
    (B) repository 〔 rɪ'pazə,torɪ 〕 *n.* 儲藏室;靈骨塔
    (C) impressible 〔 ɪm'prɛsəbḷ 〕 *adj.* 易受影響的
    (D) positive 〔'pazətɪv 〕 *adj.* 肯定的;正面的

12. (**D**) 這把剪刀是<u>特別</u>為了慣用左手的人設計的。
    (A) positively 〔'pazətɪvlɪ 〕 *adv.* 肯定地
    (B) supposedly 〔 sə'pozɪdlɪ 〕 *adv.* 據稱
    (C) reposefully 〔 rɪ'pozfəlɪ 〕 *adv.* 平靜地
    (D) *expressly* 〔 ɪk'sprɛslɪ 〕 *adv.* 明確地;特別地
    scissors 〔'sɪzəz 〕 *n.pl.* 剪刀   design 〔 dɪ'zaɪn 〕 *v.* 設計

13. (**C**) 一定有某件事困擾著珍;我從沒看過她如此<u>沮喪</u>。
    (A) pressing 〔'prɛsɪŋ 〕 *adj.* 緊急的
    (B) pressed 〔 prɛst 〕 *adj.* 緊壓的;困難的
    (C) *depressed* 〔 dɪ'prɛst 〕 *adj.* 沮喪的
    (D) impressed 〔 ɪm'prɛst 〕 *adj.* 印象深刻的

14. (**D**) 湯姆沒有察覺到,他外在的行為<u>正表達出</u>他內心的想法。
    (A) corrective 〔 kə'rɛktɪv 〕 *adj.* 改正的
    (B) indisposed 〔,ɪndɪ'spozd 〕 *adj.* 不願意的;不適的
    (C) compressive 〔 kəm'prɛsɪv 〕 *adj.* 壓縮的
    (D) *expressive* 〔 ɪk'sprɛsɪv 〕 *adj.* 表達的
    outward 〔'autwəd 〕 *adj.* 外在的   inner 〔'ɪnə 〕 *adj.* 內在的

15. (**D**) 科學家正在研究,人蔘根部對普通感冒的<u>抑制</u>效果。
    (A) interposal 〔,ɪntə'pozḷ 〕 *n.* 插入
    (B) suggestive 〔 sə(g)'dʒɛstɪv 〕 *adj.* 暗示的
    (C) imposing 〔 ɪm'pozɪŋ 〕 *adj.* 宏偉的
    (D) *suppressive* 〔 sə'prɛsɪv 〕 *adj.* 壓抑的;抑制的
    ginseng 〔'dʒɪnsɛŋ 〕 *n.* 人蔘   root 〔 rut 〕 *n.* 根

請連中文一起背,背至50秒內,終生不忘。 ★

1

press	壓
oppress	壓迫
suppress	鎮壓
impress	使印象深刻
express	表達
compress	壓縮
depress	使沮喪
repress	鎮壓

2

pressing	迫切的
pressure	壓力
pressurize	逼迫
oppression	壓迫
oppressor	壓迫者
oppressive	壓迫的
suppression	鎮壓
suppressor	鎮壓者
suppressive	鎮壓的

3

impression	印象
impressive	令人印象深刻的
impressible	易受影響的
impressionable	易受影響的
impressionism	印象主義
impressionist	印象主義者

字根 press

expression	表達
expresso	濃縮咖啡
expressive	表達的
expressible	可表達的
expressly	明確地
expressage	快遞費
compression	壓縮
compressor	壓縮機
compressive	壓縮的

4

depression	沮喪
depressor	壓抑者
depressive	憂鬱的
depressing	令人沮喪的
depressed	沮喪的
depressant	鎮靜劑
repression	鎮壓
repressor	鎮壓者
repressive	鎮壓的

※ 本頁可影印後,隨身攜帶,方便背誦。

Group 3 字 根 *ply*

目 標： ① 先將72個字放入短期記憶。
② 加快速度至1分鐘之內，成為長期記憶。

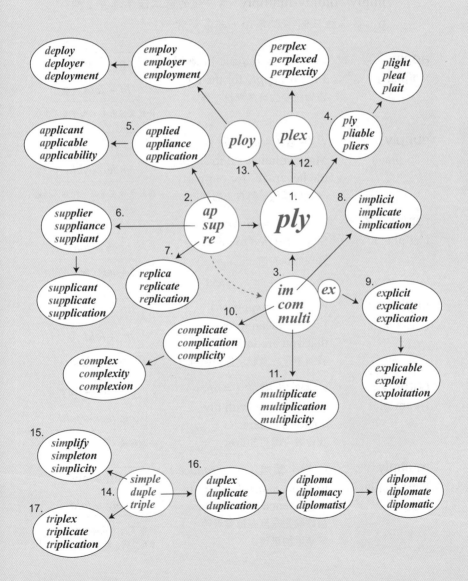

1. 字根 *ply* 核心單字

ply 的核心單字共有 6 個，apply-supply-reply，imply-comply-multiply，第一組的前二個字都有 2 個 p，第二組三個字都有 m，非常好背。

apply[2]
〔ə'plaɪ〕

v. 申請（= *request*）；應用
Jim will *apply* for the job.
吉姆將要去應徵那份工作。

ap +	ply
to +	fold 摺疊

折起來寄出去，為了要「申請」

supply[2]
〔sə'plaɪ〕

v. 供給（= *provide*）
Mary volunteered to *supply* the beverages for our party.
瑪麗自願供給舞會上的飲料。

sup +	ply
under +	fold

折起來放在下面，即為「供給」

reply[2]
〔rɪ'plaɪ〕

v. 回答（= *answer*）
Susan *replied* to my letter.
蘇珊回我的信。

re +	ply
back +	fold

折起來寄回去，即是「回答」

imply[4]
〔ɪm'plaɪ〕

v. 暗示（= *suggest*）
I didn't mean to *imply* that you are lazy.
我並不是故意暗示你很懶惰。

im +	ply
in +	fold

折在裡面，叫「暗示」

comply
〔kəm'plaɪ〕

v. 服從；遵從（= *obey*）
I will *comply* with my doctor's orders.
我會遵守醫生的指示。

com +	ply
together +	fold

一起折疊，表示「服從；遵從」

multiply[2]
〔'mʌltə,plaɪ〕

v. 乘；繁殖（= *reproduce*）
Rodents *multiply* faster in the absence of predators.
齧齒動物在沒有掠食者時，繁殖更加迅速。

multi +	ply
many +	fold

折很多次，就會越來越多，表示「乘；繁殖」

ply
〔 plaɪ 〕

v. 忙於；定期往返　n. 一股；一層
Many ferry boats *ply* the waters between Hong Kong and Macau.
許多渡輪定期往返於香港和澳門之間。

pliable
〔'plaɪəbḷ 〕

adj. 易折的；柔軟的
Gold is the most *pliable* of precious metals.
黃金是最柔軟的貴金屬。

pli	+	able
fold	+	易～的

pliers
〔'plaɪɚz 〕

n.pl. 鉗子
Use a pair of *pliers* to remove the rusty nail. 用鉗子把生鏽的釘子拔出來。

pliers

plight[6]
〔 plaɪt 〕

n. 困境
Seeing the *plight* of those homeless people brought tears to my eyes.
看到那些無家可歸的人的困境，使我眼淚盈眶。

pleat
〔 plit 〕

v. (衣服) 打褶　n. 褶
Sandy bought a *pleated* skirt.
珊蒂買了一件打褶的裙子。

pleated skirt

plait
〔 plet 〕

n. 辮子 (= braid)　v. 編辮子
She wears her hair in *plaits*.
她的頭髮編成辮子。

plait

【背誦祕訣】

　　這一回除了 6 個核心單字之外，再加上 ply 的變化有 6 個字，前三個字都有 /plaɪ/ 的發音，總共 12 個字，要背到 7 秒之內。

2. *applied-appliance-application*

　　第二回有 15 個字，來自 apply-supply-reply 的變化，apply 除「申請」外，也有「應用」之意；supply 的變化有 6 個字，除了 supplier 之外，其餘皆是「懇求」家族；而 replica-replicate-replication 都和「複製」有關。

字根 ply

applied[2]
(ə'plaɪd)

adj. 應用的 (= *practical*)
Ashley has a master's degree in *applied* chemistry.
愛希莉擁有應用化學的碩士學位。

appliance[4]
(ə'plaɪəns)

n. 用具；用品 (= *device*)
Refrigerators are the most common household *appliance*. 冰箱是最常見的家電用品。

application[4]
(,æplə'keʃən)

n. 申請 (= *request*)
Make sure to sign and date the *application* form.
要確定在申請表上簽名，並註明日期。

applicant[4]
('æpləkənt)

n. 申請人；應徵者 (= *candidate*)
Potential *applicants* should have at least three years' teaching experience.

applic + ant
| 　　 |
申請 ＋ 人

可能的應徵者應有至少三年的教學經驗。

applicable[6]
('æplɪkəbḷ)

adj. 適用的 (= *valid*)
The new anti-smoking law is not *applicable* in all public places.
這項新的禁煙法，並不適用於所有公共場所。

applicability
(,æplɪkə'bɪlətɪ)

n. 適用性 (= *relevance*)
International laws have no *applicability* in outer space. 國際法在外太空就不適用了。

supplier
(sə'plaɪɚ)

n. 供應者 (= *provider*)
The company is the leading wholesale *supplier* of semiconductors.
那家公司是半導體的主要批發供應商。

suppliance
('sʌpliəns)

n. 懇求 (= *appeal* ; *plea*)
The worshipers bowed in *suppliance* when the priest appeared.
當牧師出現時，膜拜者都鞠躬懇求。

sup	+	pli	+	ance	
under	+	fold	+	n.	

把身體向下折，即是彎腰，表示「懇求」

字根 ply

suppliant
('sʌpliənt)

adj. 懇求的 (= *begging*)   *n.* 懇求者
She hoped her *suppliant* words would change his mind.
她希望她懇求的話語可以改變他的心意。

supplicant
('sʌplɪkənt)

n. 懇求者 (= *suppliant* ; *beggar*)
The streets of New Delhi are filled with *supplicants*.
新德里的街道上充滿了乞丐。

supplicate
('sʌplɪˌket)

v. 懇求 (= *appeal* ; *plead* ; *beg*)
The child *supplicated* his mother for permission to attend the party.
那個小孩懇求他的媽媽允許他去參加派對。

supplication
(ˌsʌplɪ'keʃən)

n. 懇求 (= *suppliance*)
Prayer is the most common form of *supplication*.
祈禱是最常見的懇求形式。

字根 ply

replica
('rɛplɪkə)

n. 複製品 (= *replication*)
The museum features life-sized *replicas* of dinosaurs.
這座博物館的特色，是實體大小的恐龍複製品。

replicate
('rɛplɪˌket)

v. 複製 (= *copy*)
The scientist hoped to *replicate* the success of his previous experiment.
科學家希望能複製他前一次實驗的成功。

re	+ plic +	ate
|	|	|
again	+ *fold* +	*v.*

再折一次，也就是再做一次，即表示「複製」

replication
(ˌrɛplɪ'keʃən)

n. 複製 (品) (= *copy*)
Diana bought a cheap *replication* of a Gucci bag at the night market.
戴安娜在夜市買了一個便宜的 Gucci 仿冒包。

【背誦祕訣】

比較後面三組：

{ supplier
  suppliance
  suppliant

除了第一個字唸 (sə'plaɪə) 之外，其他 2 個字都唸成 ('sʌplɪ-)。

{ supplicant
  supplicate
  supplication

第一、二字重音唸 /ʌ/，第三字次重音唸 /ʌ/。
第一字爲「人」，第二、三字爲動詞和名詞。

{ replica
  replicate
  replication

第一、二字重音唸 /ɛ/，第三字次重音唸 /ɛ/。
第一字爲「物」，第二、三字爲動詞和名詞。

3. *implicit-implicate-implication*

　　第三回總共 18 個字，除了 imply-comply-multiply 的變化之外，還多了 ex 的變化，英文沒有 exply，但有其他的詞類衍生，都列在這一回裡，18 個字要背到 10 秒之內，就永遠不會忘記了。

字根 ply

implicit[6]
〔ɪmˈplɪsɪt〕

adj. 暗示的（= *implied*）
His smile gave *implicit* consent.
他的微笑表示默許。

im + plic + it
in + fold + *adj.*

implicate
〔ˈɪmplɪˌket〕

v. 牽連；涉入（= *involve*）
Several government officials were *implicated* in the corruption scandal.　數名政府官員涉入這場貪污醜聞。

implication
〔ˌɪmplɪˈkeʃən〕

n. 牽連；暗示（= *involvement*）
Global warming may have severe *implications* for future generations.
全球暖化可能會嚴重牽連到未來的世代。

explicit[6]
〔ɪkˈsplɪsɪt〕

adj. 明白的（= *obvious*；*clear*）
This text cannot be copied without *explicit* consent of the author.
這段內文若沒有作者明白表示同意，不得抄襲。

explicate
〔ˈɛksplɪˌket〕

v. 詳細說明（= *explain*）
The senator refused to *explicate* his controversial statements.
參議員拒絕說明他的極具爭議性的論點。

ex + plic + ate
out + fold + *v.*

把折疊處打開，即「說明」

explication
〔ˌɛksplɪˈkeʃən〕

n. 詳細說明（= *explanation*）
The teacher did not accept *explication* for my many absences.　老師不接受我多次缺席的解釋。

字根 ply

explicable
〔'ɛksplɪkəbḷ ,
ɪk'splɪkəbḷ 〕

adj. 可說明的；可解釋的（= *explainable* ）
There was no *explicable* reason for his actions.
他的行為沒有原因可解釋。

exploit[6]
〔 ɪk'splɔɪt 〕

v. 開發；利用；剝削（= *use* ）
Bernie won the game by *exploiting* his opponent's
weakness. 伯尼利用對手的弱點贏得這場比賽。

> ex ＋ ploit
> ｜　　｜
> *out* ＋ *fold*
>
> 把折在裡面未利用的物品「開發」出來，
> 過度開發則變成「利用；剝削」

exploitation
〔͵ɛksplɔɪ'teʃən 〕

n. 開發；利用；剝削（= *use* ）
Capitalism depends on the *exploitation* of cheap
labor. 資本主義有賴於對廉價勞工的利用。

【背誦祕訣】

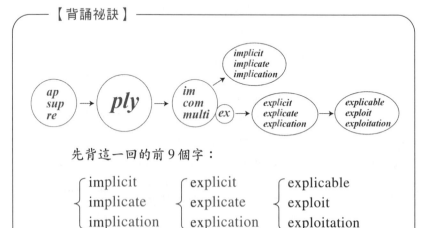

先背這一回的前 9 個字：

　┌ implicit　　　┌ explicit　　　┌ explicable
　│ implicate　　│ explicate　　│ exploit
　└ implication　└ explication　└ exploitation

前二組除了字首之外，完全相同，非常好背。

complicate[4]

(ˈkɑmpləˌket)

v. 使複雜

Our travel plans were *complicated* by bad weather.

我們的旅行計劃因為天氣惡劣，變得很複雜。

```
com + plic + ate
 |      |      |
all  + fold  +  v.
```
全部折在一起，就「變得很複雜」

complication[6]

(ˌkɑmpləˈkeʃən)

n. 複雜 (= *difficulty*)；併發症

He died from *complications* during heart surgery.

他因為動心臟手術時產生併發症而死亡。

complicity

(kəmˈplɪsətɪ)

n. 共謀；共犯 (= *involvement*)

He denied *complicity* in the murder case.

他否認是這宗謀殺案的共犯。

complex[3]

(kəmˈplɛks)

adj. 複雜的 (= *complicated*)

It's a *complex* problem with no easy solution.

這個複雜的問題不容易解決。

```
com + plex
 |      |
all  + fold
```

complexity[6]

(kəmˈplɛksətɪ)

n. 複雜 (= *complication*)

I failed to grasp the *complexity* of the situation.

我無法了解這個情況的複雜性。

complexion[6]

(kəmˈplɛkʃən)

n. 臉色；膚色 (= *skin*)

Gigi has a very fair *complexion*.

Gigi 膚色非常白皙。

multiplicate	*adj.* 多重的 (= *with many parts*)
('mʌltəplɪˌket)	A *multiplicate* flower has an unusual amount of petals.
	多瓣花有非常多的花瓣。

multiplication	*n.* 乘法;繁殖 (= *reproduction*)
(ˌmʌltəpləˈkeʃən)	Games are a fun way to learn your *multiplication* tables.
	利用遊戲學習乘法表,是一種很有趣的方法。

multiplicity	*n.* 多重;多樣 (= *variety*)
(ˌmʌltəˈplɪsətɪ)	There is a *multiplicity* of food vendors on Da An Road.
	大安路上有多種食物的小販。

字根 ply

【背誦祕訣】

complicate
complication
complicity

第一字重音讀 /ɑ/
第二字次重音讀 /ɑ/

complex
complexity
complexion

這三個字重音都在 plex 上,母音都唸成 /ɛ/

multiplicate
multiplication
multiplicity

重音讀 /ʌ/
次重音讀 /ʌ/
次重音讀 /ʌ/

這三組都是第一個字為動詞或形容詞,再搭配二個名詞。

4 perplex-perplexed-perplexity

這一回9個字，字根是 plex 和 ploy，plex 和 ploy 都是 ply 的變體，非常好背，5秒鐘背9個字，一定沒有問題。

字根 ply

perplex
〔 pɚˋplɛks 〕

v. 使複雜；使困惑（ = confuse ）
Your question really *perplexed* me.
你的問題真是使我困惑。

per	+	plex
thoroughly	+	fold

完全被摺進去，也就是完全捲入，即「使複雜；使困惑」

perplexed
〔 pɚˋplɛkst 〕

adj. 困惑的（ = confused ）
I am *perplexed* by your rude behavior.
我對你粗魯的行為感到困惑。

perplexity
〔 pɚˋplɛksətɪ 〕

n. 困惑；複雜；困難（ = confusion ）
Many comedians joke about the *perplexity* of modern life. 許多喜劇演員會嘲諷現代生活的難處。

employ[3]
〔 ɪmˋplɔɪ 〕

v. 雇用（ = hire ）
Our company will eventually *employ* over 300 people.
我們公司最後會雇用超過 300 人。

em	+	ploy
in	+	fold

折入工作中，即「雇用」

employer[3]
〔 ɪmˋplɔɪɚ 〕

n. 雇主（ = boss ; company ）
The Indian Railway Company is the world's largest *employer*. 印度鐵路公司是全世界最大的公司。

employment[3]
〔 ɪmˋplɔɪmənt 〕

n. 職業；工作（ = job ）
Many Americans are seeking full-time *employment*.
許多美國人正在尋找全職的工作。

deploy
(dɪ'plɔɪ)

v. 部署 (= *arrange*)
North Korea threatened to
deploy their nuclear missiles.
北韓威脅要部署核子飛彈。

de	+ ploy
apart	+ fold

將重疊的分散，即「部署」

deployer
(dɪ'plɔɪə)

n. 部署者；調度者 (= *arranger*)
Despite being a first time *deployer* in Iraq, Sgt.
White was asked to command a battalion.
儘管是第一次在伊拉克負責部署，懷特中士被要求
指揮一整個營。

deployment
(dɪ'plɔɪmənt)

n. 部署；調度 (= *arrangement*)
The soldiers awaited their *deployment* orders.
士兵們等待著調度命令。

字根 ply

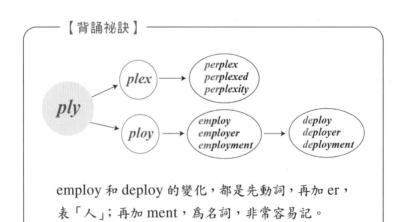

【背誦祕訣】

employ 和 deploy 的變化，都是先動詞，再加 er，
表「人」；再加 ment，為名詞，非常容易記。

5. simple-duple-triple

　　第 5 回 18 個字，來自 simple-duple-triple 的衍生，
ple 也是 ply 的變體，simple 是一折，duple 是二折，triple
是三折，非常好背，18 字只要 10 秒鐘，就終生難忘。

simple[1] (ˈsɪmpḷ)	*adj.* 簡單的 (= *easy*) The job is not as *simple* as you might think. 這份工作沒有你想的那麼簡單。	sim + ple ｜　　｜ *one + fold* 只有一折，所以很「簡單」
duple (ˈdjupḷ)	*adj.* 兩倍的；雙重的 The couple danced in *duple* time. 這對舞者跳著二拍子的舞。	du + ple ｜　　｜ *two + fold*
triple[5] (ˈtrɪpḷ)	*adj.* 三倍的　*v.* 成為三倍 The price of oil has *tripled* during the last month. 油價在上個月漲成三倍。	tri　+ ple ｜　　　｜ *three + fold*

字根 ply

simplify[6] (ˈsɪmpləˌfaɪ)	*v.* 簡化 (= *make ~ simpler*) You'll need to *simplify* your message if you want to be heard. 如果你想要被聽懂的話，你必須把你的訊息簡化。
simpleton (ˈsɪmpḷtən)	*n.* 傻子；笨蛋 (= *fool*) Charles is a *simpleton* and can't be trusted with money.　查爾斯是個傻子，不能把錢交付給他。
simplicity[6] (sɪmˈplɪsətɪ)	*n.* 簡單；簡樸 (= *easiness* ; *uncomplicatedness*) We admired the *simplicity* of the design. 我們很欣賞這個簡單的設計。

duplex
('djuplɛks)

adj. 雙重的（ = *containing two parts* ）
Howard owns a *duplex* apartment
in Boston.
豪爾德在波士頓擁有一間雙層公寓。

a duplex department

duplicate
('djuplə‚ket)

v. 複製（ = *copy* ; *replicate* ）
Your performance will be hard to *duplicate*.
你的表現很難再重現了。

duplication
(‚djuplə'keʃən)

n. 複製（品）（ = *replication* ）
You had better keep a *duplication* of the letter,
just in case.
你最好保存這封信的複本，以防萬一。

字根 ply

【背誦祕訣】

simple   sim 表示 one
duple   du 表示 two
triple   tri 表示 three

simplify
simpleton   只折一折，即為「簡化」，重音在第一音節
simplicity   頭腦簡單就是「傻子」，重音也在第一音節

duplex   除了第一個字之外，第二、三字為動詞和名
duplicate   詞，變化和 implicit-implicate-implication，
duplication   explicit-explicate-explication 相同。

diploma[4]
(dɪˈplomə)

n. 文憑;畢業證書 (= *certificate*)
Mary framed her *diploma* and hung it on the wall behind her desk.
瑪麗把她的畢業證書裱框,掛在她書桌後面的牆上。

di	+ plo	+ ma
two +	*fold* +	*n.*

「畢業證書」常常被折成二層

diplomacy[6]
(dɪˈploməsɪ)

n. 外交 (= *international relations*);外交手腕
The road to world peace will be paved by *diplomacy*. 世界和平之路要靠外交來進行。

diplomatist
(dɪˈplomətɪst)

n. 外交家 (= *diplomat*)
The young *diplomatist* learned to choose his friends wisely. 這位年輕的外交家學會了明智地擇友。

字根 ply

diplomat[4]
(ˈdɪpləˌmæt)

n. 外交官 (= *diplomatist*)
A team of bodyguards escorted the Cuban *diplomat* to the airport.
有一組保鏢護送這位古巴外交官到機場。

di	+ plo	+ mat
two +	*fold* +	*n.*

「外交官」需要精通雙方的語言及文化

diplomate
(ˈdɪpləˌmet)

n. 專科醫生 (= *specialist*)
Dr. Wu is a *diplomate* of veterinary surgery at that hospital. 吳醫師是那間醫院裡的專科獸醫。

diplom	+ ate
文憑	+ *n.*

「專科醫生」一定要有「文憑」

diplomatic[6]
(ˌdɪpləˈmætɪk)

adj. 外交的 (= *relating to diplomacy*)
The two leaders hoped for a *diplomatic* solution to the crisis. 兩位領導人希望透過外交解決這個危機。

字根 ply

triplex
〔'trɪplɛks 〕

adj. 三倍的；三重的（ = *threefold* ）
The operation is a *triplex* procedure.
這項手術需要三組程序。

triplicate
〔'trɪplə,ket 〕

v. 成為三倍（ = *make three copies* ）
adj. 一式三份的　*n.* 一式三份中之一
I saved *triplicate* copies of the file on my hard drive.
我把這份檔案儲存三份在我的硬碟裡。

triplication
〔,trɪplə'keʃən 〕

n. 分成三份；三重
Genetic *triplication* is a rare condition.
遺傳學上細胞分裂成三個，是很罕見的情況。

【背誦祕訣】

⎰ diploma
⎱ diplomacy　　重音都在第二音節 /plo/ 上
⎰ diplomatist

⎰ diplomat　　重音在第一音節，唸成 /dɪ/
⎱ diplomate　　重音在第一音節，唸成 /dɪ/
⎰ diplomatic　　次重音在第一音節，也唸成 /dɪ/

⎰ triplex
⎱ triplicate　　這三個字的順序和 duplex-duplicate-
⎰ triplication　　duplication 相同。

Exercise : Choose the correct answer. ★

1. The _____ of your silence is that you are bored.
   (A) exploitation   (B) supplication
   (C) complication   (D) implication

2. This isn't a real Rolex watch; it's a cheap _____ I picked up in Hong Kong.
   (A) supplicant   (B) replica
   (C) plight   (D) complexion

3. The key to winning at chess is to _____ your opponent's weaknesses.
   (A) employ   (B) exploit
   (C) deploy   (D) supply

4. Don't _____ matters by getting your sister involved.
   (A) complicate   (B) explicate
   (C) replicate   (D) duplicate

5. The audience looked at the lecturer, _____. They couldn't follow his speech at all.
   (A) suppliant   (B) duplex
   (C) applied   (D) perplexed

6. Prospective students may now _____ online for admission to the university.
   (A) ply   (B) multiply
   (C) apply   (D) simplify

7. Apple's iPod is appreciated for its _____ of design and ease of use.
   (A) complicity   (B) explicitly
   (C) simplicity   (D) multiplicity

8. I sent Mary a letter but she never _____.
   (A) complied　　　　(B) implied
   (C) replied　　　　(D) supplied

9. After decades of conflict, North and South Korea have resumed _____ relations.
   (A) diplomatic　　　　(B) diploma
   (C) diplomate　　　　(D) diplomat

10. This insurance form must be filled out in _____.
    (A) triplicate　　　　(B) triplication
    (C) triple　　　　(D) triplex

11. There was no evidence to _____ him in the robbery.
    (A) perplex　　　　(B) implicate
    (C) supplicate　　　　(D) pleat

12. He left _____ instructions not to disturb the items on his desk.
    (A) multiplicate　　　　(B) explicit
    (C) complicit　　　　(D) pliable

13. It is a privilege to work for such an excellent _____.
    (A) employer　　　　(B) simpleton
    (C) appliance　　　　(D) employment

14. The professor attempted to give a clear _____ of modern physics.
    (A) multiplication　　　　(B) applicability
    (C) duplication　　　　(D) explication

15. The business deal was closed with a(n) _____ handshake.
    (A) duple　　　　(B) diplomatist
    (C) simple　　　　(D) applicable

字根 ply

字彙測驗詳解

1. (**D**)　你的沈默暗示你很無聊。

    (A) exploitation〔͵ɛksplɔɪˈteʃən〕*n.* 利用；剝削

    (B) supplication〔͵sʌplɪˈkeʃən〕*n.* 懇求

    (C) complication〔͵kɑmpləˈkeʃən〕*n.* 複雜；併發症

    (D) *implication*〔͵ɪmplɪˈkeʃən〕*n.* 暗示；牽連

    silence〔ˈsaɪləns〕*n.* 沈默　　bored〔bord〕*adj.* 無聊的

2. (**B**)　這不是眞正的勞力士手錶；這是我在香港買的便宜的仿冒品。

    (A) supplicant〔ˈsʌplɪkənt〕*n.* 懇求者

    (B) *replica*〔ˈrɛplɪkə〕*n.* 複製品

    (C) plight〔plaɪt〕*n.* 困境

    (D) complexion〔kəmˈplɛkʃən〕*n.* 膚色

Rolex

    Rolex〔ˈrolɛks〕*n.* 勞力士【瑞士名牌手錶】　　*pick up* 買

3. (**B**)　下西洋棋要贏，關鍵就是要利用對手的弱點。

    (A) employ〔ɪmˈplɔɪ〕*v.* 雇用

    (B) *exploit*〔ɪkˈsplɔɪt〕*v.* 利用；開發；剝削

    (C) deploy〔dɪˈplɔɪ〕*v.* 部署

    (D) supply〔səˈplaɪ〕*v., n.* 供給

chess

    key〔ki〕*n.* 關鍵　　chess〔tʃɛs〕*n.* 西洋棋

    opponent〔əˈponənt〕*n.* 對手　　weakness〔ˈwiknɪs〕*n.* 弱點

4. (**A**)　不要把你的妹妹牽扯進來，使事情變得很複雜。

    (A) *complicate*〔ˈkɑmpləͺket〕*v.* 使複雜

    (B) explicate〔ˈɛksplɪͺket〕*v.* 詳細說明

    (C) replicate〔ˈrɛplɪͺket〕*v.* 複製

    (D) duplicate〔ˈdjupləͺket〕*v.* 複製

    matter〔ˈmætɚ〕*n.* 事情；事務　　involve〔ɪnˈvɑlv〕*v.* 使牽連

5. (**D**) 觀眾們看著這位演講者，<u>一臉困惑</u>。他們完全聽不懂他的演講。

(A) suppliant 〔'sʌpliənt〕 *adj.* 懇求的

(B) duplex 〔'djuplɛks〕 *adj.* 雙重的

(C) applied 〔ə'plaɪd〕 *adj.* 應用的

(D) ***perplexed*** 〔pɚ'plɛkst〕 *adj.* 困惑的

perplexed

audience 〔'ɔdɪəns〕 *n.* 觀眾；聽眾

lecturer 〔'lɛktʃərɚ〕 *n.* 演講者　　follow 〔'falo〕 *v.* 聽懂

6. (**C**) 有希望的學生，現在可以在網路上<u>申請</u>該大學的入學許可。

(A) ply 〔plaɪ〕 *v.* 忙於；定期往返

(B) multiply 〔'mʌltə,plaɪ〕 *v.* 乘；繁殖

(C) ***apply*** 〔ə'plaɪ〕 *v.* 申請；應用

(D) simplify 〔'sɪmplə,faɪ〕 *v.* 簡化

prospective 〔prə'spɛktɪv〕 *adj.* 未來的；有希望的

online 〔'an,laɪn〕 *adv.* 在網路上；線上

admission 〔əd'mɪʃən〕 *n.* 入學許可

7. (**C**) 蘋果的 iPod 因為設計<u>簡單</u>及使用容易而頗受欣賞。

(A) complicity 〔kəm'plɪsətɪ〕 *n.* 共謀；共犯

(B) explicitly 〔ɪk'splɪsɪtlɪ〕 *adv.* 明白地

(C) ***simplicity*** 〔sɪm'plɪsətɪ〕 *n.* 簡單；簡樸

(D) multiplicity 〔,mʌltə'plɪsətɪ〕 *n.* 衆多；多<u>重</u>

iPod

appreciate 〔ə'priʃɪ,et〕 *v.* 欣賞

design 〔dɪ'zaɪn〕 *n.* 設計　　***ease of use*** 使用容易

8. (**C**) 我寄給瑪麗一封信，但她都沒有<u>回</u>。

(A) comply 〔kəm'plaɪ〕 *v.* 服從；遵從

(B) imply 〔ɪm'plaɪ〕 *v.* 暗示

(C) ***reply*** 〔rɪ'plaɪ〕 *v., n.* 回答

(D) supply 〔sə'plaɪ〕 *v., n.* 供給

9. (**A**) 在數十年的衝突之後，北韓和南韓已恢復<u>外交</u>關係。

(A) *diplomatic*〔͵dɪpləˋmætɪk〕*adj.* 外交的

(B) diploma〔dɪˋplomə〕*n.* 文憑；畢業證書

(C) diplomate〔ˋdɪplə͵met〕*n.* 專科醫生

(D) diplomat〔ˋdɪplə͵mæt〕*n.* 外交官

decade〔ˋdɛked〕*n.* 十年

conflict〔ˋkɑnflɪkt〕*n.* 衝突

Korea〔koˋriə〕*n.* 韓國

resume〔rɪˋzum〕*v.* 恢復

relation〔rɪˋleʃən〕*n.* 關係

10. (**A**) 這份保險表格必須填寫<u>一式三份</u>。

(A) *triplicate*〔ˋtrɪplə͵ket〕*adj.* 一式三份的

n. 一式三份中之一　　*in triplicate* 一式三份的

(B) triplication〔͵trɪpləˋkeʃən〕*n.* 分成三份；三重

(C) triple〔ˋtrɪpḷ〕*adj.* 三倍的　*v.* 成為三倍

(D) triplex〔ˋtrɪplɛks〕*adj.* 三倍的；三重的

insurance〔ɪnˋʃurəns〕*n.* 保險

form〔fɔrm〕*n.* 表格　　*fill out* 填寫

11. (**B**) 沒有證據顯示他<u>涉入</u>這宗搶案。

(A) perplex〔pɚˋplɛks〕*v.* 使困惑；使複雜

(B) *implicate*〔ˋɪmplɪ͵ket〕*v.* 牽連；涉入

(C) supplicate〔ˋsʌplɪ͵ket〕*v.* 懇求

(D) pleat〔plit〕*v.*（衣服）打褶　*n.*（衣服的）褶

evidence〔ˋɛvədəns〕*n.* 證據

involvement〔ɪnˋvɑlvmənt〕*n.* 牽涉在內

robbery〔ˋrɑbərɪ〕*n.* 搶劫；搶案

12. (**B**) 他留下<u>明白的</u>指示，不要弄亂他書桌上的物品。

    (A) multiplicate〔'mʌltəplɪ,ket〕*adj.* 多重的

    (B) *explicit*〔ɪk'splɪsɪt〕*adj.* 明白的

    (C) complicit〔kəm'plɪsɪt〕*adj.* 共謀的

    (D) pliable〔'plaɪəbl̩〕*adj.* 易折的；柔軟的

    instruction〔ɪn'strʌkʃən〕*n.* 指示

    disturb〔dɪ'stɝb〕*v.* 擾亂；打擾　　item〔'aɪtəm〕*n.* 物品

13. (**A**) 為這樣一個優秀的<u>老板</u>工作是一項殊榮。

    (A) *employer*〔ɪm'plɔɪɚ〕*n.* 老板；公司

    (B) simpleton〔'sɪmpl̩tən〕*n.* 傻子；笨蛋

    (C) appliance〔ə'plaɪəns〕*n.* 用具；用品

    (D) employment〔ɪm'plɔɪmənt〕*n.* 職業；工作

    privilege〔'prɪvl̩ɪdʒ〕*n.* 特權；殊榮　　*work for* 為～工作

14. (**D**) 教授試著為現代物理學做一個清楚而<u>詳細的說明</u>。

    (A) multiplication〔,mʌltəplə'keʃən〕*n.* 乘法；繁殖

    (B) applicability〔,æplɪkə'bɪlətɪ〕*n.* 適用性

    (C) duplication〔,djuplə'keʃən〕*n.* 複製（品）

    (D) *explication*〔,ɛksplɪ'keʃən〕*n.* 詳細說明

    professor〔prə'fɛsɚ〕*n.* 教授

    attempt〔ə'tɛmpt〕*v.* 嘗試；企圖　　physics〔'fɪzɪks〕*n.* 物理學

15. (**C**) 這項商業交易以一個<u>簡單的</u>握手就完成了。

    (A) duple〔'djupl̩〕*adj.* 兩倍的；雙重的

    (B) diplomatist〔dɪ'plomətɪst〕*n.* 外交家

    (C) *simple*〔'sɪmpl̩〕*adj.* 簡單的

    (D) applicable〔'æplɪkəbl̩〕*adj.* 適用的

    deal〔dil〕*n.* 交易　　close〔kloz〕*v.* 完成；談妥

    close a deal 完成交易；議妥　　handshake〔'hænd,ʃek〕*n.* 握手

請連中文一起背，背至一分半鐘內，終生不忘。

1

apply	申請
supply	供給
reply	回答
imply	暗示
comply	服從
multiply	乘

ply	忙於
pliable	易折的
pliers	鉗子
plight	困境
pleat	打褶
plait	辮子

2

applied	應用的
appliance	用具
application	應用
applicant	申請人
applicable	適用的
applicability	適用性

supplier	供應者
suppliance	懇求
suppliant	懇求者
supplicant	懇求者
supplicate	懇求
supplication	懇求
replica	複製品
replicate	複製
replication	複製

字根 ply

3

implicit	暗示的
implicate	牽連
implication	牽連
explicit	明白的
explicate	詳細說明
explication	詳細說明
explicable	可說明的
exploit	開發
exploitation	開發

字根 ply

complicate	使複雜
complication	複雜
complicity	共謀
complex	複雜的
complexity	複雜
complexion	臉色
multiplicate	多重的
multiplication	乘法
multiplicity	多重

5

simple	簡單的
duple	兩倍的
triple	三倍的
simplify	簡化
simpleton	傻子
simplicity	簡單
duplex	雙重的
duplicate	複製
duplication	複製品

4

perplex	使困惑
perplexed	困惑的
perplexity	困惑
employ	雇用
employer	雇主
employment	職業
deploy	部署
deployer	部署者
deployment	部署

diploma	文憑
diplomacy	外交
diplomatist	外交家
diplomat	外交官
diplomate	專科醫生
diplomatic	外交的
triplex	三倍的
triplicate	成為三倍
triplication	分成三份

※ 本頁可影印後，隨身攜帶，方便背誦。

Group 4 字根 *sign*

目標： ① 先將60個字放入短期記憶。
② 加快速度至50秒之內，成為長期記憶。

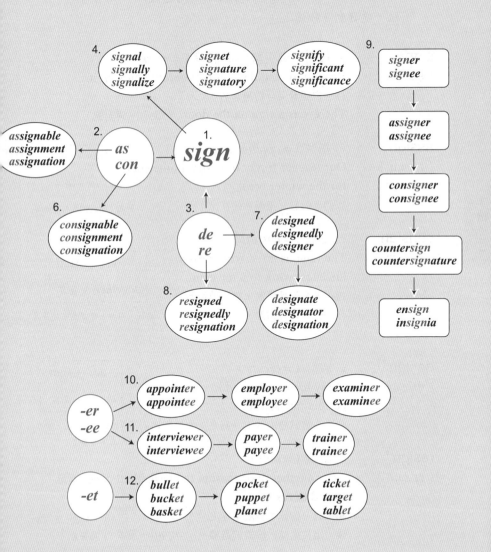

1. 字根 *sign* 核心單字

字根 sign 核心單字只有 5 個，<u>s</u>ign-as<u>s</u>ign-con<u>s</u>ign 的 s 都發 /s/ 音，de<u>s</u>ign-re<u>s</u>ign 的 s 則唸成 /z/，用發音分組，要背到 3 秒鐘之內。

sign[2]
〔 saɪn 〕

v. 簽名；做手勢　　*n.* 記號（＝*mark*）
Be sure to read the contract before you *sign* it.
你一定要看完合約再簽名。
There was a *sign* on the door. 門上有一個記號。

assign[4]
〔 ə'saɪn 〕

v. 指派（＝*appoint*）
Our teacher forgot to *assign* homework
for the winter break.
我們老師忘記指派寒假作業了。

```
as  +  sign
|      |
to  +  簽名
```
簽名「指派」某人去做事

consign
〔 kən'saɪn 〕

v. 委託（＝*entrust*）
The famous artist will *consign*
his latest work to a museum.
這位著名的藝術家，要將他最新的
作品委託給博物館。

```
con    +  sign
 |         |
together + 簽名
```
「委託」別人，雙方要一起簽名

design[2]
〔 dɪ'zaɪn 〕

v. 設計（＝*create*）
Many have attempted to *design* a
perfect mousetrap.
許多人嘗試要設計出一個完美的捕鼠器。

```
de   +  sign
 |       |
down +  簽名
```
「設計」作品後，會在
作品下面簽名

resign[4]
〔 rɪ'zaɪn 〕

v. 辭職（＝*quit*）
After another poor season, the basketball coach was
forced to *resign*.
繼另外一個球季表現不佳之
後，這位籃球教練被迫辭職。

```
re   +  sign
 |       |
again + 簽名
```
「辭職」要一再
地簽名

2. signal-signally-signalize

這一回共有 15 個單字，前 9 個來自 sign 的變化，後 6 個則是 assign 和 consign 的變化，記住這一組的 sign，s 都發 /s/ 音。要背到 8 秒鐘之內，就終生難忘。

signal[3]
〔'sɪgnḷ〕

n. 信號 (= *sign* ; *mark*)
Raise your right hand as a *signal* that you have finished the exam.
當你完成考試，請舉起右手表示。

```
sign  + al
 |      |
做手勢  + n.
```

signally
〔'sɪgnḷɪ〕

adv. 顯著地 (= *notably* ; *remarkably*)
He has *signally* failed to solve the problem.
他顯然無法解決這個問題。

```
signal + ly
  |      |
信號   + adv.
```
有信號就很「顯著」

signalize
〔'sɪgnḷ͵aɪz〕

v. 使顯著 (= *make sth. stand out*)
The president *signalized* his term in office with many good deeds.
這位總統任期內政績卓著。

```
signal + ize
  |      |
信號   + v.
```

signet
〔'sɪgnɪt〕

n. 印章 (= *seal*)
Once you apply a *signet* to the contract, the car is yours. 你只要在合約
上蓋個章，車子就是你的了。

```
sign + et
 |     |
簽名  + n.
```
代替簽名的小東西，就是「印章」

signature[4]
〔'sɪgnətʃɚ〕

n. 簽名 (= *signed name*)
These documents require your *signature*. 這些文件需要你的簽名。

```
sign + ature
 |      |
簽名  + n.
```

signatory
〔'sɪgnə͵torɪ〕

n. 簽署者 (= *signee*)
The agreement must be authorized by three *signatories*.
這份協議需要三名簽署者授權。

```
sign + atory
 |      |
簽名  + 人
```

signify[6]
〔ˈsɪgnəˌfaɪ〕

v. 表示（＝*express*；*show*）
In many cultures, the color red
signifies love.
在許多文化中，紅色表示愛情。

sign	+	ify
記號	+	*make*

significant[3]
〔sɪgˈnɪfəkənt〕

adj. 意義重大的（＝*meaningful*；*important*）
The result is highly *significant* for the future
development. 這個結果對於未來的發展意義重大。

sign	+	ifi	+	cant
記號	+	*make*	+	*adj.*

significance[4]
〔sɪgˈnɪfəkəns〕

n. 意義；重要性（＝*meaning*；*importance*）
I don't see the *significance* of your comment.
我看不出你的評論有何意義。

字根 sign

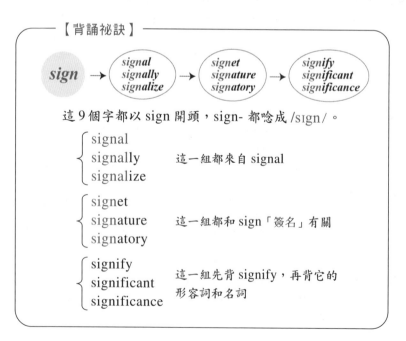

【背誦祕訣】

sign → signal / signally / signalize → signet / signature / signatory → signify / significant / significance

這 9 個字都以 sign 開頭，sign- 都唸成 /sɪgn/。

signal
signally　　這一組都來自 signal
signalize

signet
signature　　這一組都和 sign「簽名」有關
signatory

signify
significant　　這一組先背 signify，再背它的
significance　　形容詞和名詞

assignable
〔 ə'saɪnəbḷ 〕

adj. 可指派的；可認定的（ = *able to be assigned* ）
Doctors failed to find an *assignable* cause for
Oscar's illness. 醫生無法認定奧斯卡的病因。

```
assign + able
  |       |
 指派  + 可～的
```

assignment[4]
〔 ə'saɪnmənt 〕

n. 任務；功課（ = *task* ; *homework* ）
I asked Mr. Brown for more time
to complete my *assignment.*
我要求布朗老師多給我一點時間，
完成我的功課。

```
assign + ment
  |        |
 指派  +   n.
```

assignation
〔 ,æsɪg'neʃən 〕

n. 幽會；約會（ = *rendezvous* ）
Against her parent's wishes,
Heidi kept an *assignation*
with the boy from Tokyo.

```
assign + ation
  |        |
 指派  +   n.
```

海蒂違背父母的意願，和那個來自東京的男生偷偷幽會。

consignable
〔 kən'saɪnəbḷ 〕

adj. 可委託的；可交付的（ = *deliverable* ）
Nuclear waste is not *consignable* to ordinary
methods of disposal.
核子廢料不能交付一般的處理方法。

consignment
〔 kən'saɪnmənt 〕

n. 委託（物）（ = *delivery* ）
The first *consignment* of relief supplies reached
the flood victims.
第一批委託的救援物資，已經送達洪水災民那裡。

consignation
〔 ,kɑnsɪg'neʃən 〕

n. 委託
The judge will decide if our *consignation* was
made properly.
法官將會判定我們的委託方式是否妥當。

字根 sign

3. *designed-designedly-designer*

這一回有 9 個字，前 6 個字是 design 的變化，後 3 個字是 resign 的衍生，9 個字背到 5 秒鐘之內，就永遠不會忘記了。

designed[2]
〔 dɪ'zaɪnd 〕

adj. 設計好的；故意的 (= *intentional*)
I tripped him, but it was not *designed*.
我害他絆倒，但不是故意的。

designedly
〔 dɪ'zaɪnɪdlɪ 〕

adv. 故意地 (= *intentionally*)
We didn't know if he did so *designedly*.
我們不知道他這麼做是不是故意的。

designer[3]
〔 dɪ'zaɪnɚ 〕

n. 設計師
Designer clothing is often ridiculously over-priced.
設計師品牌的服裝價錢常常是貴得離譜。

字根
sign

designate[6]
〔 'dɛzɪɡ,net 〕

v. 指定；任命 (= *appoint*)
We will vote to *designate* a
spokesperson for our group.
我們即將投票指定我們這一組的發言人。

```
de  + sign + ate
 |      |      |
完全 + 標記 +  v.
```

designator
〔 'dɛzɪɡ,netɚ 〕

n. 指定者 (= *appointer*)
A laser *designator* is a light source
used to locate a target for guided
bombs and missiles. 雷射標定器是
一個光源，被用來爲導彈找到目標。

laser designator

designation
〔 ,dɛzɪɡ'neʃən 〕

n. 指定；任命 (= *appointment*)
In the U.S., private property is not eligible for
national landmark *designation*.
在美國，私人財產不適合被指定爲全國性的地標。

resigned[4]
〔 rɪ'zaɪnd 〕

adj. 辭職的；認命的 (= *unresisting*)
Ted is *resigned* to being a failure all his life.
泰德對於終生做個失敗者很認命。

resignedly
〔 rɪ'zaɪnɪdlɪ 〕

adv. 認命地 (= *unresistingly*)
I *resignedly* accepted her apology.
我很認命地接受她的道歉。

resignation[4]
〔 ‚rɛzɪg'neʃən 〕

n. 辭職；認命 (= *acceptance*)
Jasper wore a look of *resignation* as I told him the bad news.
當我告訴傑斯伯這個壞消息時，他一副認命的表情。

字根 sign

【背誦祕訣】

designed
designedly　　這三個字重音都是 /aɪ/
designer

designate　　　這個字重音讀 /ɛ/
designator　　　這個字重音讀 /ɛ/
designation　　這個字次重音讀 /ɛ/

resigned
resignedly　　前二個字重音都讀 /aɪ/
resignation

4. *signer-signee-assigner-assignee*

這一回共有 10 個字，二個二個一組，前三組是 sign，assign，consign 字尾各加上 er，ee，接下來是 sign 和 signature 前加上 counter，這 10 個字 5 秒鐘就可背完。

signer
〔'saɪnɚ 〕

n. 簽名者（ = *one who signs his name* ）
Thomas Jefferson was one of the original *signers* of the Declaration of Independence.
傑弗遜是獨立宣言最初的三位簽名者之一。

signee
〔 saɪ'ni 〕

n. 簽署者（ = *signatory* ）
This document is not legally binding until it has been endorsed by the appropriate *signee*.
這份文件要等到適合的簽署者簽名之後，法律上才有效。

assigner
〔 ə'saɪnɚ 〕

n. 分配人（ = *one who assigns* ）
The *assigner* will tell you which line to join.
分配人會告訴你要排哪一行隊伍。

assignee
〔ˌæsaɪ'ni 〕

n.（ 財產 ）受讓人（ = *one who receives property* ）
A suitable *assignee* for the ancient castle could not be found. 這座古老的城堡找不到適合的受讓人。

consigner
〔 kən'saɪnɚ 〕

n. 委託者；寄件人
We have developed a significant number of regular *consigners*. 我們已經有相當多固定的委託者。

consignee
〔ˌkɑnsaɪ'ni 〕

n. 受託者；收件人
It is unlawful to deliver the goods to anyone but the authorized *consignee*. 除了有授權的收件人之外，把這些商品送給任何人都是違法的。

countersign
（'kaʊntɚˌsaɪn）

v. 副署；連署（= *cosign*）
A rental contract must be *countersigned* by the
landlord to be valid.
租賃契約需要房東副署，
才是有效文件。

```
counter + sign
   |       |
  對應    + 簽名
```

countersignature
（ˌkaʊntɚ'sɪgnətʃɚ）

n. 副署；連署
This report will require my supervisor's
countersignature.
這份報告需要我的上司副署。

ensign
（'ɛnsaɪn）

n. 徽章（= *badge*）
A pirate ship's *ensign* has traditionally been
the white skull and crossbones on a black
background.　海盜船的傳統標章是，黑色的旗
子配上白色的骷髏頭和交叉的骨頭。

```
en + sign
 |     |
 on  + 記號    「徽章」的上面有記號
```

pirate ship

insignia
（ɪn'sɪgnɪə）

n. 徽章（= *ensign*）
The Iron Cross was an *insignia* used on German
aircraft during World War II.
第二次世界大戰中，德國的飛機
上有鐵十字徽章的圖案。

```
in  + sign + ia
 |     |     |
on  + 記號 + 物
```

Iron Cross

字根 sign

5. *appointer-appointee*

這一回共有 12 個單字，字尾 er 常表「主動者」，
ee 常表「被動者」，兩兩一組做比較，共 6 組，而且按
照字母順序排列，非常好背，要背到 6 秒之內。

appointer
〔 ə'pɔɪntə 〕

n. 任命者（= *selector*）
The President also serves as the
appointer for the Supreme Court.
總統同時也有最高法院的任命權。

> appoint + er
> |　　　　|
> 任命　+ 主動者

appointee
〔 əpɔɪn'ti ,
ˌæpɔɪn'ti 〕

n. 被任命者（= *functionary*）
George Jetson is the latest *appointee* to the regulatory
commission on nuclear energy.
喬治・傑生是核能管制局最新被任命者。

employer[3]
〔 ɪm'plɔɪə 〕

n. 老板（= *boss*）
Many *employers* regard a high EQ
as an important quality in a worker.
許多老板認爲，高 EQ（情緒商數）是
員工應有的一個重要特質。

> employ + er
> |　　　　|
> 雇用　+ 主動者

employee[3]
〔ˌɛmplɔɪ'i 〕

n. 員工（= *worker*）
Sally was a diligent *employee* who never missed a day's
work in ten years. 莎莉是勤奮的員工，十年來工作從不缺席。

examiner[4]
〔 ɪg'zæmɪnə 〕

n. 主考官；檢查者（= *inspector*）
Lisa answered the questions of
the *examiner* nervously.
麗莎很緊張地回答主考官的問題。

> examin(e) + er
> |　　　　　|
> 考試　+ 主動者

examinee[4]
〔 ɪgˌzæmə'ni 〕

n. 考生（= *responder*）
During the oral test, a teacher will assess the
knowledge of each *examinee* individually.
在口試時，老師會個別評估每位考生的知識。

interviewer
〔ˈɪntɚˌvjuɚ〕

n. 面試者；訪問者（= *questioner*）
The *interviewer* did his best to get the truth out of the witness.
訪問者盡全力從目擊者口中得到真相。

> interview　+　er
> 　　|　　　　　|
> 面試；訪問　+ 主動者

interviewee
〔ˌɪntɚvjuˈi〕

n. 被面試者；受訪者（= *respondent*）
Asking easy questions at the beginning of an interview helps to make the *interviewee* more receptive to tougher inquiries later in the conversation.
在訪問一開始先問簡單的問題，有助於讓受訪者較容易接受後面對話中更困難的問題。

payer
〔ˈpeɚ〕

n. 付款人（= *renter*）
The cost of the election will be passed on to the tax *payers*.
選舉的費用會被轉嫁給納稅人。

> pay　+　er
> 　|　　　　|
> 付款　+ 主動者

字根 sign

payee
〔peˈi〕

n. 收款人（= *recipient*）
The check was made out to the *payee* in the amount of one thousand dollars.
這張支票被開給收款人，面額是一千元美金。

trainer
〔ˈtrenɚ〕

n. 訓練者；教練（= *coach*）
The circus tiger did not respond to the commands of his *trainer*.
馬戲團的老虎對訓練師的命令不予回應。

> train　+　er
> 　|　　　　|
> 訓練　+ 主動者

trainee
〔trenˈi〕

n. 受訓者（= *student*）
Bill spent six months as a *trainee* in the accounting department before being promoted to clerk.
比爾在會計部門受訓六個月之後，才升為職員。

6. *bullet-bucket-basket*

最後這一回共有 9 個單字，都是 et 結尾，字尾
et 常表「小東西」，第一組 b 開頭，第二組全是 p 開
頭，第三組為 t，5 秒背 9 字，終生不忘。

bullet[3]
(ˈbʊlɪt)

n. 子彈 (= *cartiridge*)
Surgeons were unable to remove the *bullet*
lodged in the shooting victim's skull.
外科醫生無法將遭槍擊的受害者腦中的子彈取出。

bull	+ et
公牛	+ 小

bucket[3]
(ˈbʌkɪt)

n. 水桶 (= *pail*)
There's an old saying that goes, "A leaky
bucket holds no water."
有一句古老的諺語說：「漏水的水桶裝不了水。」

buck	+ et
元	+ 小

basket[1]
(ˈbæskɪt)

n. 籃子 (= *container*)
Another common idiom is that you should
"never put all your eggs in one *basket*."
另一個常見的成語是，你「不該把所有的雞蛋放在一個籃子裡」。

bask	+ et
曬太陽	+ 小

pocket[1]
(ˈpɑkɪt)

n. 口袋 (= *pouch*)
Money burns a hole in my *pocket*, which
means that I spend everything I get.
錢會在我的口袋裡燒出一個洞，意思就是我會把所有的錢都花光。

pock	+ et
麻子；痘疤	+ 小

puppet[2]
(ˈpʌpɪt)

n. 木偶 (= *marionette*)
The children put on a *puppet* show to
entertain their teacher.
孩子們演出一場木偶秀來娛樂老師。

pup	+ pet
小狗	+ 小

planet[2]
(ˈplænɪt)

n. 行星 (= *celestial body*)
Earth is the third *planet* from the sun
in the solar system.
地球是太陽系中距離太陽第三位的行星。

plan	+ et
計畫	+ 小

ticket[1]
〔ˈtɪkɪt〕

n. 票（= *pass*）

Tickets for A-mei's concert at Taipei Arena sold out in a matter of minutes.

阿妹在台北小巨蛋演唱會的門票，大約幾分鐘之內就賣光了。

tick	+ et
滴答聲	+ 小

target[2]
〔ˈtɑrgɪt〕

n. 靶子；目標（= *point*）

Expert predictions of our company's revenues were right on *target*.

專家對我們公司收入的預測很準確。

tablet[3]
〔ˈtæblɪt〕

n. 藥片（= *pill*）

Helen's medication plan requires her to take four *tablets* of aspirin every day.

海倫的藥單中包括她每天要吃四片阿斯匹靈藥片。

字根
sign

【背誦祕訣】

tablet 這個字背不下來，可先背 table（桌子），利用比較法背單字，也是不錯的方法之一，但要注意發音。

　　table〔ˈtebḷ〕*n.* 桌子

　　tablet〔ˈtæblɪt〕*n.* 藥片【像桌子一樣平的】

再背一個字：

　　stable〔ˈstebḷ〕*adj.* 穩定的【像桌子一樣穩】

Exercise : Choose the correct answer. ✦

1. It seems to me that certain drivers have little or no practical knowledge of how to use a turn _____.
   (A) signal   (B) signet
   (C) signatory   (D) signature

2. The airport security guard ordered me to empty my _____.
   (A) bullets   (B) puppets
   (C) pockets   (D) buckets

3. John recently became an editorial _____ at the China Post.
   (A) payee   (B) trainee
   (C) payer   (D) appointee

4. Drifting for days on the open water, the shipwreck survivor was _____ to his fate until he spotted a speck of land on the horizon.
   (A) consigned   (B) signalized
   (C) signed   (D) resigned

5. Frances stayed up late last night to finish the _____.
   (A) consignation   (B) assignment
   (C) designation   (D) assignation

6. A medical _____ is responsible for determining the cause of death.
   (A) employee   (B) appointer
   (C) examinee   (D) examiner

7. Applicants for a U.K. passport are required to provide a(n) _____ before the document can be issued.
   (A) countersignature   (B) insignia
   (C) ensign   (D) consigner

字根 sign

8. We've had a _____ amount of rainfall last month.
   (A) signally   (B) consignable
   (C) designedly   (D) significant

9. Since we can't seem to agree, we'll have to draw straws to
   _____ a driver for the party. Shortest straw loses.
   (A) designate   (B) resign
   (C) design   (D) countersign

10. Due to the dockworkers' strike, cargo ships loaded with
    goods ready for _____ were forced to idle in the harbor.
    (A) resignation   (B) appointment
    (C) consignment   (D) designator

11. He fired five shots, but none of them hit the _____.
    (A) baskets   (B) tablets
    (C) targets   (D) tickets

12. If you are injured on the job, you should notify your _____
    immediately.
    (A) interviewer   (B) employer
    (C) designer   (D) signer

13. The widow wore black to _____ her mourning.
    (A) signify   (B) assign
    (C) interview   (D) examine

14. There are more convenience stores per square kilometer in
    Taipei than anywhere else on the _____.
    (A) puppet   (B) trainer
    (C) signee   (D) planet

15. The increased size and frequency of storms in the world may
    be _____ to global warming.
    (A) interviewee   (B) assignable
    (C) significant   (D) significance

字彙測驗詳解

1. (**A**) 對我而言，某些駕駛人似乎不太知道，或完全不知道如何打方向燈。
    (A) *signal* (ˈsɪgnl̩) *n.* 信號　　*turn signal* 方向燈
    (B) signet (ˈsɪgnɪt) *n.* 印章
    (C) signatory (ˈsɪgnəˌtorɪ) *n.* 簽署者
    (D) signature (ˈsɪgnətʃɚ) *n.* 簽名

2. (**C**) 機場安全警衛命令我把口袋清空。
    (A) bullet (ˈbʊlɪt) *n.* 子彈　　(B) puppet (ˈpʌpɪt) *n.* 木偶
    (C) *pocket* (ˈpakɪt) *n.* 口袋　　(D) bucket (ˈbʌkɪt) *n.* 水桶
    security guard 安全　　empty (ˈɛmptɪ) *v.* 倒空；清空

3. (**B**) 約翰最近在英文中國郵報的編輯部受訓。
    (A) payee (peˈi) *n.* 收款人　　(B) *trainee* (trenˈi) *n.* 受訓者
    (C) payer (ˈpeɚ) *n.* 付款人
    (D) appointee (əpɔɪnˈti, ˌæpɔɪnˈti) *n.* 被任命者

4. (**D**) 在遼闊的水面上漂流了好幾天，這名船難生還者原先已認命，
    直到他看到了水平線上有一小點陸地。
    (A) consign (kənˈsaɪn) *v.* 委託
    (B) signalize (ˈsɪgnl̩ˌaɪz) *v.* 使顯著
    (C) sign (saɪn) *v.* 簽名　　*n.* 記號；標記
    (D) *resigned* (rɪˈzaɪnd) *adj.* 辭職的；認命的
    drift (drɪft) *v.* 漂流　　open (ˈopən) *adj.* 開闊的；無障礙物的
    shipwreck (ˈʃɪpˌrɛk) *n.* 船難　　spot (spat) *v.* 看到
    speck (spɛk) *n.* 小點　　horizon (həˈraɪzn̩) *n.* 地平線；水平線

5. (**B**) 法蘭西絲昨晚爲了完成作業，熬夜熬到很晚。
    (A) consignation (ˌkansɪgˈneʃən) *n.* 委託
    (B) *assignment* (əˈsaɪnmənt) *n.* 作業；任務
    (C) designation (ˌdɛzɪgˈneʃən) *n.* 指定；任命
    (D) assignation (ˌæsɪgˈneʃən) *n.* 幽會；指派

6. (**D**) <u>驗屍官</u>負責判定死因。
    (A) employee〔͵ɛmplɔɪ'i〕*n.* 員工
    (B) appointer〔ə'pɔɪntɚ〕*n.* 任命者
    (C) examinee〔ɪg͵zæmə'ni〕*n.* 應試者；受檢者
    (D) *examiner*〔ɪg'zæmɪnɚ〕*n.* 主考官；檢查者
       medical examiner 驗屍官；體檢醫生

7. (**A**) 要申請英國護照的人，在發給文件之前，必須提供<u>第二人簽名</u>。
    (A) *countersignature*〔͵kaʊntɚ'sɪgnətʃɚ〕*n.* 連署；第二人簽名
    (B) insignia〔ɪn'sɪgnɪə〕*n.* 徽章
    (C) ensign〔'ɛnsaɪn〕*n.* 徽章
    (D) consigner〔kən'saɪnɚ〕*n.* 委託者；寄件人

8. (**D**) 我們上個月的降雨量<u>相當大</u>。
    (A) signally〔'sɪgn̩ɪ〕*adv.* 明顯地
    (B) consignable〔kən'saɪnəbḷ〕*adj.* 可委託的
    (C) designedly〔dɪ'zaɪnɪdlɪ〕*adv.* 故意地
    (D) *significant*〔sɪg'nɪfəkənt〕*adj.* 重大的；顯著的；相當大的

9. (**A**) 因爲我們似乎意見不一致，所以必須抽吸管，<u>指定</u>去參加派對時由誰開車。吸管最短的人就輸。
    (A) *designate*〔'dɛzɪg͵net〕*v.* 指定
    (B) resign〔rɪ'zaɪn〕*v.* 辭職　(C) design〔dɪ'zaɪn〕*v.* 設計
    (D) countersign〔'kaʊntɚ͵saɪn〕*v.* 副署；連署
    draw〔drɔ〕*v.* 拉；抽　　straw〔strɔ〕*n.* 稻草；吸管

10. (**C**) 因爲碼頭工人罷工，原本準備好要<u>托運</u>的滿載貨物的貨船，被迫閒置在港口。
    (A) resignation〔͵rɛzɪg'neʃən〕*n.* 辭職
    (B) appointment〔ə'pɔɪntmənt〕*n.* 約會
    (C) *consignment*〔kən'saɪnmənt〕*n.* 委託；托運
    (D) designator〔'dɛzɪg͵netɚ〕*n.* 指定者
    dockworker〔'dɑk͵wɝkɚ〕*n.* 碼頭工人　　strike〔straɪk〕*n.* 罷工
    cargo〔'kɑrgo〕*n.* 貨物　　*be loaded with* 滿載
    idle〔'aɪdḷ〕*v.* 閒置；(引擎)空轉　　harbor〔'hɑrbɚ〕*n.* 港口

字根 sign

11. (**C**) 他發射五發子彈，但沒有一發中靶。
    (A) basket〔'bæskɪt〕*n.* 籃子
    (B) tablet〔'tæblɪt〕*n.* 藥片
    (C) *target*〔'tɑrgɪt〕*n.* 靶子；目標
    (D) ticket〔'tɪkɪt〕*n.* 票

12. (**B**) 如果你在工作時受傷，應該要立刻通知你的老板。
    (A) interviewer〔'ɪntɚ,vjuɚ〕*n.* 面試者；訪問者
    (B) *employer*〔ɪm'plɔɪɚ〕*n.* 雇主；老板
    (C) designer〔dɪ'zaɪnɚ〕*n.* 設計師
    (D) signer〔'saɪnɚ〕*n.* 簽名者
    on the job 工作時；勤務中   notify〔'notə,faɪ〕*v.* 通知

13. (**A**) 這位寡婦穿黑色衣服，表示她正在服喪。
    (A) *signify*〔'sɪgnə,faɪ〕*v.* 表示
    (B) assign〔ə'saɪn〕*v.* 指派
    (C) interview〔'ɪntɚ,vju〕*v., n.* 面試；訪問
    (D) examine〔ɪg'zæmɪn〕*v.* 檢查
    widow〔'wɪdo〕*n.* 寡婦   mourning〔'mɔrnɪŋ〕*n.* 哀悼；服喪

14. (**D**) 台北每平方公里的便利商店，比地球上其他地方都要多。
    (A) puppet〔'pʌpɪt〕*n.* 木偶
    (B) trainer〔'trenɚ〕*n.* 訓練者；教練
    (C) signee〔saɪ'ni〕*n.* 簽署者
    (D) *planet*〔'plænɪt〕*n.* 行星【在此指「地球」】

15. (**B**) 全世界暴風雨的規模和頻率增加，原因可被認定是全球暖化。
    (A) interviewee〔,ɪntɚvju'i〕*n.* 被面試者；受訪者
    (B) *assignable*〔ə'saɪnəbḷ〕*adj.* 可指派的；可認定的
    (C) significant〔sɪg'nɪfəkənt〕*adj.* 意義重大的
    (D) significance〔sɪg'nɪfəkəns〕*n.* 意義；重要性
    frequency〔'frikwənsɪ〕*n.* 頻率
    global warming 全球暖化

字根 sign

請連中文一起背，背至75秒內，終生不忘。 ★

1

sign	簽名
assign	指派
consign	委託
design	設計
resign	辭職

assignable	可指派的
assignment	任務
assignation	幽會
consignable	可委託的
consignment	委託物
consignation	委託

2

signal	信號
signally	顯著地
signalize	使顯著
signet	印章
signature	簽名
signatory	簽署者
signify	表示
significant	意義重大的
significance	意義

3

designed	故意的
designedly	故意地
designer	設計師
designate	指定
designator	指定者
designation	指定
resigned	認命的
resignedly	認命地
resignation	辭職

字根 sign

4

signer	簽名者
signee	簽署者
assigner	分配人
assignee	財產受讓人
consigner	委託者
consignee	受託者

countersign	連署
countersignature	連署
ensign	徽章
insignia	徽章

字根 sign

5

appointer	任命者
appointee	被任命者
employer	老板
employee	員工
examiner	主考官
examinee	考生

interviewer	面試者
interviewee	被面試者
payer	付款人
payee	收款人
trainer	教練
trainee	受訓者

6

bullet	子彈
bucket	水桶
basket	籃子
pocket	口袋
puppet	木偶
planet	行星
ticket	票
target	靶子
tablet	藥片

※ 本頁可影印後，隨身攜帶，方便背誦。

Group 5 字根 *serve*

目標： ① 先將56個字放入短期記憶。
② 加快速度至47秒之內，成為長期記憶。

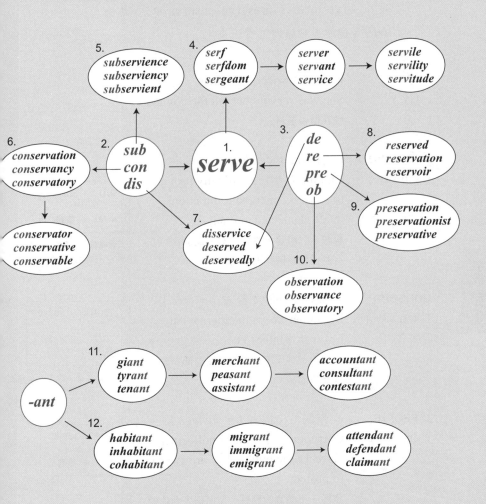

1. 字根 *serve* 核心單字

　　這一課核心單字共有 8 個字，第一組 serve-subserve-conserve-disserve 中，s 都唸 /s/，第二組 deserve-reserve-preserve-observe 中，s 都唸 /z/，8 個字 5 秒鐘即可背出來。

---

serve[1]
〔 sɝv 〕

v. 服務（ = *work for sb.* ）
She was *serving* behind the counter.
她在櫃檯服務。

---

subserve
〔 səb'sɝv 〕

v. 有助於（ = *help* ）
Vitamin C is scientifically proven to *subserve* metabolic functions in all plants and animals.
科學上已證實，維他命 C 有助於所有動植物新陳代謝的功能。

```
sub  + serve
 |       |
under +  服務
```
在下面服務，如幫你洗腳按摩，「有助於」健康

---

conserve[5]
〔 kən'sɝv 〕

v. 保存；保護；節省（ = *save* ）
My father keeps the thermostat lower in winter to *conserve* energy.
我父親在冬天將恆溫器溫度調低一點，以節省能源。

```
con   + serve
 |        |
all   +  keep
together
```
大家一起保留，即「節省」

---

disserve
〔 dɪs'sɝv 〕

v. 幫倒忙；損害（ = *damage* ）
Corrupt and dishonest policemen *disserve* the public they are sworn to protect.
貪污、不誠實的警察，反而損害到他們宣誓要保護的民眾。

```
dis  + serve
 |       |
not  +  服務
```

---

deserve[4]
〔 dɪˈzɝv 〕

v. 應得（ = *be worthy of* ）
Young people should treat their
elders with the respect they *deserve*.
年輕人應該以長輩應得的尊重來對待長輩。

```
de  + serve
 |      |
加強 + 服務
```

reserve[3]
〔 rɪˈzɝv 〕

v. 保留；預約（ = *book* ）
I'll *reserve* a table for four in the
restaurant around the corner.
我要到轉角那家餐廳去預約一桌
四人座。

```
re   + serve
 |       |
back + keep
```
保留到未來再用，即「預約」

preserve[4]
〔 prɪˈzɝv 〕

v. 保存（ = *keep* ; *maintain* ）
A group of local retirees formed a
committee to *preserve* some of
the historical buildings in town.
一群當地的退休者組成一個委員會，
來保存鎮上一些有歷史性的建築物。

```
pre    + serve
  |        |
before + keep
```
保留在以前的狀態，
即「保存」

observe[3]
〔 əbˈzɝv 〕

v. 觀察（ = *watch* ）；遵守（ = *comply with* ）
With my new telescope, I can *observe*
distant planets in the solar system.
有了我的新望遠鏡，我可以觀察
太陽系中遙遠的行星。

```
ob  + serve
 |      |
eye + keep
```
保留在眼前，表示「觀察；遵守」

字根 serve

【背誦祕訣】

本課核心單字分成二組，各四個單字 serve-
subserve-conserve-disserve，第 4 個字唸成
〔 dɪsˈsɝv 〕，s 發無聲的 /s/ 音，剛好接下一組
第一字 deserve〔 dɪˈzɝv 〕，s 唸有聲的 /z/ 音。

2. *serf-serfdom-sergeant*

這一回都是 serve 的變化，共有 9 個字，記得要背到 5 秒鐘之內，就可終生難忘。

serf
〔 sɝf 〕

n. 農奴（= *farm worker*）
Before rising to the throne, King Arthur began life as the son of an emancipated *serf.* 在成為國王之前，亞瑟王出生時，是被解放的農奴之子。

```
ser  +    f
 |        |
serve + farmer
```

serfdom
〔'sɝfdəm 〕

n. 農奴制度（= *slavery*）
History portrays many Russian noblemen as sponsors of *serfdom.* 歷史記載，許多俄國的貴族都支持農奴制度。

sergeant[5]
〔'sɑrdʒənt 〕

n. 士官
By refusing to meet the enemy in battle, the cowardly *sergeant* lost the respect of the soldiers under his command. 拒絕上戰場與敵人交戰，這位膽小的士官失去了他麾下士兵的尊敬。

字根 serve

server[5]
〔'sɝvɚ 〕

n. 侍者（= *waiter*）
Our dining experience there was dreadful. The *server* confused our order and by the time the food came to the table, we were no longer hungry.
我們在那裡的用餐經驗很糟。侍者把我們點的菜搞錯，等食物送上桌時，我們早就不餓了。

servant[2]
〔'sɝvənt 〕

n. 僕人（= *domestic worker*）
The spoiled princess treated everyone like a *servant.*
這位被寵壞的公主把每個人都當成僕人對待。

```
serv + ant
 |      |
服務  +  人
```

service[1]
〔'sɝvɪs 〕

n. 服務（= *work for sb.*）
Many American doctors charge outrageous sums for their *services.* 許多美國的醫生為他們的服務收取過高的費用。

servile
〔'sɝvḷ 〕

adj. 奴隸的；卑屈的（= *submissive* ）

This project requires strong leadership.　Eddie is far too *servile* to direct our group.

這項計劃需要強勢的領導人。艾迪太卑躬屈膝，不宜來領導我們的團隊。

```
serv ＋ ile
 │      │
serve ＋ adj.
```

servility
〔 sə'vɪlətɪ 〕

n. 奴性；卑躬屈膝（= *flattery* ）

I hate seeing him showing *servility* to his boss.

我討厭看到他對老闆表現出卑屈的姿態。

servitude
〔'sɝvə,tjud 〕

n. 奴役；勞役（= *slavery* ）

The murderer was sentenced to fifty years of penal *servitude*.

這名謀殺犯被判處五十年監禁勞役。

【背誦祕訣】

serf
serfdom
sergeant

這一組是 serve 的變化形，變成 serf，serge。

server
servant
service

這一組都和「服務」有關，二個「人」和一個名詞。

servile
servility
servitude

這一組都有「奴隸」之意，一個形容詞加上二個名詞。

字根 serve

3. subservience-subserviency-subservient

這一回是 subserve 和 conserve 的衍生字，背起來有點
長，但不要害怕，快速背到 6 秒鐘之內，你就不會忘記了。

subservience
〔 səb'sɜvɪəns 〕

n. 卑屈；從屬；有益（ = *servility* ）
I don't want to be kept in *subservience* to his power.
我不想屈從於他的力量之下。

subserviency
〔 səb'sɜvɪənsɪ 〕

n. 卑屈；有益（ = *subservience* ）
Sarah's boss demands total *subserviency* from his
employees. 莎拉的老闆要求員工完全順從。

subservient
〔 səb'sɜvɪənt 〕

adj. 卑屈的；附屬的（ = *servile* ）
In a Communist state, the needs of the individual
are seen as *subservient* to the whole of society.
在共產國家，個人的需要被視為在整體社會之下。

字根 serve

conservation[6]
〔 ˌkɑnsə'veʃən 〕

n. 保存；保護（ = *upkeep* ; *protection* ）
The World Wildlife Federation (WWF) is dedicated
to the *conservation* of all endangered animal species.
世界自然基金會致力於保護所有瀕臨絕種的動物。

conservancy
〔 kən'sɜvənsɪ 〕

n. 保存；保護（ = *conservation* ）
One of the biggest problems facing the world today
is the issue of fresh water *conservancy*.
現在全世界所面臨的最大問題之一，就是淡水的保存問題。

conservatory
〔 kən'sɜvəˌtorɪ 〕

n. 溫室（ = *greenhouse* ）
Many cities in cold climates have built *conservatories*
to display tropical plants and
hold flower displays.
許多寒冷氣候區的都市都建有溫室，
以展示熱帶植物，及舉行花展。

conserv + atory
| |
keep + 地方

conservator
〔 kənˈsɝvətɚ 〕

n. 保護者；文物保護員（ = *protector* ; *restorer* ）
An accredited *conservator* will be able to assess the value of this antique clock.
被認定合格的文物保護員，就能夠評估出這個古董鐘的價值。

conservative[4]
〔 kənˈsɝvətɪv 〕

adj. 保守的（ = *traditional* ）
In certain *conservative* cultures, practices such as homosexuality are considered immoral.
在某些保守文化中，如同性戀這些習慣，是被視爲不道德的。

conservable
〔 kənˈsɝvəbḷ 〕

adj. 可保存的；可節省的（ = *able to be conserved* ）
Time is one of the most *conservable* and costly resources we have at our disposal.
時間是我們可以隨意支配的資源中，最可節省，也是最珍貴的之一。

【背誦祕訣】

subservience
subserviency
subservient
先背二個相等的名詞，再加上形容詞，這一組重音都在字根上

conservation
conservancy
conservatory
先背二個相等的名詞，再加上「場所名詞」；第二、三字重音都在字根上

conservator
conservative
conservable
這一組重音也都在字根上，先背「人」，再搭配二個形容詞

字根 serve

4. disservice-deserved-deservedly

這一回共有 12 個字，包含 disserve-deserve-reserve-
preserve-observe 的變化，disserve 的衍生字只有一個，所
以和 deserve 二個衍生字併成一組，其他三個核心單字也各
有三個衍生字，這一回要快速背至 8 秒鐘之內。

disservice
〔 dɪs'sɝvɪs 〕

n. 幫倒忙的行為；損害（= *damage*）
Parents who put too much emphasis on studying do
their children a great *disservice* by denying them a
social life. 太過於強調小孩要讀書，而不給他們社交生
活的父母親，反而給孩子幫了倒忙。

deserved[4]
〔 dɪ'zɝvd 〕

adj. 應得的
Richard's bad behavior resulted in a *deserved*
punishment. 理察的不當行為導致了應得的處罰。

deservedly
〔 dɪ'zɝvɪdlɪ 〕

adv. 應得地；當然地（= *justly*）
The restaurant serves excellent food and is *deservedly*
popular. 這家餐廳東西很好吃，當然很受歡迎。

reserved[3]
〔 rɪ'zɝvd 〕

adj. 預訂的（= *booked*）
He managed to get two *reserved* seats for the concert.
他設法弄到了這場演唱會的二個保留位。

reservation[4]
〔 ˌrɛzɚ'veʃən 〕

n. 預約（= *booking*）
It's almost impossible to get a table in a decent restaurant
on Valentine's Day without a *reservation*. 在情人節當
天，在不錯的餐廳裡，沒有預約幾乎不可能有位子。

reservoir[6]
〔 'rɛzɚˌvɔr 〕

n. 水庫
Thanks to the extraordinary amount of rainfall we've
had this year, the local *reservoir* is at maximum capacity.
因為今年的需雨量異常的多，所以當地的水庫已達到最高水位。

字根 serve

preservation[4]
〔͵prɛzɚˋveʃən〕

n. 保存;保護 (= *protection*)
Taiwanese aboriginal tribes are fighting for the *preservation* of their cultural heritage.
台灣的原住民部落正在努力保存他們的文化遺產。

preservationist
〔͵prɛzɚˋveʃənɪst〕

n. 保護者 (= *conservator*)
The film explores the life and death of a bear expert and wildlife *preservationist*.
這部電影探索一位熊的專家,也是野生動物保護者的生與死。

preservative
〔 prɪˋzɝvətɪv 〕

adj. 防腐的 (= *preserving* = *antibacterial*)
n. 防腐劑
Western cedar grows in North America and contains natural *preservatives* which protect the wood from insects and disease.
西洋杉生長在北美洲,含有天然的防腐劑,可以保護木頭不受昆蟲和疾病的侵害。

observation[4]
〔͵ɑbzɚˋveʃən 〕

n. 觀察 (= *watching*)
Recent satellite *observations* have detected the presence of water on the moon.
近來衛星的觀察發現,月球上有水的存在。

observance
〔 əbˋzɝvəns 〕

n. 遵守 (= *compliance*)
The non-profit group monitors the *observance* of human rights throughout the world.
這個非營利團體,負責監督全世界人權標準是否被遵守。

observatory
〔 əbˋzɝvə͵torɪ 〕

n. 天文台;觀測站
The world's highest astronomy *observatory* is located in India and sits 4,500 meters above sea level. 全世界最高的天文觀測站,位於印度,海拔4,500 公尺。

5. *giant-tyrant-tenant*

這一回我們共列入 18 個 ant 結尾的單字，字尾 ant 可表示「人」，9 字一組，非常好背，18 個字背到 10 秒鐘之內，你就非常熟練，不會忘記了。

giant[2]
〔'dʒaɪənt 〕

n. 巨人
Albert Einstein is considered one of the *giants* of twentieth-century physics.
愛因斯坦被認爲是二十世紀物理學的巨人之一。

tyrant[5]
〔'taɪrənt 〕

n. 暴君
The ruthless German dictator Adolph Hitler is a good example of a *tyrant*.
殘暴的德國獨裁者希特勒，是暴君的一個很好的例子。

Adolph Hitler

tenant[5]
〔'tɛnənt 〕

n. 房客
A good landlord will pay attention to the needs of his *tenant*.
好的房東會注意房客的需求。

```
ten  + ant
 |      |
hold + 人
```

merchant[3]
〔'mɝtʃənt 〕

n. 商人
In the late fifteenth-century, Dutch *merchants* landed on Penghu.
在十五世紀末期，荷蘭商人在澎湖登陸。

```
merch      + atory
 |            |
merchandise + 人
商品
```

peasant[5]
〔'pɛznt 〕

n. 農夫 (= *farmer*)
Disputes over land or economic exploitation were frequent causes of *peasant* revolts in colonial Mexico.
土地或是經濟剝削的爭議，常常是殖民時代的墨西哥農夫反叛的原因。

```
peas + ant
 |      |
pea  + 人
碗豆
```

assistant[2]
〔 ə'sɪstənt 〕

n. 助手 (= *helper*)
Donald applied for the position of part-time research *assistant*. 唐納德去應徵兼職研究助理的職位。

accountant[4]
〔əˋkaʊntənt〕
n. 會計師
Reimbursement for travel expenses must first be approved by the company *accountant*.
旅費退款必須先經過公司會計的核准。

```
account + ant
   |      |
  帳戶   + 人
```

consultant[4]
〔kənˋsʌltənt〕
n. 顧問
Based upon recommendations from a *consultant*, our firm decided to upgrade its computer software.
根據顧問的建議，我們公司決定將電腦軟體升級。

```
consult + ant
   |      |
  請教   + 人
```

contestant[6]
〔kənˋtɛstənt〕
n. 參賽者
Three *contestants* in the diving competition were disqualified when they tested positive for steroids.
跳水比賽的三名參賽者被取消資格，
因為他們類固醇檢驗呈陽性反應。

```
contest + ant
   |      |
  比賽   + 人
```

字根 serve

【背誦祕訣】

giant
tyrant
tenant
這一、二字重音節母音都是 /aɪ/
第二、三字都是 t 開頭

merchant
peasant
assistant
這一組都是「職業」

accountant
consultant
contestant
這三個字都有 tant 結尾，和上一組的 assistant 一致。

habitant
〔ˈhæbətənt〕

n. 居民（= *resident*）
A research group was sent on a
mission to secretly observe the
habitants of the small village.
一個研究小組被派出去，任務是暗中觀察這
個小村莊的居民。

```
habit  + ant
  |        |
live in +  人
```

inhabitant[6]
〔ɪnˈhæbətənt〕

n. 居民（= *habitant*）
Invading troops expelled the
inhabitants of the town,
confiscating their land and property.
入侵的軍隊將鎮上居民逐出，沒收他們的土地和財產。

```
in + habit  + ant
 |     |        |
in + live in +  人
```

cohabitant
〔koˈhæbətənt〕

n. 同居者
Unmarried couples who live together are considered
to be *cohabitants*.
沒有結婚就住在一起的男女，被認為是同居者。

---

migrant[5]
〔ˈmaɪgrənt〕

n. 移民　*adj.* 移居的
During the Lunar New Year Festival, millions of
migrant workers leave the cities and
return to their home provinces.
在農曆春節期間，數百萬移居的工人離
開都市，回到家鄉各省。

```
migr + ant
  |      |
move +  人
```

immigrant[4]
〔ˈɪməgrənt〕

n.（移入的）移民（= *settler*）
Much of the America's farm labor is done by poorly
paid *immigrants* from Mexico.
美國許多農場上的苦工，是由薪水很低的墨西哥移民做的。

emigrant[6]
〔ˈɛməgrənt〕

n.（移出的）移民；僑民
During the famine of the 1840s, many Irish *emigrants*
went to the U.S. or Canada.
在 1840 年代發生飢荒時，許多愛爾蘭移民移居到美國
或加拿大。

字根 serve

attendant[6]
〔 ə'tɛndənt 〕

n. 出席者；服務者
Frank doesn't feel comfortable leaving his new Mercedes with an unfamiliar parking *attendant*.
法蘭克把他的新賓士車交給一位不熟悉的停車服務員，覺得不太安心。

attend　+ ant
　|　　　|
參加；照護　+　人

defendant
〔 dɪ'fɛndənt 〕

n. 被告（ = *the accused* ）
Facing charges of first-degree murder, the *defendant* claimed innocence on grounds of temporary insanity.
面對一級謀殺的控訴，被告宣稱自己因爲暫時性精神錯亂，所以是無辜的。

defend + ant
　|　　　|
辯護　+　人

claimant
〔 'klemənt 〕

n. 原告；要求者（ = *the accuser* ）
Finding the defendant at fault, the court awarded five million dollars to the injured *claimant*.
法院判定被告有過失，所以裁定賠償受傷的原告五百萬元。

claim + ant
　|　　　|
要求　+　人

字根 serve

【背誦祕訣】

habitant
inhabitant　　這一組都和「居住者」有關
cohabitant

migrant
immigrant　　這一組都提到「移民」
emigrant

attendant
defendant　　第二、三字「被告」和「原告」
claimant　　　剛好相反

Exercise : Choose the correct answer.

1. Not enough is being done to _____ the world's rainforests.
   (A) dispose
   (B) disserve
   (C) consign
   (D) conserve

2. David was upset because he felt that he didn't _____ to be punished.
   (A) subserve
   (B) suppress
   (C) deserve
   (D) design

3. The suspect was _____ standing in front of the store just minutes before the robbery.
   (A) observed
   (B) opposed
   (C) compressed
   (D) oppressed

4. The travel agency charges a small fee for its _____.
   (A) disservice
   (B) services
   (C) conservatory
   (D) serfdom

5. The café _____ coffee, tea, and pastries.
   (A) poses
   (B) presses
   (C) serves
   (D) signs

6. Wearing _____ clothing is recommended when traveling in foreign countries.
   (A) applicable
   (B) preservative
   (C) assignable
   (D) conservative

7. My mother has a set of expensive silverware which is _____ for use on special occasions.
   (A) reserved
   (B) resigned
   (C) depressed
   (D) composed

字根 serve

8. Our writers' group is dedicated to the _____ of literary traditions.
   (A) compression
   (B) observation
   (C) preservation
   (D) servitude

9. The manager trusted his _____ to oversee the day-to-day operation of the store.
   (A) tyrant
   (B) giant
   (C) depressor
   (D) assistant

10. Most of California's fruits and vegetables are picked by _____ workers from Mexico.
    (A) inhabitant
    (B) migrant
    (C) cohabitant
    (D) tenant

11. The jury found the _____ not guilty of all charges.
    (A) depressant
    (B) significant
    (C) defendant
    (D) claimant

12. The king's every need is attended to by a large staff of _____.
    (A) servants
    (B) accountants
    (C) contestants
    (D) merchants

13. Women no longer play a _____ role in society.
    (A) conservable
    (B) subservient
    (C) consignable
    (D) complicated

14. Sandra Bullock _____ won the Academy Award for best actress.
    (A) resignedly
    (B) deservedly
    (C) designedly
    (D) signally

15. I have made all the _____ for my trip.
    (A) designations
    (B) complexions
    (C) reservations
    (D) conservations

字根 serve

字彙測驗詳解

1. (**D**) 對於全世界雨林的<u>保護</u>，我們所做的還不夠。
   (A) dispose〔dɪ'spoz〕 *v.* 處置
   (B) disserve〔dɪs'sɝv〕 *v.* 幫倒忙；損害
   (C) consign〔kən'saɪn〕 *v.* 委託
   (D) *conserve*〔kən'sɝv〕 *v.* 保存；保護；節省
   rainforest〔'ren,fɔrɪst〕 *n.* 雨林

2. (**C**) 大衛很不高興，因為他覺得自己<u>不應該</u>被處罰。
   (A) subserve〔səb'sɝv〕 *v.* 有助於
   (B) suppress〔sə'prɛs〕 *v.* 鎮壓；壓抑
   (C) *deserve*〔dɪ'zɝv〕 *v.* 應得（賞罰）
   (D) design〔dɪ'zaɪn〕 *v.* 設計
   upset〔ʌp'sɛt〕 *adj.* 不高興的

3. (**A**) 就在搶案發生前幾分鐘，那名嫌疑犯被看到站在那家店的前面。
   (A) *observe*〔əb'zɝv〕 *v.* 觀察；遵守；看到
   (B) oppose〔ə'poz〕 *v.* 反對
   (C) compress〔kəm'prɛs〕 *v.* 壓縮
   (D) oppress〔ə'prɛs〕 *v.* 壓迫

4. (**B**) 旅行社會收取小額的<u>服務</u>費。
   (A) disservice〔dɪs'sɝvɪs〕 *n.* 幫倒忙行為；損害
   (B) *service*〔'sɝvɪs〕 *n.* 服務
   (C) conservatory〔kən'sɝvə,torɪ〕 *n.* 溫室
   (D) serfdom〔'sɝfdəm〕 *n.* 農奴制度
   travel agency 旅行社　　charge〔tʃɑrdʒ〕 *v.* 索取（費用）

5. (**C**) 那家咖啡廳<u>供應</u>咖啡、茶，和糕點。
   (A) pose〔poz〕 *v.* 擺姿勢　　(B) press〔prɛs〕 *v.* 壓
   (C) *serve*〔sɝv〕 *v.* 服務；供應　　(D) sign〔saɪn〕 *v.* 簽名
   pastry〔'pestrɪ〕 *n.* 糕餅

6. (**D**)　在國外旅行時，我們建議穿著<u>保守的</u>衣服。
　　(A) applicable〔`ˈæplɪkəbl̩`〕*adj.* 適用的
　　(B) preservative〔`prɪˈzɝvətɪv`〕*adj.* 防腐的
　　(C) assignable〔`əˈsaɪnəbl̩`〕*adj.* 可指派的；可認定的
　　(D) *conservative*〔`kənˈsɝvətɪv`〕*adj.* 保守的
　　recommend〔`ˌrɛkəˈmɛnd`〕*v.* 推薦；建議

7. (**A**)　我媽媽有一套昂貴的銀製餐具，是<u>保留</u>給特殊場合使用的。
　　(A) *reserve*〔`rɪˈzɝv`〕*v.* 保存；保留；預約
　　(B) resign〔`rɪˈzaɪn`〕*v.* 辭職
　　(C) depress〔`dɪˈprɛs`〕*v.* 使沮喪
　　(D) compose〔`kəmˈpoz`〕*v.* 組成

silverware

　　silverware〔`ˈsɪlvɚˌwɛr`〕*n.* 銀製餐具　occasion〔`əˈkeʒən`〕*n.* 場合

8. (**C**)　我們的寫作小組致力於<u>保存</u>文學的傳統。
　　(A) compression〔`kəmˈprɛʃən`〕*n.* 壓縮
　　(B) observation〔`ˌabzɚˈveʃən`〕*n.* 觀察
　　(C) *preservation*〔`ˌprɛzɚˈveʃən`〕*n.* 保存；保護
　　(D) servitude〔`ˈsɝvəˌtjud`〕*n.* 奴役
　　be dedicated to 致力於　literary〔`ˈlɪtəˌrɛrɪ`〕*adj.* 文學的

9. (**D**)　這位經理委託他的<u>助手</u>，監督這家店每天的營運。
　　(A) tyrant〔`ˈtaɪrənt`〕*n.* 暴君　　(B) giant〔`ˈdʒaɪənt`〕*n.* 巨人
　　(C) depressor〔`dɪˈprɛsɚ`〕*n.* 壓抑者；壓板
　　(D) *assistant*〔`əˈsɪstənt`〕*n.* 助手
　　trust〔`trʌst`〕*v.* 信任；委託　oversee〔`ˌovɚˈsi`〕*v.* 監督；管理
　　day-to-day *adj.* 每天的　operation〔`ˌɑpəˈreʃən`〕*n.* 營運；經營

10. (**B**)　都是由來自墨西哥的<u>移居的</u>工人摘的。
　　(A) inhabitant〔`ɪnˈhæbətənt`〕*n.* 居民
　　(B) *migrant*〔`ˈmaɪgrənt`〕*n.* 移民；(到處尋找工作的) 流動工人
　　　　　adj. 移居的　　*migrant worker* 移居的工人；農業季節工人
　　(C) cohabitant〔`koˈhæbətənt`〕*n.* 同居者
　　(D) tenant〔`ˈtɛnənt`〕*n.* 房客

字根 serve

11. (**C**) 陪審團判定，所有的指控<u>被告</u>都無罪。
- (A) depressant〔dɪ'prɛsənt〕*n.* 鎮靜劑
- (B) significant〔sɪg'nɪfəkənt〕*adj.* 意義重大的
- (C) ***defendant***〔dɪ'fɛndənt〕*n.* 被告
- (D) claimant〔'klemənt〕*n.* 原告

jury〔'dʒʊrɪ〕*n.* 陪審團
find〔faɪnd〕*v.*（陪審團）判決；判定
guilty〔'gɪltɪ〕*adj.* 有罪的 < *of* >　　charge〔tʃɑrdʒ〕*n.* 控告

12. (**A**) 國王的每項需求，都有大批的<u>僕人</u>照料。
- (A) ***servant***〔'sɝvənt〕*n.* 僕人
- (B) accountant〔ə'kaʊntənt〕*n.* 會計師
- (C) contestant〔kən'tɛstənt〕*n.* 競賽者
- (D) merchant〔'mɝtʃənt〕*n.* 商人

attend to 照顧；照料　　staff〔stæf〕*n.* 員工；全體職員

13. (**B**) 女性在社會上不再扮演<u>附屬的</u>角色。
- (A) conservable〔kən'sɝvəbl̩〕*adj.* 可保存的
- (B) ***subservient***〔səb'sɝvɪənt〕*adj.* 卑屈的；附屬的
- (C) consignable〔kən'saɪnəbl̩〕*adj.* 可委託的
- (D) complicated〔'kɑmplə,ketɪd〕*adj.* 複雜的

14. (**B**) 珊卓布拉克獲得奧斯卡最佳女演員獎是<u>應該</u>的。
- (A) resignedly〔rɪ'zaɪnɪdlɪ〕*adv.* 認命地
- (B) ***deservedly***〔dɪ'zɝvɪdlɪ〕*adv.* 應得地；當然地
- (C) designedly〔dɪ'zaɪndlɪ〕*adv.* 故意地
- (D) signally〔'sɪgnl̩ɪ〕*adv.* 顯著地

Sandra Bullock

15. (**C**) 我這趟旅行全都<u>預訂</u>好了。
- (A) designation〔,dɛzɪg'neʃən〕*n.* 指定
- (B) complexion〔kəm'plɛkʃən〕*n.* 膚色
- (C) ***reservation***〔,rɛzɚ'veʃən〕*n.* 預訂
- (D) conservation〔,kɑnsɚ'veʃən〕*n.* 保存；保護

字根 serve

請連中文一起背，背至70秒內，終生不忘。

1

serve	服務
subserve	有助於
conserve	節省
disserve	幫倒忙
deserve	應得
reserve	預約
preserve	保存
observe	觀察

2

serf	農奴
serfdom	農奴制度
sergeant	士官
server	侍者
servant	僕人
service	服務
servile	奴隸的
servility	奴性
servitude	奴役

3

subservience	有益
subserviency	有益
subservient	有益的
conservation	保存
conservancy	保存
conservatory	溫室
conservator	文物保護員
conservative	保守的
conservable	可保存的

【劉毅老師的話】

　　一個單字往往有很多意思，先背一個主要意思，其他的意思也會逐漸知道。

字根 serve

4

disservice　幫倒忙行為
deserved　應得的
deservedly　應得地

reserved　預訂的
reservation　預約
reservoir　水庫

preservation　保存
preservationist　文物保護員
preservative　防腐的

observation　觀察
observance　遵守
observatory　天文台

字根 serve

5

giant　巨人
tyrant　暴君
tenant　房客

merchant　商人
peasant　農夫
assistant　助手

accountant　會計師
consultant　顧問
contestant　競賽者

habitant　居民
inhabitant　居民
cohabitant　同居者

migrant　移民
immigrant　（移入的）移民
emigrant　（移出的）移民

attendant　出席者
defendant　被告
claimant　原告

※ 本頁可影印後，隨身攜帶，方便背誦。

Group 6 字根 *tend*

目標： ① 先將69個字放入短期記憶。
② 加快速度至57秒之內，成為長期記憶。

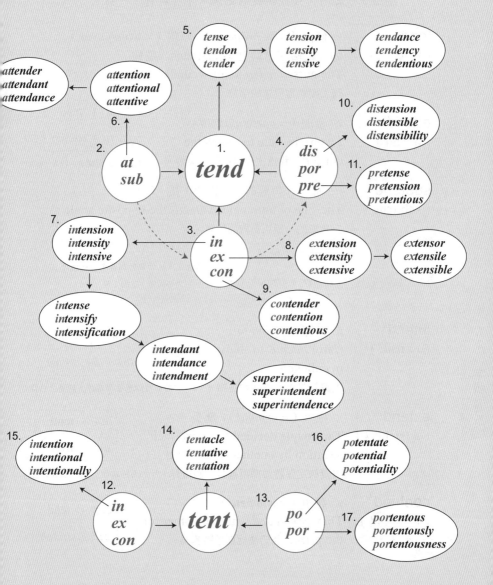

5.
tense
tendon
tender

tension
tensity
tensive

tendance
tendency
tendentious

attender
attendant
attendance

attention
attentional
attentive

6.

2.
at
sub

1.
tend

4.
dis
por
pre

10.
distension
distensible
distensibility

11.
pretense
pretension
pretentious

7.
intension
intensity
intensive

3.
in
ex
con

8.
extension
extensity
extensive

extensor
extensile
extensible

intense
intensify
intensification

9.
contender
contention
contentious

intendant
intendance
intendment

superintend
superintendent
superintendence

15.
intention
intentional
intentionally

14.
tentacle
tentative
tentation

16.
potentate
potential
potentiality

12.
in
ex
con

tent

13.
po
por

17.
portentous
portentously
portentousness

1. 字根 *tend* 核心單字

這9個字，3個一組一起背，可先背6個再背3個，背
熟至5秒之內，可成為長期記憶，才可再背下一組。

tend[3]
〔tɛnd〕

v. 傾向（= *be prone to*）；照料（= *watch over*）
tend 這個字根的意思是 stretch「延伸」
The nurse *tended* to his wounds.
護士照料他受傷的部位。

attend[2]
〔ə'tɛnd〕

v. 參加（= *participate in*）
I won't be able to *attend* the
concert. 我無法參加這個音樂會。

at	+	tend
to	+	stretch

想往那方向延伸，即是「參加」

subtend
〔səb'tɛnd〕

v.（弦、三角形的邊）正對（弧、角）
The side of a triangle *subtends* the opposite angle.
三角形的一邊正對對面的角。

sub	+	tend
under	+	stretch

三角形的邊往下延伸會對到其中的一個角，
即「（弦、三角形的邊）正對（弧、角）」

intend[4]
〔ɪn'tɛnd〕

v. 打算（= *plan to*）
Carol *intends* to study biology
in college.
卡蘿打算上大學時唸生物。

in	+	tend
toward	+	stretch

發自內心想往那延伸，即是「打算」

extend[4]
〔ɪk'stɛnd〕

v. 擴大（= *expand*）；延長
The couple decided to *extend* their
vacation by another week. 這對
夫妻決定要將假期再延長一個禮拜。

ex	+	tend
out	+	stretch

向外延伸，即是「擴大；延長」

contend[5]
〔kən'tɛnd〕

v. 競爭（= *compete*）
They *contended* with each other for
the prize. 他們彼此競爭該獎品。

con	+	tend
all	+	stretch

distend
〔 dɪ'stɛnd 〕

v. 膨脹（ = *swell* ）
The hungry child had a *distended* belly.
這飢餓的孩子有著脹大的肚子。

```
dis  +  tend
 |       |
apart + stretch
```

向外圍四周延伸，即是「膨脹」

portend
〔 por'tɛnd 〕

v. 預示；是…的前兆（ = *predict* ）
The results of the survey *portend* that the majority of people are not happy with the government.
這個調查結果顯示大部分的民眾對政府不滿意。

```
por  +  tend
 |       |
forward + stretch
```

向前伸展，看到未來的事物，即是「預示」

pretend[3]
〔 prɪ'tɛnd 〕

v. 假裝（ = *make believe* ）
Let's *pretend* this incident never happened.
我們就假裝這件事從沒發生過吧。

```
pre  +  tend
 |       |
before + stretch
```

向前伸展開來，即是「假裝」

【背誦祕訣】

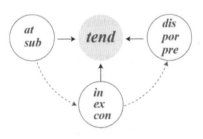

字根 tend 衍生出這九個字，按照以下的背誦順序和要訣，你馬上就背得起來。

$\left\{\begin{array}{l} \text{tend} \\ \text{attend} \\ \text{subtend} \end{array}\right.$ $\left\{\begin{array}{l} \text{intend} \\ \text{extend} \\ \text{contend} \end{array}\right.$ $\left\{\begin{array}{l} \text{distend} \\ \text{portend} \\ \text{pretend} \end{array}\right.$

字根 tend

2. *tense-tendon-tender*

這一組有 9 個字，3 個一組一起背，可先背 6 個
再背 3 個，背熟至 5 秒之內，變成直覺。

tense[4]
(tɛns)

adj. 緊張的 (= *strained*)　　*n.* 時態
The sentence is written in the past *tense*.
這個句子是用過去式寫的。

tendon
('tɛndən)

n. 腱
Polly strained a *tendon* in her ankle
while playing volleyball.
波莉在打排球的時候，扭傷腳踝的肌腱。

tend	+ on
stretch +	*n.*

tender[3]
('tɛndɚ)

adj. 柔軟的 (= *soft*)；溫柔的 (= *gentle*)
John acts like a tough guy but he really has a *tender*
heart.
約翰行事作風像個剛強的人，但他其實有個溫柔的心。

tension[4]
('tɛnʃən)

n. 緊張 (= *nervousness*)
There was *tension* in the air as I
entered the room.　當我進入這房間
的時候，可以感覺到緊張的氣氛。

tens	+ ion
stretch +	*n.*

tensity
('tɛnsətɪ)

n. 緊張
Ruan's poems are about the *tensity*
of everyday life.
盧恩的詩是關於日常生活的緊張。

tens	+ ity
stretch +	*n.*

tensive
('tɛnsɪv)

adj. 緊張的 (= *nervous*)
Dennis often chews his fingernails
during *tensive* moments.
丹尼斯在緊張的時候，常常咬他的指甲。

tens	+ ive
stretch +	*adj.*

字根 tend

tendance
（ˈtɛndəns ）

n. 照料（ = *care* ）

If not for your *tendance*, I might never have recovered from the accident.

要不是有你的照顧，我可能無法從那場車禍中復原。

```
tend   + ance
 |         |
stretch +  n.
```

tendency[4]
（ˈtɛndənsɪ ）

n. 傾向（ = *inclination* ）

Louis has a *tendency* to exaggerate when telling a story.

路易斯在講故事時，有誇張的傾向。

```
tend   + ency
 |         |
stretch +  n.
```

tendentious
（ tɛnˈdɛnʃəs ）

adj. 有特定傾向的；有偏見的（ = *biased* ）

The Bible presents a *tendentious* view of history.

聖經在對歷史的觀點上有特定的傾向。

```
tend   + entious
 |         |
stretch +  adj.
```

【背誦祕訣】

字根 tend 衍生出 9 個字，按照下列背誦順序和要訣，你馬上就背得起來。

tense	依字義可串連成一個口訣
tendon	「make tense tendons tender」
tender	使緊繃的肌腱變柔軟

tension	
tensity	這三個字的重音皆在第一音節
tensive	

ˈtendance	
ˈtendency	前兩個字的重音在第一音節
tenˈdentious	

字根 tend

3. *attention-attentional-attentive*

這一組有 18 個字，分成兩組，第一組是 attend 的衍生字，
第二組是 intend 的衍生字，背熟至 10 秒之內，變成直覺。

attention[2]
〔 ə'tɛnʃən 〕

n. 注意（= *concentration*）
This matter requires your
immediate *attention*.
這件事情需要你立刻去注意。

```
at  +  tent   + ion
|       |        |
to + stretch +  n.
```
身體向那延伸，表示想「注意」

attentional
〔 ə'tɛnʃənḷ 〕

adj. 注意的（= *attentive*）
Children exposed to television at an early age often
develop *attentional* problems later in life. 過早接觸
電視的孩子，通常日後在生活中會產生注意力的問題。

attentive
〔 ə'tɛntɪv 〕

adj. 專注的；體貼的（= *considerate*）
She was a kind and *attentive* mother.
她是個既仁慈又體貼的母親。

attender
〔 ə'tɛndɚ 〕

n. 出席者
The concert *attenders* were
disappointed by the singer's
performance. 去聽這場演唱會
的人，對歌手的表現感到失望。

```
at  +  tend   + er
|       |        |
to + stretch +  人
```

attendant[6]
〔 ə'tɛndənt 〕

n. 服務員（= *servant*）；出席者
The parking *attendant* said the lot
was full.
停車服務員說，停車場已經滿了。

```
attend + ant
|         |
參加   +  人
```

attendance[5]
〔 ə'tɛndəns 〕

n. 出席（= *presence*）
There were 5,000 people in
attendance in the seminar.
有五千個人出席這場研討會。

```
attend + ance
|         |
參加   +  n.
```

字根 tend

intension
〔ɪnˈtɛnʃən〕

n. 強度；決心（= *determination*）
Tom shows his *intension* of winning a lot of
money. 湯姆展現出要贏很多錢的決心。

in	+	tens	+ ion
inward	+	stretch	+ *n.*

內心只想往那延展，
即是心中的「決心」

intensity[4]
〔ɪnˈtɛnsətɪ〕

n. 強度（= *strength*）
We were surprised by the *intensity* of the storm.
我們都對這暴風雨的強度感到驚訝。

in	+	tens	+ ity
inward	+	stretch	+ *n.*

intensive[4]
〔ɪnˈtɛnsɪv〕

adj. 密集的（= *concentrated*）
This course requires *intensive* study.
這課程需要密集的研讀。

intense[4]
〔ɪnˈtɛns〕

adj. 強烈的（= *strong*）
Most people stay indoors during the *intense*
afternoon heat.
在午後的高溫下，大部分的人都待在室內。

intensify[4]
〔ɪnˈtɛnsəˌfaɪ〕

v. 加強（= *make strong*）
The police have *intensified* their
search for the missing children.
警方加強尋找失蹤兒童。

intens	+	ify
強烈的	+	*make*

intensification
〔ɪnˌtɛnsəfəˈkeʃən〕

n. 加強
Only the *intensification* of farming will help
improve the economy.
只有加強農業，才有助於改善經濟。

字根 tend

intendant
(ɪn'tɛndənt)

n. 管理者 (= *administrator*);監督官
The *intendant's* decision was final; there would
be no appeal.
監督官的決定已確立;不得上訴。

intendance
(ɪn'tɛndəns)

n. 管理;監督 (= *supervision*)
This park was built under the *intendance* of the
mayor's office.
這個公園是在市長室的監督下建造的。

```
in    +  tend  + ance
 |        |       |
inward + stretch +  n.      心之所向,即是「管理;監督」
```

intendment
(ɪn'tɛndmənt)

n. 真意;涵義
The *intendment* of the Egyptian pyramids is not
completely understood.
埃及金字塔的真正涵義還沒被完全了解。

superintend
(ˌsupərɪn'tɛnd)

v. 監督 (= *supervise*)
His position of assistant manager did not
superintend the sales department.
副理的職位無法監督業務部。

```
super  +   in   +  tend
  |        |        |
above + toward + stretch     向~之上伸展注意力,
                             即是「監督」
```

superintendent
(ˌsupərɪn'tɛndənt)

n. 監督者 (= *intendant*)
The building *superintendent* is responsible for
all maintenance and repairs.
這個大樓的監督者負責所有的保養和維修。

superintendence
(ˌsupərɪn'tɛndəns)

n. 監督 (= *intendance*)
Thanks to your *superintendence*, the project was
completed on time and under budget. 由於你的
監督,才能使這個計畫準時且在預算內完成。

4. *extension-extensity-extensive*

這一組有 15 個字，分成四組，第一組是 extend 的衍生字，
第二組是 contend 的衍生字，第三組是 distend 的衍生字，第
四組是 pretend 的衍生字，背熟至 7 秒之內，變成直覺。

extension[5]
〔 ɪk'stɛnʃən 〕

n. 擴大；延長；（電話）分機
You will need to apply for a visa *extension* if you want to stay in the country. 如果你想要待在這個國家的話，就需要申請簽證延長。

```
ex +  tens  + ion
 |      |      |
out + stretch +  n.
```
向外延伸，即是「擴大；延長」

extensity
〔 ɛk'stɛnsətɪ 〕

n. 擴張性
The growing *extensity* of trade has complicated relations between the U.S. and China.
貿易逐漸的擴張，使中美關係變複雜。

extensive[5]
〔 ɪk'stɛnsɪv 〕

adj. 廣泛的（ = *widespread* ）；大規模的
Wilbur needed *extensive* dental work after the accident.
威爾伯在事故發生之後，需要大規模的牙齒治療。

extensor
〔 ɪk'stɛnsɚ 〕

n. 伸展肌
This exercise will stretch the *extensors* in your lower back.
這個運動可以伸展你下背部的伸展肌。

```
ex +  tens  + or
 |      |      |
out + stretch +  n.
```
可以向外延伸的肌肉，
即是「伸展肌」

extensile
〔 ɪk'stɛnsɪl 〕

adj. 可延伸的（ = *extensible* ）
The human tongue has amazing *extensile* abilities.
人類的舌頭有驚人的延展力。

extensible
〔 ɪk'stɛnsəbḷ 〕

adj. 可延伸的（ = *extensile* ）
The road was constructed to be *extensible* for widening in the future. 這條路的建造是可以在未來延伸拓寬。

字根 tend

contender
(kən'tɛndə)

n. 競爭者 (= *competitor*)
George participated but was not a *contender* in the race. 喬治參加了，但不是這場比賽的競爭者。

contend + er
|　　　　|
爭論　＋　人　　會和你爭論的人，即是「競爭者」

contention
(kən'tɛnʃən)

n. 爭論 (= *argument*)；競爭
Ownership of the Moon is a matter of international *contention*.
月球的所有權是個引起國際爭論的事情。

contentious
(kən'tɛnʃəs)

adj. 有爭論的 (= *argumentative*)
Wearing fur is a highly *contentious* subject between animal rights groups and the fashion industry.
在動物權益團體和時尚業之間，穿著皮草是個高度爭論的主題。

【背誦祕訣】

字根 extend 衍生出 6 個字，按照下列背誦順序和要訣，你馬上背得起來。

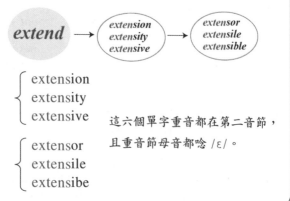

extend → extension / extensity / extensive → extensor / extensile / extensible

extension
extensity
extensive

extensor
extensile
extensibe

這六個單字重音都在第二音節，且重音節母音都唸 /ɛ/。

字根 tend

distension
〔 dɪ'stɛnʃən 〕

n. 膨脹（ = *swelling* ）
A symptom of extreme
hunger is a *distension*
of the stomach.
胃的膨脹是極度飢餓的症狀。

dis	+	tens	+ ion
apart	+	stretch	+ *n.*

distensible
〔 dɪ'stɛnsəbḷ 〕

adj. 會膨脹的
The human heart is a fairly *distensible* organ.
人類的心臟是非常會膨脹的器官。

dis	+	tens	+ ible
apart	+	stretch	+ 可～的

distensibility
〔 dɪsˌtɛnsə'bɪlətɪ 〕

n. 膨脹性；擴張
Bronchitis is a disease that limits the *distensibility*
of the lungs. 支氣管炎是一種會限制肺部擴張的疾病。

pretense
〔 prɪ'tɛns 〕

n. 假裝（ = *pretension* ）
I make no *pretense* of being able to solve all the
world's problems.
我並沒有假裝一副可以解決世界所有問題的樣子。

pretension
〔 prɪ'tɛnʃən 〕

n. 假裝；做作（ = *pretense* ）
He was well-liked for his honesty and lack
of *pretension*.
因為他既誠實又不做作，所以很受大家喜歡。

pre	+	tens	+ ion
before	+	stretch	+ *n.*

pretentious
〔 prɪ'tɛnʃəs 〕

adj. 虛偽的；自大的（ = *pompous* ）
Paul sounds *pretentious* when he talks about
himself.
保羅談論自己的時候，總是聽起來很自大。

字根 tend

5. intent-extent-content

這一組有 5 個字，是字根 tend 的變化型 tent，3 個
一組一起背，可先背 3 個，再背 2 個，背熟至 3 秒之內，
變成直覺。

intent[5]
〔 ɪnˈtɛnt 〕

n. 意圖 (= *intention*)
It is not my *intent* to cause you any harm.
我並不想對你造成任何的傷害。

in	+	tent
toward	+	stretch

內心想延伸到的地方，即是「意圖」

extent[4]
〔 ɪkˈstɛnt 〕

n. 程度 (= *degree*)；範圍
It will take some time to assess the
full *extent* of the damage caused by
the fire. 這場火災所造成的全部損害
程度，需要一些時間來評估。

ex	+	tent
out	+	stretch

向外能延伸到的地方，
即是「範圍」

content[4]
〔 kənˈtɛnt 〕

n. 滿足 (= *satisfaction*)
〔ˈkɑntɛnt 〕 *n.* 內容
Content is happiness.
知足常樂。

con	+	tent
all	+	stretch

大家都可伸手獲得，即是「滿足」

potent
〔ˈpotn̩t 〕

adj. 有力的 (= *powerful*)
Rice wine is a very *potent* liquor.
米酒是非常烈的酒。

portent
〔ˈportɛnt 〕

n. 預兆 (= *omen*)
The dark sky is a *portent* of rain.
天色昏暗是要下雨的預兆。

6. *tentacle-tentative-tentation*

第一組有 12 個字，是字根 tent 的衍生字，3 個一組一起背，
可先背 6 個再背 6 個，背熟至 7 秒之內，變成直覺。

tentacle
〔'tɛntəkḷ〕

n. 觸鬚；觸手
The octopus got its *tentacle*
caught in the fishing net.
這隻章魚的觸手被魚網絆住了。

```
tent    + acle
  |         |
stretch +   n.
```

可延伸出去的東西，即是「觸鬚」

tentative[5]
〔'tɛntətɪv〕

adj. 試驗性的（= *experimental*）；暫時的
The two sides signed a *tentative* agreement to a
ceasefire.　雙方簽署了一個暫時性的停火協定。

tentation
〔tɛn'teʃən〕

n. 試驗調整
The new product was perfected through *tentation*.
這項新產品透過試驗調整而變得完美。

intention[4]
〔ɪn'tɛnʃən〕

n. 意圖（= *intent*）
Thomas announced his *intention* to
run for class president.
湯姆士宣佈他有意要選班長。

```
intent + ion
   |       |
 意圖   +   n.
```

intentional
〔ɪn'tɛnʃənḷ〕

adj. 故意的（= *deliberate*）
I can assure you the mistake was
not *intentional*.　我可以向你保證，
這個錯誤不是故意的。

```
intention + al
    |         |
  意圖    +  adj.
```

有意圖去做事，即是「故意的」

intentionally
〔ɪn'tɛnʃənḷɪ〕

adv. 故意地（= *on purpose*）
Felix *intentionally* stayed out of his father's sight
for the next two days.
菲利克斯在接下來的兩天，都故意不要讓他的父親看到。

字根 tend

potentate
('potṇ,tet)

n. 統治者 (= *ruler*)；當權者
North Korea is governed by a
ruthless *potentate*.
北韓被殘忍的統治者統治。

potent + ate
|　　|
有力的 + 人

potential⁵
(pə'tɛnʃəl)

n. 潛力　*adj.* 可能的 (= *possible*)
Sarah has the *potential* to be a great dancer.
莎拉有潛力能成爲一個很棒的舞者。

potentiality
(pə,tɛnʃɪ'æləti)

n. 潛力；可能性 (= *possibility*)
The *potentialities* of the human brain are
incredible.
人腦的潛力是不可思議的。

portentous
(por'tɛntəs)

adj. 預兆的；不祥的 (= *ominous*)
There was nothing *portentous* about Betty's
manner.　貝蒂的行爲舉止並沒有任何的預兆。

portent + ous
|　　　|
預兆　+ *adj.*

portentously
(por'tɛntəslɪ)

adv. 有預兆地 (= *ominously*)
Dark clouds gathered *portentously* in the sky;
a storm was on its way.
天空烏雲密佈，預兆了暴風雨要來了。

portentousness
(por'tɛntəsnɪs)

n. 預兆 (= *omen*)
I did not notice any *portentousness* in Yvonne's
reply.
在伊凡的回答中，我並沒有注意到任何的預兆。

Exercise : Choose the correct answer.

1. Over 5,000 people are expected to _____ the festival.
   (A) contain   (B) impress
   (C) detain   (D) attend

2. Laura and Sally are in _____ for the same scholarship.
   (A) petition   (B) approbation
   (C) contention   (D) expression

3. This test was designed to determine the _____ of your knowledge.
   (A) audacity   (B) extent
   (C) passion   (D) conflict

4. Mel speaks with a _____ British accent.
   (A) impetuous   (B) notorious
   (C) pretentious   (D) generous

5. This road will be _____ another 30 kilometers and connect with Highway 1.
   (A) extended   (B) generated
   (C) navigated   (D) attained

6. Skydiving is one of the most _____ experiences I've ever had.
   (A) tactile   (B) intense
   (C) prompt   (D) perennial

7. The matter was resolved after two days of _____ discussions.
   (A) pregnant   (B) compatible
   (C) sacred   (D) intensive

字根 tend

8. My car is in need of _____ repairs before I can drive it again.
   (A) extensive
   (B) inexorable
   (C) expatriate
   (D) exanimate

9. George doesn't _____ to know all the answers.
   (A) render
   (B) sanction
   (C) battle
   (D) pretend

10. The violent _____ of the film is not suitable for children.
    (A) authority
    (B) illusion
    (C) content
    (D) ransom

11. Wilma left work early under the _____ of a family emergency.
    (A) pretense
    (B) example
    (C) gender
    (D) annotation

12. The new health care system is highly _____ among politicians.
    (A) devious
    (B) obvious
    (C) previous
    (D) contentious

13. Jane has a _____ to lose interest in her boyfriend after a few weeks.
    (A) tendency
    (B) alimony
    (C) dowry
    (D) fancy

14. Most students struggle to remain _____ during the professor's long, boring lectures.
    (A) native
    (B) combative
    (C) impassive
    (D) attentive

15. I'm sorry; it was not my _____ to offend you.
    (A) compassion
    (B) intention
    (C) sanction
    (D) contagion

字彙測驗詳解

1. (**D**) 預計會超過五千個人<u>參加</u>這個節慶。

    (A) contain〔kən'ten〕*v.* 包含

    (B) impress〔ɪm'prɛs〕*v.* 使印象深刻

    (C) detain〔dɪ'ten〕*v.* 留住；使耽擱

    (D) ***attend***〔ə'tɛnd〕*v.* 參加

    expect〔ɪk'spɛkt〕*v.* 期待；預期   festival〔'fɛstəvl̩〕*n.* 節慶

2. (**C**) 蘿拉和莎莉在<u>競爭</u>同樣的獎學金。

    (A) petition〔pə'tɪʃən〕*n.* 請願

    (B) approbation〔͵æprə'beʃən〕*n.* 許可

    (C) ***contention***〔kən'tɛnʃən〕*n.* 競爭；爭論

    (D) expression〔ɪk'sprɛʃən〕*n.* 表達

    scholarship〔'skɑlə͵ʃɪp〕*n.* 獎學金

scholarship

3. (**B**) 這個測驗是設計來測定你的知識<u>程度</u>。

    (A) audacity〔ɔ'dæsətɪ〕*n.* 大膽

    (B) ***extent***〔ɪk'stɛnt〕*n.* 程度；範圍

    (C) passion〔'pæʃən〕*n.* 熱情

    (D) conflict〔'kɑnflɪkt〕*n.* 衝突

    design〔dɪ'zaɪn〕*v.* 設計   determine〔dɪ'tɜmɪn〕*v.* 測定

4. (**C**) 梅爾用<u>做作的</u>英國口音說話。

    (A) impetuous〔ɪm'pɛtʃʊəs〕*adj.* 衝動的

    (B) notorious〔no'torɪəs〕*adj.* 惡名昭彰的

    (C) ***pretentious***〔prɪ'tɛnʃəs〕*adj.* 假裝的；做作的

    (D) generous〔'dʒɛnərəs〕*adj.* 大方的

    accent〔'æksɛnt〕*n.* 口音；腔調

字根 tend

5. (**A**) 這條路會再<u>延長</u>三十公里,和一號公路連結。

    (A) *extend* ﹝ ɪk'stɛnd ﹞ *v.* 延長

    (B) generate ﹝'dʒɛnə,ret ﹞ *v.* 產生

    (C) navigate ﹝'nævə,get ﹞ *v.* 航行

    (D) attain ﹝ ə'ten ﹞ *v.* 達到

    kilometer ﹝'kɪlə,mitɚ ﹞ *n.* 公里

    connect ﹝ kə'nɛkt ﹞ *v.* 連接   highway ﹝'haɪ'we ﹞ *n.* 公路

6. (**B**) 高空跳傘是我曾經擁有過最<u>刺激的</u>經驗之一。

    (A) tactile ﹝'tæktɪl ﹞ *adj.* 有觸覺的

    (B) *intense* ﹝ ɪn'tɛns ﹞ *adj.* 強烈的;緊張的

    (C) prompt ﹝ prɑmpt ﹞ *adj.* 迅速的

    (D) perennial ﹝ pə'rɛnɪəl ﹞ *adj.* 常年的

    skydiving ﹝'skaɪ,daɪvɪŋ ﹞ *n.* 高空跳傘

skydiving

7. (**D**) 在兩天<u>密集</u>的討論後,這件事終於解決了。

    (A) pregnant ﹝'prɛgnənt ﹞ *adj.* 懷孕的

    (B) compatible ﹝ kəm'pætəbḷ ﹞ *adj.* 相容的

    (C) sacred ﹝'sekrɪd ﹞ *adj.* 神聖的

    (D) *intensive* ﹝ ɪn'tɛnsɪv ﹞ *adj.* 密集的

    matter ﹝'mætɚ ﹞ *n.* 事情   resolve ﹝ rɪ'zɑlv ﹞ *v.* 解決

8. (**A**) 我的車子需要<u>大規模的</u>修理,才能再開。

    (A) *extensive* ﹝ ɪk'stɛnsɪv ﹞ *adj.* 大規模的

    (B) inexorable ﹝ ɪn'ɛksərəbḷ ﹞ *adj.* 無法改變的

    (C) expatriate ﹝ ɛks'petrɪɪt ﹞ *adj.* 流放的

    (D) exanimate ﹝ ɪg'zænəmɪt ﹞ *adj.* 無生氣的

    in need of 需要   repair ﹝ rɪ'pɛr ﹞ *n.* 修理

9. (**D**) 喬治沒有<u>假裝</u>知道所有的答案。

    (A) render〔'rɛndɚ〕*v.* 使成為；給予

    (B) sanction〔'sæŋkʃən〕*v.* 批准

    (C) battle〔'bætḷ〕*v.* 作戰

    (D) ***pretend***〔prɪ'tɛnd〕*v.* 假裝

10. (**C**) 這電影暴力的<u>內容</u>不適合小孩子觀賞。

    (A) authority〔ə'θɔrətɪ〕*n.* 權威

    (B) illusion〔ɪ'ljuʒən〕*n.* 錯覺

    (C) ***content***〔'kɑntɛnt〕*n.* 內容

    (D) ransom〔'rænsəm〕*n.* 贖金

    violent〔'vaɪələnt〕*adj.* 暴力的

    suitable〔'sutəbḷ〕*adj.* 適合的

11. (**A**) 威爾瑪<u>假裝</u>家裡有急事提早下班了。

    (A) ***pretense***〔prɪ'tɛns〕*n.* 假裝

    (B) example〔ɪg'zæmpḷ〕*n.* 例子

    (C) gender〔'dʒɛndɚ〕*n.* 性別

    (D) annotation〔͵æno'teʃən〕*n.* 註解

    leave work 下班

    emergency〔ɪ'mɝdʒənsɪ〕*n.* 緊急情況

12. (**D**) 新的醫療照護系統在政治人物之間<u>爭論</u>不斷。

    (A) devious〔'divɪəs〕*adj.* 迂迴的

    (B) obvious〔'ɑbvɪəs〕*adj.* 明顯的

    (C) previous〔'privɪəs〕*adj.* 之前的

    (D) ***contentious***〔kən'tɛnʃəs〕*adj.* 有爭論的

    health care 醫療照護　　highly〔'haɪlɪ〕*adv.* 高度地；非常地

    politician〔͵pɑlə'tɪʃən〕*n.* 政治人物

字根 tend

13. (**A**) 珍有一個傾向，在幾週後就會對男朋友失去興趣。

    (A) *tendency* 〔'tɛndənsɪ 〕 *n.* 傾向

    (B) alimony 〔'ælə,monɪ 〕 *n.* 贍養費

    (C) dowry 〔'daʊrɪ 〕 *n.* 嫁妝

    (D) fancy 〔'fænsɪ 〕 *n.* 愛好

14. (**D**) 在教授冗長又無聊的授課中，大多數的學生都努力保持注意力集中。

    (A) native 〔'netɪv 〕 *adj.* 出生地的

    (B) combative 〔 kəm'bætɪv 〕 *adj.* 好戰的

    (C) impassive 〔 ɪm'pæsɪv 〕 *adj.* 無情的

    (D) *attentive* 〔 ə'tɛntɪv 〕 *adj.* 專注的

lecture

struggle 〔'strʌgḷ 〕 *v.* 努力；奮鬥

remain 〔 rɪ'men 〕 *v.* 保持

lecture 〔'lɛktʃɚ 〕 *n.* 授課；講課

15. (**B**) 很抱歉；我並非有意要冒犯你。

    (A) compassion 〔 kəm'pæʃən 〕 *n.* 同情

    (B) *intention* 〔 ɪn'tɛnʃən 〕 *n.* 意圖

    (C) sanction 〔'sæŋkʃən 〕 *n.* 批准

    (D) contagion 〔 kən'tedʒən 〕 *n.* 感染

offend 〔 ə'fɛnd 〕 *v.* 冒犯

字根 tend

【劉毅老師的話】

    目標鎖定後，背的時候遇到挫折，休息幾天、幾個星期、甚至幾個月，只要繼續朝目標前進，終有成功的一天，無論是背單字，或是做其他事業，都是一樣。

請連中文一起背，背至85秒內，終生不忘。

1

tend	傾向
attend	參加
subtend	正對角
intend	打算
extend	擴大
contend	競爭
distend	膨脹
portend	預示
pretend	假裝

2

tense	緊張的
tendon	腱
tender	柔軟的
tension	緊張
tensity	緊張
tensive	緊張的
tendance	照料
tendency	傾向
tendentious	有特定傾向的

3

attention	注意
attentional	注意的
attentive	專注的
attender	出席者
attendant	服務員
attendance	出席

intension	強度
intensity	強度
intensive	密集的
intense	強烈的
intensify	加強
intensification	加強
intendant	管理者
intendance	管理
intendment	真意
superintend	監督
superintendent	監督者
superintendence	監督

字根 tend

4

extension　擴大
extensity　擴張性
extensive　廣泛的

extensor　伸展肌
extensile　可延伸的
extensible　可延伸的

contender　競爭者
contention　爭論
contentious　有爭論的

distension　膨脹
distensible　會膨脹的
distensibility　膨脹性

pretense　假裝
pretension　假裝
pretentious　虛偽的

5

intent　意圖
extent　程度
content　滿足

potent　有力的
portent　預兆

6

tentacle　觸鬚
tentative　試驗性的
tentation　試驗調整

intention　意圖
intentional　故意的
intentionally　故意地

potentate　統治者
potential　潛力
potentiality　潛力

portentous　預兆的
portentously　有預兆地
portentousness　預兆

字根 tend

※ 本頁可影印後，隨身攜帶，方便背誦。

Group 7 字根 *pel*

目標: ① 先將48個字放入短期記憶。
② 加快速度至40秒之內，成為長期記憶。

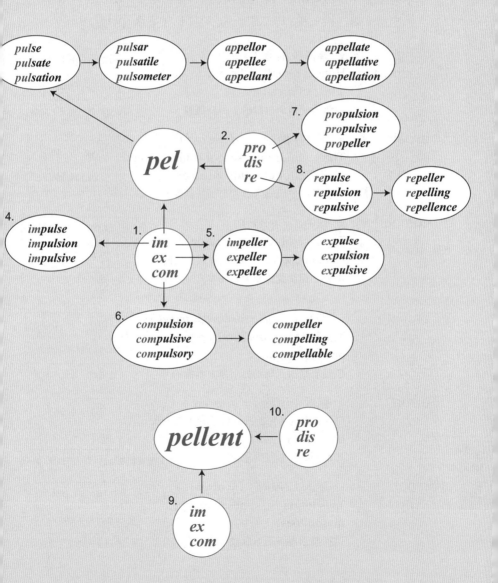

1. 字根 *pel* 核心單字

　　字根 pel 意思是 drive「驅趕」，核心單字共有 6 個，這 6 個字的字首 im-ex-com，pro-dis-re，和第一課中 pose 的核心單字中間 6 個一模一樣，只要你 pose 的變化背下來，pel 就背好了。

impel
〔 ɪmˈpɛl 〕

v. 驅使；推進 (= *drive*)
Hunger *impelled* the boy to steal a loaf of bread.
飢餓驅使這個男孩偷了一條麵包。

im + pel
|　　|
in + *drive*

在心裡驅趕，即是「驅使」

expel[6]
〔 ɪkˈspɛl 〕

v. 驅逐；開除 (= *drive out*)
Three junior high school students were *expelled* for cheating on an exam.
三名國中生因為考試作弊而被開除。

ex + pel
|　　|
out + *drive*

compel[5]
〔 kəmˈpɛl 〕

v. 強迫 (= *force*)
The lack of rain this season *compels* us to conserve water. 這個季節雨水缺乏迫使我們要節約用水。

com + pel
|　　　|
together + *drive*

驅趕你一起做，就是「強迫」你

propel[6]
〔 prəˈpɛl 〕

v. 推進 (= *push forward* = *impel*)
The boat is *propelled* by a gas-powered engine.
這艘船是由瓦斯動力引擎來推進的。

pro + pel
|　　　|
forward + *drive*

向前驅趕，即是「推進」

dispel
〔 dɪˈspɛl 〕

v. 驅散；消除 (= *disperse*)
Diana has tried everything to *dispel* her fear of flying. 黛安娜非常努力想消除她對飛行的恐懼。

dis + pel
|　　|
apart + *drive*

驅趕四散分開，即是「驅散；消除」

repel
〔 rɪˈpɛl 〕

v. 逐退；使厭惡 (= *disgust*)
This lotion is supposed to *repel* mosquitoes.
這種藥水應該可以驅蚊。

re + pel
|　　|
back + *drive*

趕回去，即是「逐退」

字根 pel

2. *pulse-pulsate-pulsation*

　　字根 pel 的變化形很多都變成 pulse，血液驅趕流
通全身，就會變成「脈搏；脈動」了，這一回 6 個字都
來自 pulse「脈搏」。

---

pulse[5]
〔 pʌls 〕

n. 脈搏（ = *beat* ）　　*v.* 脈動；跳動
The doctor felt my *pulse*. 醫生幫我量脈搏。
His heart *pulsed* with pleasure. 他的心因喜悅而狂跳。

pulsate
〔ˈpʌlset 〕

v. 脈動；跳動（ = *throb* ）
The city seemed to *pulsate* with
excitement. 整座都市似乎興奮地脈動著。

```
puls + ate
 |      |
脈搏  +  v.
```

pulsation
〔 pʌlˈseʃən 〕

n. 脈搏（ = *pulse* ）；跳動（ = *beat* ）
We danced to the rhythmic *pulsations* of the music.
我們隨著音樂節奏性的節拍而起舞。

---

pulsar
〔ˈpʌlsɚ 〕

n. 脈衝星
A new survey has found over 100
pulsars in our solar system.
一項新的調查發現，我們的太陽系
裡有超過 100 顆脈衝星。

```
puls + ar
 |      |
脈搏  +  n.
```

發出「脈衝波」的星球，
稱為「脈衝星」

pulsatile
〔ˈpʌlsətḷ , -tɪl 〕

adj. 脈動的；跳動的（ = *vibrating* ）
I was awakened by the *pulsatile* vibrations
coming from next door. 我被來自隔壁的震動吵醒。

pulsometer
〔 pʌlˈsɑmətɚ 〕

n. 脈搏計（ = *pulsimeter* ）
A *pulsometer* is a medical instrument used to measure
a person's heart rate.
脈搏計是一種醫療儀器，用
來測量一個人的心跳速率。

pulsometer

```
puls + ometer
 |       |
脈搏  +  measure
```

字根 pel

3. *appellor-appellee-appellant*

　　這一回的前 4 個字，都來自動詞 appeal「懇求；上訴」，字尾 or 表「主動者」，ee 表「被動者」，ant 可表「人」，都是前面學過的。而最後 2 個字，要懇求、要上訴，要有具體的「稱呼」。這 6 個字比較難，只要背到 6 秒鐘之內，就不會忘記了。

appellor (ə'pɛlɔr)	*n.* 上訴者 The defendant refused to answer the *appellor*'s questions. 被告拒絕回答上訴者的問題。

```
ap + peal
 |     |
to  + drive
```
驅使、拜託你去做，
即是「懇求；上訴」

appellee (ˌæpə'li)	*n.* 被上訴者 The *appellee* continued to deny the charges brought against him.　被上訴者持續否認對他的指控。
appellant (ə'pɛlənt)	*n.* 上訴者 (= *appellor*)　　*adj.* 上訴的 The *appellant*'s attorney filed a brief with the Supreme Court.　上訴者的律師向最高法院提出案情摘要。

appellate (ə'pɛlɪt)	*adj.* 上訴的 (= *appellant*) We will take our case to the *appellate* court.　我們會將我們的案子交給受理上訴的法院。

```
ap + pell + ate
 |     |     |
to  + drive + adj.
```

appellative (ə'pɛlətɪv)	*adj.* 稱呼的　　*n.* 名稱；稱呼 Homo sapien is the most common *appellative* for all human beings. 人類所有的名稱中，最常見的是 "home sapiens"。

```
ap + pell + ative
 |     |      |
to  + drive + adj., n.
```

appellation (ˌæpə'leʃən)	*n.* 名稱；稱呼 (= *appellative* = *name*) "Your Majesty" is the most appropriate *appellation* to use when addressing a king or queen. 「陛下」是尊稱國王或皇后時，最適當的稱呼。

4. *impulse-impulsion-impulsive*

這一回共有 15 個字，來自 impel-expel-compel 的變化，前 9 個字中，impeller 後沒有其他變化，所以和 expeller-expellee 併成一組。這一回不難背，要背到 8 秒鐘之內。

impulse[5] （'ɪmpʌls）	*n.* 衝動（ = *urge* ） Yolanda resisted an *impulse* to laugh out loud. 尤蘭達忍住一股想大聲笑出來的衝動。

> im + pulse
> ｜　　｜
> *in* + *drive*
>
> 在心中推動，即是「衝動」

impulsion （ ɪm'pʌlʃən ）	*n.* 衝動（ = *impulse* ） The thief is driven by an *impulsion* to steal. 這名小偷會行竊是因為一時的衝動。
impulsive[5] （ ɪm'pʌlsɪv ）	*adj.* 衝動的（ = *hasty* ） James is too *impulsive* to be a responsible team leader. 詹姆斯太衝動了，無法成為負責任的小組領導人。
impeller （ ɪm'pɛlɚ ）	*n.* 推動者；（ 渦輪 ）葉片 A bird got caught in the airplane's *impeller*, forcing the pilot to make an emergency landing. 一隻鳥捲入飛機的渦輪葉片中，迫使飛行員緊急降落。

impeller

expeller （ ɛk'spɛlɚ ）	*n.* 驅逐者；開除者 Natural oils like pressed olive oil and coconut butter, can be *expellers* of harmful microbes. 天然的油，如榨出的橄欖油和椰子油，可以驅除有害的細菌。
expellee （ ͵ɛkspɛ'li ）	*n.* 被逐出者；被開除者 The *expellee* felt deep hostility toward his former employer. 這名被開除者對之前的雇主懷有很深的敵意。

expulse
〔 ɪk'spʌls 〕

v. 驅逐（= *expel*）
The rebels were *expulsed* from their mountain hideaway by government troops.
叛軍被政府軍隊從山裡的隱藏處逐出。

expulsion
〔 ɪk'spʌlʃən 〕

n. 驅逐；開除（= *dismissal*）
The liver is mainly responsible for the *expulsion* of waste products from the blood stream.
肝臟主要是負責將血液中的廢物排出。

expulsive
〔 ɪk'spʌlsɪv 〕

adj. 驅逐的；開除的
The cat remained in the tree despite the fireman's *expulsive* efforts.
儘管消防隊員努力想把那隻貓趕出來，貓咪還是待在樹上。

【背誦祕訣】

impulse
impulsion
impulsive
→
impeller
expeller
expellee
→
expulse
expulsion
expulsive

1. 第一組和第三組變化完全相同。

2. 第二組先 **im**peller 再 **ex**peller，只改字首，而 expeller-expellee 則是「主動者」和「被動者」。

字根 pel

compulsion
〔 kəm'pʌlʃən 〕

n. 強迫 (= *force*)；衝動 (= *impulse*)
Harriet felt a *compulsion* to talk about her problems.
哈莉艾特覺得有一股想談論自己問題的衝動。

compulsive
〔 kəm'pʌlsɪv 〕

adj. 強迫的；無法克制的 (= *obsessive*)
John has a *compulsive* desire to play jokes on
his friends.
約翰忍不住想要對他的朋友惡作劇。

compulsory
〔 kəm'pʌlsərɪ 〕

adj. 強制的；義務的；必修的 (= *required*)
Most countries have *compulsory* education for
school-aged children.
大部分的國家對學齡兒童都實施義務教育。

compeller
〔 kəm'pɛlə 〕

n. 強迫者；強制者
A lack of money is a strong *compeller* to work hard.
缺錢是迫使人努力工作的強烈原因。

compelling
〔 kəm'pɛlɪŋ 〕

adj. 強烈的 (= *powerful*)；
令人信服的 (= *convincing*)
I can think of no *compelling* reason to approve
your request.
我想不出令人信服的理由來同意你的請求。

compellable
〔 kəm'pɛləbḷ 〕

adj. 強迫的 (= *obliging*)
Some students are simply lazy and not *compellable*
under threat of punishment.
有些學生就是懶惰，威脅要處罰也強迫不動。

5. *propulsion-propulsive-propeller*

這一回9個字，包括 propel 和 repel 的變化，但是
沒有 dispel，背誦順序和前面各回大致相同，非常好背，
要背到5秒鐘之內。

propulsion
〔 prə'pʌlʃən 〕

n. 推進力 (= *push*)
Solar *propulsion* may be the key to future space travel.
太陽能推進力可能是未來太空旅行的關鍵。

propulsive
〔 prə'pʌlsɪv 〕

adj. 推進的 (= *propelling*)
The faster a jet plane goes, the greater its *propulsive* efficiency.
噴射機速度越快，它的推進效率就越大。

propeller[6]
〔 prə'pɛlɚ 〕

n. 推進器；螺旋槳
One torpedo damaged the battleship's *propeller*.
一枚魚雷損壞了戰艦的推進器。

propeller

repulse
〔 rɪ'pʌls 〕

v. 擊退 (= *repel*)；拒絕 (= *reject*)
Jane is *repulsed* by the sight of worms.
珍看到蟲就感到很厭惡。

repulsion
〔 rɪ'pʌlʃən 〕

n. 擊退；嫌惡 (= *disgust*)
The sight of worms fills Jane with *repulsion*.
看到那些蟲使珍充滿厭惡。

repulsive
〔 rɪ'pʌlsɪv 〕

adj. 令人厭惡的；討厭的 (= *disgusting*)
As far as Jane is concerned, worms are the most *repulsive* creatures on Earth.
就珍而言，蟲是世界上最令人厭惡的生物。

字根
pel

repeller

〔 rɪ'pɛlə 〕

n. 擊退者；抵制者

Certain flowers have natural aromas that act as insect *repellers*.

某些花有天然的氣味，可以作為驅蟲劑。

repelling

〔 rɪ'pɛlɪŋ 〕

adj. 令人厭惡的（ = *disgusting* ）

Stinky tofu is the most *repelling* odor I've ever come across.

臭豆腐的味道是我所遇過最令人厭惡的。

repellence

〔 rɪ'pɛləns 〕

n. 抵抗性（ = *resistance* ）

A protective wax may be applied to provide additional water *repellence*.

上一層保護性的蠟，可以提供額外的防水性。

【背誦祕訣】

propulsion
propulsive   沒有 *propulse*，
propeller   但加入 propeller

repulse
repulsion   和第四回第一、三組順序相同
repulsive

repeller
repelling   先 -er，再 -ing，和 compeller-
repellence   compelling 一樣。

字根 pel

6. impellent-expellent-compellent

第六回是字根 pel 的變化，變成 pellent，一樣配
合 im-ex-com，pro-dis-re 六個字首，皆變成形容詞，
非常好背。

impellent
〔 ɪmˊpɛlənt 〕
adj. 推進的 (= *propulsive*)；強迫的
Charles has a reputation as an *impellent* public
speaker.
查爾斯是一位有名的公開演說者，以論點強而有力著稱。

expellent
〔 ɛkˊspɛlənt 〕
adj. 驅除的；有驅逐力的　*n.* 驅除劑；排毒劑
Oil and water are naturally *expellent* toward each
other. 油和水天生就會互相排斥。

compellent
〔 kəmˊpɛlənt 〕
adj. 引人注目的
The Captain approved only *compellent* defensive
actions. 隊長只同意顯著的防衛行動。

propellent
〔 prəˊpɛlənt 〕
adj. 推進的 (= *propulsive*)　*n.* 推進劑
Gasoline is a dangerous and highly flammable
propellent. 汽油是很危險，而且高度可燃的推進劑。

dispellent
〔 dɪˊspɛlənt 〕
adj. 分散的 (= *scattering*)
Scott paid no attention to Nancy's *dispellent* advice.
南西的勸告過於分散，史考特完全不予理會。

repellent
〔 rɪˊpɛlənt 〕
adj. 排斥的；不透…的 (= *proof* = *resistant*)
n. 防水劑；驅蟲劑
This jacket is made of water-*repellent* nylon.
這件夾克是由防水尼龍材料製成的。

字根 pel

Exercise : Choose the correct answer. ✦

1. Scientists have concerns about insect _____ that contain toxic chemicals.
   - (A) expositions
   - (B) impressions
   - (C) applications
   - (D) repellents

2. Several students faced _____ for fighting on school grounds.
   - (A) expulsion
   - (B) explication
   - (C) expressage
   - (D) extension

3. Doctor Smith didn't like his patients to use his formal _____, so everyone called him "Bob."
   - (A) reposition
   - (B) countersign
   - (C) supplication
   - (D) appellation

4. Recent events _____ us to make changes for the future.
   - (A) deposit
   - (B) compel
   - (C) imply
   - (D) observe

5. Over twenty countries have _____ voting, which requires citizens to participate in elections.
   - (A) composedly
   - (B) preservative
   - (C) contentious
   - (D) compulsory

6. Our troops were able to _____ the enemy's invasion.
   - (A) reserve
   - (B) repose
   - (C) reply
   - (D) repel

7. After a long day of hiking, Joe's feet _____ with pain.
   - (A) perplexed
   - (B) resigned
   - (C) pulsed
   - (D) extended

8. Kitty's first _____ was to leave the scene as quickly as possible.
   (A) impulse
   (B) implication
   (C) imposture
   (D) impressionism

9. Nancy _____ Kenneth's attempt to apologize.
   (A) intended
   (B) decomposed
   (C) replicated
   (D) repulsed

10. The speaker tried to _____ the misconceptions of global warming.
    (A) dispel
    (B) duplicate
    (C) design
    (D) disserve

11. A rocket will _____ the spacecraft into orbit.
    (A) pretend
    (B) posit
    (C) propel
    (D) ply

12. We are under _____ from the boss to complete the project ahead of schedule.
    (A) consignment
    (B) composure
    (C) complexity
    (D) compulsion

13. Edward is a _____ liar; you can't believe a word he says.
    (A) compulsive
    (B) complex
    (C) composite
    (D) compressive

14. Leo made no effort to excuse his own _____ behavior.
    (A) significant
    (B) repulsive
    (C) portentous
    (D) disposable

15. "Take your time," his father said. "Make an _____ decision now, and you may be sorry some day."
    (A) imposing
    (B) imposturous
    (C) impulsive
    (D) impressible

字彙測驗詳解

1. (**D**) 科學家擔心<u>驅蟲劑</u>含有有毒的化學物質。

    (A) exposition〔͵ɛkspə'zɪʃən〕 n. 展覽會;解說

    (B) impression〔ɪm'prɛʃən〕 n. 印象

    (C) application〔͵æplə'keʃən〕 n. 申請;應用

    (D) *repellent*〔rɪ'pɛlənt〕 adj. 排斥的 n. 驅蟲劑

    concern〔kən'sɝn〕 n. 關心;擔心   insect〔'ɪnsɛkt〕 n. 昆蟲
    contain〔kən'ten〕 v. 包含   toxic〔'taksɪk〕 adj. 有毒的
    chemical〔'kɛmɪkl̩〕 n. 化學物質

2. (**A**) 數名學生因為在校園裡打架,面臨<u>開除</u>的處分。

    (A) *expulsion*〔ɪk'spʌlʃən〕 n. 驅逐;開除

    (B) explication〔͵ɛksplɪ'keʃən〕 n. 詳細說明

    (C) expressage〔ɪk'sprɛsɪdʒ〕 n. 快遞費

    (D) extension〔ɪk'stɛnʃən〕 n. 擴大;延伸;(電話)分機

    fight〔faɪt〕 v. 打架   grounds〔graʊndz〕 n. pl. 場地;用地

3. (**D**) 史密斯醫生不喜歡病人用他的正式<u>名字</u>,所以大家都叫他「鮑伯」。

    (A) reposition〔͵ripə'zɪʃən〕 n., v. 放回

    (B) countersign〔'kaʊntɚ͵saɪn〕 v. 副署;連署

    (C) supplication〔͵sʌplɪ'keʃən〕 n. 懇求

    (D) *appellation*〔͵æpə'leʃən〕 n. 名稱;稱呼

    patient〔'peʃənt〕 n. 病人   formal〔'fɔrml̩〕 adj. 正式的

4. (**B**) 最近的事件<u>迫使</u>我們將來要做一些改變。

    (A) deposit〔dɪ'pazɪt〕 v. 存款;存放;沈積

    (B) *compel*〔kəm'pɛl〕 v. 強迫

    (C) imply〔ɪm'plaɪ〕 v. 暗示

    (D) observe〔əb'zɝv〕 v. 觀察;遵守

    recent〔'risn̩t〕 adj. 最近的   event〔ɪ'vɛnt〕 n. 事件

5. (**D**) 超過 20 個國家有投票<u>義務</u>，要求國民參與選舉。

    (A) composedly〔kəm'pozɪdlɪ〕*adv.* 鎮靜地

    (B) preservative〔prɪ'zɝvətɪv〕*adj.* 保護的；防腐的

    (C) contentious〔kən'tɛnʃəs〕*adj.* 爭論的

    (D) *compulsory*〔kəm'pʌlsərɪ〕*adj.* 強制的；義務的

    voting〔'votɪŋ〕*n.* 投票   require〔rɪ'kwaɪr〕*v.* 要求

    citizen〔'sɪtəzn̩〕*n.* 國民

    participate〔pəˈtɪsəˌpet〕*v.* 參加

6. (**D**) 我們的部隊能夠<u>逐退</u>敵人的入侵。

    (A) reserve〔rɪ'zɝv〕*v.* 預訂；保留

    (B) repose〔rɪ'poz〕*v., n.* 休息

    (C) reply〔rɪ'plaɪ〕*v., n.* 回答

    (D) *repel*〔rɪ'pɛl〕*v.* 逐退；驅逐

    troop〔trup〕*n.* 部隊   *be able to + V.* 能夠~

    enemy〔'ɛnəmɪ〕*n.* 敵人

    invasion〔ɪn'veʒən〕*n.* 入侵

7. (**C**) 走了漫長的一天之後，喬的雙腳陣陣<u>抽痛</u>。

    (A) perplex〔pəˈplɛks〕*v.* 使困惑

    (B) resign〔rɪ'zaɪn〕*v.* 辭職

    (C) *pulse*〔pʌls〕*n.* 脈搏   *v.* 脈動；跳動

    (D) extend〔ɪk'stɛnd〕*v.* 擴大；延長

    hike〔haɪk〕*v.* 健行；徒步旅行

8. (**A**) 吉蒂第一個<u>衝動</u>是盡快離開現場。

    (A) *impulse*〔'ɪmpʌls〕*n.* 衝動

    (B) implication〔ˌɪmplɪ'keʃən〕*n.* 牽連；暗示

    (C) imposture〔ɪm'pɑstʃɚ〕*n.* 欺騙

    (D) impressionism〔ɪm'prɛʃənˌɪzəm〕*n.* 印象主義

    scene〔sin〕*n.* 現場

    as~as possible 盡可能地~

字根 pel

9. (**D**) 肯尼斯試著要道歉，但是南西<u>拒絕</u>了。

    (A) intend〔 ɪn'tɛnd 〕*v.* 打算

    (B) decompose〔ˌdikəm'poz 〕*v.* 分解

    (C) replicate〔'rɛplɪˌket 〕*v.* 複製

    (D) *repulse*〔 rɪ'pʌls 〕*v.* 擊退；拒絕

    attempt〔 ə'tɛmpt 〕*n.* 企圖；嘗試

    apologize〔 ə'paləˌdʒaɪz 〕*v.* 道歉

10. (**A**) 演講者試圖<u>消除</u>大家對全球暖化的錯誤觀念。

    (A) *dispel*〔 dɪ'spɛl 〕*v.* 驅散；消除

    (B) duplicate〔'djuplə,ket 〕*v.* 複製

    (C) design〔 dɪ'zaɪn 〕*v.* 設計

    (D) disserve〔 dɪs'sɝv 〕*v.* 幫倒忙；損害

    misconception〔ˌmɪskən'sɛpʃən 〕*n.* 錯誤的觀念；誤解

11. (**C**) 火箭能<u>推動</u>太空船進入軌道。

    (A) pretend〔 prɪ'tɛnd 〕*v.* 假裝

    (B) posit〔'pazɪt 〕*v.* 假定

    (C) *propel*〔 prə'pɛl 〕*v.* 推進

    (D) ply〔 plaɪ 〕*v.* 忙於；定期往返

    rocket〔'rakɪt 〕*n.* 火箭

    spacecraft〔'spes,kræft 〕*n.* 太空船

    orbit〔'ɔrbɪt 〕*n.*（天體運行的）軌道

rocket-propelled

12. (**D**) 我們受到老闆的<u>強迫</u>，要超前進度完成這項計劃。

    (A) consignment〔 kən'saɪnmənt 〕*n.* 委託

    (B) composure〔 kəm'poʒə 〕*n.* 鎮靜

    (C) complexity〔 kəm'plɛksətɪ 〕*n.* 複雜

    (D) *compulsion*〔 kəm'pʌlʃən 〕*n.* 強制；強迫

    project〔'pradʒɛkt 〕*n.* 計劃

    ahead of schedule 在預定進度之前

字根 pel

13. (**A**) 愛德華總是<u>忍不住</u>想要說謊；他說的話你一個字都不能相信。

    (A) *compulsive* 〔 kəm'pʌlsɪv 〕 *adj.* 強迫的；無法克制的

    (B) complex 〔 kəm'plɛks 〕 *adj.* 複雜的

    (C) composite 〔 kəm'pazɪt 〕 *adj.* 混合的；合成的

    (D) compressive 〔 kəm'prɛsɪv 〕 *adj.* 壓縮的

    liar 〔'laɪɚ〕 *n.* 說謊者

14. (**B**) 里歐完全不努力為他自己<u>討厭的</u>行為辯解。

    (A) significant 〔 sɪg'nɪfəkənt 〕 *adj.* 重要的

    (B) *repulsive* 〔 rɪ'pʌlsɪv 〕 *adj.* 討厭的

    (C) portentous 〔 por'tɛntəs 〕 *adj.* 有凶兆的

    (D) disposable 〔 dɪ'spozəbl̩ 〕 *adj.* 用完即丟的

        disposable chopsticks 免洗筷

    make no effort 不努力   excuse 〔 ɪk'skjuz 〕 *v.* 為～辯解

    behavior 〔 bɪ'hevjɚ 〕 *n.* 行為；舉止

15. (**C**) 「慢慢來，」他爸爸說。「現在做一個<u>衝動的</u>決定，有一天你可能會後悔。」

    (A) imposing 〔 ɪm'pozɪŋ 〕 *adj.* 宏偉的

    (B) imposturous 〔 ɪm'pastʃərəs 〕 *adj.* 欺騙的

    (C) *impulsive* 〔 ɪm'pʌlsɪv 〕 *adj.* 衝動的

    (D) impressible 〔 ɪm'prɛsəbl̩ 〕 *adj.* 易受影響的

    take one's time 慢慢來

    make a～decision 做～決定

    some day （將來）有一天

請連中文一起背，背至一分鐘內，終生不忘。 ✦

1

impel	驅使
expel	驅逐
compel	強迫
propel	推進
dispel	驅散
repel	逐退

2

pulse	脈搏
pulsate	脈動
pulsation	脈搏
pulsar	脈衝星
pulsatile	脈動的
pulsometer	脈搏計

3

appellor	上訴者
appellee	被上訴者
appellant	上訴者
appellate	上訴的
appellative	稱呼的
appellation	名稱

【劉毅老師的話】

養成嘴裡唸唸有辭背單字的習慣，一組一組地背，越背速度越快。

字根 pel

4

impulse	衝動
impulsion	衝動
impulsive	衝動的
impeller	推動者
expeller	驅逐者
expellee	被逐出者
expulse	驅逐
expulsion	驅逐
expulsive	驅逐的

compulsion	強迫
compulsive	強迫的
compulsory	強制的
compeller	強迫者
compelling	強烈的
compellable	強迫的

5

propulsion	推進力
propulsive	推進的
propeller	推進器
repulse	擊退
repulsion	擊退
repulsive	令人厭惡的
repeller	擊退者
repelling	令人厭惡的
repellence	抵抗性

6

impellent	推進的
expellent	驅逐的
compellent	引人注目的
propellent	推進的
dispellent	分散的
repellent	排斥的

字根 pel

※ 本頁可影印後，隨身攜帶，方便背誦。

Group 8 字根 *fer*

目標: ① 先將60個字放入短期記憶。
② 加快速度至50秒之內,成為長期記憶。

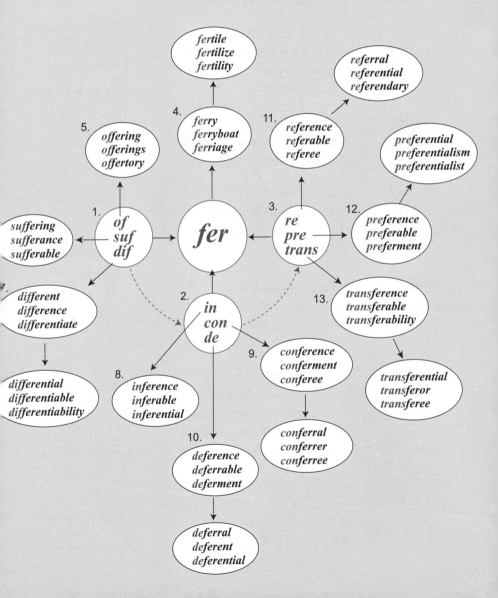

1. 字根 *fer* 核心單字

　　這 9 個字，3 個一組一起背，可先背 6 個，再背 3 個，背熟至 5 秒之內，可成爲長期記憶，才可再背下一組。

offer[2]
〔ˈɔfɚ〕

v. 提供（= *provide*）
fer 這個字根的意思是 carry「攜帶」
May I *offer* you a cup of tea?
我可以請你喝杯茶嗎？

```
of  +  fer
|      |
near + carry
```
帶到你面前，即是「提供」

suffer[3]
〔ˈsʌfɚ〕

v. 遭受（= *undergo*）
William *suffers* from seasonal allergies. 威廉罹患季節性的過敏。

```
suf  +  fer
 |       |
under + carry
```

differ[4]
〔ˈdɪfɚ〕

v. 不同（= *vary*）
Our teachers *differ* in method and style. 我們的老師在教學方式和風格上都不相同。

```
dif  +  fer
 |       |
apart + carry
```
一個個分開帶，即是「不同」

infer[6]
〔ɪnˈfɝ〕

v. 推論（= *conclude*）
From what I can *infer*, you seem to be having a bad day.
依我推斷，你今天似乎過得不太好。

```
in  +  fer
|      |
into + carry
```
把想法引入心中，即是「推論」

confer[6]
〔kənˈfɝ〕

v. 商議（= *consult*）
I will have to *confer* with your mother before I agree to that.
在我同意這件事情之前，我必須先跟你的母親商議一下。

```
con  +  fer
 |       |
all  + carry
```
把大家都叫進來，即是「商議」

defer
〔dɪˈfɝ〕

v. 延期（= *delay*）；服從
Ashley applied to *defer* payments on her student loan.
愛旭力申請學生貸款的延遲付款。

```
de  +  fer
 |      |
down + carry
```

拿到人之下，即是「服從」

refer[4]
〔 rɪˋfɝ 〕

v. 參考 (= *consult*)；提及；是指
Please *refer* to the last page of
the book for answers.
要找答案，請參考書的最後一頁。

```
re  +  fer
|      |
back + carry
```
帶回去看看，即是「參考」

prefer[2]
〔 prɪˋfɝ 〕

v. 比較喜歡 (= *favor*)
Lisa *prefers* reading to watching
television.
麗莎比較喜歡閱讀勝過電視。

```
pre  +  fer
|       |
before + carry
```

看到要先拿，即是「比較喜歡」

transfer[4]
〔 trænsˋfɝ 〕

v. 轉移 (= *move*)；傳送
The clerk agreed to *transfer* my
medical records to Dr. Jones.
這個職員同意將我的醫療紀錄轉給
瓊斯醫生。

```
trans +  fer
|        |
A→B  + carry
```

從 A 運到 B，即是「轉移」

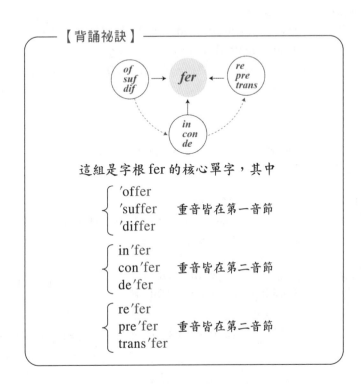

【背誦祕訣】

這組是字根 fer 的核心單字，其中

$$
\begin{cases}
ˋoffer \\
ˋsuffer \\
ˋdiffer
\end{cases}
\text{重音皆在第一音節}
$$

$$
\begin{cases}
inˋfer \\
conˋfer \\
deˋfer
\end{cases}
\text{重音皆在第二音節}
$$

$$
\begin{cases}
reˋfer \\
preˋfer \\
transˋfer
\end{cases}
\text{重音皆在第二音節}
$$

2. ferry-ferryboat-ferriage

這一組有 6 個字，3 個一組一起背，可先背 3 個，
再背 3 個，背熟至 3 秒之內，變成直覺。

ferry[4]
('fɛrɪ)
n. 渡輪 (= *boat*)　*v.* 運送 (= *carry*)
Paula took a *ferry* from Hong Kong to Macau.
寶拉從香港搭渡輪到澳門。

ferryboat
('fɛrɪ,bot)
n. 渡輪 (= *ferry*)
Traveling by *ferryboat* is a pleasant alternative to other
forms of transport.
搭渡輪旅行是其他交通工具以外，另一個很棒的選擇。

ferriage
('fɛrɪɪdʒ)
n. 渡船費
The shipment of goods will be held
in storage until we pay the *ferriage.*
在我們支付渡船費之前，船貨將會先放
在倉庫裡。

ferri	+ age
ferry +	*n.*

這三個字都和「船」有關，
且重音都在第一音節。

fertile[4]
('fɜtḷ)
adj. 肥沃的；多產的 (= *productive*)
The land is very *fertile.* 這個土地很肥沃。

fertilize[6]
('fɜtḷ,aɪz)
v. 使肥沃；給…施肥
The farmer used compost to *fertilize* his crops.
農夫使用堆肥來替他的農作物施肥。

fertility[6]
(fɜ'tɪlətɪ)
n. 繁殖力 (= *productivity*)
Smoking can have harmful effects
on a woman's *fertility.*
抽菸對女性的生殖力有不好的影響。

fertil	+ ity
fertile +	*n.*

這三個字都和「生產」有關，
且開頭皆爲 fertil。

3. *offering-offerings-offertory*

這一組有 12 個字，分成三組，第一組是 offer 的衍生字，第二組是 suffer 的衍生字，第三組是 differ 的衍生字，背熟至 7 秒之內，變成直覺。

offering[6]
〔'ɔfərɪŋ〕
n. 提供 (= *contribution*)
Toy Story 3 is the latest animated *offering* from Pixar Films. 「玩具總動員 3」是皮克斯公司所提供的最新動畫片。

offerings[6]
〔'ɔfərɪŋz〕
n. pl. 捐獻物 (= *charity*)
The schoolhouse was constructed with funds from local church *offerings*. 這學校校舍的建造經費是來自當地教堂的捐贈。

offer	+	ings
提供	+	*n.*

這三個字都與「貢獻」有關，且重音皆在第一音節。

offertory
〔'ɔfɚ͵torɪ〕
n. 奉獻儀式；奉獻金
Father Reilly presided over the *offertory*.
瑞利神父主持奉獻儀式。

suffering[3]
〔'sʌfərɪŋ〕
n. 痛苦 (= *pain*)；苦難
Tina bore her *sufferings* bravely.
蒂娜勇敢地忍受著痛苦。

sufferance
〔'sʌfərəns〕
n. 寬容 (= *tolerance*)
All people should practice *sufferance* and live in peace. 所有的人都應該實踐習寬容並且和平相處。

suffer	+	ance
遭受	+	*n.*

願意忍受痛苦，即是「寬容」

sufferable
〔'sʌfərəbḷ〕
adj. 可忍受的 (= *endurable*)
Some forms of punishment are more *sufferable*.
有些形式的處罰較可以忍受。

字根 fer

different[1]
(ˈdɪfərənt)

adj. 不同的 (= *distinct*)
It is important to let students see *different* aspects of the issue.
讓學生看到這議題的不同方面是很重要的。

difference[2]
(ˈdɪfərəns)

n. 差異 (= *dissimilarity*)
There is a big *difference* between sympathy and empathy. 同情和移情作用之間有很大的差異。

differentiate[6]
(ˌdɪfəˈrɛnʃɪˌet)

v. 區分 (= *distinguish*)
Oscar doesn't have the ability to *differentiate* between his imagination and reality.
奧斯卡並沒有能力來區別想像和現實。

differ	+ ent	+ iate	
|	|	|	
不同	+ *adj.*	+ *v.*	把不同處找出來，即是「區分」

differential
(ˌdɪfəˈrɛnʃəl)

adj. 差別的 (= *distinctive*)   *n.* 差異
They pay *differential* rents according to their income.
他們根據自己的收入來付差別的租金。

differ	+ ent	+ ial
|	|	|
不同	+ *adj.*	+ *n.*

differentiable
(ˌdɪfəˈrɛnʃɪəbl̩)

adj. 可分辨的
Under a microscope, cancer cells are easily *differentiable* from normal, healthy cells. 在顯微鏡下，可以輕易地分辨癌細胞和正常、健康的細胞。

differ	+ ent	+ iable
|	|	|
不同	+ *adj.*	+ 可~的

differentiability
(ˌdɪfəˌrɛnʃɪəˈbɪlətɪ)

n. 可辨性
The professor explained the idea of *differentiability* in mathematics. 教授解釋數學中的可辨性的觀念。

* 這六個單字為 differ 的詞類變化，意思都與「不同；區別」有關。

4. *inference-inferable-inferential*

這一組有 15 個字，分成三組，第一組是 infer 的衍生字，第二組是 confer 的衍生字，第三組是 defer 的衍生字，背熟至 8 秒之內，變成直覺。

---

inference[6]
〔ˈɪnfərəns〕

n. 推論 (= *conclusion*)
What *inferences* can we draw from these facts?
我們可以從這些事實中推論出什麼？

inferable
〔ɪnˈfɝəbḷ〕

adj. 能推論的 (= *derivable*)
There is no *inferable* reason for Betty's bad attitude.
貝蒂態度不良的原因無從推論。

```
infer + able
  |      |
推論  + 可～的
```

inferential
〔͵ɪnfəˈrɛnʃəl〕

adj. 推論的 (= *derivative*)
His statements were not based upon facts but upon *inferential* references to rumors.
他的陳述並非依據事實，而是參考謠言來推論的。

---

conference[4]
〔ˈkɑnfərəns〕

n. 會議 (= *meeting*)
The president invited his advisors to a *conference* on education.
總統邀請他的顧問來參加教育會議。

```
confer + ence
  |        |
商談   +   n.
```

conferment
〔kənˈfɝmənt〕

n. 授與 (= *presentation*)
The *conferment* of this award is indeed a special honor.
這個獎項的授與真的是一個特別的榮耀。

```
confer + ment
  |        |
授與   +   n.
```

conferee
〔͵kɑnfəˈri〕

n. 參加會議者
The *conferees* warned that global warming has serious implications for the future.
與會者警告，全球暖化對未來會有嚴重的影響。

conferral
〔kən'fɝrəl〕

n. 授與（＝*conferment*）；商量
In most societies, parents will have a *conferral* when
Choosing the name of a new-born. 在大部分的社會中，
選新生兒的名字時，父母親會商量一下。

conferrer
〔kən'fɝ〕

n. 授與者
The *conferrer* of the prize is very famous.
這個獎項的頒獎人非常有名。

conferree
〔ˌkɑnfə'ri〕

n. 參加會議者（＝*conferee*）
The conference will be open to questions from the
conferees.
這個會議將開放給與會者提問。

【背誦祕訣】

confer → conference conferment conferee → conferral conferrer conferree

後面 6 個字為 confer 的詞類變化單
字，其中

　conference
　conferment　這組僅有一個 r
　conferee

　conferral
　conferrer　這組皆有兩個 r
　conferree

deference
（'dɛfərəns）

n. 服從（= *obedience*)；敬意
Stanley bowed in *deference* to
his superiors.
史丹利向他的主管鞠躬，表示敬意。

defer + ence
服從 + *n.*

deferrable
（dɪ'fʒəbḷ）

adj. 可延期的
This credit card offers *deferrable* payments for up to
six months.
這張信用卡提供最高延期六個月繳款的服務。

deferment
（dɪ'fʒmənt）

n. 延期（= *postponement*)
Victor was granted a temporary
deferment from military service.
維克特被給予暫時性的兵役延期。

defer + ment
延遲 + *n.*

deferral
（dɪ'fʒəl）

n. 延期（= *deferment*)
Critics argue that most people have already paid their
taxes, so a *deferral* will be of little help.
評論家說，大部分的人已繳稅了，所以延期並不會有太大
的幫助。

deferent
（'dɛfərənt）

adj. 恭敬的（= *respectful*)
I was puzzled by my cousin's *deferent* attitude toward
the stranger.
我表弟對那個陌生人恭敬的態度使我很困惑。

deferential
（,dɛfə'rɛnʃəl）

adj. 恭敬的（= *deferent*)
The woman kept a *deferential* silence.
那位婦人恭敬地保持著沈默。

---

* 這六個字為 defer 的詞類變化，所以意思皆與「延遲」或「服從」有關。

5. *reference-referable-referee*

這一組有 18 個字,分成三組,第一組是 refer 的衍生字,第二組是 prefer 的衍生字,第三組是 transfer 的衍生字,背熟至 10 秒之內,變成直覺。

reference[4]
('rɛfərəns)

n. 參考;提及 (= *mention*)
This book contains several *references* to World War II. 這本書裡有好幾次提到第二次世界大戰。

```
refer + ence
  |      |
 提及  +  n.
```

referable
('rɛfərəbḷ)

adj. 可歸因的;可參考的
Most of the patient's symptoms are *referable* to his cancer. 這個病人大部份的症狀都可歸因於他的癌症。

```
refer + able
  |      |
 參考  + 可～的
```

referee[5]
(,rɛfə'ri)

n. 裁判 (= *judge*)
The *referee* called a foul on number 24.
裁判說 24 號球員犯規。

referral
(rɪ'fɝəl)

n. 參考;推薦
The best way to find a new doctor is by *referral* from your friends.
找一個新醫生的最好方法,就是經由朋友的推薦。

```
refer + ral
  |      |
 提及  +  n.
```

referential
(,rɛfə'rɛnʃəl)

adj. 參考的;相關的
In this instance, a *referential* knowledge of physics is required. 在這個例子中,物理學的相關知識是需要的。

referendary
(,rɛfə'rɛndɛrɪ)

n. 仲裁者 (= *judge*)
The mother acted as a *referendary* in her children's disputes. 在孩子的爭論中,這位母親擔任仲裁者。

---

* 這六個字為 refer 的詞類變化,所以意思皆與「提及;參考」有關。

preference[5] ('prɛfərəns)	*n.* 偏愛 (= *partiality*) Steve enjoys all types of music but his *preference* is hip-hop. 史蒂夫喜歡所有類型的音樂， 但是偏愛嘻哈樂。

```
prefer   + ence
  |          |
比較喜歡  +  n.
```

字根 fer

preferable[4] ('prɛfərəbḷ)	*adj.* 較合人意的；較好的 (= *better*) Shopping online is *preferable* to going to the mall. 線上購物比去購物中心好。

preferment (prɪ'fɜmənt)	*n.* 晉升 (= *promotion*) The executive's son used his connection to gain *preferment* in the company. 那位主管的兒 子利用他的關係在公司獲得升遷。

```
prefer + ment
  |        |
較喜歡  +  n.
```

＊這三個字皆與「偏好」有關。

preferential (ˌprɛfə'rɛnʃəl)	*adj.* 優先的；優惠的 The bank is offering loans with *preferential* interest rates to long-time customers. 這家銀行提供長期顧客較優惠的貸款利率。

preferentialism (ˌprɛfə'rɛnʃəlɪzm̩)	*n.* 優惠主義 We expect *preferentialism* to play a major role in trade between the U.S. and Canada. 在美國和加拿大的貿易中， 我們預期優惠主義將會扮演 重要的角色。

```
preferential + ism
     |           |
   優惠的      + ～主義
```

preferentialist (ˌprɛfə'rɛnʃəlɪst)	*n.* 優惠主義論者 The trade *preferentialists* have a serious dispute with some senators. 貿易優惠主義論者和一些參議員有嚴重的爭執。

＊這三個字為 preferential 的衍生字，意思都與「優惠」有關。

transference
(træns'fɜəns)

n. 轉移；傳遞 (= *transmission*)
The *transference* of information is impossible unless both parties are willing to listen.
除非雙方都願意聆聽，否則訊息的傳遞是不可能的。

transferable
(træns'fɜəbḷ)

adj. 可轉移的 (= *transmissible*)
The Supreme Court ruled that basic human rights are not *transferable* to non-citizens.
最高法院裁定，基本人權是無法轉移給非公民者。

transfer + able
轉移 ＋ 可～的

transferability
(,trænsfɜə'bɪlətɪ)

n. 可轉移性
There are laws that govern the *transferability* of property. 有規定財產轉讓的法規。

transferential
(træns'fɜənʃəl)

adj. 轉移的；轉讓的
Folk tales are an example of *transferential* knowledge.
民間故事是知識傳遞的一個例子。

transferor
(træns'fɜə)

n. 轉讓人；讓與人
All shipping costs will be paid by the *transferor*.
所有的運費將由轉讓人支付。

transfer + or
轉移 ＋ 主動者

transferee
(,trænsfə'ri)

n. 受讓人；被調動者
Once the contract is signed, the *transferee* can take possession.
一旦契約簽定，受讓人可以獲得所有權。

transfer + ee
轉移 ＋ 被動者

＊這六個字為 transfer 的詞類變化，所以意思都與「轉移」有關。

Exercise : Choose the correct answer. ✦

1. George _____ to sit in the aisle seat when taking an airplane.
   (A) resigns　　　　　　(B) assigns
   (C) differs　　　　　　(D) prefers

2. California's Central Valley is known for its _____ soil.
   (A) sufferable　　　　　(B) different
   (C) fertile　　　　　　(D) differential

3. The term "spouse" generally _____ to a partner in a marriage.
   (A) attends　　　　　　(B) extends
   (C) distends　　　　　　(D) refers

4. Mitsukoshi is _____ a fifty percent discount on all women's footwear.
   (A) offering　　　　　　(B) opposing
   (C) applying　　　　　　(D) deferring

5. They are waiting for the _____ to return.
   (A) ferriage　　　　　　(B) ferry
   (C) fertility　　　　　　(D) offerings

6. Send me your bank information and I will _____ the money into your account.
   (A) imply　　　　　　　(B) expel
   (C) transfer　　　　　　(D) fertilize

7. Bill Gates gave the opening speech at the computer _____ held in Las Vegas.
   (A) offertory　　　　　　(B) conference
   (C) sufferance　　　　　(D) difference

8. Teachers must be able to _____ the individual needs of their students.
   - (A) differentiate
   - (B) pretend
   - (C) portend
   - (D) subtend

9. My _____ is for the leg, but I will eat any part of a chicken except the feet.
   - (A) conferral
   - (B) preference
   - (C) deferral
   - (D) deference

10. He wanted to apply for a _____ from military service.
    - (A) deposition
    - (B) deferment
    - (C) conferment
    - (D) designation

11. The president often _____ with his advisers on diplomatic problems.
    - (A) conferred
    - (B) compose
    - (C) comply
    - (D) compend

12. He _____ many humiliations before he became a star.
    - (A) served
    - (B) posed
    - (C) suffered
    - (D) compelled

13. I can _____ from your silence that you do not agree with me.
    - (A) impose
    - (B) intend
    - (C) intensify
    - (D) infer

14. Your idea is _____ to mine.
    - (A) different
    - (B) referential
    - (C) preferable
    - (D) transferable

15. This movie makes _____ to several documented historical events.
    - (A) transferability
    - (B) inference
    - (C) preferment
    - (D) reference

字彙測驗詳解

1. (**D**) 搭飛機的時候，喬治<u>比較喜歡</u>坐靠走道的位子。

(A) resign〔rɪ'zaɪn〕*v.* 辭職

(B) assign〔ə'saɪn〕*v.* 指派

(C) differ〔'dɪfɚ〕*v.* 不同

(D) *prefer*〔prɪ'fɝ〕*v.* 比較喜歡

aisle〔aɪl〕*n.* 走道

2. (**C**) 加州的中央山谷以<u>肥沃的</u>土壤著名。

(A) sufferable〔'sʌfərəbl̩〕*adj.* 可容忍的

(B) different〔'dɪfərənt〕*adj.* 不同的

(C) *fertile*〔'fɝtl̩〕*adj.* 肥沃的

(D) differential〔͵dɪfə'rɛnʃəl〕*adj.* 差別的

Central Valley

central〔'sɛntrəl〕*adj.* 中央的

valley〔'vælɪ〕*n.* 山谷　　soil〔sɔɪl〕*n.* 土壤

3. (**D**) 「配偶」這個名詞通常<u>指</u>的是婚姻中的伴侶。

(A) attend〔ə'tɛnd〕*v.* 參加

(B) extend〔ɪk'stɛnd〕*v.* 擴大；延長

(C) distend〔dɪ'stɛnd〕*v.* 膨脹

(D) *refer*〔rɪ'fɝ〕*v.* 參考；提及；是指 < *to* >

term〔tɝm〕*n.* 名詞

spouse〔spauz〕*n.* 配偶

generally〔'dʒɛnərəlɪ〕*adv.* 通常

partner〔'partnɚ〕*n.* 夥伴

marriage〔'mærɪdʒ〕*n.* 婚姻

字根 fer

4. (**A**) 三越百貨正在<u>提供</u>所有女鞋五折特賣。

　　　(A) *offer* ('ɔfɚ) *v.* 提供

　　　(B) oppose (ə'poz) *v.* 反對

　　　(C) apply (ə'plaɪ) *v.* 申請

　　　(D) defer (dɪ'fɝ) *v.* 延期

　　　footwear ('fʊt,wɛr) *n.* 鞋類

5. (**B**) 他們正在等候<u>渡船</u>返回。

　　　(A) ferriage ('fɛrɪɪdʒ) *n.* 渡船費

　　　(B) *ferry* ('fɛrɪ) *n.* 渡船

　　　(C) fertility (fɝ'tɪlətɪ) *n.* 繁殖力

　　　(D) offerings ('ɔfərɪŋz) *n. pl.* 捐獻物；捐助物

6. (**C**) 把你銀行的資料寄給我，我會把錢<u>轉</u>入你的戶頭。

　　　(A) imply (ɪm'plaɪ) *v.* 暗示

　　　(B) expel (ɪk'spɛl) *v.* 驅逐；逐出

　　　(C) *transfer* (træns'fɝ) *v.* 轉移

　　　(D) fertilize ('fɝtḷ,aɪz) *v.* 使肥沃

　　　information (,ɪnfɚ'meʃən) *n.* 訊息；資料

　　　account (ə'kaʊnt) *n.* 帳戶

7. (**B**) 比爾蓋茲在拉斯維加斯舉辦的電腦<u>會議</u>中發表開場演說。

　　　(A) offertory ('ɔfɚ,torɪ) *n.* 奉獻儀式；奉獻金

　　　(B) *conference* ('kɑnfərəns) *n.* 會議

　　　(C) sufferance ('sʌfərəns) *n.* 寬容

　　　(D) difference ('dɪfərəns) *n.* 差異

　　　give a speech 發表演說

Bill Gates

8. (**A**) 老師們必須能夠<u>區別</u>學生的個別需求。

    (A) *differentiate* 〔͵dɪfə'rɛnʃɪ͵et 〕*v.* 區別

    (B) pretend 〔 prɪ'tɛnd 〕*v.* 假裝

    (C) portend 〔 por'tɛnd 〕*v.* 預示

    (D) subtend 〔 səb'tɛnd 〕*v.* 正對（弧、角）

    be able to V. 能夠～

    individual 〔͵ɪndə'vɪdʒʊəl 〕*adj.* 個別的　　need 〔 nid 〕*n.* 需求

9. (**B**) 我<u>偏好</u>腿肉的部份，但是雞的其他部位我還是會吃，除了雞
腳以外。

    (A) conferral 〔 kən'fɝəl 〕*n.* 授與；商量

    (B) *preference* 〔'prɛfərəns 〕*n.* 偏好

    (C) deferral 〔 dɪ'fɝəl 〕*n.* 延期

    (D) deference 〔'dɛfərəns 〕*n.* 服從；敬意

chicken

10. (**B**) 他想申請<u>延期</u>服兵役。

    (A) deposition 〔͵dɛpə'zɪʃən 〕*n.* 罷免

    (B) *deferment* 〔 dɪ'fɝmənt 〕*n.* 延期

    (C) conferment 〔 kən'fɝmənt 〕*n.* 授與

    (D) designation 〔͵dɛzɪg'neʃən 〕*n.* 指定

    apply for 申請　　*military service* 兵役

11. (**A**) 總統常與他的顧問<u>商議</u>外交問題。

    (A) *confer* 〔 kən'fɝ 〕*v.* 商議

    (B) compose 〔 kəm'poz 〕*v.* 組成

    (C) comply 〔 kəm'plaɪ 〕*v.* 服從；遵守

    (D) compress 〔 kəm'prɛs 〕*v.* 壓縮

    adviser 〔 əd'vaɪzɚ 〕*n.* 顧問

    diplomatic 〔͵dɪplə'mætɪk 〕*adj.* 外交的

12. (**C**) 他在成為明星前受過許多<u>屈辱</u>。

    (A) serve〔sɜv〕*v.* 服務

    (B) pose〔poz〕*v.* 擺姿勢

    (C) *suffer*〔'sʌfɚ〕*v.* 遭受

    (D) compel〔kəm'pɛl〕*v.* 強迫

    humiliation〔hju‚mɪlɪ'eʃən〕*n.* 羞辱

    star〔stɑr〕*n.* 明星

13. (**D**) 我可以從你的沉默<u>推論</u>出，你不同意我。

    (A) impose〔ɪm'poz〕*v.* 強加

    (B) intend〔ɪn'tɛnd〕*v.* 打算

    (C) intensify〔ɪn'tɛnsə‚faɪ〕*v.* 加強

    (D) *infer*〔ɪn'fɜ〕*v.* 推論

    silence〔'saɪləns〕*n.* 沉默

silence

14. (**C**) 你的主意比我的<u>更好</u>。

    (A) different〔'dɪfərənt〕*adj.* 不同的

    (B) referential〔‚rɛfə'rɛnʃəl〕*adj.* 參考的；相關的

    (C) *preferable*〔'prɛfərəbḷ〕*adj.* 較合人意的；較好的

    (D) transferable〔træns'fɝəbḷ〕*adj.* 可轉移的

15. (**D**) 這部電影<u>提及</u>好幾個有證據的歷史事件。

    (A) transferability〔‚trænsfɝə'bɪlətɪ〕*n.* 可移轉性

    (B) inference〔'ɪnfərəns〕*n.* 推論

    (C) preferment〔prɪ'fɝmənt〕*n.* 晉升

    (D) *reference*〔'rɛfərəns〕*n.* 參考；提及

    documented〔'dɑkjə‚mɛntɪd〕*adj.* 有文件證明的；有證據的

    historical〔hɪs'tɔrɪkḷ〕*adj.* 歷史的

    event〔ɪ'vɛnt〕*n.* 事件

請連中文一起背，背至75秒內，終生不忘。　　　✦

字根 fer

1

offer	提供
suffer	遭受
differ	不同
infer	推論
confer	商議
defer	延期
refer	參考
prefer	比較喜歡
transfer	轉移

2

ferry	渡輪
ferryboat	渡輪
ferriage	渡船費
fertile	肥沃的
fertilize	使肥沃
fertility	繁殖力

3

offering	提供
offerings	捐獻物
offertory	奉獻儀式
suffering	痛苦
sufferance	寬容
sufferable	可忍受的

different	不同的
difference	差異
differentiate	區分
differential	差別的
differentiable	可分辨的
differentiability	可辨性

字根 fer

4

inference	推論
inferable	能推論的
inferential	推論的

conference	會議
conferment	授與
conferee	參加會議者

conferral	授與
conferrer	授與者
conferee	參加會議者

deference	服從
deferrable	可延期的
deferment	延期

deferral	延期
deferent	恭敬的
deferential	恭敬的

5

reference	參考
referable	可歸因的
referee	裁判

referral	參考
referential	參考的
referendary	仲裁者

preference	偏愛
preferable	較合人意的
preferment	晉升

preferential	優先的
preferentialism	優惠主義
preferentialist	優惠主義論者

transference	轉移
transferable	可轉移的
transferability	可轉移性

transferential	轉移的
transferor	轉讓人
transferee	受讓人

※本頁可影印後，隨身攜帶，方便背誦。

Group 9 字根 *pend*

目標： ① 先將57個字放入短期記憶。
② 加快速度至48秒之內，成為長期記憶。

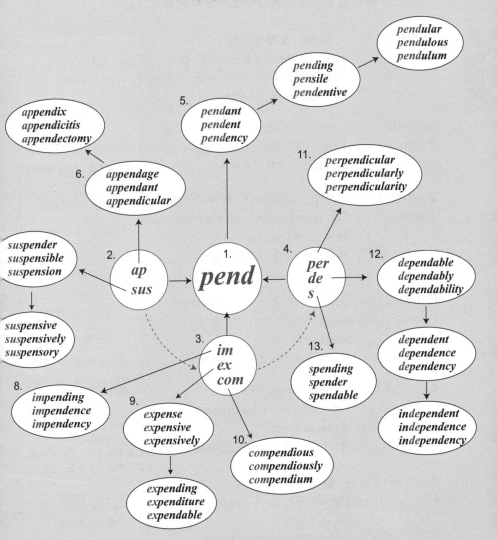

1. 字根 *pend* 核心單字

這 9 個字，3 個一組，一起背，可先背 6 個，再背 3 個，背熟至 5 秒之內，可成為長期記憶，才可再背下一組。

字根 pend

pend
〔 pɛnd 〕

v. 懸掛；使懸而未決
pend 這個字根的意思是 hang「懸掛」；weigh「衡量」
They *pended* the settlement of a patent application.
他們擱置一項專利申請。

append
〔 ə'pɛnd 〕

v. 附加（= *attach*）
There was no signature *appended* to the letter. 這封信並沒有附上簽名。

ap + pend
|　　|
to + hang

掛上去，即是「附加」

suspend[5]
〔 sə'spɛnd 〕

v. 懸掛（= *hang*）；暫停（= *stop*）
The typhoon forced the government to *suspend* high-speed rail service.
颱風迫使政府暫停高鐵的服務。

sus + pend
|　　|
under + hang

垂吊而下，即是「懸掛」

impend
〔 ɪm'pɛnd 〕

v. 迫近；逼近（= *approach*）
Black clouds are signs that a storm *impends*.
烏雲是暴風雨就要來臨的前兆。

im + pend
|　　|
on + hang

懸在上面，即是「逼近」

expend
〔 ɪk'spɛnd 〕

v. 花費（= *spend*）
Jason *expends* a lot of energy on his hobbies.
傑森花了很多的精力在他的嗜好上。

ex + pend
|　　|
out + hang

東西掛在外頭，別人就知道
錢花哪去了，即是「花費」

compend
〔 'kɑmpɛnd 〕

n. 概略（= *brief*）
The witness gave a *compend* of the incident.
目擊者簡略的敘述了這個事件。

com + pend
|　　|
all + hang

該掛的都掛起來，即是「概略」

perpend
〔 pɚˊpɛnd 〕

v. 仔細考慮（ = *think over* ）
I will *perpend* all the facts before making my decision.
我在做決定之前會仔細考慮所有的事實。

per	+ pend
thoroughly	+ *hang*

全部的心思都懸在那裡，即是「仔細考慮」

depend[2]
〔 dɪˊpɛnd 〕

v. 依賴（ = *rely* ）
Children are forced to *depend* on their parents until they are old enough to think for themselves.
孩子在大到可以獨立思考前，不得不依賴他們的父母。

de	+ pend
down	+ *hang*

挨著什麼東西下面掛著，即是「依賴」

spend[1]
〔 spɛnd 〕

v. 花費（ = *expend* ）；渡過
Tina is curious to know how I will *spend* the summer vacation.
蒂娜好奇想知道我暑假要怎麼過。

s	+ pend
apart	+ *hang*

把買的東西分開掛出來，即是「花費」

【背誦祕訣】

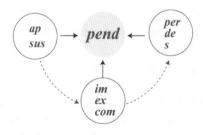

這組是 pend 的核心單字，重音多在第二音節，即在字根上，且詞性皆為動詞，唯一例外為 compend〔ˊkɑmpɛnd〕，重音在第一音節，且詞性為名詞。

2. pendant-pendent-pendency

這一組有 9 個單字，3 個一組一起背，可先背
6 個，再背 3 個，背至 5 秒之內，變成直覺。

pendant
（'pɛndənt）

n. 垂飾
Jackie wore a jade *pendant* on a
silver chain around her neck.
賈姬在她的脖子上掛了一條上面有
玉墜飾的銀鍊子。

> pend + ant
> | |
> *hang* + *n.*

掛著的東西，即是「垂飾」

pendent
（'pɛndənt）

adj. 垂下的　*n.* 垂飾
Hector reached up for a *pendent* bunch of grapes.
海克特伸手向上拿了一串垂吊的葡萄。

pendency
（'pɛndənsɪ）

n. 未決定
The court is looking for ways to
cut down on the *pendency* of
certain cases. 法院正尋找能
減少某些案件懸而未決的方法。

> pend + ency
> | |
> *hang* + *n.*

事情處於懸掛的狀態，
即是「未決定」

pending
（'pɛndɪŋ）

adj. 懸而未決的（= *undecided*）；迫近的
Alan's application to Harvard is
still *pending*.
艾倫申請哈佛的結果還沒確定。

> pend + ing
> | |
> *hang* + *adj.*

現在分詞當形容詞用

pensile
（'pɛnsḷ）

adj. 懸垂的
Most species of birds utilize a *pensile* nest, usually found
in trees. 大部分的鳥類都使用懸吊式的鳥巢，通常是在樹上。

pendentive
（pɛn'dɛntɪv）

n. 三角穹窿
The first use of *pendentives* occurred in a
2nd century Roman cathedral. 三角穹窿的
使用最早是在西元二世紀的羅馬教堂上。

pendentive

pendular
〔'pɛndjələ 〕

adj. 鐘擺運動的；擺動的

My personal trainer recommended *pendular* exercises to increase my flexibility.

我的私人教練建議我做搖擺式的運動，以增加我的柔軟度。

pendulous
〔'pɛndʒələs 〕

adj. 搖擺的；動盪不定的

Bulldogs are known for their *pendulous* lower jaws.

鬥牛犬以牠們搖搖擺擺的下顎聞名。

bulldog

字根 pend

pendulum
〔'pɛndʒələm 〕

n. 鐘擺

The little girl was fascinated by the *pendulum* which swung back and forth.

來回擺動的鐘擺吸引了小女孩的注意。

【背誦祕訣】

這組九個字為字根 pend 衍生出的詞類變化單字。

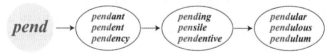

'pendant
'pendent
'pendency

這六個意思皆與「懸吊；懸而未決」有關，重音皆在第一音節，只有 pendentive 重音在第二音節，背誦時請注意。

'pending
'pensile
pen'dentive

'pendular
'pendulous
'pendulum

這組的意思皆與「搖擺；擺動」有關，重音皆在第一音節。

3. appendage-appendant-appendicular

這一組有 12 個字，分成兩組，第一組是 append 的衍生字，
第二組是 suspend 的衍生字，背熟至 7 秒之內，變成直覺。

字根 pend

appendage
[ə'pɛndɪdʒ]

n. 附加物（= *addition*）；附屬物
Some species of fish have skin *appendages* that
make them resemble coral or
rocks. 有些種類的魚皮膚上有
附屬物，使牠們很像珊瑚或岩石。

```
append + age
   |       |
  附加  +   n.
```

appendant
[ə'pɛndənt]

adj. 附加的（= *additional*）
Walter has an *appendant* reason for being late.
華特遲到還有附帶的理由。

appendicular
[ˌæpən'dɪkjələ]

adj. 附屬物的；四肢的（= *affiliated*）
Walking is an example of *appendicular* locomotion.
走路是四肢運動的例子。

appendix
[ə'pɛndɪks]

n. 附錄（= *addendum*）；盲腸
Rules for punctuation are typically listed in an
appendix. 標點符號的規則通常都會列在附錄中。

appendicitis
[əˌpɛndə'saɪtɪs]

n. 盲腸炎
Harvey has a case of acute
appendicitis.
哈維得了急性盲腸炎。

```
append + icitis
   |        |
  附加  +   發炎
```

-itis = inflammation 發炎

appendectomy
[ˌæpən'dɛktəmɪ]

n. 盲腸切除手術
The doctor performed an *appendectomy* yesterday.
那位醫生昨天施行了盲腸切除手術。

```
 append  + ec  + tom + y
    |       |      |     |
appendix + out + cut  + n.
```

suspender
〔 sə'spɛndɚ 〕

n.（褲子的）吊帶（ = *brace* ）
My grandfather always wore *suspenders*.
我祖父總是穿著吊帶。

sus	+ pend +	er
under	+ *hang* +	*n.*

suspenders

suspensible
〔 sə'spɛnsəbḷ 〕

adj. 可懸掛的；可懸浮的
Boats are reliable forms of water-*suspensible*
transportation. 船是可靠的水上懸浮式運輸工具。

suspens +	ible
懸掛 +	可～的

suspension[6]
〔 sə'spɛnʃən 〕

n. 懸掛；暫停（ = *pause* ）
The volcano erupted, resulting in the *suspension* of
all air traffic in or out of Europe.
火山爆發導致進出歐洲的空中交通全部暫停。

suspensive[6]
〔 sə'spɛnsɪv 〕

adj. 懸疑的；未決定的（ = *undecided* ）
Last night's episode of the serial
had a *suspensive* ending.
昨晚的那集連續劇結尾很懸疑。

suspens +	ive
未決定 +	*adj.*

suspensively
〔 sə'spɛnsɪvlɪ 〕

adv. 未決定地；暫停地
The judge paused *suspensively* before announcing
the verdict. 法官在宣布判決之前，先行暫停。

suspensory
〔 sə'spɛnsərɪ 〕

adj. 懸吊的   *n.* 懸垂肌
The athlete injured a *suspensory* ligament and will
miss the competition.
這個運動員一處懸垂肌韌帶受傷了，將無法參加比賽。

＊這六個字為 suspend 的詞類變化，故意思都與「懸掛；未決定」有關，
　且重音皆在第二音節。

4. *impending-impendence-impendency*

這一組有 12 個字，分成三組，第一組是 impend 的衍生字，第二組是 expend 的衍生字，第三組是 compend 的衍生字，背熟至 7 秒之內，變成直覺。

字根 pend

impending
〔 ɪmˈpɛndɪŋ 〕

adj. 即將發生的；逼近的 (= *imminent*)
Teresa watched the sunset and waited for the *impending* darkness.
泰瑞莎看著日落，等待即將來臨的黑暗。

> impend + ing
> |　　　 |
> 迫近 　 + *adj.*
>
> 現在分詞當形容詞用

impendence
〔 ɪmˈpɛndəns 〕

n. 來臨 (= *coming*)
Scientists are worried about the *impendence* of another strong earthquake.
科學家擔心另一個強烈地震的來臨。

> impend + ence
> |　　　 |
> 迫近 　 + *n.*

impendency
〔 ɪmˈpɛndənsɪ 〕

n. 來臨 (= *coming*)
The doctor emphasized the *impendency* of another heart attack if I didn't change my habits.
醫生強調，如果我再不改變習慣，我會再次心臟病發。

* 這三個字為 impend 的詞類變化，意思皆與「即將到來」有關，且重音皆在第二音節。

expense[3]
〔 ɪkˈspɛns 〕

n. 花費 (= *expenditure*)；代價
She completed the work at the *expense* of her health.
她完成了工作，但卻付出了健康的代價。

expensive[2]
〔 ɪkˈspɛnsɪv 〕

adj. 昂貴的 (= *costly*)
That was the most *expensive* meal I've eaten in my life.
這是我這輩子吃過最昂貴的一餐。

> expens + ive
> |　　　 |
> 花費 　 + *adj.*

expensively
〔 ɪkˈspɛnsɪvlɪ 〕

adv. 昂貴地
An *expensively* dressed man approached the woman.
一個穿著華貴的男人朝那個女人走過去。

expending
(ɪk'spɛndɪŋ)

n. 支出

More and more companies are increasing their *expending* on Internet advertising.

有越來越多的公司持續增加他們在網路廣告上的支出。

expenditure
(ɪk'spɛndɪtʃɚ)

n. 支出;費用 (= *expense*)

The government is aiming to reduce *expenditures* on defense. 政府想要減少國防的支出。

```
expend + iture
   |       |
  花費   +  n.
```

字根 pend

expendable
(ɪk'spɛndəbḷ)

adj. 可消耗的;可拋棄的 (= *dispensable*)

His manager made it clear to him that he was *expendable*.

他的經理明確告訴他,他是可有可無的。

```
expend + able
   |       |
  消耗  + 可～的
```

compendious
(kəm'pɛndɪəs)

adj. 摘要的;簡明的 (= *concise*)

The professor gave a *compendious* explanation of nuclear physics.

教授簡略地說明核子物理學。

```
compend + ious
   |        |
  概略   +  adj.
```

compendiously
(kəm'pɛndɪəslɪ)

adv. 摘要地;簡潔地 (= *briefly*)

The author spoke *compendiously* about his latest work. 這個作者扼要地說明他最新的作品。

compendium
(kəm'pɛndɪəm)

n. 手冊;大全 (= *collection*)

The book is a *compendium* of amusing quotations from famous people.

這本書是名人幽默語錄大全。

```
compend + ium
   |        |
  概略   +  n.
```

5. perpendicular-perpendicularly-perpendicularity

這一組有 15 個字，分成三組，第一組是 perpend 的衍生字，第二組是 depend 的衍生字，第三組是 spend 的衍生字，背熟至 8 秒之內，變成直覺。

字根 pend

perpendicular
(ˌpɝpənˈdɪkjələ˞)

adj. 垂直的 (= *vertical*)
Central Street and Park Road run *perpendicular* to each other. 中央街和公園路彼此垂直。

per	+ pend + icular
through + hang + *adj.*	

直接懸垂而下的

perpendicularly
(ˌpɝpənˈdɪkjələ˞lɪ)

adv. 垂直地 (= *vertically*)
The Red Line MRT runs *perpendicularly* to the Blue Line. 捷運紅線和藍線彼此垂直行駛。

perpendicularity
(ˌpɝpənˌdɪkjəˈlærətɪ)

n. 垂直 (= *verticality*)
I knew it was almost at two o'clock by the *perpendicularity* of the sun's rays. 按照太陽光垂直照射的情況，我知道時間差不多是下午兩點鐘。

dependable[4]
(dɪˈpɛndəbḷ)

adj. 可靠的 (= *trustworthy*)
Daniel is a good friend and a *dependable* companion.
丹尼爾是個好朋友，也是個可靠的同伴。

depend + able
依賴 ＋ 可～的

dependably
(dɪˈpɛndəblɪ)

adv. 可靠地 (= *trustworthily*)
My car has run *dependably* for over ten years.
我的車子很可靠地行駛了十多年。

dependability
(dɪˌpɛndəˈbɪlətɪ)

n. 可靠性；可信任 (= *trustworthiness*)
Rick was a good worker, known for his *dependability*. 瑞克是個好員工，以值得信任聞名。

dependent[4]
〔 dɪ'pɛndənt 〕

adj. 依靠的（ = *reliant* ）；視～而定的
Our picnic is *dependent* upon the weather; if it rains, we'll have to stay home. 我們的野餐要視天氣而定；如果下雨，我們就得待在家裡。

```
depend + ent
  |        |
依賴   + adj.
```

dependence
〔 dɪ'pɛndəns 〕

n. 依賴（ = *reliance* ）
Most doctors consider alcohol *dependence* to be a disease. 大部分的醫生認為，酒精依賴是一種疾病。

dependency
〔 dɪ'pɛndənsɪ 〕

n. 依賴（ = *dependence* ）
Elaine tried to break her *dependency* on caffeine. 伊蓮試著戒除她對咖啡因的依賴。

* 這三個字為 depend 的詞類變化。

independent[2]
〔 ˌɪndɪ'pɛndənt 〕

adj. 獨立的（ = *self-reliant* ）
The U.S. education system emphasizes *independent* thought over memorization.
美國的教育體系強調獨立思考勝過死記。

```
in + depend + ent
 |      |       |
not +  依賴   + adj.       不依賴的，即是「獨立的」
```

independence[2]
〔 ˌɪndɪ'pɛndəns 〕

n. 獨立（ = *self-government* ）
The Declaration of *Independence* was signed in 1777. 獨立宣言在 1777 年簽署。

independency
〔 ˌɪndɪ'pɛndənsɪ 〕

n. 獨立（ = *independence* ）
The Southern rebels fought for *independency* from the Northern regime. 南方的叛軍主要是為了脫離北方的統治，為爭取獨立而戰。

spending[1]
〔'spɛndɪŋ〕

n. 開銷;花費 (= *expenditure*)
The company will reduce *spending* in the next year to help ease its debt.
公司將會減少明年的開銷,以減輕債務。

spend	+ ing
花費	+ *n.*

spender
〔'spɛndɚ〕

n. 揮霍者
Bob is a big *spender* who likes to throw money around.
鮑伯是個很揮霍的人,他喜歡把錢亂花。

spendable
〔'spɛndəbl̩〕

adj. 可花費的
The U.S. dollar is *spendable* in many foreign countries.
美元在國外的很多國家都可以花用。

spend	+ able
花費	+ 可~的

【背誦祕訣】

這九個字為 depend 的詞類變化,其中:

depend → dependable / dependably / dependability → dependent / dependence / dependency → independent / independence / independency

de'pendable
de'pendably
dependa'bility
　　這組單字皆是在 depend 的後面接 a 再做變化

de'pendent
de'pendence
de'pendency
　　這組單字皆是在 depend 的後面接 e 再做變化,且重音皆在第二音節

inde'pendent
inde'pendence
inde'pendency
　　這組單字為 dependent 的反義字,須在字首加 in 表否定,重音皆在第三音節

Exercise : Choose the correct answer.

1. We can _____ on Michael to deliver the message.
   (A) pend　　　　　　　(B) append
   (C) suspend　　　　　　(D) depend

2. The book is a _____ of their poetry, religion and philosophy.
   (A) impend　　　　　　(B) compend
   (C) spend　　　　　　 (D) perpend

3. We predicted an _____ storm.
   (A) impending　　　　　(B) expending
   (C) depending　　　　　(D) suspending

4. Your hands and feet are prime examples of _____.
   (A) pendants　　　　　 (B) appendages
   (C) pendentive　　　　 (D) appendix

5. Too many traffic tickets will result in the _____ of your driving privileges.
   (A) appendicitis　　　　(B) suspenders
   (C) suspension　　　　 (D) supposition

6. The wall must be _____ to the floor.
   (A) pendulous　　　　　(B) perpendicular
   (C) pensile　　　　　　(D) suspensible

7. Thomas spared no _____ when planning his daughter's birthday party.
   (A) compendium　　　　(B) impendence
   (C) expenditure　　　　(D) expense

8. The study focused on the _____ habits of American teenagers.
   (A) independence　　　 (B) impendency
   (C) pendulum　　　　　(D) spending

字根 pend

9. He knew my examination was _____.
   (A) pending   (B) suspensive
   (C) suspensory   (D) extensive

10. Mr. and Mrs. Wang have had trouble finding a _____ babysitter for their children.
   (A) compendious   (B) dependable
   (C) distensible   (D) pendular

11. He considers the part-time employees to be _____ and easily replaced.
   (A) expendable   (B) appendent
   (C) dependent   (D) independent

12. Judging from his dirty clothing, Donald _____ little energy worrying about the way he looks.
   (A) refers   (B) tends
   (C) confers   (D) expends

13. Jessie forgot to _____ a bibliography to her report and as a result, received a much lower grade.
   (A) append   (B) defer
   (C) impend   (D) differentiate

14. The Republic of Zambia gained _____ from the United Kingdom in 1962.
   (A) perpendicularity (B) dependability
   (C) independence   (D) intensity

15. Bad weather forced the volunteers to _____ their search for the missing hikers.
   (A) fertilize   (B) suspend
   (C) transfer   (D) differ

字彙測驗詳解

1. (**D**) 我們可以<u>依賴</u>麥可傳遞訊息。

(A) pend〔pɛnd〕*v.* 懸掛；使懸而未決

(B) append〔ə'pɛnd〕*v.* 附加

(C) suspend〔sə'spɛnd〕*v.* 懸掛；暫停

(D) *depend*〔dɪ'pɛnd〕*v.* 依賴

deliver〔dɪ'lɪvɚ〕*v.* 傳遞

message〔'mɛsɪdʒ〕*n.* 訊息

字根 pend

2. (**B**) 這本書是他們詩歌、宗教和哲學的<u>概略</u>。

(A) impend〔ɪm'pɛnd〕*v.* 即將發生

(B) *compend*〔'kɑmpɛnd〕*n.* 概略

(C) spend〔spɛnd〕*v.* 花費；渡過

(D) perpend〔pɚ'pɛnd〕*v.* 仔細考慮

3. (**A**) 我們預測有個暴風雨<u>即將來臨</u>。

(A) *impending*〔'ɪmpɛndɪŋ〕*adj.* 即將發生的；逼近的

(B) expend〔ɪk'spɛnd〕*v.* 花費

(C) depend〔dɪ'pɛnd〕*v.* 依賴

(D) suspend〔sə'spɛnd〕*v.* 懸掛；暫停

4. (**B**) 你的手腳正是<u>四肢</u>的最佳範例。

(A) pendant〔'pɛndənt〕*n.* 垂飾

(B) *appendage*〔ə'pɛndɪdʒ〕*n.* 附加物；四肢

(C) pendentive〔pɛn'dɛntɪv〕*n.* 三角穹窿

(D) appendix〔ə'pɛndɪks〕*n.* 附錄

prime〔praɪm〕*adj.* 主要的；最好的

5. (**C**) 太多的交通罰單將會導致你的駕照被<u>吊銷</u>。

    (A) appendicitis〔ə͵pɛndə'saɪtɪs〕 *n.* 盲腸炎

    (B) suspender〔sə'spɛndɚ〕 *n.* (褲子的) 吊帶

    (C) *suspension*〔sə'spɛnʃən〕 *n.* 懸掛;暫停

    (D) supposition〔͵sʌpə'zɪʃən〕 *n.* 推測

appendicitis

    ticket〔'tɪkɪt〕 *n.* 罰單

    result in 導致

    privilege〔'prɪvl̩ɪdʒ〕 *n.* 特權

6. (**B**) 牆壁必須與地板成<u>直角</u>。

    (A) pendulous〔'pɛndʒələs〕 *adj.* 搖擺的

    (B) *perpendicular*〔͵pɝpən'dɪkjələ〕 *adj.* 垂直的

    (C) pensile〔'pɛnsl̩〕 *adj.* 懸垂的

    (D) suspensible〔sə'spɛndəbl̩〕 *adj.* 可懸掛的;可懸浮的

7. (**D**) 湯瑪士不惜<u>花費</u>地籌劃他女兒的生日派對。

    (A) compendium〔kəm'pɛndɪəm〕 *n.* 手冊;大全

    (B) impendence〔ɪm'pɛndəns〕 *n.* 來臨

    (C) expenditure〔ɪk'spɛndɪtʃɚ〕 *n.* 支出

    (D) *expense*〔ɪk'spɛns〕 *n.* 花費

    spare〔spɛr〕 *v.* 吝惜

8. (**D**) 這個研究著重在美國青少年的<u>消費</u>習慣。

    (A) independence〔͵ɪndɪ'pɛndəns〕 *n.* 獨立

    (B) impendency〔ɪm'pɛndənsɪ〕 *n.* 來臨

    (C) pendulum〔'pɛndʒələm〕 *n.* 鐘擺

    (D) *spending*〔'spɛndɪŋ〕 *n.* 開銷;花費

    focus on 著重於　　habit〔'hæbɪt〕 *n.* 習慣

    teenager〔'tin͵edʒɚ〕 *n.* 青少年

9. (**A**) 他知道我的考試<u>快到</u>了。

(A) *pending*〔'pɛndɪŋ〕*adj.* 懸而未決的；迫近的

(B) suspensive〔sə'spɛnsɪv〕*adj.* 懸疑的

(C) suspensory〔sə'spɛnsərɪ〕*adj.* 懸吊的

(D) extensive〔ɪk'stɛnsɪv〕*adj.* 廣大的

10. (**B**) 王先生和王太太一直很難找到<u>可靠的</u>褓姆，來照顧他們的小孩。

(A) compendious〔kəm'pɛndɪəs〕*adj.* 摘要的

(B) *dependable*〔dɪ'pɛndəbḷ〕*adj.* 可靠的

(C) distensible〔dɪ'stɛnsəbḷ〕*adj.* 可膨脹的

(D) pendular〔'pɛndjələ˞〕*adj.* 鐘擺運動的；擺動的

have trouble (*in*) *+ V-ing* 做…有困難

babysitter〔'bebɪˌsɪtə˞〕*n.* 褓姆

11. (**A**) 他認為兼職的員工是<u>可有可無的</u>，容易被取代。

(A) *expendable*〔ɪk'spɛndəbḷ〕*adj.* 可消耗的；可拋棄的

(B) appendant〔ə'pɛndənt〕*adj.* 附加的

(C) dependent〔dɪ'pɛndənt〕*adj.* 依靠的

(D) independent〔ˌɪndɪ'pɛndənt〕*adj.* 獨立的

consider〔kən'sɪdə˞〕*v.* 認為

employee〔ˌɛmplɔɪ'i〕*n.* 員工

replace〔rɪ'ples〕*v.* 取代

12. (**D**) 從唐納骯髒的衣服看來，他不太<u>花</u>心思擔心自己的外表。

(A) refer〔rɪ'fɝ〕*v.* 參考；提及

(B) tend〔tɛnd〕*v.* 傾向；照料

(C) confer〔kən'fɝ〕*v.* 商議

(D) *expend*〔ɪk'spɛnd〕*v.* 花費

13. (**A**) 潔西忘記在報告上<u>附上</u>她的參考書目,所以得到了較低的分數。

 (A) *append* 〔 ə'pɛnd 〕 v. 附加
 (B) defer 〔 dɪ'fɝ 〕 v. 延遲
 (C) impend 〔 ɪm'pɛnd 〕 v. 迫近;逼近
 (D) differentiate 〔 ͵dɪfə'rɛnʃɪ͵et 〕 v. 區別

bibliography 〔 ͵bɪblɪ'ɑgrəfɪ 〕 n. 參考書目
as a result 因此

14. (**C**) 尙比亞共和國在 1962 年脫離英國而<u>獨立</u>。

 (A) perpendicularity 〔 ͵pɝpən͵dɪkjə'lærətɪ 〕 n. 垂直
 (B) dependability 〔 dɪ͵pɛndə'bɪlətɪ 〕 n. 可靠性;可信任
 (C) *independence* 〔 ͵ɪndɪ'pɛndəns 〕 n. 獨立
 (D) intensity 〔 ɪn'tɛnsətɪ 〕 n. 強烈

republic 〔 rɪ'pʌblɪk 〕 n. 共和國
Zambia 〔 'zæmbɪə 〕 n. 尙比亞
gain 〔 gen 〕 v. 獲得   *the United Kingdom* 英國

15. (**B**) 惡劣的天候迫使義工們<u>暫停</u>尋找失蹤的健行者。

 (A) fertilize 〔 'fɝtḷ͵aɪz 〕 v. 使肥沃;給…施肥
 (B) *suspend* 〔 sə'spɛnd 〕 v. 懸掛;暫停
 (C) transfer 〔 træns'fɝ 〕 v. 轉移
 (D) differ 〔 'dɪfɚ 〕 v. 不同

force 〔 fors 〕 v. 迫使
volunteer 〔 ͵vɑlən'tɪr 〕 n. 志願者;義工
missing 〔 'mɪsɪŋ 〕 adj. 失蹤的
hiker 〔 'haɪkɚ 〕 n. 健行者

請連中文一起背，背至70秒內，終生不忘。

字根 pend

1

pend	懸掛
append	附加
suspend	懸掛
impend	迫近
expend	花費
compend	概略
perpend	仔細考慮
depend	依賴
spend	花費

2

pendant	垂飾
pendent	垂下的
pendency	未決定
pending	懸而未決的
pensile	懸垂的
pendentive	三角穹窿
pendular	鐘擺運動的
pendulous	搖擺的
pendulum	鐘擺

3

appendage	附加物
appendant	附加的
appendicular	附屬物的
appendix	附錄
appendicitis	盲腸炎
appendectomy	盲腸切除手術

suspender	褲子的吊帶
suspensible	可懸掛的
suspension	懸掛
suspensive	懸疑的
suspensively	未決定地
suspensory	懸吊的

┌─【劉毅老師的話】─┐
　　只背英文不背中文
容易忘。中英文一起背，
不會忘記。
└─────────────┘

字根 pend

4

impending　即將發生的
impendence　來臨
impendency　來臨

expense　　花費
expensive　昂貴的
expensively　昂貴地

expending　支出
expenditure　支出
expendable　可消耗的

compendious　摘要的
compendiously　摘要地
compendium　手冊

5

perpendicular　垂直的
perpendicularly　垂直地
perpendicularity　垂直

dependable　可靠的
dependably　可靠地
dependability　可靠性

dependent　依靠的
dependence　依賴
dependency　依賴

independent　獨立的
independence　獨立
independency　獨立

spending　開銷
spender　揮霍者
spendable　可花費的

※ 本頁可影印後，隨身攜帶，方便背誦。

Group 10 字根 *port*

目標： ① 先將62個字放入短期記憶。
② 加快速度至52秒之內，成為長期記憶。

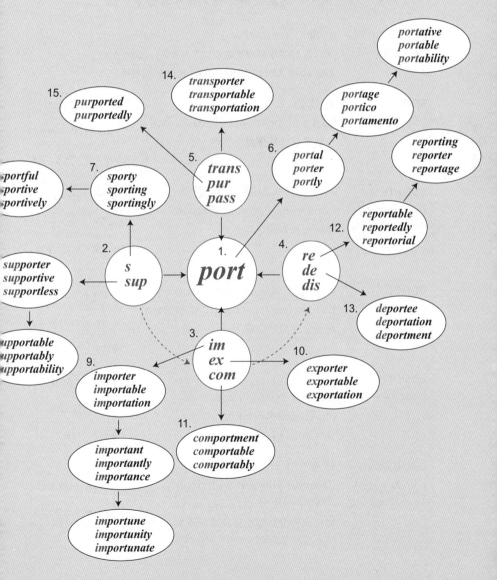

1. 字根 *port* 核心單字

　　這 12 個字，三個一組，一起背，可先背 6 個，再背 6 個，背熟至 7 秒之內，可成爲長期記憶，才可再背下一組。

port[2]
〔 port 〕

n. 港口 (= *harbor*)
port 這個字根的意思是 carry「運送」; gate「大門」
The ship sailed into *port*. 那艘船開進港口。

---

sport[1]
〔 sport 〕

n. 運動
Carl's favorite *sport* is basketball.
卡爾最喜歡的運動是籃球。

```
  s    + port
  |       |
apart + carry
```
將自己帶離工作，即是「運動」

---

support[2]
〔 sə'port 〕

v. 支持 (= *back up*)；忍受
I don't *support* your opinion.
我不支持你的意見。

```
 sup   + port
  |       |
under + carry
```
在下面撐著，即是「支持」

---

import[3]
〔 ɪm'port 〕

v. 進口 (= *bring in*)
Europe *imports* coal from America.
歐洲從美國進口煤。

```
im + port
 |     |
in + carry
```
帶進來，即是「進口」

---

export[3]
〔 ɪks'port 〕

v. 出口
Jamaica *exports* bananas to
the United Kingdom.
牙買加出口香蕉到英國。

```
 ex  + port
  |     |
out + carry
```
帶出去，即是「出口」

---

comport
〔 kəm'port 〕

v. 舉止 (= *behave*)；相稱
Comport yourself with dignity,
or you will be asked to leave.
你自己的行爲舉止要莊重，不然
別人會叫你離開。

```
 com  + port
  |      |
with + carry
```
帶在身上的，即是「舉止」

report[1]
〔 rɪ'port 〕

v. 報告 (= *narrate*); 報導
Roland returned from the jungle
and *reported* his findings.
羅蘭從叢林回來,並報告他的發現。

```
re  + port
 |      |
back + carry
```
帶回去,即是「報告」

deport
〔 dɪ'port 〕

v. 放逐 (= *exile*); 舉止
The government aims to *deport*
all illegal immigrants.
政府想要驅逐非法移民。

```
de  + port
 |      |
away + carry
```
被帶走,即是「放逐」

disport
〔 dɪ'sport 〕

v. 嬉戲 (= *play*)
The children are permitted to
disport during the mid-day recess.
在中午休息的時候,小孩可以嬉戲。

```
dis  + port
  |      |
apart + carry
```
將自己帶離工作,
即是「嬉戲」

字根 port

transport[3]
〔 træns'port 〕

v. 運輸;運送 (= *convey*)
The products were *transported* from the factory to the
station. 產品從工廠被運到車站。

```
trans + port
  |       |
A→B  + carry
```
從 A 搬到 B,即是「運輸」

purport
〔 pɚ'port 〕

v. 聲稱
Never trust a book that *purports* to tell the whole story.
千萬別相信聲稱可以說明整個事件的書。

```
pur    + port
  |       |
forward + carry
```
帶到前面去說,即是「聲稱」

passport[3]
〔 'pæs,port 〕

n. 護照
Always keep your *passport* in
a safe location.
護照一定要收在安全的地方。

```
pass + port
  |      |
通過  + carry
```
帶著通過海關的證件,即是「護照」

2. *portal-porter-portly*

這一組有 9 個字，3 個一組，一起背，可先背 6 個，
再背 3 個，背熟至 5 秒之內，變成直覺。

portal
〔'portl̩〕

n. 入口 (= *gate*)
A library is a *portal* to knowledge.
圖書館是知識的入口。

```
port + al
  |     |
gate +  n.
```

porter[4]
〔'portɚ〕

n. 行李搬運員 (= *carrier*)
The *porter* brought my suitcase to the room.
行李搬運員幫我把行李箱拿到房間。

porter

```
port + er
  |     |
carry + 人      幫你拿東西的人
```

portly
〔'portly〕

adj. 肥胖的 (= *stout*)
The new manager is a *portly* middle-aged woman.
新來的經理是個肥胖的中年婦女。

portage
〔'portɪdʒ〕

n. 搬運；運費
I paid the *portage* fee to have my
belongings shipped to Italy.
我付了運費，要將我的行李運到義大利。

```
port + age
  |      |
carry + 費用
```

portico
〔'portɪ,ko〕

n. 門廊 (= *porch*)
Socrates used to lecture from this *portico*.
蘇格拉底以前都在這座門廊授課。

portico

portamento
〔,portə'mɛnto〕

n. 滑音
Cellist Yo-Yo Ma is known for his flawless
portamento.　大提琴家馬友友以他完美的滑音著名。

portative
('pɔrtətɪv)

adj. 可攜帶的 (= *portable*)
Lionel is a collector of 15th century *portative* pipe organs. 里昂是 15 世紀可攜式管風琴的收藏者。

portable[4]
('pɔrtəbḷ)

adj. 手提的；可攜帶的 (= *movable*)
Jim took his *portable* radio wherever he went.
吉姆去哪裡都帶著他的手提收音機。

```
port  +  able
 |        |
carry  + 可~的
```

portability
(ˌpɔrtə'bɪlətɪ)

n. 可攜帶性
The *portability* of laptop computers changed the way people do business.
膝上型電腦的可攜帶性改變了人們做生意的方式。

字根 port

─── 【背誦祕訣】 ───

這組單字是字根 port 的九個衍生字：

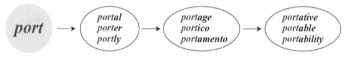

port → (*portal* / *porter* / *portly*) → (*portage* / *portico* / *portamento*) → (*portative* / *portable* / *portability*)

{ 'portal
  'porter   皆為兩個音節的單字，重音皆在
  'portly }   第一音節，且重音節母音皆為 /o/。

{ 'portage
  'portico   這組詞性皆為名詞
  porta'mento }

{ 'portative   此二字皆為三音節的單字，且重音
  'portable   皆在字根 port 上，皆發長音 /o/。
  porta'bility }

3 sporty-sporting-sportingly

這一組有 12 個字，分成兩組，第一組是 sport 的衍生字，
第二組是 support 的衍生字，背熟至 7 秒之內，變成直覺。

sporty
〔'sportɪ〕

adj. 運動時穿的；喜歡運動的
Greg went to the baseball game with
his *sporty* friends. 葛雷格和他喜歡運
動的朋友們一起去看棒球比賽。

```
sport + y
  |      |
運動   + adj.
```

sporting
〔'sportɪŋ〕

adj. 運動的（= *athletic*）
Janice is not the *sporting* type.
珍妮斯不是運動型的。

```
sport + ing
  |      |
運動   + adj.
```

分詞當形容詞用

sportingly
〔'sportɪŋlɪ〕

adv. 在運動方面；有氣度地
My mother was furious but my father took it all very
sportingly. 我媽媽發脾氣，但我爸爸非常有氣度地忍受。

sportful
〔'sportfəl〕

adj. 鬧著玩的（= *playful*）
She gave Philip's hand a *sportful* little squeeze.
她開玩笑地輕輕捏了菲利普的手。

```
sport + ful
  |      |
運動   + much
```
像在運動般的，即是「鬧著玩的」

sportive
〔'sportɪv〕

adj. 開玩笑的；愉快的（= *playful*）
Maggie is a *sportive* young woman.
瑪姬是個愛開玩笑的年輕女生。

sportively
〔'sportɪvlɪ〕

adv. 開玩笑地；愉快地
She *sportively* slapped the back of my head.
她開玩笑地拍了我的後腦勺。

* 這六個單字為 sport 的詞類變化，故意思皆與「運動」或「嬉戲」有關。

supporter
〔 sə'portə 〕

n. 支持者（ = *backer* ）
The candidate's *supporters* gathered to hear him speak.
這個候選人的支持者聚集聽他演說。

support + er
支持 + 人

supportive
〔 sə'portɪv 〕

adj. 支持的（ = *helpful* ）
His parents were *supportive* of his decision.
他的父母非常支持他的決定。

support + ive
支持 + *adj.*

supportless
〔 sə'portlɪs 〕

adj. 無支持的
Your argument is *supportless* without facts to back it up.
你的論點沒有事實根據來支持。

support + less
支持 + *little*

字根 port

supportable
〔 sə'portəbḷ 〕

adj. 可支持的；可忍受的（ = *endurable* ）
The public transit system is barely *supportable*.
大眾運輸系統幾乎令人無法忍受。

support + able
支持 + 可～的

supportably
〔 sə'portəbḷɪ 〕

adv. 可支持地；可忍受地
Albert sat *supportably* through the performance.
阿爾伯特很忍耐地一直坐到表演結束。

supportability
〔 sə,portə'bɪlətɪ 〕

n. 支持度；容忍度（ = *endurance* ）
The *supportability* of the system is in doubt.
這個系統的容忍度受到懷疑。

＊這六個單字為 support 的詞類變化，故意思皆與「支持」或「容忍」有關。

4. importer-importable-importation

這一組有 15 個字，分成三組，第一組是 import 的衍生字，第二組是 export 的衍生字，第三組是 comport 的衍生字，背熟至 8 秒之內，變成直覺。

importer
〔 ɪmˋportɚ 〕

n. 進口商
The U.S. is the world's largest
importer of electronic goods.
美國是全世界最大的電子產品進口商。

> import + er
> |　　　|
> 進口　+ 人

importable
〔 ɪmˋportəbḷ 〕

adj. 可進口的
The Department of Homeland Security has shortened
the list of *importable* items
from India. 國安局縮短了可
從印度進口的物品名單。

> import + able
> |　　　|
> 進口　+ 可～的

importation
〔 ͵ɪmporˋteʃən 〕

n. 進口
Goods headed for *importation* are subject to taxes.
要進口的物品必須課稅。

important[1]
〔 ɪmˋpɔrtṇt 〕

adj. 重要的 (= *significant*)
It's *important* that you pay
attention during class.
上課時注意聽講很重要。

> im + port + ant
> |　　|　　|
> *in + carry + adj.*

古時候房子很小，「重要的」東西才搬進來

importantly
〔 ɪmˋpɔrtṇtlɪ 〕

adv. 重要地
More *importantly*, she forgot to lock the door.
更重要的是，她忘記鎖門了。

importance[2]
〔 ɪmˋpɔrtṇs 〕

n. 重要性 (= *significance*)
This is hardly a matter of
importance.
這幾乎算不上是重要的事。

> im + port + ance
> |　　|　　|
> *in + carry +　n.*

字根 port

importune
〔͵ɪmpɚˈtjun〕

v. 不斷地要求（*= plead*）

The tourists were *importuned* by beggars wherever they went. 觀光客不管到哪裡，都被乞丐不斷地乞求。

> im + portune
> │   │
> *not* + *port*   不得進港 → 強要進港，即是「一再要求」

importunity
〔͵ɪmpɚˈtjunətɪ〕

n. 糾纏不休；強求

Wishing to avoid further *importunity*, the king granted their request.

希望能避免進一步的騷擾，國王答應了他們的請求。

importunate
〔ɪmˈpɔrtʃənɪt〕

adj. 煩人的

Lilly's secretary shielded her from *importunate* visitors.

> im + portun + ate
> │   │   │
> *not* + *port* + *adj.*

莉莉的秘書幫她擋下了很多煩人的訪客。

字根 port

【背誦祕訣】

這組字為 import 的衍生字，其中：

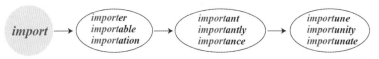

import →
- importer / importable / importation →
- important / importantly / importance →
- importune / importunity / importunate

- im′porter
- im′portable
- impor′tation

這三個字的含意皆與「進口」有關，且字根 port 的 o 皆發長音 /o/。

- im′portant
- im′portantly
- im′portance

這三個字的含意皆與「重要」有關，且重音皆在第二音節上，字根 port 的 o 皆發短音 /ɔ/。

- impor′tune
- impor′tunity
- im′portunate

這三個字的含意皆與「糾纏」或「煩人」有關，其中注意 importune 和 importunity 中，or 發 /ɚ/ 的音。

exporter
(ɪk'sportɚ)

n. 出口商
China is the world's largest
exporter of clothing.
中國是最大的成衣出口國。

```
export + er
  |      |
 出口  + 人
```

exportable
(ɛks'portəbļ)

adj. 可出口的
The government aims to increase production of the
country's *exportable* goods.
政府想增加國家出口商品的
生產。

```
export + able
  |       |
 出口   + 可～的
```

exportation
(͵ɛkspor'teʃən)

n. 出口
A large quantity of salt is ready for *exportation*.
大量的鹽已準備好要出口。

* 這三個字皆為 export 的詞類變化，故意思皆與「出口」或「輸出」有關。

comportment
(kəm'portmənt)

n. 舉止 (= *behavior*)
The man is refined in appearance and *comportment*.
這個人的外表和舉止變得較文雅了。

```
comport + ment
   |        |
  舉止    +  n.
```

comportable
(kəm'potəbļ)

adj. 合適的 (= *suitable*)
Her smile was not *comportable* with what she had
just said.　她的微笑不適合她剛剛所說的內容。

```
comport + able
   |        |
  相稱    + 可～的      可以相稱，即是「合適的」
```

comportably
(kəm'potəblɪ)

adv. 合適地
The deluxe room can *comportably* accommodate
six people.　這個豪華的房間適合六個人住。

5. *reportable-reportedly-reportorial*

　　這一組有 9 個字，分成兩組，第一組是 report 的衍生字，第二組是 deport 的衍生字，背熟至 5 秒之內，變成直覺。

字根 port

reportable
〔 rɪ'portəbḷ 〕

adj. 可報導的；值得報導的
The incident is not *reportable*.
那個事件不值得報導。

reportedly
〔 rɪ'portɪdlɪ 〕

adv. 據說（ = *allegedly* ）
The fugitive is *reportedly* hiding in the jungles of
Cambodia.　據說逃亡者藏匿在柬埔寨的叢林裡。

reportorial
〔 ˌrɛpə'tɔrɪəl 〕

adj. 記者的；報告的
He writes with a very dry, *reportorial* style.
他以很枯燥、報告般的風格寫作。

reporting[1]
〔 rɪ'portɪŋ 〕

n. 新聞報導
The anchorman has been dedicated to *reporting* for
over 30 years.　這個男主播已報導新聞超過 30 年。

reporter[2]
〔 rɪ'portɚ 〕

n. 記者（ = *journalist* ）
The actor refused to answer the
reporter's questions.
這個演員拒絕回答記者的問題。

report	+	er
報導	+	人

reportage
〔 rɪ'portɪdʒ 〕

n. 新聞報導
Newspaper editorials are usually
based on opinion and contain very
little *reportage*.　報紙的社論主要著重
在意見表達，很少有新聞報導。

report	+	age
報導	+	*n.*

＊這六個單字為 report 的詞類變化，故意思皆與「報告」或「報導」有關。

字根 port

deportee
(ˌdipor'ti)

n. 被放逐者 (= *exile*)

The *deportees* were held under armed security and not allowed to leave the airport.

被放逐者被武裝的安全人員扣留，不得離開機場。

```
deport +   ee
  |        |
驅逐   +  被動者
```

deportation
(ˌdipor'teʃən)

n. 驅逐出境 (= *exile*)

Monty over-stayed his visa and now faces *deportation*.

蒙提的簽證過期，現在面臨要被驅逐出境。

deportment
(dɪ'portmənt)

n. 舉止；禮節 (= *carriage*)

Young ladies used to have lessons in *deportment*.

以前的少女要上禮節方面的課程。

【背誦祕訣】

這六個字為 report 的衍生字，其中：

⎰ re'porting　皆為名詞，且重音皆在第二音節，
⎨ re'porter　　字根 port 上，且字根 port 的 o
⎱ re'portage　 皆發長音 /o/。

6. *transporter-transportable-transportation*

這一組有 5 個字，分成兩組，第一組是 transport 的衍生字，第二組是 purport 的衍生字，背熟至 3 秒之內，變成直覺。

transporter
〔 træns'portɚ 〕

n. 運輸者（ = *carrier* ）
The new law limits the amount of goods *transporters* can process in a single day.
新的法規限制運輸者一天可處理的商品數量。

```
trans + port + er
  |      |      |
 A→B + carry + 人
```

transportable
〔 træns'portəbḷ 〕

adj. 可運輸的
She carried as many books in her bag as were *transportable.* 她用袋子裝了很多書，裝到提不動為止。

```
trans + port + able
  |      |      |
 A→B + carry + 可~的
```

transportation[4]
〔 ͵trænspɚ'teʃən 〕

n. 運輸（ = *transport* ）；運輸工具
The goods are ready for *transportation.*
那些商品已準備好要運送。

```
trans + port + ation
  |      |      |
 A→B + carry + n.
```
注意此字的 or 發 /ɚ/ 的音

purported
〔 pɚ'portɪd 〕

adj. 傳聞的（ = *alleged* ）
The athlete signed a *purported* two-million-dollar contract.
據說這個運動員簽了兩百萬元的合約。

```
pur  + port + ed
  |     |      |
forward + carry + adj.
```

purportedly
〔 pɚ'portɪdlɪ 〕

adv. 據說（ = *allegedly* ）
Video cameras have *purportedly* been placed in hidden locations. 據說攝影機被放在隱密的地方。

Exercise : Choose the correct answer.

1. These coffee beans are —————— from Brazil.
   (A) supported (B) comported
   (C) deported (D) imported

2. The *New York Times* —————— the accident on the expressway in this morning's edition.
   (A) transported (B) disported
   (C) reported (D) supported

3. The facts don't —————— your argument.
   (A) support (B) importune
   (C) impend (D) depend

4. We'll need this —————— generator in case the power goes out.
   (A) importable (B) portable
   (C) comportable (D) sportful

5. Such heavy items are expensive to —————— by plane.
   (A) transport (B) perpend
   (C) transfer (D) pretend

6. After several items in the article were found to be untrue, the journalist was accused of sloppy ——————.
   (A) deportment (B) reporting
   (C) transporter (D) exportation

7. The man was sentenced to —————— for robbery.
   (A) porter (B) deportation
   (C) reportage (D) sports

字根 port

8. The main ———— of the cathedral is very magnificent.
   (A) portability
   (B) supportability
   (C) portal
   (D) transportation

9. The bus driver was a ———— young man.
   (A) importable
   (B) portly
   (C) portable
   (D) exportable

10. The immigration officer checked my ————.
    (A) passport
    (B) importunity
    (C) comportment
    (D) deportee

11. Switzerland is a big ———— of watches.
    (A) transporter
    (B) exporter
    (C) supporter
    (D) reporter

12. The author dedicated her new book to her ———— family.
    (A) sportive
    (B) portative
    (C) importable
    (D) supportive

13. Tina gave Tommy's cheek a ———— kiss.
    (A) reportorial
    (B) important
    (C) purported
    (D) sportful

14. Without a car, Tina relies on public ———— to get to the office.
    (A) transportation
    (B) portico
    (C) portage
    (D) passport

15. Our foreign policy does not ———— with the principles of democracy.
    (A) comport
    (B) confer
    (C) contend
    (D) compend

字彙測驗詳解

1. (**D**) 這些咖啡豆是從巴西<u>進口</u>的。
   (A) support〔 sə'port 〕 *v.* 支持
   (B) comport〔 kəm'port 〕 *v.* 舉止
   (C) deport〔 dɪ'port 〕 *v.* 放逐
   (D) *import*〔 ɪm'port 〕 *v.* 進口

coffee bean

2. (**C**) 今天早上的紐約時報<u>報導</u>了高速公路的車禍。
   (A) transport〔 træns'port 〕 *v.* 運輸；運送
   (B) disport〔 dɪ'sport 〕 *v.* 嬉戲
   (C) *report*〔 rɪ'port 〕 *v.* 報告；報導
   (D) support〔 sə'port 〕 *v.* 支持
   expressway〔 ɪk'sprɛsˌwe 〕 *n.* 高速公路　edition〔 ɪ'dɪʃən 〕 *n.* 版

3. (**A**) 這些事實無法<u>支持</u>你的論點。
   (A) *support*〔 sə'port 〕 *v.* 支持
   (B) importune〔 ˌɪmpɚ'tjun 〕 *v.* 不斷地要求
   (C) impend〔 ɪm'pɛnd 〕 *v.* 迫近；逼近
   (D) depend〔 dɪ'pɛnd 〕 *v.* 依靠
   argument〔 'ɑrgjəmənt 〕 *n.* 論點

4. (**B**) 我們需要這台<u>手提式</u>發電機，以免沒電。
   (A) importable〔 ɪm'portəbl̩ 〕 *adj.* 可進口的
   (B) *portable*〔 'portəbl̩ 〕 *adj.* 可攜帶的；手提的
   (C) comportable〔 kəm'portəbl̩ 〕 *adj.* 合適的
   (D) sportful〔 'sportfəl 〕 *adj.* 鬧著玩的

generator

   generator〔 'dʒɛnəˌretɚ 〕 *n.* 發電機

5. (**A**) 這麼重的物品用飛機<u>運送</u>很昂貴。
   (A) *transport*〔 træns'port 〕 *v.* 運輸；運送
   (B) perpend〔 pɚ'pɛnd 〕 *v.* 仔細考慮
   (C) transfer〔 træns'fɝ 〕 *v.* 轉移
   (D) pretend〔 prɪ'tɛnd 〕 *v.* 假裝

6. (**B**) 被發現文章裡有幾個不實的事件後，記者就因草率報導被控告。

    (A) deportment〔dɪ'portmənt〕*n.* 舉止；禮節

    (B) *reporting*〔rɪ'portɪŋ〕*n.* 新聞報導

    (C) transporter〔træns'portɚ〕*n.* 運輸者

    (D) exportation〔ˌɛkspor'teʃən〕*n.* 出口

    item〔'aɪtəm〕*n.* 項目   journalist〔'dʒɝnḷɪst〕*n.* 記者

    be accused of 被控告   sloppy〔'slɑpɪ〕*adj.* 草率的

7. (**B**) 這個男人因犯強盜罪而被判驅逐出境。

    (A) porter〔'portɚ〕*n.* 行李搬運員

    (B) *deportation*〔ˌdipor'teʃən〕*n.* 驅逐出境

    (C) reportage〔rɪ'portɪdʒ〕*n.* 新聞報導

    (D) sport〔sport〕*n.* 運動

8. (**C**) 這個教堂的大門很宏偉。

    (A) portability〔ˌportə'bɪlətɪ〕*n.* 可攜帶性

    (B) supportability〔sə,portə'bɪlətɪ〕*n.* 支持度；容忍度

    (C) *portal*〔'portḷ〕*n.* 門；正門

    (D) transportation〔ˌtrænspɚ'teʃən〕*n.* 運輸；運輸工具

9. (**B**) 公車司機是個胖胖的年輕人。

    (A) importable〔ɪm'portəbḷ〕*adj.* 可進口的

    (B) *portly*〔'portlɪ〕*adj.* 肥胖的

    (C) portable〔'portəbḷ〕*adj.* 可攜帶的；手提的

    (D) exportable〔ɛks'portəbḷ〕*adj.* 可出口的

portly

10. (**A**) 移民局官員檢查了我的護照。

    (A) *passport*〔'pæs,port〕*n.* 護照

    (B) importunity〔ˌɪmpɚ'tjunətɪ〕*n.* 糾纏不休；強求

    (C) comportment〔kəm'portmənt〕*n.* 舉止

    (D) deportee〔ˌdipor'ti〕*n.* 被放逐者

    immigration〔ˌɪmə'greʃən〕*n.* 移民；入境管理

    officer〔'ɔfəsɚ〕*n.* 官員

11. (**B**) 瑞士是手錶<u>出口大國</u>。
    (A) transporter〔træns'portɚ〕*n.* 輸送者
    (B) ***exporter***〔ɪk'sportɚ〕*n.* 出口商；出口國
    (C) supporter〔sə'portɚ〕*n.* 支持者
    (D) reporter〔rɪ'portɚ〕*n.* 記者

12. (**D**) 這位作家將她的新書獻給<u>支持</u>她的家人。
    (A) sportive〔'sportɪv〕*adj.* 開玩笑的
    (B) portative〔'portətɪv〕*adj.* 可攜帶的
    (C) importable〔ɪm'portəbḷ〕*adj.* 可進口的
    (D) ***supportive***〔sə'portɪv〕*adj.* 支持的
    author〔'ɔθɚ〕*n.* 作者；作家
    dedicate〔'dɛdə,ket〕*v.* 把…獻給

13. (**D**) 蒂娜<u>開玩笑地</u>親了湯米的臉頰。
    (A) reportorial〔,rɛpɚ'torɪəl〕*adj.* 記者的
    (B) important〔ɪm'portṇt〕*adj.* 重要的
    (C) purported〔pɚ'portɪd〕*adj.* 傳聞的
    (D) ***sportful***〔'sportfəl〕*adj.* 鬧著玩的

14. (**A**) 沒有車的話，蒂娜只能靠大眾<u>運輸工具</u>到辦公室。
    (A) ***transportation***〔,trænspɚ'teʃən〕*n.* 運輸；運輸工具
    (B) portico〔'portɪ,ko〕*n.* 門廊
    (C) portage〔'portɪdʒ〕*n.* 搬運；運費
    (D) passport〔'pæs,port〕*n.* 護照

15. (**A**) 我們的外交政策和民主政治的原則不<u>一致</u>。
    (A) ***comport***〔kəm'port〕*v.* 舉止；相稱
    (B) confer〔kən'fɝ〕*v.* 商議
    (C) contend〔kən'tɛnd〕*v.* 競爭
    (D) compend〔'kampɛnd〕*n.* 概略
    foreign policy 外交政策
    democracy〔dɪ'makrəsɪ〕*n.* 民主政治

請連中文一起背，背至80秒內，終生不忘。　　　　　　　　　　✦

1

port	港口
sport	運動
support	支持
import	進口
export	出口
comport	舉止

report	報告
deport	放逐
disport	嬉戲
transport	運輸
purport	聲稱
passport	護照

2

portal	入口
porter	行李搬運員
portly	肥胖的
portage	搬運
portico	門廊
portamento	滑音

portative	可攜帶的
portable	可攜帶的
portability	可攜帶性

3

sporty	運動時穿的
sporting	運動的
sportingly	在運動方面
sportful	鬧著玩的
sportive	開玩笑的
sportively	開玩笑地

supporter	支持者
supportive	支持的
supportless	無支持的
supportable	可支持的
supportably	可支持地
supportability	支持度

字根 port

字根
port

4

importer	進口商
importable	可進口的
importation	進口
important	重要的
importantly	重要地
importance	重要性
importune	不斷地要求
importunity	糾纏不休
importunate	煩人的

exporter	出口商
exportable	可出口的
exportation	出口
comportment	舉止
comportable	合適的
comportably	合適地

5

reportable	可報導的
reportedly	據說
reportorial	記者的
reporting	新聞報導
reporter	記者
reportage	新聞報導
deportee	被放逐者
deportation	驅逐出境
deportment	舉止

6

transporter	運輸者
transportable	可運輸的
transportation	運輸
purported	傳聞的
purportedly	據說

※ 本頁可影印後，隨身攜帶，方便背誦。

Group 11 字根 *tract*

目標：① 先將63個字放入短期記憶。
② 加快速度至52秒之內，成為長期記憶。

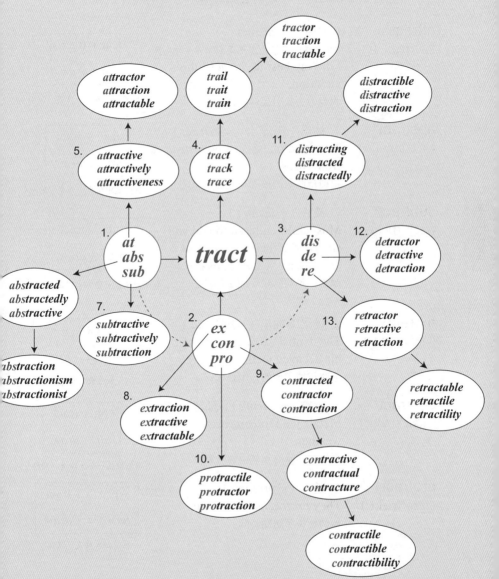

1. 字根 *tract* 核心單字

這 9 個字,三個一組一起背,可先背 6 個再背 3 個,
背熟至 5 秒之內,可成為長期記憶,才可再背下一組。

attract[3]
〔 ə'trækt 〕

v. 吸引 (= *draw*)
tract 這個字根的意思是 draw「拉;畫」
I did my best to *attract* Julie's attention.
我盡力去吸引茱莉注意。

> at + tract
> |　　　|
> to + draw

把某人拉過來,即是「吸引」

abstract[4]
〔 æb'strækt 〕

v. 抽出;提煉出 (= *extract*)
This kind of essence is *abstracted* from roses.
這種精油是由玫瑰花提煉出來的。

> abs + tract
> |　　　|
> from + draw

從～之中拉走,即是「抽出」

subtract[2]
〔 səb'trækt 〕

v. 減去 (= *deduct*)
Most children learn to add and *subtract* in their first year of schooling. 大部分的小孩在求學第一年的時候學加法和減法。

> sub + tract
> |　　　|
> under + draw

往下拉使數量變少,即是「減去」

extract[6]
〔 ɪk'strækt 〕

v. 拔出;抽出 (= *pull out*)
The dentist *extracted* one of his decayed teeth.
牙醫拔掉了他的一顆蛀牙。

> ex + tract
> |　　　|
> out + draw

拉出來,即是「拔出」

contract[3]
〔 kən'trækt 〕

v. 收縮 (= *shrink*);訂契約
Metals tend to *contract* in cold weather.
金屬在寒冷的天氣中會收縮。

> con + tract
> |　　　|
> all + draw

全部都拉在一起,即是「收縮」

protract
〔 pro'trækt 〕

v. 延長 (= *prolong*)
They *protracted* their visit.
他們延長了訪問時間。

> pro + tract
> |　　　　|
> forward + draw

往前拉,即是「延長」

distract[6]
〔 dɪ'strækt 〕

v. 使分心（= *divert* ）
Nothing can *distract* him from his work.
沒有東西可以使他工作分心。

dis + tract
| |
apart + draw

心思被拉到旁邊去，即是「分心」

detract
〔 dɪ'trækt 〕

v. 減損（= *reduce* ; *lessen* ）
She was gaining weight, but it did little to *detract* from her beauty. 她變胖了，但是她的美麗卻不減。

de + tract
| |
away + draw

把價值拉走一些，即是「減損」

retract
〔 rɪ'trækt 〕

v. 收回；縮回（= *withdraw* ）
The speaker wished to *retract* his earlier statements.
這演講者希望能收回他之前所說的。

re + tract
| |
back + draw

往回拉，即是「收回」

字根 tract

【劉毅老師的話】

　　tract 的九個核心單字中，abstract 除了做動詞外，也可做形容詞和名詞，唸成〔'æbstrækt 〕，形容詞表「抽象的」，名詞作「摘錄」解。

　　extract 也可做名詞，唸成〔'ɛkstrækt 〕，作「抽取物；摘錄」解。contract 也有名詞用法，唸成〔'kɑntrækt 〕，表「契約」之意。

2. *tract-track-trace*

這一組有 9 個字，3 個一組一起背，可先背 6 個
再背 3 個，背熟至 5 秒之內，變成直覺。

tract
〔 trækt 〕

n. 區域（＝*area*）；道
To the north of the river is an immense wooded *tract*.
河的北邊是一大片林地。

He had an infection in the upper respiratory *tract*.
他上呼吸道感染。

track[2]
〔 træk 〕

n. 足跡（＝*trace*＝*trail*）；跑道　*v.* 追蹤
The hunter followed the bear's *tracks* in the snow to a hut.
獵人沿著熊在雪地上留下的足跡走到一間小屋。

trace[3]
〔 tres 〕

n. 足跡（＝*track*＝*trail*）　*v.* 追蹤
The hikers disappeared without a *trace*.
這些健行者消失無蹤。

track

trail[3]
〔 trel 〕

n. 足跡（＝*track*＝*footprints*）；痕跡
We followed the *trail* of the wounded animal.
我們跟著這個受傷動物的足跡。

trait[6]
〔 tret 〕

n. 特性（＝*characteristic*）
Patience is not one of his strongest *traits*.
耐性不是他最強烈的特質之一。

train[1]
〔 tren 〕

v. 訓練（＝*drill*）　*n.* 火車
Pamela is *training* to run a marathon next summer.
潘蜜拉正在為明年夏天的馬拉松競賽作訓練。

tractor
〔'træktɚ〕

n. 牽引機；牽引者
Every year thousands of farm workers are injured while driving *tractors*.
每年都有數以千計的農場工人因為駕駛牽引機而受傷。

```
tract + or
  |      |
draw + n.
```

tractor

traction
〔'trækʃən〕

n. 拖曳；(輪胎與道路的) 阻力
These tires get good *traction* on slippery surfaces.
這些輪胎在滑的表面上也有很強的阻力。

tractable
〔'træktəbḷ〕

adj. 溫順的 (= *docile*)
His younger brother is very *tractable*. 他的弟弟很溫順。

```
tract + able
  |      |
draw + adj.
```

可被拉動的，即是「溫順的」

字根 tract

【背誦祕訣】

這組九個字為字根 tract 的衍生字，按照以下的背誦順序，你馬上就背得起來。

tract
track   tract 和 track 母音皆為 /æ/，
trace   且拼法皆為 trac-

trail
trait   母音皆為 /e/，且拼法皆為 trai-
train

tractor
traction   重音皆在第一音節，母音為 /æ/，
tractable   且拼法皆為 tract-

3. attractive-attractively-attractiveness

　　這一組有 15 個字，分成三組，第一組是 attract 的衍生字，第二組是 abstract 的衍生字，第三組是 substract 的衍生字，背熟至 8 秒之內，變成直覺。

attractive[3]
〔 ə'træktɪv 〕

adj. 有吸引力的（ = *charming* ）
Vivian is the most *attractive* woman in the room.
薇薇安是這房間裡最有吸引力的女性。

attractively
〔 ə'træktɪvlɪ 〕

adv. 吸引人地
The ballroom was *attractively* decorated with pink and white flowers.
這個舞廳用粉紅色和白色的花裝飾很吸引人。

attractiveness
〔 ə'træktɪvnɪs 〕

n. 吸引力（ = *charm* ）
His personality accounts for his *attractiveness* more than his looks.
他很有吸引力的原因是他的個性，而非他的外表。

attractor
〔 ə'træktɚ 〕

n. 有吸引力的人或物（ = *attracter* ）
Flowers are natural *attractors* of all sorts of insects.
花是各種昆蟲的天然吸引物。

attraction[4]
〔 ə'trækʃən 〕

n. 吸引力（ = *attractiveness* ）；有吸引力的人或物
Their *attraction* was based on a shared interest in music. 他們的吸引力建立於對音樂共同的興趣。

attractable
〔 ə'træktəbl̩ 〕

adj. 可被吸引的
Teens are more *attractable* to Internet shopping than any other age group.
青少年比其他年齡層的人更會被網路購物所吸引。

abstracted
﹝ æb'stræktɪd ﹞

adj. 心不在焉的（= *absentminded*）
He had an *abstracted* look on his face.
他一臉心不在焉。

```
abstract  +  ed
   |          |
抽取；抽離  +  adj.
```
心被抽離，即是「心不在焉」

abstractedly
﹝ æb'stræktɪdlɪ ﹞

adv. 心不在焉地（= *absently*）
Maureen *abstractedly* played with a strand of
her hair.
莫琳心不在焉地玩弄著她的一撮頭髮。

abstractive
﹝ æb'stræktɪv ﹞

adj. 抽象的（= *abstract*）
Einstein's ideas were far more *abstractive* than
practical. 愛因斯坦的想法比實際上抽象很多。

字根 tract

abstraction[6]
﹝ æb'strækʃən ﹞

n. 抽象；抽象概念；心不在焉
Truth and justice are *abstractions*.
「事實」和「正義」是抽象概念。

He was lost in *abstraction* while the professor
spoke. 當教授在說話的時候，他心不在焉。

abstractionism
﹝ æb'strækʃən,ɪzəm ﹞

n. 抽象派；抽象主義
Her work features some elements of
abstractionism.
她的作品有抽象派的特色。

abstractionism

abstractionist
﹝ æb'strækʃənɪst ﹞

n. 抽象派畫家
Woody claims to be an *abstractionist* painter.
伍迪聲稱他是個抽象派畫家。

subtractive
(səb'træktɪv)

adj. 減法的

This is a *subtractive* math problem.

這是一個減法的數學問題。

```
subtract + ive
   |        |
  減去    + adj.
```

subtractively
(səb'træktɪvlɪ)

adv. 減法地

This math problem should be solved *subtractively*.

這個數學問題應該用減法來解題。

subtraction
(səb'trækʃən)

n. 減法；扣除 (= *deduction*)

He complained about the *subtraction* of money from his paycheck.

他抱怨被扣薪水。

字根 tract

【背誦祕訣】

這組 15 個單字中，重音皆在第二音節，且重音節的母音皆為 /æ/，其中：

at'tractive
at'tractively
at'tractiveness

abs'traction
abs'tractionism
abs'tractionist

為 attractive 和 abstraction 的衍生字，依照音節數排列，在背誦時，有押韻又好背。

4. *extraction-extractive-extractable*

這一組有 15 個字，分成三組，第一組是 extract 的
衍生字，第二組是 contract 的衍生字，第三組是 protract
的衍生字，背熟至 8 秒之內，變成直覺。

extraction
〔 ɪk'strækʃən 〕

n. 拔出；抽出物（ = *drawing* ）
The *extraction* of a wisdom
tooth is a painful ordeal.
拔智齒是很痛苦的折磨。

extract + ion
拔出；抽出 + *n.*

extractive
〔 ɪk'stræktɪv 〕

adj. 萃取的
The body lotion is *extractive* from flowers.
這種身體乳液是由花朵萃取出來的。

extractable
〔 ɪk'stræktəbl̩ 〕

adj. 可萃取的；可摘錄的（ = *extractive* ）
This article is not *extractable*. 這篇文章不可摘錄。

contracted[3]
〔 kən'træktɪd 〕

adj. 收縮的（ = *shrunken* ）；狹窄的（ = *narrow* ）
Tom has no friends because of his *contracted* mind.
湯姆沒有朋友，因為他心胸狹窄。

contract + ed
收縮 + *adj.*

收縮之後就會變「狹窄的」

contractor[6]
〔 kən'træktɚ,
'kɑntræktɚ 〕

n. 承包商；收縮肌
The *contractor* is responsible
for the safety of his crew.
承包商須負責他員工的安全。

contract + or
訂契約 + 人

contraction
〔 kən'trækʃən 〕

n. 收縮（ = *tightening* ）
Her *contractions* started coming a minute apart, and
Rosalie knew the baby was coming. 羅莎莉知道寶寶
快出生了，因為她的收縮開始變成一分鐘一次。

contractive
〔 kən'træktɪv 〕

adj. 有收縮性的（= *contractile*）
The muscles in your hand are mainly *contractive*.
你手部的肌肉大部分是具有收縮性的。

contractual
〔 kən'træktʃuəl 〕

adj. 契約的
Jerry had a *contractual* obligation to finish the job on time.
傑瑞有契約上的義務，要準時完成工作。

contracture
〔 kən'træktʃɚ 〕

n. 攣縮（= *contraction*）
Severe burns result in *contractures* of the skin.
嚴重的燒傷導致了皮膚的攣縮。

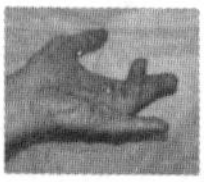
contracture

contract + ure
收縮 + *n.*

肌肉永久收縮變形，即是「攣縮」

contractile
〔 kən'træktḷ 〕

adj. 有收縮性的（= *contractible*）
The human heart is a *contractile* muscle.
人類的心臟是有收縮性的肌肉。

contract + ile
收縮 + *adj.*

contractible
〔 kən'træktəbḷ 〕

adj. 可收縮的（= *contractive*；*contractile*）
Blood vesseles are *contractible*. 血管是可收縮的。

contract + ible
收縮 + 可～的

contractibility
〔 kən,træktə'bɪlətɪ 〕

n. 收縮性
Smoking decreases the *contractibility* of blood vessels. 抽菸會降低血管的收縮性。

protractile
〔pro'træktɪl〕

adj. 能伸長的
Lobsters have *protractile* claws.
龍蝦的螯可伸長。

lobster claw

protractor
〔pro'træktə〕

n. 量角器
Timmy used a *protractor* to
measure the angle.
堤米用量角器來測量角度。

protractor

protraction
〔pro'trækʃən〕

n. 延長 (= *extension*)；拖延 (= *delay*)
The proposal will move forward without further
protraction. 這個提案會立刻進行，不會再拖延了。

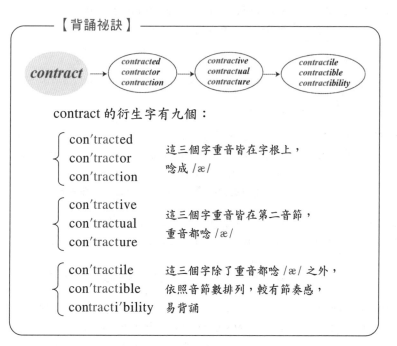

【背誦祕訣】

contract → contracted / contractor / contraction → contractive / contractual / contracture → contractile / contractible / contractibility

contract 的衍生字有九個：

con'tracted
con'tractor　　這三個字重音皆在字根上，
con'traction　　唸成 /æ/

con'tractive
con'tractual　　這三個字重音皆在第二音節，
con'tracture　　重音都唸 /æ/

con'tractile　　這三個字除了重音都唸 /æ/ 之外，
con'tractible　　依照音節數排列，較有節奏感，
contracti'bility　易背誦

字根 tract

5. distracting-distracted-distractedly

這一組有 15 個字，分成三組，第一組是 distract 的衍生字，第二組是 detract 的衍生字，第三組是 retract 的衍生字，背熟至 8 秒之內，變成直覺。

字根 tract

distracting[6]
〔 dɪ'stræktɪŋ 〕
adj. 令人分心的 (= *disturbing*)
The noise is particularly *distracting*.
這個噪音特別會令人分心。

distracted[6]
〔 dɪ'stræktɪd 〕
adj. 分心的 (= *inattentive*)
He was *distracted* by the bright lights.
他因為那些強光而分心。

distractedly
〔 dɪ'stræktɪdlɪ 〕
adv. 心煩意亂地 (= *anxiously*)
Myron is *distractedly* tapping his foot.
麥倫心煩意亂地輕踏著腳。

distract + ed + ly
|　　　 |　　 |
使分心　 + *adj.* + *adv.*　　會被分心，是因為「心煩意亂」

distractible
〔 dɪ'stræktəbḷ 〕
adj. 容易分心的
The story moves at such a pace to keep even the most *distractible* person interested.
這個故事進行流暢，連最容易分心的人都感興趣。

distractive[6]
〔 dɪ'stræktɪv 〕
adj. 分散注意力的 (= *distracting*)
Much of what politicians say is intended to be *distractive*.
政治人物說的話，很多是企圖要分散大家的注意力。

distraction[6]
〔 dɪ'strækʃən 〕
n. 分心 (= *disturbance*)；使人分心的事物
The baby's constant crying drove the father to *distraction*. 這個小嬰孩一直哭，使得爸爸分心。

detractor
〔 dɪ'træktə 〕

n. 誹謗者 (= *attacker*)

His latest performance should quiet the *detractors*.

他最近的表演應該會使那些誹謗者禁聲。

detract + or
│   │
減損 + 人

專門減損你的人，即是「誹謗者」

detractive
〔 dɪ'træktɪv 〕

adj. 貶低的

What you said is *detractive* to my ideas.

你說的話貶低了我的想法。

detraction
〔 dɪ'trækʃən 〕

n. 誹謗 (= *damaging comment*)

The candidate responded to his opponent's *detractions*.

候選人回應對手的誹謗。

字根 tract

【背誦祕訣】

這六個字是 distract 的衍生字：

dis'tracting
dis'tracted
dis'tractedly

dis'tractible
dis'tractive
dis'traction

這六個字重音皆在第二音節上，
且重音都唸 /æ/，易背誦記憶

retractor
〔rɪˈtræktɚ〕

n. 伸縮裝置；縮回者
Automobile seat belts are equipped with *retractor*.
汽車的安全帶備有伸縮裝置。

```
retract + or
   |       |
  收回  +  n.
```

retractive
〔rɪˈtræktɪv〕

adj. 可收回的（= *retractable*）
Once you submit your vote, it is not *retractive*.
一旦你交了你的選票，就不能再收回了。

retraction
〔rɪˈtrækʃən〕

n. 收回；撤回
The company denied the *retraction* of my order.
這家公司不承認我撤回了訂單。

retractable
〔rɪˈtræktəbl̩〕

adj. 可撤回的；可伸縮的（= *retractile*）
The stadium has a *retractable* roof.
這座體育館有可伸縮的屋頂。

```
retract + able
   |        |
  收回   + 可～的
```

retractile
〔rɪˈtræktl̩〕

adj. 伸縮自如的（= *retractable*；*retractive*）
Cats have *retractile* claws.
貓咪有伸縮自如的爪子。

retractile claws

retractility
〔ˌritrækˈtɪlətɪ〕

n. 伸縮性
The injury limited the *retractility* of his
tongue. 這個傷使他的舌頭伸縮性受限。

* 這六個字為 retract 的衍生字，所以意思皆與「收回；縮回」有關。

Exercise : Choose the correct answer.

1. Flies are _____ to fluorescent lights.
   (A) contracted　　　　　(B) protracted
   (C) distracted　　　　　(D) attracted

2. The somber music _____ from the pleasant atmosphere of the café.
   (A) abstracts　　　　　(B) retracts
   (C) subtracts　　　　　(D) opposes

3. Detectives _____ the suspect's whereabouts during the days leading up to the murder.
   (A) referred　　　　　(B) impended
   (C) imported　　　　　(D) traced

4. He _____ a small notebook from his pocket.
   (A) extracted　　　　　(B) exposed
   (C) expelled　　　　　(D) expressed

5. Ralph is easily _____.
   (A) contractile　　　　　(B) distracted
   (C) detractive　　　　　(D) retractile

6. The scandal will not _____ from his fame.
   (A) design　　　　　(B) deserve
   (C) detract　　　　　(D) detain

7. The low price and small size makes this phone _____ to consumers.
   (A) attractive　　　　　(B) tractable
   (C) abstractive　　　　　(D) subtractive

字根 tract

8. He runs around the _____ every morning.
   (A) trait   (B) track
   (C) tractor   (D) train

9. Please stop making that _____ noise.
   (A) propellent   (B) extractive
   (C) distracting   (D) contracted

10. Wisdom and bravery are _____.
    (A) impulsions   (B) attractiveness
    (C) contractures   (D) abstractions

11. Her teeth are so bad that she needs five _____.
    (A) extractions   (B) attractions
    (C) subtractions   (D) retractions

12. The Mayor says he pays little or no attention to his _____.
    (A) detractors   (B) retractors
    (C) protractors   (D) contractors

13. After _____ negotiations, the two sides agreed on the plan.
    (A) attractable   (B) protracted
    (C) contracted   (D) disposable

14. The committee voted to _____ an earlier decision approving the use of public land for private development.
    (A) retract   (B) repel
    (C) refer   (D) deport

15. The jet left a thin _____ of white smoke as it soared across the sky.
    (A) trail   (B) traction
    (C) distraction   (D) opposition

字彙測驗詳解

1. (**D**) 蒼蠅被螢光燈所<u>吸引</u>。
   (A) contract〔kən'trækt〕 *v.* 收縮;訂契約
   (B) protract〔pro'trækt〕 *v.* 延長
   (C) distract〔dɪ'strækt〕 *v.* 使分心
   (D) ***attract***〔ə'trækt〕 *v.* 吸引

   fluorescent

   fly〔flaɪ〕 *n.* 蒼蠅
   fluorescent〔ˌfluə'rɛsn̩t〕 *adj.* 螢光的

2. (**C**) 這憂鬱的音樂<u>減少</u>了咖啡廳裡愉快的氣氛。
   (A) abstract〔æb'strækt〕 *v.* 抽出;提煉出
   (B) retract〔rɪ'trækt〕 *v.* 縮回
   (C) ***subtract***〔səb'trækt〕 *v.* 減去
   (D) oppose〔ə'poz〕 *v.* 反對
   somber〔'sɑmbɚ〕 *adj.* 憂鬱的
   pleasant〔'plɛzn̩t〕 *adj.* 令人愉快的
   atmosphere〔'ætməsˌfɪr〕 *n.* 氣氛

3. (**D**) 警探們<u>追蹤</u>該名嫌疑犯在謀殺案發生前幾天的行蹤。
   (A) refer〔rɪ'fɝ〕 *v.* 參考;提及;是指
   (B) impend〔ɪm'pɛnd〕 *v.* 逼近;迫近
   (C) import〔ɪm'port〕 *v.* 進口
   (D) ***trace***〔tres〕 *v.* 追蹤
   detective〔dɪ'tɛktɪv〕 *n.* 偵探;警察
   suspect〔'sʌspɛkt〕 *n.* 嫌疑犯
   whereabouts〔ˌhwɛrə'bauts〕 *n. pl.* 下落
   lead up to 逐漸進入   murder〔'mɝdɚ〕 *n.* 謀殺

4. (**A**) 他從口袋裡<u>抽出</u>了一本小小的筆記本。

  (A) ***extract*** 〔ɪk'strækt〕 *v.* 抽出

  (B) expose 〔ɪk'spoz〕 *v.* 暴露

  (C) expel 〔ɪk'spɛl〕 *v.* 逐出

  (D) express 〔ɪk'sprɛs〕 *v.* 表達

  pocket 〔'pɑkɪt〕 *n.* 口袋

notebook

5. (**B**) 拉爾夫很容易<u>分心</u>。

  (A) contractile 〔kən'træktḷ〕 *adj.* 有收縮性的

  (B) ***distracted*** 〔dɪ'stræktɪd〕 *adj.* 分心的

  (C) detractive 〔dɪ'træktɪv〕 *adj.* 減損的

  (D) retractile 〔rɪ'træktḷ〕 *adj.* 收縮自如的

  Ralph 〔rælf〕 *n.* 拉爾夫【男子名】

  easily 〔'izɪlɪ〕 *adv.* 容易地

6. (**C**) 這個醜聞無<u>損</u>於他的名聲。

  (A) design 〔dɪ'zaɪn〕 *v.* 設計

  (B) deserve 〔dɪ'zɝv〕 *v.* 應得

  (C) ***detract*** 〔dɪ'trækt〕 *v.* 減損

  (D) detain 〔dɪ'ten〕 *v.* 拘留

  scandal 〔'skændḷ〕 *n.* 醜聞   fame 〔fem〕 *n.* 名聲

7. (**A**) 這款電話的低價和小尺寸很<u>吸引</u>消費者。

  (A) ***attractive*** 〔ə'træktɪv〕 *adj.* 吸引人的

  (B) tractable 〔'træktəbḷ〕 *adj.* 溫順的

  (C) abstractive 〔æb'stræktɪv〕 *adj.* 抽象的

  (D) subtractive 〔səb'træktɪv〕 *adj.* 減法的

cell phone

  consumer 〔kən'sumɚ〕 *n.* 消費者

字根 tract

8. (**B**)　他每天早上繞著<u>跑道</u>跑步。

　　(A) trait〔 tret 〕*n.* 特性

　　(B) ***track***〔 træk 〕*n.* 足跡；跑道

　　(C) tractor〔'træktɚ 〕*n.* 牽引機

　　(D) train〔 tren 〕*n.* 火車

9. (**C**)　請停止製造那種會<u>令人分心的</u>噪音。

　　(A) propellant〔 prə'pɛlənt 〕*adj.* 推進的

　　(B) extractive〔 ɪk'stræktɪv 〕*adj.* 拔出的；萃取的

　　(C) ***distracting***〔 dɪ'stræktɪŋ 〕*adj.* 令人分心的

　　(D) contracted〔 kən'træktɪd 〕*adj.* 收縮的；狹窄的

　　noise〔 nɔɪz 〕*n.* 噪音

10. (**D**)　「智慧」和「勇敢」都是<u>抽象概念</u>。

　　(A) impulsion〔 ɪm'pʌlʃən 〕*n.* 衝動

　　(B) attractiveness〔 ə'træktɪvnɪs 〕*n.* 吸引力

　　(C) contracture〔 kən'træktʃɚ 〕*n.* 攣縮

　　(D) ***abstraction***〔 æb'strækʃən 〕*n.* 抽象；抽象概念

　　wisdom〔'wɪzdəm 〕*n.* 智慧

　　bravery〔'brevərɪ 〕*n.* 勇敢

11. (**A**)　她的牙齒太糟，得<u>拔掉</u>五顆牙。

　　(A) ***extraction***〔 ɪk'strækʃən 〕*n.* 拔出；抽出物

　　(B) attraction〔 ə'trækʃən 〕*n.* 吸引力

　　(C) subtraction〔 səb'trækʃən 〕*n.* 減去

　　(D) retraction〔 rɪ'trækʃən 〕*n.* 收回

tooth extraction

12. (**A**) 市長說他不會注意那些<u>誹謗者</u>。

　　　(A) *detractor* ﹝dɪˈtræktɚ﹞ *n.* 誹謗者
　　　(B) retractor ﹝rɪˈtræktɚ﹞ *n.* 縮回者；伸縮裝置
　　　(C) protractor ﹝proˈtræktɚ﹞ *n.* 量角器
　　　(D) contractor ﹝kənˈtræktɚ﹞ *n.* 承包商
　　　mayor ﹝ˈmeɚ﹞ *n.* 市長　　***pay attention to*** 注意

13. (**B**) 在<u>長時間的</u>談判中，雙方同意了這個計畫。

　　　(A) attractable ﹝əˈtræktəbḷ﹞ *adj.* 可被吸引的
　　　(B) *protracted* ﹝proˈtræktɪd﹞ *adj.* 延長的；長時間的
　　　(C) contracted ﹝kənˈtræktɪd﹞ *adj.* 收縮的
　　　(D) disposable ﹝dɪˈspozəbḷ﹞ *adj.* 用完即丟的
　　　negotiation ﹝nɪ͵goʃɪˈeʃən﹞ *n.* 談判；協商

14. (**A**) 委員會投票<u>撤回</u>稍早同意將公用土地用於私人發展的決定。

　　　(A) *retract* ﹝rɪˈtrækt﹞ *v.* 收回
　　　(B) repel ﹝rɪˈpɛl﹞ *v.* 逐退
　　　(C) refer ﹝rɪˈfɝ﹞ *v.* 參考；提及；是指
　　　(D) deport ﹝dɪˈport﹞ *v.* 放逐
　　　committee ﹝kəˈmɪtɪ﹞ *n.* 委員會
　　　vote ﹝vot﹞ *v.* 投票　　approve ﹝əˈpruv﹞ *v.* 同意
　　　private ﹝ˈpraɪvɪt﹞ *adj.* 私人的

15. (**A**) 噴射機在飛越天空的時候，留下了一道白煙的<u>痕跡</u>。

　　　(A) *trail* ﹝trel﹞ *n.* 足跡；痕跡
　　　(B) traction ﹝ˈtrækʃən﹞ *n.* 牽引
　　　(C) distraction ﹝dɪˈstrækʃən﹞ *n.* 分心
　　　(D) opposition ﹝͵apəˈzɪʃən﹞ *n.* 反對
　　　jet ﹝dʒɛt﹞ *n.* 噴射機　　soar ﹝sor﹞ *v.* 翱翔

jet

字根 tract

請連中文一起背，背至80秒內，終生不忘。 ✦

1

attract 吸引
abstract 抽出
subtract 減去

extract 拔出
contract 收縮
protract 延長

distract 使分心
detract 減損
retract 收回

2

tract 區域
track 足跡
trace 足跡

trail 足跡
trait 特性
train 訓練

tractor 牽引機
traction 拖曳
tractable 溫順的

3

attractive 有吸引力的
attractively 吸引人地
attractiveness 吸引力

attractor 有吸引力的人或物
attraction 吸引力
attractable 可被吸引的

abstracted 心不在焉的
abstractedly 心不在焉地
abstractive 抽象的

abstraction 抽象
abstractionism 抽象派
abstractionist 抽象派畫家

subtractive 減法的
subtractively 減法地
subtraction 減法

字根 tract

4

extraction 拔出
extractive 萃取的
extractable 可萃取的

contracted 收縮的
contractor 承包商
contraction 收縮

contractive 有收縮性的
contractual 契約的
contracture 攣縮

contractile 有收縮性的
contractible 可收縮的
contractibility 收縮性

protractile 能伸長的
protractor 量角器
protraction 延長

5

distracting 令人分心的
distracted 分心的
distractedly 心煩意亂地

distractible 容易分心的
distractive 分散注意力的
distraction 分心

detractor 誹謗者
detractive 貶低的
detraction 誹謗

retractor 伸縮裝置
retractive 可收回的
retraction 收回

retractable 可撤回的
retractile 伸縮自如的
retractility 伸縮性

字根 tract

※ 本頁可影印後，隨身攜帶，方便背誦。

Group 12 字根 *ject*

目標： ① 先將53個字放入短期記憶。
② 加快速度至44秒之內，成為長期記憶。

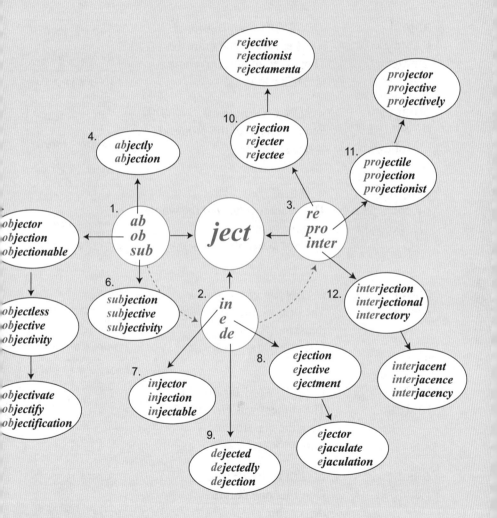

1. 字根 *ject* 核心單字

這 9 個字，3 個一組一起背，可先背 6 個，再背 3 個，背熟至 5 秒之內，可成為長期記憶，才可再背下一組。

abject
〔 æb'dʒɛkt ,
'æbdʒɛkt 〕

adj. 可憐的（= *miserable*）
ject 這個字根的意思是 throw「丟；投」
They lived in *abject* poverty.
他們的生活窮得可憐。

> ab ＋ ject
> |　　　　|
> *away* ＋ *throw*
>
> 被丟到一旁去，即是「可憐」

object[2]
〔 *v.* əb'dʒɛkt
　n. 'ɑbdʒɪkt 〕

v. 反對（= *disagree*）　*n.* 物體
Peter *objected* to the proposal.
彼得反對這個提案。

> ob ＋ ject
> |　　　　|
> *against* ＋ *throw*
>
> 投向對面，即是「反對」

subject[2]
〔 *v.* səb'dʒɛkt
　n. 'sʌbdʒɪkt 〕

v. 使服從　*n.* 主題
The general *subjected* the whole country to his rule.
這位將軍使全國服從於他的統治。

> sub ＋ ject
> |　　　　|
> *under* ＋ *throw*
>
> 投身於～之下，即是「服從」

inject[6]
〔 ɪn'dʒɛkt 〕

v. 注射（= *give a shot*）
The drug is *injected* under the skin.
這種藥物要用皮下注射。

> in ＋ ject
> |　　　　|
> *into* ＋ *throw*
>
> 投擲進來，即是「注射」

eject
〔 ɪ'dʒɛkt 〕

v. 噴出；逐出（= *expel*）
The student was *ejected* from the classroom.
這個學生被趕出教室。

> e ＋ ject
> |　　　　|
> *out* ＋ *throw*
>
> 丟出去，即是「噴出；逐出」

deject
〔 dɪ'dʒɛkt 〕

v. 使沮喪（= *depress*）
Don't let one failure *deject* you.
別讓一次失敗使你沮喪。

> de ＋ ject
> |　　　　|
> *down* ＋ *throw*
>
> 往下丟，即是「使沮喪」

reject[2]
〔 rɪˈdʒɛkt 〕

v. 拒絕（= *refuse*）
She *rejected* my offer.
她拒絕我的提議。

> re ＋ ject
> ｜　　　｜
> *back* ＋ *throw*

丟回去，即是「拒絕」

project[2]
〔 *v.* prəˈdʒɛkt
　n. ˈprɑdʒɛkt 〕

v. 投射（= *screen*）　*n.* 計劃（= *plan*）
The images were *projected*
on a screen.
這些影像被投射在銀幕上。

> pro ＋ ject
> ｜　　　　｜
> *forward* ＋ *throw*

往前丟，即是「投射」

interject
〔 ˌɪntɚˈdʒɛkt 〕

v. 突然插（話）（= *interpose*）
The professor *interjected* the lecture with clever
remarks. 教授在課堂上穿插幾個很棒的評論。

> inter ＋ ject
> ｜　　　　｜
> *between* ＋ *throw*

投入其間，即是「突然插（話）」

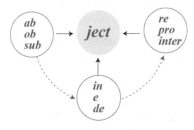

【劉毅老師的話】

　　object 也可當名詞，唸成〔ˈɑbdʒɪkt〕，作
「物體；目標；受詞」解。另外，subject 也
可做名詞和形容詞，唸成〔ˈsʌbdʒɪkt〕，名詞
表「主題；科目；主詞；臣民」之意，形容詞
的意思是「服從的；附屬的」。

2. *abjectly-abjection*

這一組有 14 個字，分成三組，第一組是 abject 的
衍生字，第二組是 object 的衍生字，第三組是 subject
的衍生字，背熟至 7 秒之內，變成直覺。

abjectly
〔 æb'dʒɛktlɪ ,
'æbdʒɛktlɪ 〕

adv. 可憐地 (= *miserably*)
The defeated athlete *abjectly* returned to the
locker room.
這個被擊敗的運動員很可憐地回到更衣室。

abjection
〔 æb'dʒɛkʃən 〕

n. 落魄；羞辱 (= *humiliation*)
He felt a sense of *abjection*.
她覺得有羞辱感。

> abject + ion
> |　　　|
> 可憐的 + *n.*

objector
〔 əb'dʒɛktɚ 〕

n. 反對者 (= *opponent*)
Henry is the only *objector* to my suggestion.
亨利是我提案的唯一反對者。

objection [4]
〔 əb'dʒɛkʃən 〕

n. 反對 (= *opposition*)
Ursula voiced her *objection*.
烏蘇拉表明她的反對。

> object + ion
> |　　　|
> 反對 + *n.*

objectionable
〔 əb'dʒɛkʃənəb̩ 〕

adj. 會引起反對的；令人討厭的 (= *offensive*)
The film contains some *objectionable* content.
這部電影包含了一些令人討厭的內容。

> object + ion + able
> |　　　|　　　|
> 反對 + *n.* + *adj.*

反對別人會「令人討厭」

objectless
('abdʒɛktlɪs)

adj. 無目的的 (= *aimless*)；無受詞的
He had an *objectless* anxiety about the future.
她對未來充滿毫無目標的焦慮。

objective⁴
(əb'dʒɛktɪv)

adj. 客觀的 (= *unbiased*)
n. 目標 (= *purpose*)
It's hard to give an *objective* opinion about this.
這件事很難表達客觀的意見。
Our *objective* is to sell a lot of products.
我們的目標是賣出很多產品。

objectivity
(,abdʒɛk'tɪvətɪ)

n. 客觀性 (= *fairness*)
Scientists must maintain a high degree of
objectivity during their experiments.
在實驗的過程中，科學家必須保有高度的客觀性。

objectivate
(əb'dʒɛktə,vet)

v. 使客觀化；使具體化 (= *objectify*)
He tends to *objectivate* his emotions.
他很容易具體表現自己的情緒。

objectify
(əb'dʒɛktə,faɪ)

v. 使客觀化；使具體化 (= *actualize*)；使物化
He failed to *objectify* his goal.
他無法將他的目標具體化。

object	+	ify
物體	+	*make*

使它變物體，即是「使具體化」
將它視為物體，即是「使物化」

objectification
(əb,dʒɛktəfə'keʃən)

n. 具體化；物化
They studied the negative results of female
objectification in the media.
他們研究媒體中將女性物化的負面結果。

字根 ject

subjection
〔 səb'dʒɛkʃən 〕

n. 服從
The prisoners were forced into *subjection*.
囚犯被迫服從。

sub	+	ject	+	ion
under	+	throw	+	*n.*

投身～之下，即是「服從」

subjective [6]
〔 səb'dʒɛktɪv 〕

adj. 主觀的 (= *personal* ; *prejudiced*)
The value of a work of art is *subjective* to the viewer. 一個藝術品的價值是在於觀看者的主觀感受。

subjectivity
〔 ˌsʌbdʒɛk'tɪvətɪ 〕

n. 主觀性 (= *prejudice*)
The *subjectivity* of the decision made some people doubt its validity. 這個決定的主觀性使得有些人懷疑它是否正確。

subjectiv	+	ity
主觀的	+	*n.*

字根 ject

【背誦祕訣】

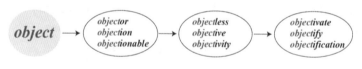

這九個字是 object 的衍生字：

ob'jector
ob'jection
ob'jectionable

這三個字重音皆在第二音節，
且重音皆唸 /ɛ/，另外此組解
釋都與「反對」有關。

'objectless
ob'jective
objec'tivity

這三個字的編排全要依據重音的位置，
第一個字重音在第一音節，第二個字重
音在第二音節，第三個字重音在第三音
節，依重音的位置排序，易於背誦。

ob'jectivate
ob'jectify
ˌobjectifi'cation

第一、二字都是動詞，第三字是第二字
的名詞，三個字都和「具體」有關。

3 injector-injection-injectable

這一組有 12 個字，分成三組，第一組是 inject 的衍生字，第二組是 eject 的衍生字，第三組是 deject 的衍生字，背熟至 7 秒之內，變成直覺。

injector
〔 ɪnˋdʒɛktɚ 〕

n. 注射者；噴射器
Toyota has announced the development of a dual *injector* system designed to improve fuel efficiency.
豐田汽車宣稱已研發出雙噴射系統，此系統主要是設計來省油。

injection[6]
〔 ɪnˋdʒɛkʃən 〕

n. 注射
The medicine will be given by *injection*.
這個藥物須用注射的方式。

injectable
〔 ɪnˋdʒɛktəbļ 〕

adj. 可注射的
Supplies of the *injectable* vaccine were sufficient.
針劑疫苗的供給是足夠的。

```
inject + able
  |        |
注射   + 可~的
```

ejection
〔 ɪˋdʒɛkʃən 〕

n. 噴出；逐出
The scandal led to the politician's *ejection* from office.
這個醜聞導致這名政治人物下台。

```
eject + ion
  |       |
噴出   + n.
```

字根 ject

ejective
〔 ɪˋdʒɛktɪv 〕

adj. 噴出的
The *ejective* force of the volcano sent a cloud of ash into the sky.　火山噴射出的力量使得一團火山灰衝入空中。

ejectment
〔 ɪˋdʒɛktmənt 〕

n. 逐出；（租用權之）剝奪
George didn't pay his rent and now the landlord is threatening an *ejectment*.
喬治沒付房租，現在房東威脅要把他趕出去。

ejector
(ɪ'dʒɛktɚ)

n. 驅逐者；噴射器 (= *expeller*)
The fighter jets are equipped with *ejector* seats in case of emergency.
戰鬥機配備了供緊急情況使用的彈射座椅。

ejector seat

ejaculate
(ɪ'dʒækjə,let)

v. 射出；突然喊叫 (= *shout out*)
"Oh no!" Donna *ejaculated*.
唐娜突然大叫：「噢，不！」

```
e  + jacul + ate
|     |       |
out + throw +  v.     jacul 是字根 ject 的變化型。
```

ejaculation
(ɪ,dʒækjə'leʃən)

n. 射出；突然的叫聲；射精
A small number of males suffer from premature *ejaculation*. 少數的男性有早洩的苦惱。

dejected
(dɪ'dʒɛktɪd)

adj. 沮喪的 (= *depressed*)
The losing candidate thanked his *dejected* supporters for their hard work and dedication to his campaign.
這即將敗選的候選人，感謝他情緒低落的支持者，在這場選戰中的努力與付出。

字根 ject

dejectedly
(dɪ'dʒɛktɪdlɪ)

adv. 沮喪地
"Tickets for the show are sold out," Carolyn said *dejectedly*. 「這場表演的票已經賣光了，」卡洛琳沮喪地說。

```
deject + ed + ly
|        |     |
使沮喪  + adj. + adv.    過去分詞當形容詞用，
                        加上 ly 形成副詞。
```

dejection
(dɪ'dʒɛkʃən)

n. 沮喪 (= *depression*)
He couldn't hide his *dejection* from losing another game. 他無法掩飾輸掉另一場比賽的沮喪。

4. rejection-rejecter-rejectee

這一組有 18 個字，分成三組，第一組是 reject 的衍
生字，第二組是 project 的衍生字，第三組是 interject
的衍生字，背熟至 10 秒之內，變成直覺。

| rejection[4]
〔 rɪˈdʒɛkʃən 〕 | *n.* 拒絕（ = *refusal* ）
He refused to accept her *rejection*.
他不願接受她的拒絕。 |
| rejecter
〔 rɪˈdʒɛktɚ 〕 | *n.* 拒絕者；拋棄者（ = *denier* ）
The terrorists are *rejecters*
of Western values.
恐怖份子是西方價值觀的摒棄者。 |

```
reject +   er
  |        |
拒絕   + 主動者
```

| rejectee
〔 rɪˌdʒɛkˈti 〕 | *n.* 遭拒絕者
Several university *rejectees* staged an on-campus
hunger strike in protest.
有好幾個被大學拒絕的人在
校園內絕食抗議。 |

```
reject +   ee
  |        |
拒絕   + 被動者
```

ee 結尾表被動者，重音必在 ee 上。

rejective 〔 rɪˈdʒɛktɪv 〕	*adj.* 拒絕的 Tony's *rejective* personality left him with few friends. 湯尼愛拒絕人的個性，使他沒有什麼朋友。
rejectionist 〔 rɪˈdʒɛkʃənɪst 〕	*adj.* 拒絕承認他人的 Critics argue that Islam is a *rejectionist* religion. 評論者認為，伊斯蘭教是個拒絕承認他人的宗教。
rejectamenta 〔 rɪˌdʒɛktəˈmɛntə 〕	*n.* 廢物（ = *waste* ） By analyzing our *rejectamenta*, we can learn hidden truths about ourselves. 藉由分析我們的排泄物，我們可以知道我們自己不 知道的身體現況。

projectile
〔 prə'dʒɛktɪl 〕

adj. 發射的
n. 發射物（尤指子彈、火箭等）
A large hole was made by the impact of the *projectile*.
這枚砲彈的衝擊力炸出了一個大洞。

project + ile
投射   + *n.* ; *adj.*

projectile

projection[6]
〔 prə'dʒɛkʃən 〕

n. 計劃（ = *plan* ）
The company struggled to meet their third-quarter sales *projections*.
這公司努力達成他們第三季的銷售計畫。

projectionist
〔 prə'dʒɛkʃənɪst 〕

n. 放映師
Donald has worked as a *projectionist* for 27 years.
唐納已經擔任電影放映師二十七年之久。

projector
〔 prə'dʒɛktɚ 〕

n. 投影機
The digital camera revolution has made slide *projectors* obsolete.
數位相機的革命已使得幻燈片投影機被淘汰了。

project + or
投射   + *n.*

可投射或投影的器具或人

projector

projective
〔 prə'dʒɛktɪv 〕

adj. 投影的；投射的
Projective tests are used to evaluate patients with personality disorders.
投射測試被用來評估性格失常的病患。

projectively
〔 prə'dʒɛktɪvlɪ 〕

adv. 投影地
I bought a *projectively* textured map of Taiwan at the airport gift shop. 我在機場的禮品店買了一個紋理投影式的台灣地圖。

projectively textured

字根 ject

* 這六個字為 project 的衍生字，故含意與「投射」有關，重音皆在第二音節，讀/ɛ/。

interjection （ˌɪntə'dʒɛkʃən ）	*n.* 插入語（= *interpolation* ）；感嘆詞（= *exclamation* ） His rude *interjection* of the President's speech resulted in several shouts of "Shut up!" from others in the crowd. 他無禮地打斷總統演講，導致人群中的其他人大喊「閉嘴！」。
interjectional （ˌɪntə'dʒɛkʃənḷ ）	*adj.* 插入的 We ignored Roger's *interjectional* observation and continued listening to Bruce's story. 我們不理會羅傑突然插入的意見，繼續聽布魯斯的故事。
interjectory （ˌɪntə'dʒɛktərɪ ）	*adj.* 插入的（= *interjectional* ） Tammy's *interjectory* remarks drew applause from the audience. 泰咪突然插入的評論贏得了觀眾的掌聲。

```
inter  +  ject  +  ory
  |         |        |
between  +  throw  +  adj.
```

interjacent （ˌɪntə'dʒesənt ）	*adj.* 在中間的（= *medial* ） Before another meeting scheduled in the afternoon, John took an *interjacent* nap. 在下午排定的另一場會議之前，約翰利用中間時間睡個午覺。
interjacence （ˌɪntə'dʒesəns ）	*n.* 在中間（= *interjacency* ） The economy seemed to recover during the *interjacence* of the two wars. 在兩場戰爭的空檔時期，經濟似乎有復甦。

```
inter  +  jac  +  ence
  |        |       |
between  +  throw  +  n.
```
jac 是字根 ject 的變化型。

interjacency （ˌɪntə'dʒesənsɪ ）	*n.* 在中間 The cities of St. Paul and Minneapolis are divided by the *interjacency* of the Mississippi River. 聖保羅市和明尼阿波利斯市中間隔了密西西比河。

* 這六個字為 interject 的衍生字，其中前三個的字根為 ject，後三個的字根為 ject 的變化型 jac。

字根 ject

Exercise : Choose the correct answer.

1. The proposal to build a nuclear plant is _____ to young people.
   - (A) portly
   - (B) injectable
   - (C) ejective
   - (D) objectionable

2. The program was a(n) _____ failure.
   - (A) rejective
   - (B) interjectional
   - (C) abject
   - (D) interjacent

3. The lawyer _____ to the testimony of the witness.
   - (A) objected
   - (B) injected
   - (C) preferred
   - (D) dejected

4. The doctor prescribed three _____.
   - (A) abjections
   - (B) injections
   - (C) objectivities
   - (D) objectifications

5. He was forcibly _____ from the nightclub.
   - (A) rejected
   - (B) projected
   - (C) ejected
   - (D) interjected

6. The memory of Kiki's _____ of his love haunts Philip to this day.
   - (A) injection
   - (B) rejection
   - (C) ejectment
   - (D) dejection

7. My opinion of the matter is purely _____.
   - (A) projective
   - (B) impending
   - (C) disposable
   - (D) subjective

8. Our study will focus on the _____ of memory.
   (A) subjectivity　　　　(B) interjacence
   (C) ejaculation　　　　 (D) purpose

9. Mary sat alone and _____ in the darkened room.
   (A) supposed　　　　　(B) dejected
   (C) abjectly　　　　　 (D) objectlessly

10. The student council voted to _____ the plan.
   (A) reject　　　　　　(B) deport
   (C) assign　　　　　　(D) contain

11. The announcer's _____ in the commentary were not appropriate.
   (A) interjacency　　　　(B) objection
   (C) interjections　　　　(D) superposition

12. Lee volunteered to oversee the _____.
   (A) ejection　　　　　(B) independence
   (C) propeller　　　　　(D) project

13. It is difficult for parents to be _____ critics of their children's behavior.
   (A) contractual　　　　(B) objective
   (C) tractable　　　　　(D) distracted

14. Bill put his hands in his pockets and _____ left the room.
   (A) dejectedly　　　　(B) distractingly
   (C) extensively　　　　(D) reportedly

15. Oscar's _____ comments were not appreciated by the committee.
   (A) interjectory　　　　(B) compulsory
   (C) reportorial　　　　(D) comportable

字根 ject

字彙測驗詳解

1. (**D**) 蓋核能電廠的提案引起年輕人的<u>反對</u>。
   (A) portly〔'portlɪ〕*adj.* 肥胖的
   (B) injectable〔ɪn'dʒɛktəbl̩〕*adj.* 可注射的
   (C) ejective〔ɪ'dʒɛktɪv〕*adj.* 噴出的
   (D) *objectionable*〔əb'dʒɛkʃənəbl̩〕*adj.* 會引起反對的；
       令人討厭的

2. (**C**) 這個計畫是個很悲慘的失敗。
   (A) rejective〔rɪ'dʒɛktɪv〕*adj.* 拒絕的
   (B) interjectional〔͵ɪntɚ'dʒɛkʃənl̩〕*adj.* 插入的
   (C) *abject*〔æb'dʒɛkt〕*adj.* 可憐的
   (D) interjacent〔͵ɪntɚ'dʒesənt〕*adj.* 在中間的
   program〔'progræm〕*n.* 節目；計畫

3. (**A**) 這個律師<u>反對</u>這個目擊者的證詞。
   (A) *object*〔əb'dʒɛkt〕*v.* 反對 < *to* >
   (B) inject〔ɪn'dʒɛkt〕*v.* 注射
   (C) prefer〔prɪ'fɝ〕*v.* 比較喜歡
   (D) deject〔dɪ'dʒɛkt〕*v.* 使沮喪
   testimony〔'tɛstə͵monɪ〕*n.* 證詞   witness〔'wɪtnəs〕*n.* 目擊者

4. (**B**) 醫生開了三支<u>注射</u>液的處方。
   (A) abjection〔æb'dʒɛkʃən〕*n.* 落魄；羞辱
   (B) *injection*〔ɪn'dʒɛkʃən〕*n.* 注射
   (C) objectivity〔͵ɑbdʒɛk'tɪvətɪ〕*n.* 客觀性
   (D) objectification〔əb͵dʒɛktəfə'keʃən〕*n.* 具體化；物化

5. (**C**) 他被強制地<u>逐出</u>夜總會。
   (A) reject〔rɪ'dʒɛkt〕*v.* 拒絕
   (B) project〔prə'dʒɛkt〕*v.* 投射
   (C) *eject*〔ɪ'dʒɛkt〕*v.* 噴出；逐出
   (D) interject〔͵ɪntɚ'dʒɛkt〕*v.* 突然插（話）
   forcibly〔'forsəblɪ〕*adv.* 強制地

nightclub

6. (**B**) 琦琦拒絕菲利浦的愛意，這段回憶至今還一直縈繞在他的腦海中。
  (A) injection〔 ɪn'dʒɛkʃən 〕 *n.* 注射
  (B) *rejection*〔 rɪ'dʒɛkʃən 〕 *n.* 拒絕
  (C) ejectment〔 ɪ'dʒɛktmənt 〕 *n.* 噴出
  (D) dejection〔 dɪ'dʒɛkʃən 〕 *n.* 沮喪
  haunt〔 hɔnt 〕 *v.* 纏繞；縈繞　　*to this day* 時到今天

7. (**D**) 我對這件事的看法是完全主觀的。
  (A) projective〔 prə'dʒɛktɪv 〕 *adj.* 投影的
  (B) impending〔 ɪm'pɛndɪŋ 〕 *adj.* 即將來臨的
  (C) disposable〔 dɪ'spozəbl̩ 〕 *adj.* 用完即丟的
  (D) *subjective*〔 səb'dʒɛktɪv 〕 *adj.* 主觀的
  purely〔'pjʊrlɪ 〕 *adv.* 完全地

8. (**A**) 我們的研究將會著重在記憶的主觀性。
  (A) *subjectivity*〔 ˌsʌbdʒɛk'tɪvətɪ 〕 *n.* 主觀性
  (B) interjacence〔 ˌɪntə'dʒesəns 〕 *n.* 在中間
  (C) ejaculation〔 ɪˌdʒækjə'leʃən 〕 *n.* 射出；突然的叫聲
  (D) purpose〔'pɝpəs 〕 *n.* 目的
  study〔'stʌdɪ 〕 *n.* 研究　　*focus on* 專注於

9. (**B**) 瑪莉獨自坐在黑暗的房間裡，感到很沮喪。
  (A) supposed〔 sə'pozd 〕 *adj.* 想像的
  (B) *dejected*〔 dɪ'dʒɛktɪd 〕 *adj.* 沮喪的
  (C) abjectly〔 æb'dʒɛktlɪ 〕 *adv.* 可憐地
  (D) objectlessly〔'ɑbdʒɛktlɪslɪ 〕 *adv.* 無目的地
  darkened〔'dɑrkənd 〕 *adj.* 黑暗的；沒有燈光的

dejected

10. (**A**) 學生會投票拒絕這個計畫。
  (A) *reject*〔 rɪ'dʒɛkt 〕 *v.* 拒絕
  (B) deport〔 dɪ'port 〕 *v.* 驅逐出境
  (C) assign〔 ə'saɪn 〕 *v.* 指派
  (D) contain〔 kən'ten 〕 *v.* 包含
  student council 學生會　　vote〔 vot 〕 *v.* 投票

11. (C) 播報員在實況轉播時所插的話很不適當。
    (A) interjacency〔͵ɪntɚ'dʒɛsənsɪ〕*n.* 在中間
    (B) objection〔əb'dʒɛkʃən〕*n.* 反對
    (C) *interjection*〔͵ɪntɚ'dʒɛkʃən〕*n.* 插入語
    (D) superposition〔͵supɚpə'zɪʃən〕*n.* 重疊
    announcer〔ə'naʊnsɚ〕*n.* 播報員
    commentary〔'kɑmən͵tɛrɪ〕*n.* 評論;實況轉播
    appropriate〔ə'proprɪɪt〕*adj.* 適當的

announcer

12. (D) 李自願監督這項計劃。
    (A) ejection〔ɪ'dʒɛkʃən〕*n.* 噴出;逐出
    (B) independence〔͵ɪndɪ'pɛndəns〕*n.* 獨立
    (C) propeller〔prə'pɛlɚ〕*n.* 推進器;螺旋槳
    (D) *project*〔'prɑdʒɛkt〕*n.* 計劃
    volunteer〔͵vɑlən'tɪr〕*v.* 自願　　oversee〔'ovɚ'si〕*v.* 監督

13. (B) 要父母對孩子的行為做客觀的評論是困難的。
    (A) contractual〔kən'træktʃʊəl〕*adj.* 契約的
    (B) *objective*〔əb'dʒɛktɪv〕*adj.* 客觀的
    (C) tractable〔'træktəbḷ〕*adj.* 溫順的
    (D) distracted〔dɪ'stræktɪd〕*adj.* 分心的
    critic〔'krɪtɪk〕*n.* 評論者

14. (A) 比爾把手放在口袋裏,沮喪地離開房間。
    (A) *dejectedly*〔dɪ'dʒɛktɪdlɪ〕*adv.* 沮喪地
    (B) distractingly〔dɪ'stræktɪŋlɪ〕*adv.* 令人分心地
    (C) extensively〔ɪk'stɛnsɪvlɪ〕*adv.* 廣泛地
    (D) reportedly〔rɪ'portɪdlɪ〕*adv.* 據說

15. (A) 奧斯卡插入的評論委員會並不欣賞。
    (A) *interjectory*〔͵ɪntɚ'dʒɛktərɪ〕*adj.* 插入的
    (B) compulsory〔kəm'pʌlsərɪ〕*adj.* 強制的;義務的
    (C) reportorial〔͵rɛpɚ'torɪəl〕*adj.* 記者的
    (D) comportable〔kəm'portəbḷ〕*adj.* 合適的
    comment〔'kɑmɛnt〕*n.* 評論　　appreciate〔ə'priʃɪ͵et〕*v.* 欣賞

請連中文一起背，背至65秒內，終生不忘。 ✦

1

abject	可憐的
object	反對
subject	使服從
inject	注射
eject	噴出
deject	使沮喪
reject	拒絕
project	投射
interject	突然插話

【劉毅老師的話】

　　第一組是核心單字，先背熟後，再背其他的。

2

abjectly	可憐地
abjection	落魄
objector	反對者
objection	反對
objectionable	會引起反對的
objectless	無目的的
objective	客觀的
objectivity	客觀性

objectivate	使具體化
objectify	使具體化
objectification	具體化
subjection	服從
subjective	主觀的
subjectivity	主觀性

字根 ject

3

injector	注射者
injection	注射
injectable	可注射的
ejection	噴出
ejective	噴出的
ejectment	噴出

ejector	驅逐者
ejaculate	射出
ejaculation	射出
dejected	沮喪的
dejectedly	沮喪地
dejection	沮喪

字根 ject

4

rejection	拒絕
rejecter	拒絕者
rejectee	遭拒絕者
rejective	拒絕的
rejectionist	拒絕承認他人的
rejectamenta	廢物

projectile	發射物
projection	計劃
projectionist	放映師
projector	投影機
projective	投影的
projectively	投影地

interjection	插入語
interjectional	插入的
interjectory	插入的
interjacent	在中間的
interjacence	在中間
interjacency	在中間

※ 本頁可影印後，隨身攜帶，方便背誦。

Group 13 字根 *dict*

目標： ① 先將51個字放入短期記憶。
②加快速度至42秒之內，成為長期記憶。

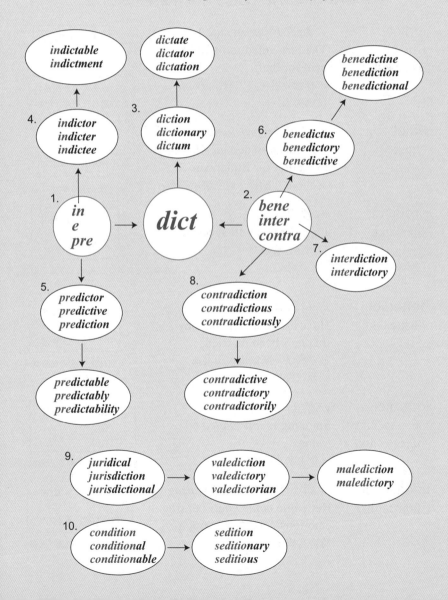

1. 字根 *dict* 核心單字

字根 dict 表示 say「說」，核心單字有 6 個，背熟至 3 秒之內，可成爲長期記憶，才可再背下一組。

---

indict
〔 ɪn'daɪt 〕
*注意發音

v. 起訴（= *prosecute*）
The jury voted to *indict* the man for theft.
陪審團投票決定以竊盜罪起訴這個男人。

> in + dict
> |　　|
> *into* + *say*

說出你心中隱藏的過錯，即是「控訴」

---

edict
〔 'idɪkt 〕

n. 詔書（= *proclamation*）；命令
The queen issued an *edict* of toleration for Buddhism.
女皇發布了詔書，宣布接納佛教。

> e + dict
> |　　|
> *out* + *say*

說出來的話，即是「命令」

---

predict[4]
〔 prɪ'dɪkt 〕

v. 預測
I *predict* you will succeed.
我預測你會成功。

> pre + dict
> |　　|
> *before* + *say*

在事情發生前先說出來，即是「預測」

---

benedict
〔 'bɛnə,dɪkt 〕

n. 已婚男子
He is called a *benedict* now that he's been married.
他結婚了，所以現在大家都叫他已婚男子。

> bene + dict
> |　　|
> *well* + *say*

看到他就要跟他說好話，即是「新婚男子」

---

interdict
〔 *v.* ,ɪntɚ'dɪkt
　n. 'ɪntɚ,dɪkt 〕

v. 禁止　*n.* 禁止
Smoking is *interdicted* on trains.
火車上禁止吸煙。

> inter + dict
> |　　　|
> *between* + *say*

插入空檔說話，即是「限制」

---

contradict[6]
〔 ,kɑntrə'dɪkt 〕

v. 與…矛盾；反駁（= *disagree*）
Her smile *contradicts* her true emotions. 她的笑容和她眞實的情緒互相矛盾。

> contra + dict
> |　　　|
> *contrary* + *say*

說相反的話，即是「反駁」

---

2. diction-dictionary-dictum

這一組有 6 個字，3 個一組一起背，可先背 3 個
再背 3 個，背熟至 3 秒之內，變成直覺。

diction
〔'dɪkʃən 〕

n. 措辭；用字（ = *wording* ）
This writing exercise will improve
your *diction*.
這個寫作練習可以改善你的遣詞用字。

```
dict + ion
  |      |
 say  +  n.
```

dictionary[2]
〔'dɪkʃən,ɛrɪ 〕

n. 字典
I borrowed Jamie's *dictionary*.　我借了傑米的字典。

dictum
〔'dɪktəm 〕

n. 格言；(專家的) 意見（ = *statement* ）
I could not accept his *dictum* that
"Fear is our greatest enemy."
我不能接受他的格言：「恐懼是我們
最大的敵人。」

```
dict + um
  |     |
 say  + n.
```

dictate[6]
〔'dɪk,tet , dɪk'tet 〕

v. 使聽寫
He will *dictate* the letter to
his assistant.
他會對他的助理口授這封信。

```
dict + ate
  |     |
 say  + v.
```

dictator[6]
〔 dɪk'tetɚ 〕

n. 獨裁者（ = *tyrant* ）；口授者
The *dictator* is known for issuing
cruel punishments to his critics.
這個獨裁者以對他的批判者處以殘酷
的處罰而著名。

```
dict + ator
  |     |
 say  + n.
```

發佈命令的人

dictation[6]
〔 dɪk'teʃən 〕

n. 聽寫；口述
His *dictation* skills have gotten noticeably worse.
他聽寫的技巧明顯變差了。

字根 dict

3. indictor-indicter-indictee

　　這一組有 11 個字，分成二組，第一組是 indict 的
衍生字，第二組是 predict 的衍生字，背熟至 7 秒之內，
變成直覺。

indictor
〔 ɪn'daɪtɚ 〕

n. 起訴者
The defendant rose to face his *indictors*.
被告站起來面對他的起訴者。

indicter
〔 ɪn'daɪtɚ 〕

n. 起訴者（ = *indictor* ）
Some of his *indicters* called
him a traitor.
有一些他的起訴者稱他為叛國賊。

```
indict +  er
  │       │
 起訴  +主動者
```

indictee
〔 ˌɪndaɪt'i 〕

n. 被告（ = *defendant* ）
The *indictee* had been arrested for robbery.
這名被告因為搶劫而被捕。

```
indict +  ee
  │       │
 起訴  +被動者
```

字根
dict

indictable
〔 ɪn'daɪtəbḷ 〕

adj. 可起訴的（ = *chargeable* ）
What you did could be *indictable*.
你所做的事可以被起訴。

```
indict + able
  │       │
 起訴  +可～的
```

indictment
〔 ɪn'daɪtmənt 〕

n. 起訴（ = *accusation* ）
The *indictment* claimed Torres was the ringleader
of a street gang.
這份起訴書聲稱托列斯為街頭幫派的首領。

　*這組單字為 indict〔 ɪn'daɪt 〕的衍生字，故含意與「起訴」有關，並注
意 c 皆不發音，且第二個 i 皆發 /aɪ/ 的音。

predictor
〔 prɪ'dɪktə 〕

n. 預測者（ = *forecaster* ）

"Scientific Kids Height *Predictor*" is a gadget allows you to predict the height of your children.

「孩童身高科學預測器」是
個可以讓你預測孩子未來的
身高的小工具。

```
pre    + dict + or
 |         |     |
before +  say  +  n.
```

predictive
〔 prɪ'dɪktɪv 〕

adj. 預言的

Some people think dreams have *predictive* value.

有些人認為夢有預測的價值。

prediction[6]
〔 prɪ'dɪkʃən 〕

n. 預測（ = *forecast* ）

Harry placed his bet according to my *prediction*.

哈利依據我的預測下賭注。

```
predict + ion
   |        |
  預測   +  n.
```

predictable
〔 prɪ'dɪktəbḷ 〕

adj. 可預測的（ = *foreseeable* ）

Zoe's angry reaction was *predictable*.

柔伊生氣的反應是可以預測的。

```
predict + able
   |        |
  預測   + 可~的
```

predictably
〔 prɪ'dɪktəblɪ 〕

adv. 如所預料；不出所料（ = *as expected* ）

She was *predictably* late for the meeting.

不出所料，她開會又遲到了。

predictability
〔 prɪ,dɪktə'bɪlətɪ 〕

n. 可預測性

A project manager is responsible for the *predictability* and efficiency of a project.

一名專案經理必須負責專案中的可預測性和效率。

```
predict + ability
   |         |
  預測   +  能力
```

4. *Benedictus-benedictory-benedictive*

這一組有 14 個字，分成三組，第一組是 benedict 的衍生字，第二組是 interdict 的衍生字，第三組是 contradict 的衍生字，背熟至 8 秒之內，變成直覺。

Benedictus
(ˌbɛnɪˈdɪktəs)

n. 天主教彌撒樂曲
The church choir sang a *Benedictus*.
教堂的唱詩班唱了天主教彌撒樂曲。

benedictory
(ˌbɛnəˈdɪktərɪ)

adj. 祝福的
The priest made a *benedictory* speech.
牧師做了祝福的演說。

```
bene + dict + ory
 |      |     |
well +  say + adj.
```
說好聽的話，即是「祝福的」

benedictive
(ˌbɛnəˈdɪktɪv)

adj. 賜福的
He was a *benedictive* speaker.　他是個賜福的演說家。

Benedictine
(ˌbɛnəˈdɪktɪn)

adj. 本篤會的　*n.* 本篤會修士
Jerome is a *Benedictine* monk.
傑洛米是個本篤會的修士。

benediction
(ˌbɛnəˈdɪkʃən)

n. 祝福的祈禱 (= *blessing*)
He closed the ceremony with a *benediction* for world peace.
他以祈求世界和平的祝福祈禱結束這個儀式。

```
bene + diction
 |       |
well +   say
```

benedictional
(ˌbɛnəˈdɪkʃənəl)

adj. 使人幸福的
This is the *benedictional* part of the ceremony.
這是這個儀式中令人感到幸福的部份。

* 字首 bene 表 well，其他常見的字還有：**bene**fit *n.* 利益；**bene**ficial *adj.* 有益的；**bene**ficient *adj.* 慈善的

interdiction
〔͵ɪntɚ'dɪkʃən〕

n. 禁止 (= *ban*)
The government's *interdiction* of alcoholic
beverages was widely ignored by the public.
政府對酒類飲料的禁令普遍被大眾所忽視。

interdictory
〔͵ɪntɚ'dɪktərɪ〕

adj. 禁止的
"Do not enter" is an example
of an *interdictory* sign.
「禁止進入」是禁止標誌
的一個範例。

> * 這兩個字爲 interdict 的衍生字，故意思皆與「禁止」有關，且重音皆在
> 字根 dict 上。

contradiction[6]
〔͵kɑntrə'dɪkʃən〕

n. 矛盾 (= *conflict*)；反駁
There is a *contradiction* between what you have
said and what you have done.
你所說的和你所做的互相矛盾。

contradictious
〔͵kɑntrə'dɪkʃəs〕

adj. 自相矛盾的；愛反駁的
We were confused by the teacher's *contradictious*
explanation.
我們被老師自相矛盾的解說搞混了。

contra	+ dict	+ ious
against	+ *say*	+ *adj.*

contradictiously
〔͵kɑntrə'dɪkʃəslɪ〕

adv. 愛反駁地；矛盾地
"No, I won't do it, "the boy declared
contradictiously.
這個男孩反駁地表示「不，我不會做的。」

字根 dict

contradictive
(͵kɑntrə'dɪktɪv)

adj. 矛盾的；愛反駁的
Monopolies are *contradictive* to the principles of capitalism.
獨占和資本主義的原則互相矛盾。

contradictory
(͵kɑntrə'dɪktərɪ)

adj. 矛盾的（= *contradicting*）
The two witnesses gave *contradictory* accounts of the accident.
這兩個目擊者對事故的描述互相矛盾。

```
contra + dict + ory
   |       |      |
against +  say  + adj.
```

contradictorily
(͵kɑntrə'dɪktərəlɪ)

adv. 反駁地（= *conflictingly*）
Steve spoke *contradictorily* with his supervisor.
史提夫以反駁的口氣跟他的主管說話。

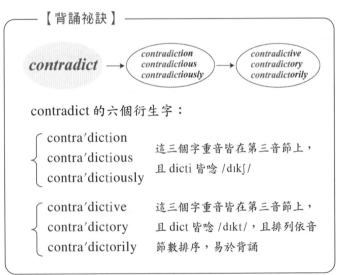

【背誦祕訣】

contradict → contradiction / contradictious / contradictiously → contradictive / contradictory / contradictorily

contradict 的六個衍生字：

contra'diction
contra'dictious   這三個字重音皆在第三音節上，
contra'dictiously   且 dicti 皆唸 /dɪkʃ/

contra'dictive   這三個字重音皆在第三音節上，
contra'dictory   且 dict 皆唸 /dɪkt/，且排列依音
contra'dictorily   節數排序，易於背誦

字根 dict

5. *juridical-jurisdiction-jurisdictional*

這一組有 8 個字，分成三組，第一組是 juri 為首的
dict 衍生字，第二組是 vale 為首的 dict 衍生字，第三
組是 male 的 dict 衍生字，背熟至 5 秒之內，變成直覺。

juridical
〔 dʒʊˈrɪdɪkḷ 〕

adj. 司法的
The police do not have
juridical powers.
警方沒有司法上的權力。

```
juri + dic + al
  |     |    |
 law + say + adj.
```
法律說的話，即是「司法上的」

jurisdiction
〔 ˌdʒʊrɪsˈdɪkʃən 〕

n. 司法權；管轄權 (= *authority*)
The island nation of Puerto Rico is under U.S.
jurisdiction. 波多黎各這個島國是美國的管轄區域。

```
juris + dict + ion
   |      |     |
  law +  say +  n.
```
法律上說的範圍，即是「管轄權」

jurisdictional
〔 ˌdʒʊrɪsˈdɪkʃənḷ 〕

adj. 管轄權的 (= *administrative*)
The proposal to redraw *jurisdictional* boundaries
was approved by the Senate.
重新畫分管轄範圍的提案已得到參議院的同意。

valediction
〔 ˌvæləˈdɪkʃən 〕

n. 告別；告別辭
Irene waved her hand in
valediction. 艾琳揮手告別。

```
vale   + dict + ion
  |       |     |
farewell + say +  n.
```
告別時說的話，即是「告別辭」

valedictory
〔 ˌvæləˈdɪktərɪ 〕

adj. 告別的 (= *farewell*)
He gave a *valedictory* speech. 他發表了告別演說。

valedictorian
〔 ˌvælədɪkˈtorɪən 〕

n. (致告別辭的) 畢業生代表
Ricky is the *valedictorian*
of his graduating class.
瑞奇是畢業班致告別辭的代表。

```
vale + dict + orian
  |      |      |
 告別 + say +  人
```
畢業典禮時，代表上台
致告別辭的畢業生

字根 dict

malediction
〔͵mælə'dɪkʃən〕

n. 詛咒（= *curse*）；誹謗
The shaman announced an evil *malediction* upon the villagers.
這個巫師對村民唸了邪惡的詛咒。

```
male + dict + ion
 |      |     |
bad  + say  + n.        說壞事，即是「詛咒」
```

maledictory
〔͵mælə'dɪktərɪ〕

adj. 詛咒的；壞話的
You can't scare me with your *maledictory* threats.
你詛咒的威脅是嚇不到我的。

【劉毅老師的話】

　　知道了字根 dict 表示「說」的含意後，加入不同的字首形成新的單字，例如：

juris-diction　法律說的內容，就是「司法」
　|　　　　|
　law　　say

vale-diction　告別說的話，就是「告別辭」
　|　　　　|
farewell　say

這樣背單字的方法，不僅中文意思記得住，也不會拼錯字。

6. *condition-conditional-conditionable*

這一組有 6 個字，分成二組，皆為字根 dict 的變化
型 dit，背熟至 3 秒之內，變成直覺。

condition[3]
〔kənˈdɪʃən〕

n. 情況；條件   *v.* 調節
I will accept your offer on one *condition*.
只有在一種條件下，我才會接受你的提議。

con	+ dit +	ion
together	+ *say* +	*n.*

說「條件」要一起說，dit 是
字根 dict 的變化型。

conditional
〔kənˈdɪʃənḷ〕

adj. 附有條件的（ = *circumstantial* ）
Mother gave *conditional* consent to our party plans.
媽媽有條件地同意了我們的派對計畫。

conditionable
〔kənˈdɪʃənəbḷ〕

adj. 可調節的
It's so hot in the room because
the temperature is not
conditionable. 這房間很熱，因為溫度沒辦法調節。

condition +	able
調節	+ 可～的

sedition
〔sɪˈdɪʃən〕

n. 煽動（ = *agitation* ）
He was charged with an act
of *sedition*.
他因煽動行為而被控告。

se	+ dit +	ion
apart	+ *say* +	*n.*

說分散人心的話，即是「煽動」

seditionary
〔sɪˈdɪʃənˌɛrɪ〕

n. 煽動叛亂者
Michael claimed to be a *seditionary*.
麥可聲稱自己是個煽動叛亂者。

seditious
〔sɪˈdɪʃəs〕

adj. 煽動性的（ = *rebellious* ）
He was accused of distributing *seditious* literature.
他因發放煽動性的印刷品而被控告。

* 這六個字皆為字根 dict 的變化型 dit 的衍生字。

字根 dict

Exercise : Choose the correct answer. ✦

1. His _____ came true; we lost the game.
   (A) dictation   (B) appellation
   (C) benediction   (D) prediction

2. The judge _____ the doctor from practicing medicine.
   (A) indicted   (B) interdicted
   (C) predicted   (D) contradicted

3. We knew he was wrong, but nobody wanted to _____ him.
   (A) contradict   (B) edict
   (C) dictate   (D) benedict

4. The miners there worked in dreadful _____.
   (A) indictments   (B) dictionaries
   (C) predictabilities   (D) conditions

5. In most countries, possession of illegal drugs is a(n) _____ offense.
   (A) predictable   (B) conditionable
   (C) indictable   (D) interdictory

6. The President's televised _____ was watched by millions.
   (A) suspension   (B) valediction
   (C) transportation   (D) sedition

7. The prisoner's statement was _____ to the one he'd made earlier.
   (A) seditionary   (B) maledictory
   (C) valedictory   (D) contradictory

字根 dict

8. Many critics say the film is an _____ of our money-oriented
   society.
   (A) indictment   (B) indictor
   (C) indicter   (D) indictee

9. "Blood is thicker than water" is an old _____.
   (A) valediction   (B) dictum
   (C) jurisdiction   (D) malediction

10. Tommy _____ ordered a medium-rare steak.
    (A) predictably   (B) contradictorily
    (C) sportively   (D) distractingly

11. A writer's "style" is a combination of structure, _____
    and figures of speech.
    (A) deposition   (B) dictum
    (C) diction   (D) depression

12. Without official _____, we expect the problem to get
    worse.
    (A) introduction   (B) production
    (C) malediction   (D) interdiction

13. Argentina's last _____ was sentenced to 25 years in prison.
    (A) predictor   (B) dictator
    (C) tractor   (D) objector

14. British police have no _____ over foreign bank accounts.
    (A) jurisdiction   (B) objectification
    (C) composition   (D) extraction

15. There seems to be a _____ between her words and actions.
    (A) contradiction   (B) contraction
    (C) conference   (D) contention

字根 dict

字彙測驗詳解

1. (**D**) 他的<u>預言</u>成眞了；我們輸了這場比賽。
    (A) dictation〔dɪkˋteʃən〕*n.* 聽寫；口述
    (B) appellation〔͵æpəˋleʃən〕*n.* 名稱；稱呼
    (C) benediction〔͵bɛnəˋdɪkʃən〕*n.* 祝福的祈禱
    (D) *prediction*〔prɪˋdɪkʃən〕*n.* 預言

2. (**B**) 法官<u>禁止</u>這名醫生行醫。
    (A) indict〔ɪnˋdaɪt〕*v.* 起訴
    (B) *interdict*〔͵ɪntɚˋdɪkt〕*v.* 禁止
    (C) predict〔prɪˋdɪkt〕*v.* 預測
    (D) contradict〔͵kɑntrəˋdɪkt〕*v.* 與～矛盾；反駁

predict

3. (**A**) 我們知道他錯了，但是沒有人想<u>反駁</u>他。
    (A) *contradict*〔͵kɑntrəˋdɪkt〕*v.* 與～矛盾；反駁
    (B) edict〔ˋidɪkt〕*n.* 詔書；命令
    (C) dictate〔dɪkˋtet〕*v.* 使聽寫
    (D) benedict〔ˋbɛnə͵dɪkt〕*n.* 已婚男子

4. (**D**) 那裡的礦工們在惡劣的<u>條件</u>下工作。
    (A) indictment〔ɪnˋdaɪtmənt〕*n.* 起訴
    (B) dictionary〔ˋdɪkʃən͵ɛrɪ〕*n.* 字典
    (C) predictability〔prɪ͵dɪktəˋbɪlətɪ〕*n.* 可預測性
    (D) *condition*〔kənˋdɪʃən〕*n.* 情況；條件

dictionary

5. (**C**) 在大部分的國家，持有非法藥物是<u>刑事罪</u>。
    (A) predictable〔prɪˋdɪktəbḷ〕*adj.* 可預測的
    (B) conditionable〔kənˋdɪʃənəbḷ〕*adj.* 可調節的
    (C) *indictable*〔ɪnˋdaɪtəbḷ〕*adj.* 可起訴的
        indictable offense 可起訴的罪；刑事罪
    (D) interdictory〔͵ɪntɚˋdɪktərɪ〕*adj.* 禁止的
    possession〔pəˋzɛʃən〕*n.* 擁有   illegal〔ɪˋligḷ〕*adj.* 非法的
    drug〔drʌg〕*n.* 藥物；毒品   offense〔əˋfɛns〕*n.* 犯罪

6. (**B**) 總統的電視<u>告別</u>演說，有數百萬人收看。

televised

    (A) suspension〔sə'spɛnʃən〕*n.* 懸掛；暫停

    (B) *valediction*〔͵vælə'dɪkʃən〕*n.* 告別；告別辭

    (C) transportation〔͵trænspə'teʃən〕*n.* 運輸；運輸工具

    (D) sedition〔sɪ'dɪʃən〕*n.* 煽動

    televised〔'tɛlə͵vaɪzd〕*adj.* 電視轉播的

7. (**D**) 那個囚犯的供詞與之前所說的<u>相矛盾</u>。

prisoner

    (A) seditionary〔sɪ'dɪʃən͵ɛrɪ〕*n.* 煽動叛亂者

    (B) maledictory〔͵mælə'dɪktərɪ〕*adj.* 詛咒的

    (C) valedictory〔͵vælɪ'dɪktərɪ〕*adj.* 告別的

    (D) *contradictory*〔͵kɑntrə'dɪktərɪ〕*adj.* 矛盾的

8. (**A**) 很多評論家說，這部電影是在<u>控訴</u>我們以金錢為導向的社會。

    (A) *indictment*〔ɪn'daɪtmənt〕*n.* 起訴；控告

    (B) indictor〔ɪn'daɪtɚ〕*n.* 起訴者

    (C) indicter〔ɪn'daɪtɚ〕*n.* 起訴者

    (D) indictee〔͵ɪndaɪt'i〕*n.* 被告

    critic〔'krɪtɪk〕*n.* 評論家

    money-oriented 以金錢為導向的

9. (**B**) 「血濃於水」是個古老的<u>格言</u>。

    (A) valediction〔͵vælə'dɪkʃən〕*n.* 告別

    (B) *dictum*〔'dɪktəm〕*n.* 格言

    (C) jurisdiction〔͵dʒurɪs'dɪkʃən〕*n.* 司法權

    (D) malediction〔͵mælə'dɪkʃən〕*n.* 詛咒

10. (**A**) <u>不出所料</u>地，湯米點了一客四分熟的牛排。

    (A) *predictably*〔prɪ'dɪktəblɪ〕*adv.* 如所預料；不出所料

    (B) contradictorily〔͵kɑntrə'dɪktərəlɪ〕*adv.* 反駁地

    (C) sportively〔'sportɪvlɪ〕*adv.* 開玩笑地

    (D) distractingly〔dɪ'stræktɪŋlɪ〕*adv.* 令人分心地

    medium-rare 四分熟　　steak〔stek〕*n.* 牛排

字根 dict

11. (**C**) 一個作者的「風格」結合了結構，<u>措辭</u>和修辭。

    (A) deposition〔͵dɛpə'zɪʃən〕*n.* 罷免

    (B) dictum〔'dɪktəm〕*n.* 格言；(專家的) 意見

    (C) *diction*〔'dɪkʃən〕*n.* 措辭；用字

    (D) depression〔dɪ'prɛʃən〕*n.* 沮喪

    combination〔͵kambə'neʃən〕*n.* 結合

    structure〔'strʌktʃɚ〕*n.* 結構   ***figure of speech*** 修辭

12. (**D**) 沒有官方的<u>禁止</u>，我們預期問題會惡化。

    (A) introduction〔͵ɪntrə'dʌkʃən〕*n.* 介紹

    (B) production〔prə'dʌkʃən〕*n.* 生產；製造

    (C) malediction〔͵mælə'dɪkʃən〕*n.* 詛咒

    (D) *interdiction*〔͵ɪntɚ'dɪkʃən〕*n.* 禁止

13. (**B**) 阿根廷最後一個<u>獨裁者</u>被判刑二十五年。

    (A) predictor〔prɪ'dɪktɚ〕*n.* 預言者

    (B) *dictator*〔dɪk'tetɚ〕*n.* 獨裁者

    (C) tractor〔'træktɚ〕*n.* 牽引機

    (D) objector〔əb'dʒɛktɚ〕*n.* 反對者

    Argentina〔͵ardʒən'tinə〕*n.* 阿根廷

    sentence〔'sɛntəns〕*v.* 判決

Argentina

14. (**A**) 英國警方對於外國銀行帳戶並無<u>司法管轄權</u>。

    (A) *jurisdiction*〔͵dʒurɪs'dɪkʃən〕*n.* 司法權；管轄權

    (B) objectification〔əb͵dʒɛktəfə'keʃən〕*n.* 具體化；物化

    (C) composition〔͵kampə'zɪʃən〕*n.* 組成；作文

    (D) extraction〔ɪk'strækʃən〕*n.* 拔出；抽出物

15. (**A**) 她的言行似乎<u>互相矛盾</u>。

    (A) *contradiction*〔͵kantrə'dɪkʃən〕*n.* 矛盾

    (B) contraction〔kən'trækʃən〕*n.* 收縮

    (C) conference〔'kanfərəns〕*n.* 會議

    (D) contention〔kən'tɛnʃən〕*n.* 爭論

請連中文一起背，背至65秒內，終生不忘。

1

indict	起訴
edict	詔書
predict	預測
benedict	已婚男子
interdict	禁止
contradict	與～矛盾

2

diction	措辭
dictionary	字典
dictum	格言
dictate	使聽寫
dictator	獨裁者
dictation	聽寫

3

indictor	起訴者
indicter	起訴者
indictee	被告
indictable	可起訴的
indictment	起訴

predictor	預測者
predictive	預言的
prediction	預測
predictable	可預測的
predictably	可預測地
predictability	可預測性

字根 dict

4

Benedictus　天主教彌撒樂曲
benedictory　　祝福的
benedictive　　賜福的

Benedictine　　本篤會的
benediction　　祝福的祈禱
benedictional　使人幸福的

interdiction　　禁止
interdictory　　禁止的

contradiction　　矛盾
contradictious　自相矛盾的
contradictiously　愛反駁地

contradictive　　矛盾的
contradictory　　矛盾的
contradictorily　反駁地

5

juridical　　司法的
jurisdiction　司法權
jurisdictional　管轄權的

valediction　告別辭
valedictory　告別的
valedictorian　畢業生代表

malediction　詛咒
maledictory　詛咒的

6

condition　　情況
conditional　　附有條件的
conditionable　可調節的

sedition　　煽動
seditionary　煽動叛亂者
seditious　　煽動性的

字根 dict

※ 本頁可影印後，隨身攜帶，方便背誦。

Group 14 字根 *sist; stitute*

目標： ① 先將56個字放入短期記憶。
② 加快速度至47秒之內，成為長期記憶。

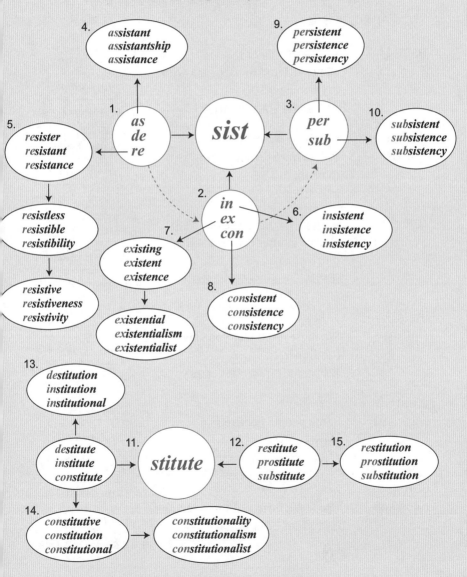

1. 字根 sist 核心單字

　　字根 sist 的意思是 stand「站」，核心單字有 9 個字，可先背 6 個，再背 3 個，背熟至 5 秒之內，可成爲長期記憶，才可再背下一組。

---

assist[3]
〔 ə'sɪst 〕

v. 幫助（ = *help* ）
James offered to *assist* me with my homework.
詹姆士提議要幫忙我做作業。

> as + sist
> |　　　|
> *to* + *stand*

站在你身邊，即是「幫助」

---

desist
〔 dɪ'zɪst 〕

v. 停止（ = *stop* ）
Please *desist* from ringing the bell.
請停止按鈴。

> de + sist
> |　　　|
> *away* + *stand*

站在旁邊，即是「停止」

---

resist[3]
〔 rɪ'zɪst 〕

v. 抵抗（ = *fight back* ）；抗拒
Norma couldn't *resist* another piece of cake.
諾瑪無法抗拒再吃另一塊蛋糕。

> re + sist
> |　　　|
> *against* + *stand*

站在反方向，即是「抵抗」

---

insist[2]
〔 ɪn'sɪst 〕

v. 堅持
We must *insist* that you stay for dinner.
我們必須堅持你留下來吃晚餐。

> in + sist
> |　　　|
> *on* + *stand*

站在上面不動，即是「堅持」

---

exist[2]
〔 ɪg'zɪst 〕

v. 存在
Some people believe that ghosts *exist*.
有人相信鬼是存在的。

> ex + ist
> |　　　|
> *out* + *stand*

站出來讓人看到，即是「存在」

---

consist[4]
〔 kən'sɪst 〕

v. 組成
The test *consists* of three sections.
這個考試由三個部份組成。

> con + sist
> |　　　|
> *all* + *stand*

通通站在一起，即是「組成」

persist[5]
〔 pəˋsɪst 〕

v. 堅持（= *insist* ）；持續（= *last* ）

You should see a doctor if those symptoms *persist*.

如果那些症狀持續的話，你就應該要去看醫生。

per	+	sist
through	+	stand

從頭到尾都站著，即是「堅持；持續」

subsist
〔 səbˋsɪst 〕

v. 生存（= *survive* ）

Conrad manages to *subsist* on one bowl of rice per day.

康拉德設法每天靠一碗飯過活。

sub	+	sist
under	+	stand

有人在下面站著撐住你，你就可以「生存」

【背誦祕訣】

這組單字為字根 sist 的核心單字

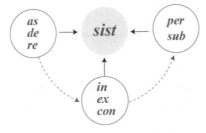

皆為兩音節，重音皆在第二音節，且讀
短母音 /ɪ/

字根 sist, stitute

2. *assistant-assistantship-assistance*

這一組有 12 個字，分成二組，第一組是 assist 的衍生字，
第二組是 resist 的衍生字，背熟至 7 秒之內，變成直覺。

assistant[2]
〔 ə'sɪstənt 〕

n. 助手（ = *helper* ）
adj. 幫助的；助理的
Lois was promoted to *assistant*
manager. 路易斯升職爲協理。

```
assist + ant
  |      |
 幫助  + adj., 人
```
幫助你的人，即是「助理」

assistantship
〔 ə'sɪstənt,ʃɪp 〕

n. 研究生助教獎學金（ = *scholarship* ）
Karl was awarded an *assistantship* at Harvard.
卡爾獲得哈佛的研究生助教獎學金。

assistance[4]
〔 ə'sɪstəns 〕

n. 幫助（ = *help* ）
I think I can manage without
your *assistance*.
我認爲不用你的幫助我也可以處理。

```
assist  + ance
  |        |
 幫助   +   n.
```

resister
〔 rɪ'zɪstɚ 〕

n. 抵抗者
The tax *resisters* organized a
protest march.
抗稅者組織了抗議遊行。

```
resist + er
  |       |
 抵抗  +   人
```

resistant[6]
〔 rɪ'zɪstənt 〕

adj. 抵抗的
The virus has proven *resistant* to the vaccines.
這種病毒已證實對疫苗產生抵抗性。

```
resist + ant
  |       |
 抵抗  +  adj.
```
注意這個字的字尾 ant 是表形容詞

resistance[4]
〔 rɪ'zɪstəns 〕

n. 抵抗
She made a stouter *resistance* than the thief had
anticipated. 她的抵抗比小偷預料的要頑強。

resistless
〔 rɪ'zɪstlɪs 〕

adj. 無法抵抗的（ = *irresistible* ）
He was *resistless* to her charms.
他無法抗拒她的魅力。

resistible
〔 rɪ'zɪstəbl̩ 〕

adj. 可抵抗的
My new jacket is *resistible*
to water.
我的新夾克是防水的。

```
resist + ible
   |       |
 抵抗  + 可～的
```

resistibility
〔 rɪˌzɪstə'bɪlətɪ 〕

n. 抵抗力
The *resistibility* of the virus to vaccines is starting
to worry health officials.
病毒對疫苗的抵抗力，開始使衛生官員擔心了。

resistive
〔 rɪ'zɪstɪv 〕

adj. 有抵抗力的（ = *resistant* ）
Sarah has always been *resistive* to change.
莎拉總是抗拒改變。

resistiveness
〔 rɪ'zɪstɪvnɪs 〕

n. 抵抗力（ = *resistance* ）
Harold refused to explain his *resistiveness* to the
proposal. 哈洛德拒絕解釋他對這提案的反抗。

```
resist + ive + ness
   |      |      |
  抗拒  + adj. +  n.     形容詞接 ness 形成抽象名詞
```

resistivity
〔 ˌrizɪs'tɪvətɪ 〕

n. 抵抗力
Nickel has the greatest *resistivity* to heat of
all metals.
鎳在所有金屬中，是最耐熱的。

3. insistent-insistence-insistency

這一組有 12 個字，分成三組，第一組是 insist 的衍生字，第二組是 exist 的衍生字，第三組是 consist 的衍生字，背熟至 7 秒之內，變成直覺。

insistent
〔 ɪn'sɪstənt 〕

adj. 堅持的
The *insistent* ringing of the telephone annoyed me a lot.
電話鈴響個不停讓我很困擾。

in +	sist +	ent
on +	stand+	*adj.*

insistence[6]
〔 ɪn'sɪstəns 〕

n. 堅持
The professor is well-known for his *insistence* on punctuality.
這個教授以他堅持準時而著名。

insistency
〔 ɪn'sɪstənsɪ 〕

n. 堅持（ = *insistence* ）
The public demand for national health care is growing in *insistency*.
大眾對全國醫療健保的要求已越來越堅持。

existing[2]
〔 ɪg'zɪstɪŋ 〕

adj. 現存的（ = *present* ）
A new building will replace the *existing* structure.
一個新的建築將會取代現有的建築。

existent
〔 ɪg'zɪstənt 〕

adj. 現存的（ = *existing* ; *current* ）
The company planned to improve *existent* products rather than focus on new developments.
公司計畫改善現有的產品，而非著重在新產品的研發上。

existence[3]
〔 ɪg'zɪstəns 〕

n. 生存
Global warming is threatening the *existence* of many plant and animal species.
全球暖化威脅了很多動植物物種的生存。

字根 sist, stitute

existential

〔͵ɛgzɪs'tɛnʃəl 〕

adj. 存在主義的

Jean-Paul Sarte was the leading *existential* philosopher of the 20th century.

保羅沙特是 20 世紀卓越的存在主義哲學家。

existentialism

〔͵ɛgzɪs'tɛnʃəl͵ɪzəm 〕

n. 存在主義

Existentialism is the idea that life is a series of personal choices.

存在主義的觀念是,「人生是一連串的個人選擇」。

```
exist + ent + ial + ism
  |      |      |      |
 存在  + adj. + adj. + 主義
```

existentialist

〔͵ɛgzɪs'tɛnʃəlɪst 〕

n. 存在主義者

Many *existentialists* regard traditional philosophy as too abstract.

很多的存在主義學家認為傳統的哲學太抽象了。

* 這三個字為 exist 的衍生字,其中文意思都與「存在主義」有關。

consistent[4]

〔 kən'sɪstənt 〕

adj. 一致的 (= *coherent*)

The testimony of the witness was *consistent* with the facts. 這個目擊證人的證詞與事實一致。

```
con    + sist  + ent
  |        |       |
together + stand + adj.      站在一起,即為「一致」
```

consistence

〔 kən'sɪstəns 〕

n. 一致;堅持

Her *consistence* of the idea won them over.

她對這個想法的堅持說服了他們。

consistency

〔 kən'sɪstənsɪ 〕

n. 一致 (= *consistence*)

Your argument lacks *consistency*.

你的論點缺乏一致性。

字根 sist, stitute

4. *persistent-persistence-persistency*

這一組有 6 個字，分成二組，第一組是 persist 的衍生字，
第二組是 subsist 的衍生字，背熟至 3 秒之內，變成直覺。

persistent[6]
〔 pə'sɪstənt 〕

adj. 堅持的；持續的
The *persistent* rain caused major
flooding in rural areas.
持續的降雨造成鄉村地區大淹水。

persist	+	ent
堅持	+	*adj.*

persistence[6]
〔 pə'sɪstəns 〕

n. 堅持
Gary credits most of his success
to sheer *persistence*.
蓋瑞將他大部分的成功歸因於完全的堅持。

persist	+	ence
堅持	+	*n.*

persistency
〔 pə'sɪstənsɪ 〕

n. 堅持；持久性（ = *persistence* ）
Chemical weapons are graded by their *persistency*.
化學武器被按它們的持久程度分級。

subsistent
〔 səb'sɪstənt 〕

adj. 生存的
The farmer's family is *subsistent*
on the crops he grows.
這農夫一家人是靠他所種植的穀物為生。

subsist	+	ent
生存	+	*adj.*

subsistence
〔 səb'sɪstəns 〕

n. 生存；生計（ = *existence* ）
Farming is a hard life of
subsistence.
農耕是一種辛苦的生計方式。

subsist	+	ence
生存	+	*n.*

subsistency
〔 səb'sɪstənsɪ 〕

n. 生計（ = *subsistence* ）
The father worked three jobs to provide for his
family's *subsistency*.
這位父親做三份工作來維持家中的生計。

【背誦歸納】

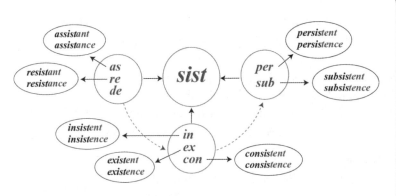

核心單字	衍生字 1	衍生字 2
assist *v.*	assistant *adj.*	assistance *n.*
resist *v.*	resistant *adj.*	resistance *n.*
insist *v.*	insistent *adj.*	insistence *n.*
exist *v.*	existent *adj.*	existence *n.*
consist *v.*	consistent *adj.*	consistence *n.*
persist *v.*	persistent *adj.*	persistence *n.*
subsist *v.*	subsistent *adj.*	subsistence *n.*

【注意 1】 核心單字中 desist 無其他衍生字。

【注意 2】 衍生字 1 中，僅有 assist 和 resist 後面接 ant，
其他均接 ent。這組的單字皆為形容詞，只有
assistant 還可當名詞。

【注意 3】 衍生字 2 中，僅有 assist 和 resist 後面接 ance，
其他均接 ence。這組的單字皆為名詞。

字根 sist, stitute

5. *destitute-institute-constitute*

這一組有 6 個字，分成二組，皆為字根 sist 的變化
型 stitute，背熟至 3 秒之內，變成直覺。

destitute
('dɛstə,tjut)

adj. 窮困的 (= *poor* ; *penniless*)
The streets of Mumbai are
crawling with *destitute* children.
孟買的街道擠滿了窮困的孩子。

de + stitute
|　　　 |
away + stand

離開衣食而生存，即是「窮困的」

institute[5]
('ɪnstə,tjut)

v. 設立；制定 (= *establish*)　　*n.* 協會
They will *institute* new rules
to improve safety. 他們將會
制定新的規則來改善安全。

in + stitute
|　　 |
up + stand

站起來給人看到，即是「創立」

constitute[4]
('kɑnstə,tjut)

v. 組成 (= *make up*)
Aboriginal peoples *constitute*
12 percent of the country's
population. 原住民族佔了
該國人口的百分之十二。

con + stitute
|　　 |
all + stand

通通站在一起，即是「組成」

restitute
('rɛstə,tjut)

v. 賠償；恢復
He was ordered to *restitute* the
victims of his crime. 他被命
令要賠償他所犯的罪的受害者。

re + stitute
|　　　 |
back + stand

站回到原處，即是「恢復；賠償」

prostitute
('prɑstə,tjut)

n. 娼妓
v. 賣淫；濫用 (才能等)
Nicholas isn't willing to
prostitute his talents. 尼可
拉斯不願濫用他的才能。

pro + stitute
|　　　 |
forth + stand

站到前面給人看，即是「出賣肉體」

substitute[5]
('sʌbstə,tjut)

v. 代替　　*n.* 代替者 (物)
Mary is ill and Laura is
to *substitute* for her.
瑪麗生病了，蘿拉要代替她。

sub + stitute
|　　　 |
under + stand

站在下面等待機會，即是「代替」

字根 sist, stitute

6. destitution-institution-institutional

這一組有 12 個字，皆爲字根 stitute 的衍生字彙，
背熟至 7 秒之內，變成直覺。

destitution
〔͵dɛstə'tjuʃən〕

n. 貧窮（= *poverty*）
Destitution has become a major problem in the city. 貧窮已經成爲該市一個重大的問題。

institution[6]
〔͵ɪnstə'tjuʃən〕

n. 設立；制度；制定；機構（= *establishment*）
The *institution* of a school is needed here.
此地需要設立一所學校。
Marriage is an *institution*.
婚姻是一種制度。

institutional
〔͵ɪnstə'tjuʃən!〕

adj. 機構的（= *established*）
He was dismissed for violating *institutional* policies. 他因違反機構的政策而被開除。

constitutive
〔'kɑnstə͵tjutɪv〕

adj. 組成的；基本的（= *essential*）
Heat is a *constitutive* property of fire.
熱是火的基本特性。

constitution[4]
〔͵kɑnstə'tjuʃən〕

n. 構成；憲法
The US *Constitution* guarantees freedom of the press. 美國憲法保障出版自由。

```
con + stitut + ion
 |      |       |
all  + stand  +  n.
```

constitutional[5]
〔͵kɑnstə'tjuʃən!〕

adj. 構成的；憲法的（= *official*）
Freedom of expression is a *constitutional* right.
表達言論的自由是憲法賦予的權利。

字根 sist, stitute

constitutionality
〔͵kɑnstə͵tjuʃən'ælətɪ 〕

n. 符合憲法
They questioned the *constitutionality* of the law.
他們質疑這條法令是否符合憲法。

constitutionalism
〔͵kɑnstə'tjuʃənḷ͵ɪzəm 〕

n. 立憲主義
American *constitutionalism* is inseparable from the culture.
美國的憲政主義和它的文化是不可分的。

constitution + al + ism
　　憲法　　+ *adj.* + 主義

constitutionalist
〔͵kɑnstə'tjuʃənḷɪst 〕

n. 立憲主義者；憲法擁護者
He is a strong *constitutionalist*.
他是個強烈的憲法擁護者。

【背誦祕訣】

constitute → *constitutive* / *constitution* / *constitutional* → *constitutionality* / *constitutionalism* / *constitutionalist*

這六個字為 constitute「組成」的衍生字

'constitutive
consti'tution
consti'tutional

這三個字的含義皆與「組成」有關

constitutio'nality
consti'tutionalism
consti'tutionalist

這三個字的含義皆與「憲法」有關

字根 sist, stitute

restitution	n. 賠償
〔͵rɛstə'tjuʃən〕	The victims are demanding *restitution*.
	受害者要求賠償。

prostitution	n. 賣淫；濫用
〔͵prɑstə'tjuʃən〕	*Prostitution* is called the world's oldest profession.
	賣淫被稱爲世界上最古老的職業。

substitution [6]	n. 代替
〔͵sʌbstə'tjuʃən〕	There is no *substitution* for hard work.
	沒有東西可以取代努力工作。

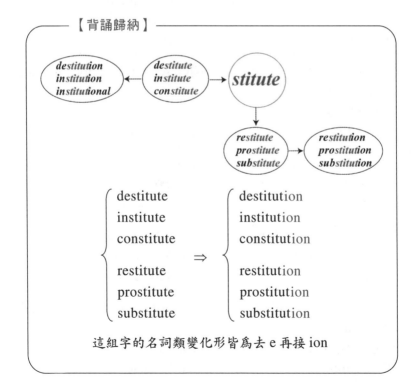

【背誦歸納】

這組字的名詞類變化形皆爲去 e 再接 ion

Exercise : Choose the correct answer. ✦

1. The children will _____ their mother with the household chores.
   (A) apply
   (B) oppose
   (C) serve
   (D) assist

2. The teacher asked the students to _____ from chewing gum in class.
   (A) deserve
   (B) depress
   (C) desist
   (D) dispel

3. Eddie found it difficult to _____ temptation.
   (A) resist
   (B) reserve
   (C) repel
   (D) resign

4. The merchant _____ on cash payment and does not accept credit cards.
   (A) intends
   (B) insists
   (C) indicts
   (D) imports

5. It remains an open question whether life _____ on Mars.
   (A) exports
   (B) extends
   (C) exists
   (D) extracts

6. The father admired the _____ of his child.
   (A) prostitution
   (B) persistence
   (C) restitution
   (D) subsistence

7. Hiking is an activity that _____ of walking in a natural environment.
   (A) comports
   (B) contradicts
   (C) contends
   (D) consists

8. There was widespread belief in ghosts, some of which _____ today.
   (A) persists
   (B) portends
   (C) perpends
   (D) prefers

9. The program provides financial _____ for students from low-income families.
   (A) sufferance
   (B) assistance
   (C) importance
   (D) subsistencey

10. George was _____ to our suggestions.
    (A) resistant
    (B) subsistent
    (C) existent
    (D) assistant

11. Jeffrey entered the talent contest at the _____ of his friends.
    (A) consistence
    (B) reference
    (C) insistence
    (D) conference

12. Water may be _____ for milk in this cookie recipe.
    (A) destituted
    (B) instituted
    (C) constituted
    (D) substituted

13. Social reformers are leading calls to legalize _____.
    (A) destitution
    (B) prostitution
    (C) institution
    (D) constitution

14. He remained _____ in his opposition to anything new.
    (A) consistent
    (B) preferable
    (C) predictable
    (D) portentous

15. No one has been able to prove or disprove the _____ of God.
    (A) existence
    (B) extension
    (C) exportation
    (D) extraction

字彙測驗詳解

1. (**D**) 孩子們會<u>協助</u>他們的母親做家事。

   (A) apply〔ə'plaɪ〕*v.* 申請；應用
   (B) oppose〔ə'poz〕*v.* 反對
   (C) serve〔sɜv〕*v.* 服務
   (D) *assist*〔ə'sɪst〕*v.* 幫助
   household chores
   household〔'haʊs,hold〕*adj.* 家庭的　　chore〔tʃɔr〕*n.* 雜事

2. (**C**) 老師要求學生<u>停止</u>在課堂上嚼口香糖。

   (A) deserve〔dɪ'zɜv〕*v.* 應得
   (B) depress〔dɪ'prɛs〕*v.* 使沮喪
   (C) *desist*〔dɪ'zɪst〕*v.* 停止
   (D) dispel〔dɪ'spɛl〕*v.* 驅散；消除
   chewing gum
   chew〔tʃu〕*v.* 咀嚼；嚼　　gum〔gʌm〕*n.* 口香糖

3. (**A**) 愛迪覺得<u>抗拒</u>誘惑是很難的。
   (A) *resist*〔rɪ'zɪst〕*v.* 對抗　　(B) reserve〔rɪ'zɜv〕*v.* 預訂
   (C) repel〔rɪ'pɛl〕*v.* 逐退　　(D) resign〔rɪ'zaɪn〕*v.* 辭職
   temptation〔tɛmp'teʃən〕*n.* 誘惑

4. (**B**) 這位商人<u>堅持</u>現金付款，不接受信用卡。
   (A) intend〔ɪn'tɛnd〕*v.* 打算
   (B) *insist*〔ɪn'sɪst〕*v.* 堅持
   (C) indict〔ɪn'daɪt〕*v.* 控訴
   (D) import〔ɪm'port〕*v.* 進口
   credit card
   merchant〔'mɜtʃənt〕*n.* 商人　　payment〔'pemənt〕*n.* 付款

5. (**C**) 火星上是否有生物<u>存在</u>還是個無法確定的問題。
   (A) export〔ɪks'port〕*v.* 出口
   (B) extend〔ɪk'stɛnd〕*v.* 延伸；延長
   (C) *exist*〔ɪg'zɪst〕*v.* 存在
   (D) extract〔ɪk'strækt〕*v.* 拔出；萃取
   open〔'opən〕*adj.* 未確定的　　Mars〔marz〕*n.* 火星

6. (**B**) 這位父親很欣賞他的孩子的<u>堅持</u>。
   (A) prostitution〔͵prɑstə'tjuʃən〕*n.* 賣淫
   (B) ***persistence***〔pə'sɪstəns〕*n.* 堅持；持續
   (C) restitution〔͵rɛstə'tjuʃən〕*n.* 賠償
   (D) subsistence〔səb'sɪstəns〕*n.* 生活

7. (**D**) 健行是一種<u>包含</u>在自然環境中走路的活動。
   (A) comport〔kəm'port〕*v.* 舉止
   (B) contradict〔͵kɑntrə'dɪkt〕*v.* 和～矛盾；反駁
   (C) contend〔kən'tɛnd〕*v.* 競爭
   (D) ***consist***〔kən'sɪst〕*v.* 組成；包含

hiking

hiking〔'haɪkɪŋ〕*n.* 健行 activity〔æk'tɪvətɪ〕*n.* 活動

8. (**A**) 以往普遍都相信有鬼，其中有些想法<u>持續</u>至今。
   (A) ***persist***〔pə'sɪst〕*v.* 堅持；持續
   (B) portend〔por'tɛnd〕*v.* 預示
   (C) perpend〔pə'pɛnd〕*v.* 仔細考慮
   (D) prefer〔prɪ'fɝ〕*v.* 比較喜歡

ghosts

widespread〔'waɪd'sprɛd〕*adj.* 普遍的
belief〔bɪ'lif〕*n.* 相信 ghost〔gost〕*n.* 鬼

9. (**B**) 這個計畫對低收入戶的學生提供了財務上的<u>協助</u>。
   (A) sufferance〔'sʌfərəns〕*n.* 苦難
   (B) ***assistance***〔ə'sɪstəns〕*n.* 協助
   (C) importance〔ɪm'portn̩s〕*n.* 重要性
   (D) subsistency〔səb'sɪstənsɪ〕*n.* 生存；生計
   program〔'progræm〕*n.* 計畫
   financial〔faɪ'nænʃəl〕*adj.* 財務的 ***low-income family*** 低收入戶

10. (**A**) 喬治<u>不接受</u>我們的建議。
   (A) ***resistant***〔rɪ'zɪstənt〕*adj.* 抵抗的
   (B) subsistent〔səb'sɪstənt〕*adj.* 生存的
   (C) existent〔ɪg'zɪstənt〕*adj.* 現存的
   (D) assistant〔ə'sɪstənt〕*adj.* 幫助的；助理的

字根 sist, stitute

11. (**C**) 傑弗瑞在他朋友的<u>堅持</u>下，參加才能競賽。
    (A) consistence〔kən'sɪstəns〕*n.* 一致
    (B) reference〔'rɛfərəns〕*n.* 參考
    (C) *insistence*〔ɪn'sɪstəns〕*n.* 堅持
    (D) conference〔'kɑnfərəns〕*n.* 會議
    enter〔'ɛntɚ〕*v.* 參加   contest〔'kɑntɛst〕*n.* 比賽

12. (**D**) 在這份餅乾食譜中，可以用水來<u>代替</u>牛奶。

recipe

    (A) destitute〔'dɛstə,tjut〕*adj.* 窮困的
    (B) institute〔'ɪnstə,tjut〕*v.* 制定
    (C) constitute〔'kɑnstə,tjut〕*v.* 組成
    (D) *substitute*〔'sʌbstə,tjut〕*v.* 代替
    cookie〔'kukɪ〕*n.* 餅乾   recipe〔'rɛsəpɪ〕*n.* 食譜

13. (**B**) 社會改革者帶頭要求<u>賣淫</u>合法化。
    (A) destitution〔,dɛstə'tjuʃən〕*n.* 貧困
    (B) *prostitution*〔,prɑstə'tjuʃən〕*n.* 賣淫；濫用
    (C) institution〔,ɪnstə'tjuʃən〕*n.* 設立；制度；機構
    (D) constitution〔,kɑnstə'tjuʃən〕*n.* 構成；憲法
    reformer〔rɪ'fɔrmɚ〕*n.* 改革者   legalize〔'ligl̩,aɪz〕*v.* 使合法化

14. (**A**) 他<u>始終</u>反對一切新事物。
    (A) *consistent*〔kən'sɪstənt〕*adj.* 始終如一的；一致的
    (B) preferable〔'prɛfərəbl̩〕*adj.* 較好的
    (C) predictable〔prɪ'dɪktəbl̩〕*adj.* 可預測的
    (D) portentous〔por'tɛntəs〕*adj.* 預兆的

15. (**A**) 沒人可以證明或反駁上帝的<u>存在</u>。

God

    (A) *existence*〔ɪg'zɪstəns〕*n.* 存在
    (B) extension〔ɪk'stɛnʃən〕*n.* 延伸；分機
    (C) exportation〔,ɛkspor'teʃən〕*n.* 出口
    (D) extraction〔ɪk'strækʃən〕*n.* 抽出；抽出物
    disprove〔dɪs'pruv〕*v.* 舉出反證；證明~錯誤；反駁

請連中文一起背，背至70秒內，終生不忘。 ★

1

assist	幫助
desist	停止
resist	抵抗
insist	堅持
exist	存在
consist	組成
persist	堅持
subsist	生存

2

assistant	助手
assistantship	研究生助教獎學金
assistance	幫助
resister	抵抗者
resistant	抵抗的
resistance	抵抗

resistless	無法抵抗的
resistible	可抵抗的
resistibility	抵抗力
resistive	有抵抗力的
resistiveness	抵抗力
resistivity	抵抗力

3

insistent	堅持的
insistence	堅持
insistency	堅持
existing	現存的
existent	現存的
existence	生存

existential	存在主義的
existentialism	存在主義
existentialist	存在主義者
consistent	一致的
consistence	一致
consistency	一致

字根 sist, stitute

4

persistent	堅持的
persistence	堅持
persistency	堅持
subsistent	生存的
subsistence	生存
subsistency	生計

5

destitute	窮困的
institute	設立
constitute	組成
restitute	賠償
prostitute	娼妓
substitute	代替

6

destitution	貧窮
institution	設立
institutional	機構的
constitutive	組成的
constitution	構成
constitutional	構成的

constitutionality	符合憲法
constitutionalism	立憲主義
constitutionalist	立憲主義者
restitution	賠償
prostitution	賣淫
substitution	代替

※ 本頁可影印後，隨身攜帶，方便背誦。

字根 sist, stitute

Group 15 字根 *scribe*

目標： ① 先將45個字放入短期記憶。

② 加快速度至37秒之內，成為長期記憶。

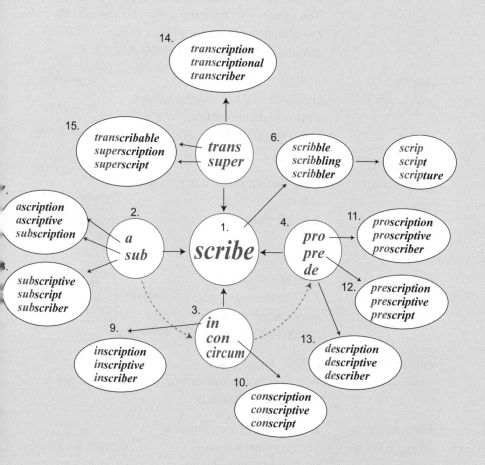

14.
transcription
transcriptional
transcriber

15.
transcribable
superscription
superscript

trans
super

6.
scribble
scribbling
scribbler

scrip
script
scripture

ascription
ascriptive
subscription

2.
a
sub

1.
scribe

4.
pro
pre
de

11.
proscription
proscriptive
proscriber

subscriptive
subscript
subscriber

12.
prescription
prescriptive
prescript

3.
in
con
circum

13.
description
descriptive
describer

9.
inscription
inscriptive
inscriber

10.
conscription
conscriptive
conscript

字根
scribe

1. 字根 *scribe* 核心單字

　　11 個字，3 個一組一起背，可先背 6 個再背 5 個，背熟至 6 秒之內，可成為長期記憶，才可再背下一組。

scribe 〔 skraɪb 〕	*n.* 抄寫員　*v.* 刻畫（線條）；書寫（＝*write*） The painter will typically *scribe* his name in the lower right-hand corner of the canvas. 那個畫家通常都把他的名字寫在畫布的右下角。

ascribe
〔 ə'skraɪb 〕

v. 歸因（＝*attribute*）
Gina *ascribed* her success to hard work and determination. 吉娜把她的成功歸因於努力和決心。

$$a + scribe$$
$$| \qquad |$$
$$to + write$$

給寫，即是「歸因」

subscribe[6]
〔 səb'skraɪb 〕

v. 訂閱
I don't *subscribe* to a newspaper at home.
我家裡沒有訂報紙。

$$sub + scribe$$
$$| \qquad |$$
$$under + write$$

把名字寫在單子下面，就是「訂閱」

inscribe
〔 ɪn'skraɪb 〕

v. 銘刻（＝*carve*）
Ancient messages were discovered *inscribed* on the walls of a cave.
在一處洞穴的牆上發現刻著古老的訊息。

$$in + scribe$$
$$| \qquad |$$
$$in , on + write$$

conscribe
〔 kən'skraɪb 〕

v. 徵召（＝*call up*）
Volunteers were *conscribed* to clean up the beach.
自願者受徵召來清理海灘。

circumscribe
〔'sɝkəm,skraɪb 〕

v. 包圍；限制（＝*restrict*）
The president's powers are *circumscribed* by the constitution.
總統的權力受制於憲法。

$$circum + scribe$$
$$| \qquad |$$
$$around + write$$

把周圍畫起來，即是「畫界線」

proscribe
〔 pro'skraɪb 〕

v. 禁止（ = *prohibit* ）
Convicted felons are *proscribed* by Federal law from owning guns. 依照聯邦法律，遭到定罪的重罪犯，禁止持有槍械。

```
pro  + scribe
 |       |
forth + write
```
把罪犯的名字公佈

prescribe[6]
〔 prɪ'skraɪb 〕

v. 開藥方
The doctor *prescribed* antibiotics for my throat infection. 醫生開抗生素來治療我的喉嚨感染。

```
pre   + scribe
 |        |
before + write
```
拿藥之前，醫生要先「開藥方」

describe[2]
〔 dɪ'skraɪb 〕

v. 描述（ = *depict* ）；形容
Even his enemies *describe* Randy as a genius.
甚至連藍帝的敵人都形容他是天才。

```
de   + scribe
 |       |
fully + write
```
寫得很詳細，即是「描述」

transcribe
〔 træn'skraɪb 〕

v. 抄寫（ = *copy* ）；將…轉譯（ 成普通文字 ）
My secretary will *transcribe* our conversation.
我的秘書會把我們的對話內容抄寫下來。

```
tran  + scribe
  |        |
across + write
```
從這邊寫到另一邊，即是「抄寫」

superscribe
〔 ˌsupɚ'skraɪb 〕

v. 把…寫上去
The teacher's comments were *superscribed* on the student's essays. 老師把他的評語寫在同學的作文上。

```
super + scribe
  |        |
above + write
```
寫在上面，即是「把…寫上去」

2. *scribble-scribbling-scribbler*

這一組有 6 個字,三個一組一起背,先背前 3 個
再背後 3 個,背熟至 3 秒之內,變成直覺。

scribble
〔'skrɪbl̩〕

v. 潦草書寫 (= *doodle*)
I *scribbled* a note in my journal as the
train left the station. 當火車離開車站的
時候,我在日記本上潦草記錄下來。

> scrib + le
> |　　　|
> *write* + *v.*

scribbling
〔'skrɪblɪŋ〕

n. 亂寫 (= *doodle*)
I can't read your writing, Edna. It looks like a bunch of
scribbling.
埃德娜,我看不懂妳在寫什麼。看起來就像是亂寫一通。

scribbler
〔'skrɪblɚ〕

n. 三流作家
Harold is a *scribbler* of
romantic poetry.
哈洛德是一位三流的浪漫詩人。

> scribble + r
> |　　　 |
> 亂寫　 + 人

亂寫的人,即是「三流的作家」

scrip
〔 skrɪp 〕

n. 紙條 (= *notepaper*)
She wrote her phone number on a *scrip* and slipped it in
his palm. 她在紙條上寫下電話號碼,然後塞到他的手裡。

script[6]
〔 skrɪpt 〕

n. 腳本;筆跡 (= *handwriting*)
She wrote the letter in an elegant *script*.
她用很漂亮的筆跡寫那封信。

scripture
〔'skrɪptʃɚ〕

n. 聖經 (= *the Bible*)
The priest quoted from the *Scriptures*.
那位神職人員引用聖經的內容。

scripture

* scrip,script,scripture 這三個字的字根,都是從 scribe 變化而來,而且
重音都在字根上。

3 ascription-ascriptive-subscription

這一組有 6 個字，分成兩組，第一組是 ascribe 的衍生字，
第二組是 subscribe 的衍生字，背熟至 3 秒之內，變成直覺。

ascription
〔 ə'skrɪpʃən 〕

n. 歸因；歸屬（ = *attribution* ）
Ascription of the fault to him was not fair.
把過錯歸因於他是不公平的。

ascriptive
〔 ə'skrɪptɪv 〕

adj. 可歸因的（ = *attributable* ）
The plane crash was *ascriptive* to bad weather.
between genders.
這場空難是歸因於天候不佳。

subscription[6]
〔 səb'skrɪpʃən 〕

n. 訂閱（ = *order* ）
Quincy cancelled his *subscription* to *Sports
Illustrated.* 昆西取消訂閱運動畫刊。

subscriptive
〔 səb'skrɪptɪv 〕

adj. 訂購的（ = *able to subscribe* ）
Tickets to the concert will not be *subscriptive.*
那場演唱會的票不開放訂購。

subscript
〔 'sʌbskrɪpt 〕

n. 寫在下面的文字
Subscripts are most commonly used in chemical
equations, for instance: H_2O.
寫在下面的文字通常用在化學方程式上，例如：H_2O。

sub	+	script
under	+	write

H_2O

subscript

subscriber
〔 səb'skraɪbɚ 〕

n. 訂閱者
Glenda has been a long-time *subscriber* to fashion
magazines. 葛蘭達是時尚雜誌長期的訂閱者。

4 *inscription-inscriptive-inscriber*

這一組有 6 個字，分成兩組，第一組是 inscribe 的衍生字，
第二組是 conscribe 的衍生字，背熟至 3 秒之內，變成直覺。

inscription
〔 ɪn'skrɪpʃən 〕

n. 題詞（ = *epigraph* ）
The statue bears an inscription which reads: "Freedom for all." 雕像上劇的字是「全民自由。」

inscriptive
〔 ɪn'skrɪptɪv 〕

adj. 銘刻的（ = *carving* ）
I am studying the *inscriptive* art of Chinese calligraphy.
我正在研究中國書法的銘刻藝術。

```
in   + script + ive
 |        |       |
upon + write  + adj.
```

inscriber
〔 ɪn'skraɪbɚ 〕

n. 銘刻者（ = *carver* ）
The *inscribers* worked all night to finish the Queen's tombstone in time for the funeral. 刻碑文的人整晚都在刻女王的墓碑，以便及時趕上她的葬禮。

conscription
〔 kən'skrɪpʃən 〕

n. 徵兵（ = *levy* ）
Military *conscription* is required of all Israeli citizens between the ages of 18 and 25 years old.
以色列人年紀在十八到二十五歲之間，都要被徵召從軍。

conscriptive
〔 kən'skrɪptɪv 〕

adj. 徵兵的（ = *levying* ）
Many young adults have chosen to avoid *conscriptive* service in the military. 許多年輕人選擇逃避兵役。

conscript
〔'kɑnskrɪpt 〕

adj. 被徵召的　*n.* 新兵（ = *recruit* ）
A group of *conscripts* were sent to relieve the weary veterans in combat.
一群新兵被派去戰場上，
支援疲累的老兵。

```
con         + script
 |             |
all, together + write
```

特別注意這個字的重音在最前面

5. *proscription-proscriptive-proscriber*

　　這一組有6個字,分成兩組,第一組是 proscribe 的衍生字,
第二組是 prescribe 的衍生字,背熟至3秒之內,變成直覺。

proscription
(pro'skrɪpʃən)

n. 禁止 (= *prohibition*)
The Muslim leader ordered the *proscription* of all
customs not conforming to religious law.
那位回教領袖下令,不符合教規的習俗都要禁止。

proscriptive
(pro'skrɪptɪv)

adj. 禁止的 (= *prohibitive*)
All students must follow a *proscriptive* set of rules.
所有學生必須遵守一套戒律。

proscriber
(pro'skraɪbɚ)

n. 禁止者 (= *prohibitor*)
Most Muslim governments are *proscribers* of
education for women.
大多數的回教政府禁止女性受教育。

prescription[6]
(prɪ'skrɪpʃən)

n. 處方 (= *formula*);規定
Certain medications are freely available without a
doctor's *prescription*.
某些藥品沒有醫生的處方也可以自由取得。

prescriptive
(prɪ'skrɪptɪv)

adj. 規定的;規範的 (= *normative*)
This dictionary is more descriptive than *prescriptive*.
這本字典客觀描述,而不是主觀規範。

prescript
('priskrɪpt)

n. 規定 (= *regulation*)
Ignoring the *prescript* against smoking in public
places, Richard lit a cigarette.
理察忽視公眾場所禁止抽煙的規定,點了一根煙。

字根 scribe

6. *description-descriptive-describer*

這一組有 9 個字，分成三組，第一組是 describe 的衍生字，第二組是 transcribe 的衍生字，第三組是 superscribe 的衍生字，背熟至 5 秒之內，變成直覺。

description[3]
〔 dɪˈskrɪpʃən 〕

n. 敘述（ = *depiction* ）
The victim was unable to give a detailed *description* of her attackers.
那位受害者無法詳細地描述攻擊她的人。

descriptive[5]
〔 dɪˈskrɪptɪv 〕

adj. 敘述的（ = *interpretative* ）
His writing is full of *descriptive* language.
他的作品充滿敘述性的語言。

describer
〔 dɪˈskraɪbɚ 〕

n. 敘述者（ = *depicter* ）
The author is a good *describer* of his environment.
這位作者擅長描述他的環境。

transcription
〔 trænˈskrɪpʃən 〕

n. 抄寫；文字記錄（ = *copy* ）
Vill's *transcription* of the interview contained many mistakes.
吉兒的面談文字記錄包含了很多錯誤。

transcriptional
〔 trænˈskrɪpʃənḷ 〕

adj. 抄寫的；改編的
Tom's job at the TV station includes *transcriptional* work. 湯姆在電視台的職務包含了抄寫工作。

transcriber
〔 trænˈskraɪbɚ 〕

n. 抄寫員
The *transcriber* can't keep up with the conversation.
那位抄寫員跟不上對話的速度。

transcribable
〔 træn'skrɪbəbḷ 〕

adj. 可抄寫的；可轉譯的
The book is *transcribable* into Braille.
這本書可轉譯成盲人的點字版。

tran	+ scrib	+ able
across	+ write	+ *adj.*

superscription
〔 ˌsupɚ'skrɪpʃən 〕

n. 題字；（信封上的）姓名地址
Without a return address *superscription*, the post office may not deliver the package.
沒有回信的姓名地址，郵局可能無法遞送包裹。

super	+ script	+ ion
above	+ write	+ *n.*

superscript
〔'supɚˌskrɪpt 〕

n. 寫在上面的文字
In mathematics, the *superscript* of X^2 is the number 2.
在數學中，X^2 寫在上面的字就是數字 2。

superscript

【背誦祕訣】

　　conscript，prescript，subscript，superscript 這四個字在 scribe 衍生出來的 45 個字當中算是很特別的，背誦的時候，要注意重音皆在第一個音節。

　　'conscript
　　'prescript
　　'subscript　　記住這四個字的重音都在最前面
　　'superscript

Exercise : Choose the correct answer. ✦

1. To receive frequent updates and special offers, simply click the _____ button and enter your e-mail address.
   (A) dispose   (B) subscribe
   (C) employ   (D) compress

2. The need for a more _____ approach to teaching English became obvious.
   (A) prescriptive   (B) distensible
   (C) reposeful   (D) oppressive

3. Without _____, our leaders fear that no one would join the armed forces.
   (A) proposition   (B) expression
   (C) conscription   (D) supplication

4. Gambling is _____ in Taiwan, but that doesn't stop people from doing it.
   (A) applied   (B) designed
   (C) proscribed   (D) expelled

5. Japan has already adopted a plan of _____ females.
   (A) extending   (B) conscribing
   (C) triplicating   (D) signalizing

6. A tall fence and armed security guards _____ the Governor's mansion.
   (A) perplex   (B) repulse
   (C) subserve   (D) circumscribe

7. She _____ her success to hard work.
   (A) ascribed   (B) attended
   (C) compelled   (D) depressed

8. Very few doctors are willing to _____ experimental medications for their patients.
   - (A) complicate
   - (B) prescribe
   - (C) ensign
   - (D) conserve

9. Words fail to _____ the natural beauty of Taroko Gorge.
   - (A) compel
   - (B) oppose
   - (C) supplicate
   - (D) describe

10. My mother's _____ for a cold is chicken soup and lots of rest.
    - (A) prescription
    - (B) complication
    - (C) designation
    - (D) tentation

11. The names of soldiers who died in the war are _____ on the memorial.
    - (A) attended
    - (B) imposed
    - (C) deposed
    - (D) inscribed

12. Every telephone call into or out of this office will be recorded and _____ for security reasons.
    - (A) resigned
    - (B) intensified
    - (C) propelled
    - (D) transcribed

13. Many news organizations are now imposing a _____ fee for access to online content.
    - (A) impulsion
    - (B) deposition
    - (C) suppression
    - (D) subscription

14. The article provides an accurate _____ of the damage caused by the typhoon.
    - (A) description
    - (B) repression
    - (C) implication
    - (D) complication

15. Your _____ of the lecture will be copied and distributed to all the students.
    - (A) triplication
    - (B) designation
    - (C) transcription
    - (D) reservation

字彙測驗詳解

1. (**B**) 要收到經常性的更新和特價資訊，只要點一下<u>訂閱</u>鍵，並且輸入你的電子郵件地址就可以了。
   (A) dispose〔dɪ'spoz〕*v.* 處置
   (B) *subscribe*〔səb'skraɪb〕*v.* 訂閱
   (C) employ〔ɪm'plɔɪ〕*v.* 雇用
   (D) compress〔kəm'prɛs〕*v.* 壓縮
   update〔'ʌpdet〕*n.* 更新　　click〔klɪk〕*v.*（用滑鼠）點

2. (**A**) 用更<u>規範性的</u>方式教英文，有其明顯的需要。
   (A) *prescriptive*〔prɪ'skrɪptɪv〕*adj.* 規定的；規範的
   (B) distensible〔dɪs'tɛnsəbl〕*adj.* 可膨脹的
   (C) reposeful〔rɪ'pozfəl〕*adj.* 平靜的
   (D) oppressive〔ə'prɛsɪv〕*adj.* 壓迫的
   approach〔ə'protʃ〕*n.* 方法

3. (**C**) 沒有<u>徵兵</u>，我們的領導人害怕沒有人會加入三軍部隊。
   (A) proposition〔,prɑpə'zɪʃən〕*n.* 提議
   (B) expression〔ɪk'sprɛʃən〕*n.* 表達；表情
   (C) *conscription*〔kən'skrɪpʃən〕*n.* 徵兵
   (D) supplication〔,sʌplɪ'keʃən〕*n.* 懇求
   armed forces 武裝部隊；三軍部隊

4. (**C**) 台灣<u>禁止</u>賭博，不過這沒辦法讓人不賭。
   (A) apply〔ə'plaɪ〕*v.* 申請　　(B) design〔dɪ'zaɪn〕*v.* 設計
   (C) *proscribe*〔pro'skraɪb〕*v.* 禁止
   (D) expel〔ɪk'spɛl〕*v.* 逐出；驅逐

5. (**B**) 日本已經採用一項計畫，要<u>徵召</u>女性從軍。
   (A) extend〔ɪk'stɛnd〕*v.* 延長；延伸
   (B) *conscribe*〔kən'skraɪb〕*v.* 徵召入伍
   (C) triplicate〔,trɪplə'ket〕*v.* 使成三倍
   (D) signalize〔'sɪgnə,laɪz〕*v.* 使大放異彩；顯示

6. (**D**) 高築的圍牆和武裝保全把州長的豪宅整個<u>包圍</u>起來。
   - (A) perplex〔pɚˈplɛks〕 *v.* 使困惑
   - (B) repulse〔rɪˈpʌls〕 *v.* 擊退；拒絕
   - (C) subserve〔səbˈsɝv〕 *v.* 促進；有助於
   - (D) *circumscribe*〔ˌsɝkəmˈskraɪb〕 *v.* 包圍；限制

   security guard 保全　　governor〔ˈɡʌvənɚ〕 *n.* 州長
   mansion〔ˈmænʃən〕 *n.* 豪宅

7. (**A**) 她把自己的成功<u>歸因</u>於勤勞。
   - (A) *ascribe*〔əˈskraɪb〕 *v.* 歸因
   - (B) attend〔əˈtɛnd〕 *v.* 參加
   - (C) compel〔kempɛl〕 *v.* 強電
   - (D) depress〔dɪˈprɛs〕 *v.* 使沮喪

8. (**B**) 很少有醫生願意<u>開</u>實驗性藥物的<u>藥方</u>給他們的病人。
   - (A) complicate〔ˈkɑmpləˌket〕 *v.* 使複雜
   - (B) *prescribe*〔prɪˈskraɪb〕 *v.* 開藥方
   - (C) ensign〔ˈɛnsaɪn〕 *n.* 徽章
   - (D) conserve〔kənˈsɝv〕 *v.* 保存；節約

   willing〔ˈwɪlɪŋ〕 *adj.* 願意的
   medication〔ˌmɛdɪˈkeʃən〕 *n.* 藥物

9. (**D**) 文字無法<u>描述</u>太魯閣自然的美。
   - (A) compel〔kəmˈpɛl〕 *v.* 強迫
   - (B) oppose〔əˈpoz〕 *v.* 反對
   - (C) supplicate〔ˈsʌplɪˌket〕 *v.* 懇求
   - (D) *describe*〔dɪˈskraɪb〕 *v.* 描述

   fail to + *V.* 無法~；未能~　　gorge〔ɡɔrdʒ〕 *n.* 峽谷

10. (**A**) 我媽媽治感冒的<u>藥方</u>是雞湯和多休息。
    - (A) *prescription*〔prɪˈskrɪpʃən〕 *n.* 藥方
    - (B) complication〔ˌkɑmpləˈkeʃən〕 *n.* 複雜
    - (C) designation〔ˌdɛzɪɡˈneʃən〕 *n.* 指定；指派
    - (D) tentation〔tɛnˈteʃən〕 *n.* 試驗調整

11. (**D**) 在戰爭中捐軀的士兵，他們的名字被刻在紀念碑上。
    (A) attend〔ə'tɛnd〕v. 參加
    (B) impose〔ɪm'poz〕v. 強加於
    (C) depose〔dɪ'poz〕v. 罷免
    (D) *inscribe*〔ɪn'skraɪb〕v. 銘刻
    memorial〔mə'morɪəl〕n. 紀念碑

12. (**D**) 每一通打進或打出辦公室的電話，基於安全的理由，都會被錄音
    並且轉譯成文字。
    (A) resign〔rɪ'zaɪn〕v. 辭職
    (B) intensify〔ɪn'tɛnsə,faɪ〕v. 加強
    (C) propel〔prə'pɛl〕v. 驅使；推動
    (D) *transcribe*〔træn'skraɪb〕v. 抄寫；將…轉譯（成普通文字）

13. (**D**) 許多新聞機構現在加收上網瀏覽網站內容的訂閱費。
    (A) impulsion〔ɪm'pʌlʃən〕n. 衝動；推進（力）
    (B) deposition〔,dɛpə'zɪʃən〕n. 罷免
    (C) suppression〔sə'prɛʃən〕n. 鎮壓；抑制
    (D) *subscription*〔səb'skrɪpʃən〕n. 訂閱
    access〔'æksɛs〕n. 接近或使用權   content〔'kantɛnt〕n. 內容

14. (**A**) 這篇文章將這次颱風造成的損害做了正確的敘述。
    (A) *description*〔dɪ'skrɪpʃən〕n. 敘述
    (B) repression〔rɪ'prɛʃən〕n. 鎮壓；抑制
    (C) implication〔,ɪmplɪ'keʃən〕n. 暗示；關連
    (D) complication〔,kamplə'keʃən〕n. 複雜

15. (**C**) 你這份演講的文字記錄內容，將會被影印並發給所有同學。
    (A) triplication〔,trɪplə'keʃən〕n. 分成三份
    (B) designation〔,dɛzɪg'neʃən〕n. 指定；指派
    (C) *transcription*〔træn'skrɪpʃən〕n. 謄寫
    (D) reservation〔,rɛzɚ'veʃən〕n. 預約
    lecture〔'lɛktʃɚ〕n. 演說；講課
    distribute〔dɪ'strɪbjut〕v. 分發

請連中文一起背，背至55秒內，終生不忘。

1

scribe	抄寫員
ascribe	歸因
subscribe	訂閱
inscribe	銘刻
conscribe	徵召
circumscribe	包圍
proscribe	禁止
prescribe	開藥方
describe	描述
transcribe	抄寫
superscribe	把…寫上去

2

scribble	潦草書寫
scribbling	亂寫
scribbler	三流作家

scrip	紙條
script	腳本
scripture	聖經

3

ascription	歸因
ascriptive	可歸因的
subscription	訂閱
subscriptive	可訂購的
subscript	寫在下面的文字
subscriber	訂閱者

字根 scribe

4

inscription	碑文
inscriptive	銘刻的
inscriber	銘刻者
conscription	徵兵
conscriptive	徵兵的
conscript	被徵召的

5

proscription	禁止
proscriptive	禁止的
proscriber	禁止者
prescription	處方
prescriptive	規定的
prescript	規定

6

description	敘述
descriptive	敘述的
describer	敘述者
transcription	抄寫
transcriptional	抄寫的
transcriber	抄寫員
transcribable	可抄寫的
superscription	題字
superscript	寫在上面的文字

※ 本頁可影印後，隨身攜帶，方便背誦。

Group 16 字根 *tain*

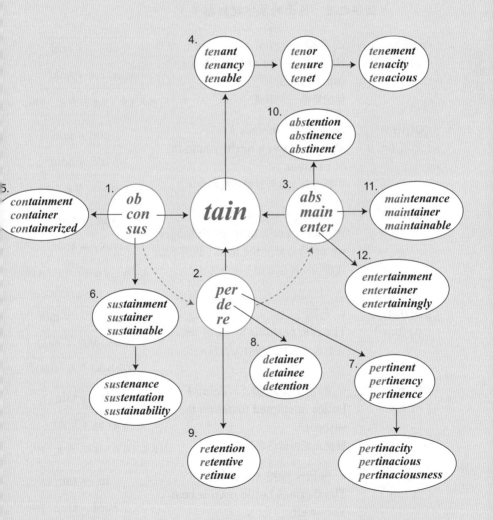

1. 字根 *tain* 核心單字

字根 tain

　　字根 tain 表 hold；keep「抓住；保持」之意，核心單字有 9 個，3 個一組，一起背，很容易背。背熟這 9 個字之後，後面的單字就輕鬆了。

obtain[4]
〔əbˈten〕

v. 獲得（= *gain*）
He was able to *obtain* a large sum of money.
他能獲得一大筆錢。

ob	+ tain
near, eye	+ *hold*

抓在身旁（眼旁），即是「獲得」

contain[2]
〔kənˈten〕

v. 包含（= *include*）
Milk *contains* a healthy amount of calcium.
牛奶含有大量有益健康的鈣質。

con	+ tain
all	+ *hold*

全部抓住，即是「包含」

sustain[5]
〔səˈsten〕

v. 維持（= *support*）
We don't know how much longer we can *sustain* the heat. 我們不知道還可以維持這個熱度多久。

sus	+ tain
under	+ *hold*

在下面支撐住你，即是「維持」

pertain
〔pɚˈten〕

v. 有關
The rule *pertains* to all of us.
這個規則和我們所有人有關。

per	+ tain
thoroughly	+ *hold*

完全抓住，即是「有關」

detain[6]
〔dɪˈten〕

v. 拘留；使耽擱（= *delay*）
Police attempted to *detain* the suspect.
警察企圖拘留這名嫌犯。

de	+ tain
away	+ *hold*

抓住你不讓別人靠近，即是「拘留」

retain[4]
〔rɪˈten〕

v. 保留；保持（= *hold*）
The thermos bottle *retains* heat Very well.
這保溫瓶的保溫效果很好。

re	+ tain
back	+ *keep*

保持到以後，即是「保留」

abstain
〔əbˈsten〕

v. 抑制；戒除（= *refrain*）
Please *abstain* from smoking.
請勿吸菸。

```
abs  +  tain
 |       |
from  +  keep
```
離開某物，即是「抑制」

maintain[2]
〔menˈten〕

v. 維持（= *keep*）
Margaret *maintained* her composure.
瑪格麗特保持冷靜。

```
main  +  tain
 |        |
hand  +  hold
```
保有於手中，即是「維持」

entertain[4]
〔ˌɛntɚˈten〕

v. 娛樂（= *amuse*）
She *entertained* us by singing a song.
她唱一首歌來娛樂我們。

```
enter    +  tain
  |          |
between  +  hold
```
抱著兩個人，就是「娛樂」

字根 tain

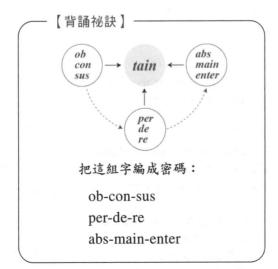

【背誦祕訣】

把這組字編成密碼：

ob-con-sus

per-de-re

abs-main-enter

2. *tenant-tenancy-tenable*

這一組由 tain 衍生出九個單字,一起背,很順口,
必須背到 5 秒之內,成為長期記憶,就沒有負擔了。

字根 tain

tenant[5]
(ˈtɛnənt)
n. 房客 (= *renter*)
I've been a *tenant* in this building for five years.
我在這棟大樓租房子已經五年了。

ten	+	ant
hold, keep	+	*person*

擁有的人,即是「房客」

tenancy
(ˈtɛnənsɪ)
n. 租賃;租賃期間
Review the terms of *tenancy* before signing the lease.
簽租約前要再看一次租賃的條件。

tenable
(ˈtɛnəbḷ)
adj. 可維持的;(理論)站得住腳的 (= *defensible*)
I am not in a *tenable* position to
argue with you.
和你爭吵我站不住腳。

ten	+	able
keep	+	可~的

tenor
(ˈtɛnɚ)
n. 大意 (= *purport*)
I caught the *tenor* of the conversation.
我抓到這次談話的大意了。

tenure
(ˈtɛnjɚ)
n. 任期
He achieved great things during
his *tenure* as president.
他在總統任期內完成許多偉大的事。

ten	+	ure
hold	+	*n.*

擔任職位的期間,即是「任期」

tenet
(ˈtɛnɪt)
n. 主義 (= *principle*);教義
Non-violence is one of the *tenets*
of the Buddhist faith.
佛教的教義之一是禁止暴力。

ten	+	et
hold	+	小東西

緊緊保護的東西,就是「主義」

tenement
〔'tɛnəmənt 〕

n. 租屋；廉價公寓
Kyle grew up in a *tenement* on the south side of town.
凱爾在城裡南方的一間廉價公寓內長大。

> tene + ment
> | |
> *hold* +   *n.*

tenacity
〔 tɪ'næsətɪ 〕

n. 堅持；不屈不撓（ = *perseverance* ）
I admire people who have the *tenacity* to reach their goals.
我欣賞那些堅持達成目標的人。

> ten + acity
> | |
> *hold* +   傾向

抓住這個傾向不變

字根 tain

tenacious
〔 tɪ'neʃəs 〕

adj. 堅持的；不屈不撓的（ = *persistent* ）
He is *tenacious* of his opinions.
他固執己見。

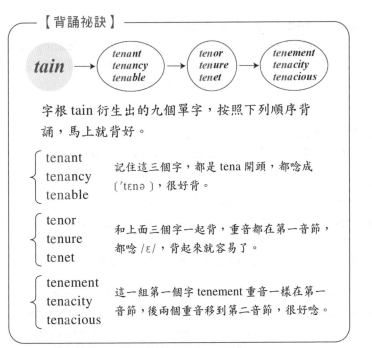

【背誦祕訣】

tain → (tenant / tenancy / tenable) → (tenor / tenure / tenet) → (tenement / tenacity / tenacious)

字根 tain 衍生出的九個單字，按照下列順序背誦，馬上就背好。

⎧ tenant
⎨ tenancy　　記住這三個字，都是 tena 開頭，都唸成
⎩ tenable　　〔'tɛnə 〕，很好背。

⎧ tenor
⎨ tenure　　和上面三個字一起背，重音都在第一音節，
⎩ tenet　　都唸 /ɛ/，背起來就容易了。

⎧ tenement
⎨ tenacity　　這一組第一個字 tenement 重音一樣在第一
⎩ tenacious　音節，後兩個重音移到第二音節，很好唸。

3. containment-container-containerized

這一回也有 9 個字，分成二組，第一組是 contain 的衍生字，第二組源自 sustain，快速背誦，就變成直覺了。

字根 tain

containment
〔 kən'tenmənt 〕

n. 抑制（= *control*）
Containment of the epidemic is a global concern. 抑制這個傳染病是全球共同都很關心的事。

con + tain + ment
|　　　　|　　　　|
all + *hold* +　*n.*

全部都抓住了，即是「抑制」

container[4]
〔 kən'tenɚ 〕

n. 容器（= *vessel*）；貨櫃
Connie keeps her dirty laundry in a plastic *container*.
康妮把她的髒衣服放在一個塑膠容器內。

containerized
〔 kən'tenɚ,raɪzd 〕

adj. 用貨櫃運送的
Armor Metals, Inc. is the world's leading trader in *containerized* scrap metal. 阿莫金屬公司，是全球首屈一指的用貨櫃運送廢五金的公司之一。

sustainment
〔 sə'stenmənt 〕

n. 支持（= *support*）
His family gave him *sustainment* during those difficult times. 他的家人支持他度過許多低潮。

sustainer
〔 sə'stenɚ 〕

n. 支持者（= *supporter*）
They are *sustainers* of traditional values and customs.
他們是傳統價值觀和習俗的支持者。

sustainable
〔 sə'stenəbl̩ 〕

adj. 可支撐的（= *supportable*）；永續的
Sustainable agriculture is a way of farming that is healthy for consumers and the environment.
永續農業是有益於消費者和環境的農耕方式之一。

sustenance
〔'sʌstənəns 〕

n. 營養物；食物 (= *nourishment*)
His only *sustenance* was a stale piece of bread.
他唯一的食物就是一塊不新鮮的麵包。

sus	+	ten	+	ance	
under	+	hold	+	*n.*	

支持、維持著你健康的東西，
即是「營養物；食物」

sustentation
〔,sʌstɛn'teʃən 〕

n. 支撐；支持 (= *sustention*)
Her theory lacked scientific *sustentation*.
她的理論缺少科學的支持。

字根 tain

sustainability
(sə,stenə'bɪlətɪ)

n. 持續性
Critics question the *sustainability* of the system.
評論家質疑這個系統的持續性。

sustain	+	ability
支持	+	能力

可支持下去的能力，即是「持續性」

【背誦祕訣】

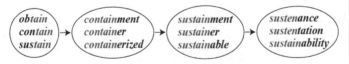

由核心單字 ob-con-sus 衍生出的九個單字很好
背，obtain 沒有衍生字。

第一組 ⎰ containment
⎱ container　　三個字很好背。
　　containerized

前兩個字都由 contain 開頭，後兩個字都有
container，可以用比較字根的方式來背，很
快就背下來了。

4. pertinent-pertinency-pertinence

這一回共有 12 個字，先背前 6 個，pertain 的變化，再
背後 6 個，detain 和 retain 的變化，背完壓力都沒有了。

字根 tain

pertinent
(ˈpɝtṇənt)

adj. 有關的（= *relevant* ）
They asked questions *pertinent* to the subject.
他們問了跟這個主題有關的問題。

per	+	tin	+	ent
thoroughly	+	*hold*	+	*adj.*

完全抓住這個主題，
即是「有關的」

pertinency
(ˈpɝtṇənsɪ)

n. 相關性（= *relevancy* ）
A judge will determine the *pertinency* of the
evidence. 法官會判定這項證據的相關性。

pertinence
(ˈpɝtṇəns)

n. 相關性（= *pertinency* ）
That you are angry has no *pertinence* to the matter
at hand. 你生氣和手邊這個問題無關。

pertinacity
(ˌpɝtṇˈæsətɪ)

n. 固執（= *obstinacy* ）
Raymond has the *pertinacity* of an old mule.
雷蒙像老騾子般的固執。

pertin	+	acity
pertain	+	傾向

附屬於這個傾向不變，即是「固執」

pertinacious
(ˌpɝtṇˈeʃəs)

adj. 固執的（= *obstinate* ）
Nicole was a *pertinacious* child.
妮可是個固執的孩子。

mule

pertinaciousness
(ˌpɝtṇˈeʃəsnɪs)

n. 固執（= *pertinacity* ）
The panel members were not pleased with his
pertinaciousness. 研究小組的成員對他的固執不滿。

detainer
〔dɪˈtenɚ〕

n. 拘留者；非法侵占
I sued my landlord for being an unlawful *detainer*.
我告我的房東非法侵占。

> detain + er
> │   │
> 拘留 + *n.*   把別人的東西拘留起來，即是「非法侵占」

detainee
〔dɪˌteˈni〕

n. 被拘留者（= *prisoner*）
The foreign *detainees* were
held without bail.
這些外籍犯被收押不得保釋。

> detain + ee
> │   │
> 拘留 + 被動者

detention
〔dɪˈtɛnʃən〕

n. 拘留（= *custody*）
The lawyer said his client's *detention* was
politically motivated.
這名律師說他的客戶被拘留是有政治目的。

retention
〔rɪˈtɛnʃən〕

n. 保留（= *holding*）；記憶力（= *memory*）
The brain tumor severely affected his memory
retention.
大腦腫瘤嚴重影響他的記憶力。

retentive
〔rɪˈtɛntɪv〕

adj. 記性好的
Eleanor has a *retentive* mind.
愛麗諾有很好的記性。

retinue
〔ˈrɛtn̩ˌju〕

n. 侍從（= *attendants*）
The king entered the palace with his *retinue* of soldiers.
國王進入皇宮，他的士兵侍從們隨侍在後。

> re + tin + ue
> │   │   │
> *back* + *hold* + *n.*   跟隨在其後，即是「侍從」

字根 tain

5. *abstention-abstinence-abstinent*

　　第五回是 abs-main-enter 這組核心單字的衍生字，共有 9 字，須背至 5 秒鐘內，變成直覺，才能終生不忘。

abstention
〔 æb'stɛnʃən 〕

n. 戒除 (= *refusal*)
Nutritionists recommend *abstention* from products with high levels of saturated fat.
營養師建議戒除含有高單位飽和脂肪的產品。

$$
\begin{array}{ccc}
abs & + \ ten & + \ tion \\
| & | & | \\
from & + \ keep & + \ n.
\end{array}
$$

abstinence
〔 'æbstənəns 〕

n. 禁慾；節制 (= *temperance*)
Monks practice *abstinence* and reject worldly possessions. 修道士實踐禁慾且拒絕擁有財產。

abstinent
〔 'æbstənənt 〕

adj. 節制的 (= *temperate*)；禁慾的
Louis was *abstinent* from alcohol until he turned 21.
路易士被禁止喝酒，直到滿二十一歲為止。

maintenance[5]
〔 'mentənəns 〕

n. 保養 (= *upkeep*)
Such an expensive car will require a lot of *maintenance*. 如此昂貴的車將要常常保養。

maintainer
〔 men'tenə 〕

n. 養護者
The *maintainers* of democracy will face many challenges in the future.
民主維護者在未來將面對許多挑戰。

maintainable
〔 men'tenəbl̩ 〕

adj. 可維持的
Reggie has yet to realize that his lifestyle is not *maintainable* on such a small salary. 雷奇尚未了解，他的生活方式不是如此微薄的薪水可以維持的。

entertainment[4]
〔͵ɛntɚ'tenmənt〕

n. 娛樂（ = *amusement* ）
Cruise ships generally offer a wide range of *entertainment*.
一般而言郵輪上都會提供很多種娛樂。

entertainer
〔͵ɛntɚ'tenɚ〕

n. 演藝人員
Elvis Presley was the most popular *entertainer* of his time.
貓王是他那個時代最受歡迎的藝人。

entertainingly
〔͵ɛntɚ'tenɪŋlɪ〕

adv. 有趣地
Byron's memoirs are *entertainingly* well-written.
拜倫的回憶錄寫得很棒，趣味盎然。

Byron

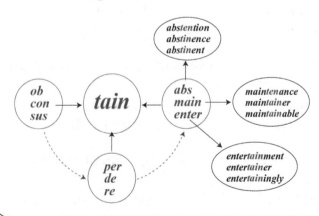

【背誦祕訣】

把 abs-main-enter 這串密碼想成「absmain 這個人走進來」之後，再背誦這組衍生字。

Exercise : Choose the correct answer.

1. Mike is the most _____ fighter of all the neighborhood boys.
   (A) tenacious   (B) suppliant
   (C) subservient   (D) distensible

2. Your comments don't _____ to the discussion.
   (A) pretend   (B) pertain
   (C) propel   (D) posture

3. Mary failed to _____ her driver's license.
   (A) observe   (B) depress
   (C) obtain   (D) compose

4. The pillars _____ the roof of the pit.
   (A) sustain   (B) deserve
   (C) expell   (D) repose

5. Franklin will move to a new apartment at the end of his _____ here.
   (A) extensity   (B) intention
   (C) tensity   (D) tenancy

6. The hotel was built in 1849 and _____ most of its original charm.
   (A) designs   (B) retains
   (C) observes   (D) contends

7. The foreigners were _____ by authorities at the border crossing.
   (A) replicated   (B) pressurized
   (C) interposed   (D) detained

8. The two countries _____ good relations.
   (A) dispel (B) superimpose
   (C) maintain (D) compress

9. Most children are easy to _____.
   (A) entertain (B) conserve
   (C) signalize (D) imply

10. The library _____ a large collection of books.
    (A) expels (B) pretends
    (C) disserves (D) contains

11. The mother's womb has everything necessary for the baby's _____.
    (A) postage (B) sustenance
    (C) complicity (D) propulsion

12. While I admire your _____, I'm afraid I can't offer you the job.
    (A) repulsion (B) distensibility
    (C) pertinacity (D) complexion

13. Most people have limited _____ of their dreams.
    (A) intension (B) retention
    (C) position (D) compulsion

14. The landlord has the right to evict a(n) _____ who doesn't pay the rent.
    (A) tenant (B) employee
    (C) appellor (D) puppet

15. Rick has allergies and must _____ from eating certain foods.
    (A) implicate (B) expose
    (C) compel (D) abstain

字彙測驗詳解

1. (**A**) 麥克是鄰居男孩中最<u>不屈不撓</u>的鬥士。
   (A) ***tenacious***〔tɪˈneʃəs〕*adj.* 不屈不撓的
   (B) suppliant〔ˈsʌplɪənt〕*adj.* 懇求的；哀求的
   (C) subservient〔səbˈsɜvɪənt〕*adj.* 卑屈的；附屬的
   (D) distensible〔dɪˈstɛnsəbḷ〕*adj.* 可擴張的
   fighter〔ˈfaɪtɚ〕*n.* 鬥士

2. (**B**) 你的評論與這次的討論無<u>關</u>。
   (A) pretend〔prɪˈtɛnd〕*v.* 假裝
   (B) ***pertain***〔pɚˈten〕*v.* 有關　(C) propel〔prəˈpɛl〕*v.* 推動
   (D) posture〔ˈpɑstʃɚ〕*n.* 姿勢；態度
   comment〔ˈkɑmɛnt〕*n.* 評論

3. (**C**) 瑪莉無法考到<u>駕照</u>。
   (A) observe〔əbˈzɜv〕*v.* 觀察；遵守
   (B) depress〔dɪˈprɛs〕*v.* 使沮喪
   (C) ***obtain***〔əbˈten〕*v.* 獲得
   (D) compose〔kəmˈpoz〕*v.* 組成

   driver's license

   driver's license 駕照　　***fail to V.*** 未能…

4. (**A**) 坑道須用柱子<u>支撐</u>著。
   (A) ***sustain***〔səˈsten〕*v.* 支撐；維持
   (B) deserve〔dɪˈzɜv〕*v.* 應得
   (C) expel〔ɪkˈspɛl〕*v.* 驅逐　　(D) repose〔rɪˈpoz〕*v.* 休息

5. (**D**) 富蘭克林在這裡的<u>租約</u>到期後，將搬到新的公寓。
   (A) extensity〔ɛkˈstɛnsətɪ〕*n.* 延展
   (B) intention〔ɪnˈtɛnʃən〕*n.* 意圖
   (C) tensity〔ˈtɛnsətɪ〕*n.* 緊張
   (D) ***tenancy***〔ˈtɛnənsɪ〕*n.* 租賃；租賃期間

6. (**B**) 這家飯店建於 1849 年，並<u>保留</u>其大部分原有的魅力。
　　(A) design〔dɪ'zaɪn〕*v.* 設計
　　(B) ***retain***〔rɪ'ten〕*v.* 保持；保留
　　(C) observe〔əb'zɝv〕*v.* 觀察；遵守
　　(D) contend〔kən'tɛnd〕*v.* 聲稱；爭奪
　　original〔ə'rɪdʒənḷ〕*adj.* 原本的　　charm〔tʃɑrm〕*n.* 魅力

7. (**D**) 這群外籍人士在過境時被當局<u>拘留</u>。
　　(A) replicate〔'rɛplɪ,ket〕*v.* 複製
　　(B) pressurize〔'prɛʃə,raɪz〕*v.* 使有壓力
　　(C) interpose〔,ɪntə'poz〕*v.* 插入；介入
　　(D) ***detain***〔dɪ'ten〕*v.* 拘留

border crossing

　　authorities〔ə'θɔrətɪz〕*n. pl.* 當局
　　border〔'bɔrdə〕*n.* 邊界　　crossing〔'krɔsɪŋ〕*n.* 過境處

8. (**C**) 這兩國<u>維持</u>良好的關係。
　　(A) dispel〔dɪ'spɛl〕*v.* 驅散
　　(B) superimpose〔,supərɪm'poz〕*v.* 使重疊
　　(C) ***maintain***〔men'ten〕*v.* 維持
　　(D) compress〔kəm'prɛs〕*v.* 壓縮

9. (**A**) 大多數的孩子很容易<u>取悅</u>。
　　(A) ***entertain***〔,ɛntə'ten〕*v.* 娛樂；使快樂
　　(B) conserve〔kən'sɝv〕*v.* 節約；保存
　　(C) signalize〔'sɪgnḷ,aɪz〕*v.* 顯示
　　(D) imply〔ɪm'plaɪ〕*v.* 暗示

10. (**D**) 這間圖書館<u>有</u>大量的藏書。
　　(A) expel〔ɪk'spɛl〕*v.* 逐出
　　(B) pretend〔prɪ'tɛnd〕*v.* 假裝
　　(C) disserve〔dɪs'sɝv〕*v.* 幫倒忙；損害
　　(D) ***contain***〔kən'ten〕*v.* 包含
　　a large collection of 大量的…收藏

字根 tain

11. (**B**) 母親的子宮裡擁有嬰兒所需要的所有<u>營養</u>。

    (A) postage〔'postɪdʒ〕*n.* 郵資

    (B) ***sustenance***〔'sʌstənəns〕*n.* 營養物；食物

    (C) complicity〔kəm'plɪsətɪ〕*n.* 共謀

    (D) propulsion〔prə'pʌlʃən〕*n.* 推進力

    womb〔wum〕*n.* 子宮

12. (**C**) 雖然我很佩服你的<u>不屈不撓</u>，但我恐怕無法給你這份工作。

    (A) repulsion〔rɪ'pʌlʃən〕*n.* 憎惡；排斥力

    (B) distensibility〔dɪs,tɛnsə'bɪlətɪ〕*n.* 膨脹性

    (C) ***pertinacity***〔,pɝtn̩'æsətɪ〕*n.* 固執；不屈不撓

    (D) complexion〔kəm'plɛkʃən〕*n.* 氣色

13. (**B**) 大多數人只能有限地<u>保有</u>他們的夢想。

    (A) intension〔ɪn'tɛnʃən〕*n.* 緊張

    (B) ***retention***〔rɪ'tɛnʃən〕*n.* 保留

    (C) position〔pə'zɪʃən〕*n.* 位置

    (D) compulsion〔kəm'pʌlʃən〕*n.* 強迫

14. (**A**) 房東有權驅逐不付租金的<u>房客</u>。

    (A) ***tenant***〔'tɛnənt〕*n.* 房客

    (B) employee〔,ɛmplɔɪ'i〕*n.* 員工

    (C) appellor〔ə'pɛlor〕*n.* 上訴人

    (D) puppet〔'pʌpɪt〕*n.* 木偶

puppet

    landlord〔'lænd,lord〕*n.* 房東   right〔raɪt〕*n.* 權力

    evict〔ɪ'vɪkt〕*v.* 驅逐   rent〔rɛnt〕*n.* 租金

15. (**D**) 瑞克有過敏，必須<u>避免</u>吃某些食物。

    (A) implicate〔'ɪmplɪ,ket〕*v.* 使牽涉

    (B) expose〔ɪk'spoz〕*v.* 暴露

    (C) compel〔kəm'pɛl〕*v.* 強迫

    (D) ***abstain***〔əb'sten〕*v.* 抑制；戒除

allergy

    allergy〔'ælədʒɪ〕*n.* 過敏症   certain〔'sɝtn̩〕*adj.* 某些

請連中文一起背，背至一分鐘內，終生不忘。 ★

1

obtain	獲得
contain	包含
sustain	維持
pertain	有關
detain	拘留
retain	保留
abstain	抑制
maintain	維持
entertain	娛樂

2

tenant	房客
tenancy	租賃
tenable	可維持的
tenor	大意
tenure	任期
tenet	主義

tenement	租屋
tenacity	堅持
tenacious	不屈不撓的

字根 tain

3

containment	抑制
container	容器
containerized	用貨櫃運送的
sustainment	支持
sustainer	支持者
sustainable	可支撐的
sustenance	營養物
sustentation	支撐
sustainability	持續性

4

pertinent　　　　有關的
pertinency　　　　相關性
pertinence　　　　相關性

pertinacity　　　固執
pertinacious　固執的
pertinaciousness　固執

detainer　　　拘留者
detainee　　　被拘留者
detention　　　拘留

retention　　　保留
retentive　　　記性好的
retinue　　　　侍從

字根 tain

5

abstention　　戒除
abstinence　　禁慾
abstinent　　　節制的

maintenance　保養
maintainer　　養護者
maintainable　可維持的

entertainment 娛樂
entertainer　　演藝人員
entertainingly 有趣地

【劉毅老師的話】

　　背以前，先聽錄音，聽熟後，
背起來就輕鬆。

Group 17 字根 *form*

目標： ①先將51個字放入短期記憶。
②加快速度至42秒之內，成為長期記憶。

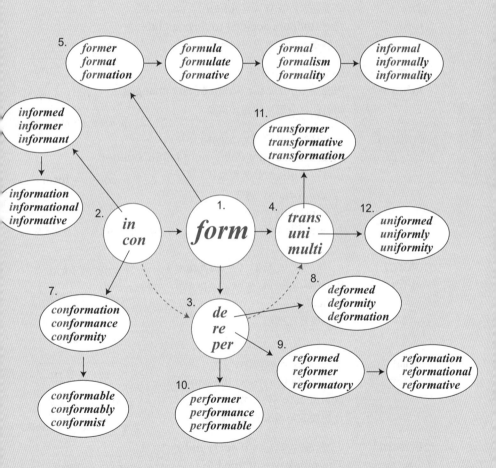

1. 字根 *form* 核心單字

這 9 個字，3 個一組一起背，可先背 6 個，再背 3 個，背熟至 5 秒之內，可成爲長期記憶，才可再背下一組。

form[2]
〔 fɔrm 〕

v. 形成；成立（= *found*）　　*n.* 形狀
The students decided to *form* a club.
這群學生決定成立一個社團。

---

inform[3]
〔 ɪnˈfɔrm 〕

v. 通知（= *notify*）
Please *inform* the group of any changes.
如有任何改變，請通知集團。

> in ＋ form
> ｜　　　｜
> *into* ＋ *form*
>
> 在心裡形成，即是「通知」

---

conform[6]
〔 kənˈfɔrm 〕

v. 順從；遵守（= *comply*）
The law does not *conform* to public opinion.
法律不會順從於公眾輿論。

> conform to 遵守
> = comply with
> = abide by

> con ＋ form
> ｜　　　｜
> *together* ＋ *form*
>
> 讓所有人形狀相同，即是「順從」

---

deform
〔 dɪˈfɔrm 〕

v. 變形；使畸形（= *disfigure*）
Plastic *deforms* when exposed to heat.
塑膠遇熱就變形了。

> de ＋ form
> ｜　　　｜
> *away* ＋ *form*
>
> 正常形狀跑掉，即是「變形；使畸形」

---

reform[4]
〔 rɪˈfɔrm 〕

v. 改革（= *improve*）
He wants to *reform* the nation's health care system.
他想要改革國家的醫療制度。

> re ＋ form
> ｜　　　｜
> *again* ＋ *form*
>
> 再造一個形狀，即是「改革」

---

perform[3]
〔 pɚˈfɔrm 〕

v. 表演；執行（= *carry out*）
The monkey is trained to *perform* tricks. 這隻猴子被訓練來表演特技。

> per ＋ form
> ｜　　　｜
> *thoroughly* ＋ *form*
>
> 把形狀完全表現出來，即是「表演；執行」

transform[4]
〔 træns'fɔrm 〕

v. 使轉變（= *transfigure*）
The new technology will *transform*
the publishing industry.
這項新科技將會改變出版業。

```
trans + form
  |        |
A→B  + form
```

轉移形狀，即是「使轉變」

uniform[2]
〔 'junə‚fɔrm 〕

n. 制服
The soldiers marched
in *uniform*.
這批軍人穿著制服行軍。

```
uni + form
 |      |
one + form
```

所有的人看起來一個外形，
因為穿著「制服」

multiform
〔 'mʌltə‚fɔrm 〕

adj. 多樣的
The aim of science is to understand
the *multiform* universe.
科學的目標就是要了解多樣的宇宙。

```
multi + form
  |       |
many + form
```

有許多形狀，即是「多樣的」

字根
form

【背誦祕訣】

字根 form 的九個核心單字，按照以下的背誦順序
和要訣，你馬上就背得起來。

form
inform　　in 是「進入」，con 是「一起」，用字首的
conform　　意思聯想，背起來就容易了。

deform
reform　　記住這三個字，第二個字母都是 e，背起
perform　　來就容易了。

transform
uniform　　第 2、3 個字重音都在第一音節，uni 表
multiform　　示 one「一」，multi 表示 many「多」。

2. *former-format-formation*

這一組有 12 個字，3 個一組一起背，可先背 6 個，
再背 6 個，背熟至 8 秒之內，變成直覺。

former[2]
('fɔrmɚ)

adj. 以前的（ = *previous*)；前者的
She was on good terms with her
former husband.
她與前夫保持良好的關係。

```
form + er
 |      |
form  + adj.
```

可以形成別的東西，表示它是「以前的」

format[5]
('fɔrmæt)

n. 格式（ = *form*)
The document is accessible in a
variety of *formats*.
這份文件有各種格式。

```
form + at
 |      |
form  + n.
```

按照固定的形狀，即是「格式」

formation[4]
(fɔr'meʃən)

n. 構成；結構（ = *creation*)
The tourists took pictures of the beautiful rock
formations. 遊客們對著美麗的岩石結構拍照。

formula[4]
('fɔrmjələ)

n. 公式
There is a special formula for calculating distance, if
speed and time are known.
如果已知速度和時間，就可利用一個特別的公式來計算距離。

```
form + ula
 |      |
form  + n.
```

每個題目都按相同的形式來算，即是「公式」，
注意其複數型為 formulae/formulas

formulate[6]
('fɔrmjə,let)

v. 使公式化；明確陳述
I don't know enough about the subject to *formulate* an
opinion. 我對這個主題瞭解得不夠，不能明確說出一種看法。

formative
('fɔrmətɪv)

adj. 形成的
Education has a *formative* effect
on a child's mind.
教育對孩子的心靈有塑造力。

```
form + ative
 |      |
form  + adj.
```

字根 form

formal[2]
〔'fɔrml̩〕

adj. 正式的（ = *official* ）
The government has to make
a *formal* announcement.
政府必須發布正式的公告。

```
form + al
 |      |
form  + adj.
```

formalism
〔'fɔrml̩,ɪzəm〕

n. 形式主義
He argued that the term "literary *formalism*" is
outdated. 他認為「文學的形式主義」這個名詞已經過時了。

```
form + al + ism
 |      |     |
form + adj. + 主義
```
ism 是名詞字尾，表示「主義」、
「學說」或「特性」

formality
〔fɔr'mælətɪ〕

n. 拘泥形式；正式手續（ = *ceremony* ）
Chester was not aware of the legal *formalities*
involved in selling his house.
契斯特不知道賣房子時相關的法律手續。

字根 form

informal[2]
〔ɪn'fɔrml̩〕

adj. 非正式的（ = *casual* ）
It was an *informal* gathering of
friends. 這是朋友間非正式的聚會。

```
in + form + al
 |     |     |
not + form + adj.
```

informal

informally
〔ɪn'fɔrməlɪ〕

adv. 非正式地（ = *casually* ）
The children were dressed *informally* in shorts
and T-shirts. 孩子們穿著輕便的短褲與 T 恤。

informality
〔,ɪnfɔr'mælətɪ〕

n. 非正式；不拘禮節
Kevin was surprised by the doctor's friendly
informality. 凱文驚訝於醫生的友善、不拘禮節。

```
in + form + al + ity
 |     |     |    |
not + form + adj. + n.
```

3. *informed-informer-informant*

　　這一組有 12 個字，分成兩組，第一組是 inform 的衍生字，
第二組是 conform 的衍生字，背熟至 8 秒之內，變成直覺。

informed[3]
〔 ɪn'fɔrmd 〕

adj. 有知識的（= *well-informed*）
The new regulations will help people make *informed* decisions about the food they eat.
這些新規定將有助於人們對自己吃的
食物做出有知識的決定。

```
inform + ed
  |        |
 通知    + adj.
```

informer
〔 ɪn'fɔrmɚ 〕

n. 線民
Evidence suggests that he was a government *informer*.
證據顯示他是政府的線民。

informant
〔 ɪn'fɔrmənt 〕

n. 線民（= *informer*）
Police recruited *informants* from the local community.
警方從當地社區招募線民。

information[4]
〔 ͵ɪnfɚ'meʃən 〕

n. 資訊（= *data*）
The website contains a great deal of useful *information*. 這個網站包含了許多有用的資訊。

informational
〔 ͵ɪnfɚ'meʃənl̩ 〕

adj. 新聞的
We watched an *informational* program about global warming.
我們觀賞了一個關於全球暖
化的新聞節目。

```
information + al
     |         |
    資訊     + adj.
```
與許多資訊有關，即是「新聞的」

informative[4]
〔 ɪn'fɔrmətɪv 〕

adj. 知識性的；有教育性的（= *instructive*）
Nancy read an *informative* article about lung cancer.
南西讀了一篇關於肺癌的知識性文章。

```
inform + ative
  |        |
 通知    + adj.
```
通知別人許多事情，即是「知識性的」

conformation
〔͵kɑnfɔr'meʃən 〕

n. 構造；形態（= *structure* ）
The horse has a graceful *conformation*.
這匹馬的形態相當優雅。

conformance
〔 kən'fɔrməns 〕

n. 遵照（= *compliance* ）；一致
The proposal was written in *conformance* to the client's needs.
這個提案是遵照客戶的需求而寫成的。

conformity
〔 kən'fɔrmətɪ 〕

n. 遵照（= *conformance* ）
Joseph acted in *conformity* with his principles.
約瑟夫的行動都遵照他自己的原則。

字根 form

conformable
〔 kən'fɔrməbḷ 〕

adj. 符合的（= *compliant* ）
I hope that our plans are *conformable* to your wishes.
希望我們的計畫符合您的期望。

conformably
〔 kən'fɔrməblɪ 〕

adv. 服從地（= *obediently* ）
They live *conformably* to Jewish customs.
他們的生活服從猶太人的習俗。

```
conform + ab + ly
   |         |     |
  順從      + adj. + adv.
```

conformist
〔 kən'fɔrmɪst 〕

n. 循規蹈矩的人（= *complier* ）
Leonard was taught to be a *conformist*.
里奧納多被教育為循規蹈矩的人。

4. *deformed-deformity-deformation*

這一組有 12 個字，分成三組，第一組是 deform 的
衍生字，第二組是 reform 的衍生字，第三組是 perform
的衍生字，背熟至 8 秒之內，變成直覺。

字根 form

deformed
〔dɪˈfɔrmd〕
adj. 畸形的（ = *malformed* ）
Tony was born with a *deformed* left hand.
東尼生來左手就是畸形的。

deformity
〔dɪˈfɔrmətɪ〕
n. 畸形（ = *malformation* ）
Some *deformities* are not present at birth but
develop later in life.
有些畸形出生時看不到，稍長之後才看得出來。

deformation
〔ˌdifɔrˈmeʃən〕
n. 畸型（ = *malformation* ）
The *deformation* of his legs was the result of a
genetic disorder.
他腿上的畸形是遺傳疾病的結果。

reformed[4]
〔rɪˈfɔrmd〕
adj. 已改善的（ = *improved* ）；改過自新的
His life is *reformed* because of this experience.
因為這次的經驗，他的生活已改善了。

reformer
〔rɪˈfɔrmɚ〕
n. 改革者（ = *improver* ）
Johnson was the leading social *reformer* of the
19th century.
強森是十九世紀主要的社會改革者。

reformatory
〔rɪˈfɔrməˌtorɪ〕
adj. 改革的；矯正的（ = *reformational* ）
Her punishment was intended to be *reformatory*.
處罰她的目的是要矯正她。

reformation
〔ˌrɛfəˈmeʃən 〕

n. 改革（ = *improvement* ）
The U.S. is currently in the middle of an economic *reformation*.
美國目前正處於經濟改革中。

reformational
〔ˌrɛfəˈmeʃənḷ 〕

adj. 革新的（ = *reformatory* ）
Glenn is a student of philosophy and *reformational* thought. 格蘭在學習哲學以及革新的想法。

```
reform  +  ation  +  al
  |            |         |
 改革    +    n.     +  adv.
```

reformative
〔 rɪˈfɔrmətɪv 〕

adj. 改革的（ = *reformational* ）
Another party criticized the government's *reformative* policy.
另一個政黨批評政府的改革政策。

```
reform  +  ative
  |           |
 改革    +   adj.
```

想要進行改革，即是「改革的」

performer[5]
〔 pəˈfɔrmə 〕

n. 表演者（ = *player* ）
Angela is an energetic *performer*.
安琪拉是個充滿活力的表演者。

performance[3]
〔 pəˈfɔrməns 〕

n. 表演（ = *show* ）
The audience cheered his *performance*.
觀衆爲他的表演喝采。

performance

performable
〔 pəˈfɔrməbḷ 〕

adj. 可實行的；可完成的
Some of these calculations are not *performable*.
這些計算中，有些是無法完成的。

```
perform  +  able
  |            |
 執行     +   adj.
```

字根 form

5. *transformer-transformative-transformation*

　　這一組有 6 個字，分成兩組，第一組是 transform 的衍生字，第二組是 uniform 的衍生字，背熟至 4 秒之內，變成直覺。

字根 form

transformer
〔 træns'fɔrmɚ 〕

n. 變壓器
I noticed an electrical *transformer* on a power pole behind the house.
我注意到屋子後面的電線竿上有個變壓器。

transform + er	
| |	
使轉變 + *n.*	使電壓轉變，即是「變壓器」

transformative
〔 træns'fɔrmətɪv 〕

adj. 變化的
A clean room has a *transformative* effect on my mood. 乾淨的房間對我有變化心情的效果。

transformation[6]
〔ˌtrænsfɚ'meʃən 〕

n. 轉變（ = *change* ）
The village underwent a *transformation* from a sleepy little town to a busy tourist destination.
這個村莊由沒有活力的小鎮轉變為熱鬧的旅遊景點。

uniformed
〔'junəˌfɔrmd 〕

adj. 穿制服的
He was escorted to the exit by a *uniformed* security guard. 他被一名穿制服的保全護送到出口。

uniformly
〔'junəˌfɔrmlɪ 〕

adv. 一樣地（ = *equally* ）
The soldiers have a *uniformly* stern appearance.
軍人有著一樣的嚴肅外表。

uniform + ly	
| |	
一樣的 + *adv.*	

uniformity
〔ˌjunə'fɔrmətɪ 〕

n. 一樣；一律（ = *monotony* ）
Nature does not follow the rule of consistency or *uniformity*. 大自然並未遵守一致或千篇一律的規則。

Exercise : Choose the correct answer. ★

1. The committee supported the adoption of _____ measures.
   (A) reformative   (B) contender
   (C) appellant   (D) depressant

2. The suspects in custody have been _____ of their rights.
   (A) complicated   (B) informed
   (C) expelled   (D) designed

3. The ambassador received a _____ invitation from the President.
   (A) formal   (B) significant
   (C) preservative   (D) servile

4. Her face was _____ by anger.
   (A) disserved   (B) deformed
   (C) portended   (D) impeled

5. A tip from a(n) _____ led the police to the fugitive's hideout.
   (A) informant   (B) migrant
   (C) appellate   (D) tentacle

6. The students have to memorize many mathematical _____ for the exam.
   (A) propellers   (B) formulas
   (C) postages   (D) replicas

7. The government is attempting to _____ the nation's education system.
   (A) reform   (B) deposit
   (C) expel   (D) repose

字根 form

8. He never failed to _____ his duties.
   (A) oppose
   (B) perform
   (C) posit
   (D) comply

9. Clouds are _____ of condensed water vapor.
   (A) formations
   (B) applications
   (C) impulsions
   (D) distensions

10. Their _____ was essential to the success of our mission.
    (A) conformity
    (B) repository
    (C) perplexity
    (D) imposture

11. We were amazed by her _____ from an awkward young girl into a beautiful young woman.
    (A) transformation
    (B) opposition
    (C) complication
    (D) assignation

12. The professor preferred _____ discussions to lectures.
    (A) puppet
    (B) signal
    (C) repressive
    (D) informal

13. Critics praised the dancer's most recent _____.
    (A) performance
    (B) uniform
    (C) target
    (D) servility

14. I found the lecture to be very _____.
    (A) suppressive
    (B) informative
    (C) multiplicative
    (D) signatory

15. Kosher foods _____ to the rules of the Jewish religion.
    (A) distend
    (B) conform
    (C) repulse
    (D) propose

字根 form

字 彙 測 驗 詳 解

1. (**A**) 委員會支持採取改革的措施。

(A) *reformative* 〔 rɪˈfɔrmətɪv 〕 *adj.* 改革的

(B) contender 〔 kənˈtɛndɚ 〕 *n.* 競爭者

(C) appellant 〔 əˈpɛlənt 〕 *adj.* 上訴的

(D) depressant 〔 dɪˈprɛsənt 〕 *adj.* 有鎮靜作用的　*n.* 鎮靜劑

committee 〔 kəˈmɪtɪ 〕 *n.* 委員會

adoption 〔 əˈdɑpʃən 〕 *n.* 採用　　measure 〔ˈmɛʒɚ 〕 *n.* 措施

2. (**B**) 被羈押的嫌犯已經被告知他們的權利。

(A) complicate 〔ˈkɑmpləˌket 〕 *v.* 使複雜

(B) *inform* 〔 ɪnˈfɔrm 〕 *v.* 通知；告知 < *of* >

(C) expel 〔 ɪkˈspɛl 〕 *v.* 驅逐

(D) design 〔 dɪˈzaɪn 〕 *v.* 設計

suspect 〔ˈsʌspɛkt 〕 *n.* 嫌犯

custody 〔ˈkʌstədɪ 〕 *n.* 拘留

3. (**A**) 大使收到來自總統的正式邀請。

(A) *formal* 〔ˈfɔrml̩ 〕 *adj.* 正式的

(B) significant 〔 sɪgˈnɪfəkənt 〕 *adj.* 重要的；意義重大的

(C) preservative 〔 prɪˈzɜvətɪv 〕 *adj.* 保護的

(D) servile 〔ˈsɜvl̩ 〕 *adj.* 奴隸的；奴性的

ambassador 〔 æmˈbæsədɚ 〕 *n.* 大使

4. (**B**) 她氣得臉都變形了。

(A) disserve 〔 dɪsˈsɜv 〕 *v.* 幫倒忙；損害

(B) *deform* 〔 dɪˈfɔrm 〕 *v.* 使成畸形；變形

(C) portend 〔 pɔrˈtɛnd 〕 *v.* 預示

(D) impel 〔 ɪmˈpɛl 〕 *v.* 驅使

字根 form

5. (**A**) <u>線民</u>所提供的線索讓警方找到了逃犯的藏身處。

    (A) ***informant*** ﹝ ɪnˈfɔrmənt ﹞ *n.* 線民

    (B) migrant ﹝ˈmaɪgrənt ﹞ *n.* 移民

    (C) appellate ﹝ əˈpɛlɪt ﹞ *adj.* 上訴的

    (D) tentacle ﹝ˈtɛntəkḷ﹞ *n.* 觸鬚；觸角；觸手

tip ﹝ tɪp ﹞ *n.* 線索   lead ﹝ lid ﹞ *v.* 引導

fugitive ﹝ˈfjudʒətɪv ﹞ *n.* 逃犯；逃亡者

hideout ﹝ˈhaɪd͵aut ﹞ *n.* 藏身處；藏匿處

6. (**B**) 學生必須爲考試背下許多數學的<u>公式</u>。

    (A) propeller ﹝ prəˈpɛlə ﹞ *n.* 螺旋槳

    (B) ***formula*** ﹝ˈfɔrmjələ ﹞ *n.* 公式

    (C) postage ﹝ˈpostɪdʒ ﹞ *n.* 郵資

    (D) replica ﹝ˈrɛplɪkə ﹞ *n.* 複製品

memorize ﹝ˈmɛmə͵raɪz ﹞ *v.* 記憶；背誦

mathematical ﹝͵mæθəˈmætɪkḷ﹞ *adj.* 數學的

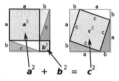

mathematical formula

7. (**A**) 政府正嘗試<u>改革</u>國家的教育體制。

    (A) ***reform*** ﹝ rɪˈfɔrm ﹞ *v.* 改革；改良

    (B) deposit ﹝ dɪˈpɑzɪt ﹞ *v.* 存（款）

    (C) expel ﹝ ɪkˈspɛl ﹞ *v.* 驅逐

    (D) repose ﹝ rɪˈpoz ﹞ *v.* 休息

attempt ﹝ əˈtɛmpt ﹞ *v.* 嘗試

8. (**B**) 他每次都有盡自己的<u>義務</u>。

    (A) oppose ﹝ əˈpoz ﹞ *v.* 反對

    (B) ***perform*** ﹝ pəˈfɔrm ﹞ *v.* 執行；表演

    (C) posit ﹝ˈpɑzɪt ﹞ *v.* 假定

    (D) comply ﹝ kəmˈplaɪ ﹞ *v.* 遵守；服從

fail to V. 未能

duty ﹝ˈdjutɪ ﹞ *n.* 責任；義務

9. (**A**) 雲是水氣凝結<u>而成</u>。

    (A) *formation*〔 fɔr'meʃən 〕*n.* 構成

    (B) application〔͵æplə'keʃən 〕*n.* 申請；應用

    (C) impulsion〔 ɪm'pʌlʃən 〕*n.* 驅使；推動；衝動

    (D) distension〔 dɪ'stɛnʃən 〕*n.* 膨脹

10. (**A**) 他們的<u>服從</u>對我們任務的成功是必要的。

    (A) *conformity*〔 kən'fɔrmətɪ 〕*n.* 遵照；服從

    (B) repository〔 rɪ'pazə͵torɪ 〕*n.* 存放處；貯藏室

    (C) perplexity〔 pɚ'plɛksətɪ 〕*n.* 困惑

    (D) imposture〔 ɪm'pastʃɚ 〕*n.* 欺騙

    essential〔 ə'sɛnʃəl 〕*adj.* 必要的

    mission〔'mɪʃən 〕*n.* 任務

11. (**A**) 對於她從個笨拙的小女孩<u>轉變</u>成美麗的小女人，我們都非常驚訝。

    (A) *transformation*〔͵trænfɚ'meʃən 〕*n.* 轉變

    (B) opposition〔͵apə'zɪʃən 〕*n.* 反對

    (C) complication〔͵kamplə'keʃən 〕*n.* 複雜

    (D) assignation〔͵æsɪg'neʃən 〕*n.* 約會；幽會

    amaze〔 ə'mez 〕*v.* 使驚訝

    awkward〔'ɔkwɚd 〕*adj.* 笨拙的

12. (**D**) 比起演講，教授比較喜歡<u>非正式的</u>討論。

    (A) puppet〔'pʌpɪt 〕*n.* 傀儡；木偶

    (B) signal〔'sɪgnḷ 〕*n.* 信號　*adj.* 顯著的

    (C) repressive〔 rɪ'prɛsɪv 〕*adj.* 專制的

    (D) *informal*〔 ɪn'fɔrmḷ 〕*adj.* 非正式的

    professor〔 prə'fɛsɚ 〕*n.* 教授

    lecture〔'lɛktʃɚ 〕*n.* 演講；講課

字根 form

13. (**A**) 評論家讚賞這位舞者最近的<u>表演</u>。

    (A) *performance* ﹝ pəˋfɔrməns ﹞ *n.* 表演

    (B) uniform ﹝ˋjunəˏfɔrm ﹞ *n.* 制服

    (C) target ﹝ˋtɑrgɪt ﹞ *n.* 目標；靶

    (D) servility ﹝ səˋvɪlətɪ ﹞ *n.* 奴役

    critic ﹝ˋkrɪtɪk ﹞ *n.* 評論家

    most recent 最近的；最新的 (= *latest*)

14. (**B**) 我覺得這場演講非常<u>有知識性</u>。

    (A) suppressive ﹝ səˋprɛsɪv ﹞ *adj.* 壓抑的

    (B) *informative* ﹝ ɪnˋfɔrmətɪv ﹞ *adj.* 知識性的

    (C) multiplicative ﹝ˏmʌltɪˋplɪkətɪv ﹞ *adj.* 增加的

    (D) signatory ﹝ˋsɪgnəˏtɔrɪ ﹞ *n.* 簽署者

15. (**B**) 潔淨衛生的食物<u>與</u>猶太人的信仰<u>一致</u>。

    (A) distend ﹝ dɪˋstɛnd ﹞ *v.* 膨脹

    (B) *conform* ﹝ kənˋfɔrm ﹞ *v.* 順從；一致 < *to* >

    (C) repulse ﹝ rɪˋpʌls ﹞ *v.* 使厭惡；拒絕

    (D) propose ﹝ prəˋpoz ﹞ *v.* 提議

    kosher ﹝ˋkoʃɚ ﹞ *adj.* 潔淨的；衛生的

    Jewish ﹝ˋdʒuɪʃ ﹞ *adj.* 猶太人的；猶太教的

    religion ﹝ rɪˋlɪdʒən ﹞ *n.* 宗教

【劉毅老師的話】

    一個人背單字較無聊，找個朋友一起背，用比賽的方式，輪流背誦，效果較好，歡迎參加劉毅英文「字根記憶班」，大家一起背誦，效果最佳。

字根 form

請連中文一起背，背至65秒內，終生不忘。　　　　✦

1

form	形成
inform	通知
conform	順從
deform	變形
reform	改革
perform	表演
transform	使轉變
uniform	制服
multiform	多樣的

2

former	以前的
format	格式
formation	構成
formula	公式
formulate	使公式化
formative	形成的
formal	正式的
formalism	形式主義
formality	拘泥形式

informal	非正式的
informally	非正式地
informality	非正式

3

informed	有知識的
informer	線民
informant	線民
information	資訊
informational	新聞的
informative	知識性的

conformation	構造
conformance	遵照
conformity	遵照
conformable	符合的
conformably	服從地
conformist	循規蹈矩的人

字根 form

字根 form

4

deformed	畸形的
deformity	畸形
deformation	畸形

reformed	已改善的
reformer	改革者
reformatory	改革的

reformation	改革
reformational	革新的
reformative	改革的

performer	表演者
performance	表演
performable	可實行的

5

transformer	變壓器
transformative	變化的
transformation	轉變

uniformed	穿制服的
uniformly	一樣地
uniformity	一樣

【劉毅老師的話】

　　對於不知道如何用的單字，可參考例句，也可做做練習題。

Group 18 字根 *mit*

目標： ① 先將48個字放入短期記憶。
② 加快速度至40秒之內，成為長期記憶。

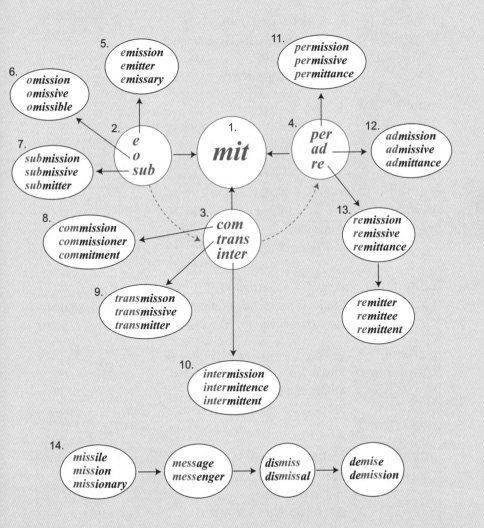

1. 字根 *mit* 核心單字

　　這九個核心單字，3 個一組，一起背，很容易就背起來了。把九個單字背到 5 秒之內，變成長期記憶，接下來的單字就很簡單。

emit
〔 ɪˋmɪt 〕

v. 發射（ = *send out* ）
The sun *emits* a massive amount of heat and energy.
太陽發出大量的熱與能量。

```
e  +  mit
|       |
out + send
```
送出去，即是「發射」

omit[2]
〔 oˋmɪt 〕

v. 省略（ = *neglect* ）
A revised edition of the book *omits* the graphic language.
這本書的修訂版省略了圖解。

```
o  +  mit
|       |
away + send
```
把不用的送走，即是「省略」

submit[5]
〔 səbˋmɪt 〕

v. 屈服；投降（ = *yield* ）
We were forced to *submit* to their demands.
我們被迫屈服於他們的要求。

```
sub  +  mit
|         |
under + send
```
把自己送到下面，即是「屈服」

commit[4]
〔 kəˋmɪt 〕

v. 委託（ = *consign* ）；犯（罪）
Students must *commit* these vocabulary words to their long-term memory. 學生們必須把這些單字放入長期記憶中。

transmit[6]
〔 trænsˋmɪt 〕

v. 傳送（ = *pass on* ）；傳染；傳導
Please *transmit* this message to all the employees.
請把這則訊息傳達給所有員工。

```
trans  +  mit
|           |
across + send
```
從一個地方送到另一個地方，即是「傳送」

intermit
〔 ͵ɪntəˋmɪt 〕

v. 中斷（ = *pause* ）
Let's *intermit* the meeting and have lunch.
讓我們暫停會議，先吃午餐。

```
inter  +  mit
|           |
between + send
```
送到中間，即是「中斷」

permit[3]
〔 pɚˋmɪt 〕

v. 允許（＝*allow*）
The park does not *permit* dogs without a leash.
沒有繫狗鍊的狗不得進入這個公園。

```
  per   +  mit
   |        |
through + send      要通過就要先取得的，即是「允許」
```

admit[3]
〔 ədˋmɪt 〕

v. 承認（＝*acknowledge*）
Oliver refused to *admit* his
involvement in the robbery.
奧利佛拒絕承認參與搶案。

```
 ad  +  mit
  |       |
 to  + send
```
把事實送出來，即是「承認」

remit
〔 rɪˋmɪt 〕

v. 匯款
I'll *remit* the money to you
as soon as possible.
我會儘快把錢匯給你。

```
 re   +  mit
  |        |
back  + send
```
把錢寄回去要「匯款」

字根 mit

【背誦祕訣】

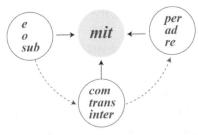

這組 9 個核心單字，重音都在 mit 上，很好記。
記住第一個就「發射」，往外跑，用 re 做結束，
有「休息」的意思。

commit
transmit   記住中間三個字，都是在兩者或兩地
intermit   之間的關係，背起來就很簡單

2. emission-emitter-emissary

這一組由 emit、omit、submit 衍生出九個單字，三個
一組一起背，很容易就能背至 5 秒之內，沒有負擔。

emission
〔 ɪ'mɪʃən 〕

n. 發射；排放（= *release*）
International laws regulate the *emission* of greenhouse
gases into the atmosphere.
國際法限制溫室氣體排放至大氣中的量。

```
e  + miss + ion
|     |      |
out + send +  n.
```
直接往外送的名詞，即是「發射」，
miss 是 mit 的變化形。

emitter
〔 ɪ'mɪtɚ 〕

n. 發射器
The television remote control won't work if you have
your thumb over the *emitter*.
如果你的大拇指擋住發射器，電視遙控器就起不了作用。

字根 mit

emissary
〔'ɛmə,sɛrɪ 〕

n. 特使（= *agent*）
The president sent one of his
emissaries to attend the
memorial service.
總統派遣一位特使去參加追悼儀式。

```
e  + miss + ary
|     |      |
out + send +  人
```
送出消息的人，即是「特使」

omission
〔 o'mɪʃən 〕

n. 省略（= *skip*）
The editor found several noticeable *omissions* of fact in
the article. 編輯發現這篇文章中有一些對事實的明顯省略。

omissive
〔 o'mɪsɪv 〕

adj. 疏忽的
We are *omissive* of responsibility in the matter.
我們疏忽了這件事的責任。

omissible
〔 o'mɪsəbl̩ 〕

adj. 可省略的
There are several *omissible* passages in the text.
文章中有很多可省略的段落。

submission
〔 səb'mɪʃən 〕

n. 屈服（ = *surrender* ）
I will not stop fighting until I gain your total *submission*.
直到你完全屈服於我，我才會停止作戰。

submissive
〔 səb'mɪsɪv 〕

adj. 屈服的（ = *yielding* ）
The dog sat back on its hind legs in a *submissive* posture. 這隻狗用一種服從的姿勢坐在自己後腿上。

sub	+ miss	+ ive	
|	|	|	把自己送往較低下的位置，
under	+ *send*	+ *adj.*	即是「屈服的」

submitter
〔 səb'mɪtɚ 〕

n. 屈服者
The problem of feeding the enemy *submitters* became a pressing issue.
供養敵方投降者的問題，變成一個迫切的議題。

字根 mit

【背誦祕訣】

　　這一組九個字，每一小組第一個字都是 sion 結尾的名詞，這樣記就不會記錯。

　　除了 emissary 以外，其他字的重音都在第二音節上，記住這個特例，就很容易背了。

3. *commission-commissioner-commitment*

這一回一樣 9 個字,由核心單字 commit、transmit、intermit 各衍生出三個字,快速背誦至 5 秒內,變成不思考的直覺,才會記得久。

commission[5]
〔 kə'mɪʃən 〕

n. 委員會 (= *committee*);佣金
A *commission* was established to investigate the financial crisis. 有個委員會被成立來調查金融危機。

commissioner
〔 kə'mɪʃənɚ 〕

n. 委員
The office of *commissioner* is a lifetime appointment. 這個委員職位是終身職。

commitment[6]
〔 kə'mɪtmənt 〕

n. 承諾 (= *promise*);投入 (= *dedication*)
Dale is a good drummer but he lacks the *commitment* to play at a professional level.
戴爾是一個很好的鼓手,但他不夠投入,無法晉升專業水平。

transmission[6]
〔 træns'mɪʃən 〕

n. 傳送 (= *transmitting*)
Frequent hand washing cuts down on the *transmission* of disease. 常洗手可減少疾病的傳播。

transmissive
〔 trænz'mɪsɪv 〕

adj. 傳送的;傳染的
Transmissive LCDs are commonly used in laptop computers.
透射式液晶顯示器常被用於筆記型電腦。

transmissive LCD

transmitter
〔 træns'mɪtɚ 〕

n. 傳播物
A bolt of lightning struck the radio *transmitter*, interrupting the broadcast.
一道閃電擊中了電台發射器,中斷了廣播。

radio transmitter

字根 mit

intermission
〔͵ɪntəˈmɪʃən〕

n. 休息時間（= *break*）；中止；中斷
We will resume our meeting after a brief *intermission.*
我們短暫休息後會再繼續我們的會議。

intermittence
〔͵ɪntəˈmɪtn̩s〕

n. 間歇性
The *intermittence* of her speech made it hard to follow. 她斷斷續續的演說讓人很難聽懂。

inter	+ mitt	+	ence
|	|		|
between	+ *send*	+	抽象名詞字尾

中斷的名詞，即是「間歇性」

intermittent
〔͵ɪntəˈmɪtn̩t〕

adj. 間歇的（= *periodic*）
After two hours of *intermittent* rain, the skies finally cleared. 斷斷續續下了兩小時的雨後，天空終於放晴。

inter	+ mitt	+ ent
|	|	|
between	+ *send*	+ *adj.*

送到中間打斷進行，即是「間歇的」

字根 mit

――【背誦祕訣】――

　　這一組九個字，和上一組一樣都以 sion 結尾的名詞做每組的開頭，非常好記。

　　記住重音都在字根 mis 或 mit 上面，就不會記錯。

commission
commissioner
commitment
→
transmisson
transmissive
transmitter
→
intermission
intermittence
intermittent

4. *permission-permissive-permittance*

　　這一組只有6個字，由 permit 和 admit 分別衍生出三個，背至3秒內，一下就變成長期記憶，煩惱都消了。

permission[3]
〔 pɚ'mɪʃən 〕

n. 許可（= *allowance*）
I don't need your *permission* to sit here.
我坐在這裡不需要你的同意。

permissive
〔 pɚ'mɪsɪv 〕

adj. 許可的；寬容的（= *tolerant*）
Natalie is a *permissive* teacher who allows her students to sleep in class.
娜塔莉是一位寬容的老師，她容許學生在上課時睡覺。

permittance
〔 pɚ'mɪtn̩s 〕

n. 許可（= *permission*）
The mission will continue with the Captain's *permittance*. 在船長的同意之下任務將繼續進行。

per	+ mitt +	ance
through	+ *send* +	抽象名詞字尾

能夠通過，就是抽象名詞「許可」

admission[4]
〔 əd'mɪʃən 〕

n. 准許進入；承認（= *acknowledgement*）
He was given free *admission* to the exhibition.
他獲准免費進入展覽會。

ad +	miss +	ion
to +	*send* +	*n.*

「承認」你就「准許你進入」

admissive
〔 əd'mɪsɪv 〕

adj. 准許進入的；許可的
The client was *admissive* to our proposal.
客戶同意我們的提案。

admittance
〔 əd'mɪtn̩s 〕

n. 入場權（= *entry*）；入場許可
Gloria was denied *admittance* to the club.
葛洛瑞亞不得進入俱樂部。

5. *remission-remissive-remittance*

這一組有 6 個字，全部由 remit 衍生出來，remit 除
「匯款」之外，也有「減輕；寬恕」之意。

remission
〔 rɪˋmɪʃən 〕

n. 減輕
His cancer is in *remission*.
他的癌症情況有好轉。

```
re  + miss + ion
 |     |      |
back + send +  n.
```

生病時身體回到原來的狀
態，就「減輕」病痛了

remissive
〔 rɪˋmɪsɪv 〕

adj. 寬恕的（ = *forgiving* ）
"Sorry," I said, and she gave me a *remissive* glance.
我說：「對不起」，她給了我一個寬恕的眼神。

remittance
〔 rɪˋmɪtn̩s 〕

n. 匯款（ = *payment* ）
Once we receive your *remittance* of $19.95, the product
will be shipped to you.
一旦我們收到你所匯的款項 19.95 元，貨品就會運送給你。

字根 mit

remitter
〔 rɪˋmɪtɚ 〕

n. 匯款人
The government provides a service to *remitters* for
sending money overseas.
政府為匯款人提供匯款至
海外的服務。

```
remit +  ter
  |       |
匯款   + 主動者
```

remittee
〔 ͵rɪmɪˋti 〕

n. 受款人
The *remittee* must be the direct relative of the remitter.
受款人必須是匯款人的直系親屬。

```
remit +  tee
  |       |
匯款   + 被動者
```

remittent
〔 rɪˋmɪtn̩t 〕

adj. 時好時壞的；間歇的
She has suffered from *remittent* bouts of nausea.
她的噁心症狀時好時壞。

6. *missile-mission-missionary*

最後一組字共有 9 個，由 mit 的變體 mis 和 mess
衍生出來，根據發音很快就背好了。

missile[3]
('mɪsḷ)

n. 飛彈 (= *projectile*)
Iran is threatening to launch
a *missile* at Israel.
伊朗威脅要對以色列發射飛彈。

> miss + ile
> | |
> *send* + *n.*

投擲出來的東西，即是「飛彈」

mission[3]
('mɪʃən)

n. 任務 (= *assignment*)
Their *mission* was to irrigate the desert.
他們的任務是要灌溉沙漠。

missionary[6]
('mɪʃən‚ɛrɪ)

n. 傳教士 (= *preacher*)
Missionaries are not welcome
in this town.
在這個鎮上，傳教士是不受歡迎的。

> miss + ion + ary
> | | |
> *send* + *n.* + 人

被派出進行傳教任務的人，
即是「傳教士」

message[2]
('mɛsɪdʒ)

n. 訊息
I didn't receive your *message*.
我沒有收到你的訊息。

> mess + age
> | |
> *send* + *n.*

送給別人的消息，即是「訊息」

messenger[4]
('mɛsn̩dʒɚ)

n. 信差
The package will be delivered by a bicycle *messenger*.
這個包裹將由騎腳踏車的信差遞送。

dismiss[4]
(dɪs'mɪs)

v. 解散；解僱；駁回
The judge *dismissed* all charges against the defendant.
法官駁回對這位被告的所有指控。

dismissal
(dɪs'mɪsḷ)

n. 解散；解職
Such an action would result in his *dismissal* from the
board of directors. 這樣的舉動會致使他被董事會免職。

字根 mit

demise
〔 dɪˋmaɪz 〕

n. 死亡（= *death*）
Who is to blame for Michael
Jackson's sudden *demise*?
麥可的猝死是誰的責任？

$$\begin{array}{ccc} de & + & mise \\ | & & | \\ away & + & send \end{array}$$

放手離開，即是「死亡」

demission
〔 dɪˋmɪʃən 〕

n. 辭職（= *resignation*）
The corrupt politician was forced into *demission*.
貪污的政客被迫下台。

【背誦祕訣】

這一組由 mit 的變體 mis 做衍生：

$\left\{\begin{array}{l} missile \\ mission \\ missionary \end{array}\right.$　這一組很好背，記住重音節都在第一音節，都是 /ɪ/ 的發音，就背起來了。

$\left\{\begin{array}{l} message \\ messenger \end{array}\right.$　這一組，記住重音也在第一音節，唸 /ɛ/ 的音，就背起來了。

$\left\{\begin{array}{l} dismiss \\ dismissal \end{array}\right.$

$\left\{\begin{array}{l} demise \\ demission \end{array}\right.$　這二組，記住第一音節母音都發 /ɪ/ 的音，重音在第二音節，就能背起來了。

字根 mit

📝 **Exercise** : Choose the correct answer. ✦

1. The factory _____ a large amount of carbon dioxide into the atmosphere.
   (A) replies
   (B) deploys
   (C) signifies
   (D) emits

2. Susan _____ ten percent of her weekly salary to charity.
   (A) expresses
   (B) portends
   (C) commits
   (D) impels

3. The army intends to occupy the city and force its inhabitants into _____.
   (A) compulsion
   (B) deposition
   (C) explication
   (D) submission

4. Paris Hilton was shocked by her _____ from the guest list.
   (A) complexion
   (B) assignation
   (C) omission
   (D) reservation

5. Despite our differences, we made a(n) _____ to continue working together.
   (A) contestant
   (B) intendant
   (C) pretension
   (D) commitment

6. The city council voted to _____ the sale of alcoholic beverages at sporting events.
   (A) repel
   (B) compose
   (C) permit
   (D) replicate

7. Vanessa chose to _____ her date of birth on the application form.
   (A) triple
   (B) signal
   (C) preserve
   (D) omit

字根 mit

8. Mosquitoes _____ deadly diseases to humans.
   (A) attend
   (B) superintend
   (C) transmit
   (D) repulse

9. The rebels would rather die fighting than _____ to the enemy.
   (A) pulsate
   (B) oppose
   (C) depress
   (D) submit

10. The men worked 15 hours straight without _____.
    (A) repression
    (B) exploitation
    (C) intermission
    (D) impulsion

11. You have to _____, the other team played a better game.
    (A) subserve
    (B) repose
    (C) impress
    (D) admit

12. Christine serves on a _____ that regulates commercial development in rural areas of the country.
    (A) diploma
    (B) merchant
    (C) commission
    (D) attendance

13. Timothy asked for _____ to leave the room.
    (A) pulsation
    (B) impression
    (C) complication
    (D) permission

14. Single parents are more likely to be _____ with their children.
    (A) explicable
    (B) assignable
    (C) permissive
    (D) extensive

15. Isaac was denied _____ to the university.
    (A) admission
    (B) pretension
    (C) expulsion
    (D) supposition

字彙測驗詳解

1. (**D**) 工廠<u>排放</u>大量的二氧化碳到大氣中。
   (A) reply〔rɪˋplaɪ〕v. 回答　　(B) deploy〔dɪˋplɔɪ〕v. 部署
   (C) signify〔ˋsɪgnəˏfaɪ〕v. 表示
   (D) *emit*〔ɪˋmɪt〕v. 發射；排放
   atmosphere〔ˋætməsˏfɪr〕n. 大氣

2. (**C**) 蘇珊把她週薪的百分之十<u>交付</u>慈善機構。
   (A) express〔ɪkˋsprɛs〕v. 表達
   (B) portend〔porˋtɛnd〕v. 預示
   (C) *commit*〔kəˋmɪt〕v. 委託；交付；犯（罪）
   (D) impel〔ɪmˋpɛl〕v. 驅使
   charity〔ˋtʃærətɪ〕n. 慈善機構

3. (**D**) 軍隊打算佔領城市，然後迫使居民<u>投降</u>。
   (A) compulsion〔kəmˋpʌlʃən〕n. 強制；衝動
   (B) deposition〔ˏdɛpəˋzɪʃən〕n. 罷免
   (C) explication〔ˏɛksplɪˋkeʃən〕n. 說明
   (D) *submission*〔səbˋmɪʃən〕n. 屈服；投降
   occupy〔ˋɑkjəˏpaɪ〕v. 佔據；佔用
   force〔fors〕v. 強迫　　inhabitant〔ɪnˋhæbətənt〕n. 居民

4. (**C**) 芭莉絲希爾頓為她被從賓客名單中<u>刪除</u>感到震驚。
   (A) complexion〔kəmˋplɛkʃən〕n. 膚色
   (B) assignation〔ˏæsɪgˋneʃən〕n. 幽會
   (C) *omission*〔oˋmɪʃən〕n. 省略；刪除
   (D) reservation〔ˏrɛzɚˋveʃən〕n. 預訂

   Paris Hilton

5. (**D**) 儘管我們意見分歧，我們做出<u>承諾</u>要繼續合作。
   (A) contestant〔kənˋtɛstənt〕n. 競爭者
   (B) intendant〔ɪnˋtɛndənt〕n. 管理者；監督者
   (C) pretension〔prɪˋtɛnʃən〕n. 假裝；做作
   (D) *commitment*〔kəˋmɪtmənt〕n. 承諾；委託

6. (**C**) 市議會投票決定<u>允許</u>在體育活動中出售含酒精的飲料。

    (A) repel〔rɪ'pɛl〕*v.* 驅逐；拒絕

    (B) compose〔kəm'poz〕*v.* 組成；作（曲）

    (C) ***permit***〔pɚ'mɪt〕*v.* 允許

    (D) replicate〔'rɛplɪˌket〕*v.* 複製

beverage

city council 市議會　　beverage〔'bɛvrɪdʒ〕*n.* 飲料

event〔ɪ'vɛnt〕*n.* 大型活動；（比賽）項目

7. (**D**) 凡妮莎選擇<u>忽略</u>她申請表格內的出生日期。

    (A) triple〔'trɪpl̩〕*v.* 使成三倍

    (B) signal〔'sɪgnl̩〕*v.* 打信號

    (C) preserve〔prɪ'zɝv〕*v.* 保存

    (D) ***omit***〔o'mɪt〕*v.* 省略

8. (**C**) 蚊子<u>傳染</u>致命的疾病給人類。

    (A) attend〔ə'tɛnd〕*v.* 出席；參加

    (B) superintend〔ˌsuprɪn'tɛnd〕*v.* 監督

    (C) ***transmit***〔træns'mɪt〕*v.* 傳送；傳染；傳導

    (D) repulse〔rɪ'pʌls〕*v.* 拒絕；擊退

mosquito〔mə'skito〕*n.* 蚊子　　deadly〔'dɛdlɪ〕*adj.* 致病的

9. (**D**) 這些反叛份子寧可戰死也不願向敵人<u>投降</u>。

    (A) pulsate〔'pʌlset〕*v.* 脈動　　(B) oppose〔ə'poz〕*v.* 反對

    (C) depress〔dɪ'prɛs〕*v.* 使沮喪

    (D) ***submit***〔səb'mɪt〕*v.* 服服；投降 < *to* >

rebel〔'rɛbl̩〕*n.* 反叛者

10. (**C**) 這些人連續工作十五個小時沒有<u>中斷</u>。

    (A) repression〔rɪ'prɛʃən〕*n.* 抑制；鎮壓

    (B) exploitation〔ˌɛksplɔɪ'teʃən〕*n.* 開發；剝削；利用

    (C) ***intermission***〔ˌɪntɚ'mɪʃən〕*n.* 休息時間；中止；中斷

    (D) impulsion〔ɪm'pʌlʃən〕*n.* 衝動；刺激

straight〔stret〕*adv.* 連續地；無間斷地

11. (**D**) 你必須<u>承認</u>，另一隊打出了更漂亮的比賽。
    (A) subserve〔səb'sɝv〕v. 有助於
    (B) repose〔rɪ'poz〕v. 休息
    (C) impress〔ɪm'prɛs〕v. 使印象深刻
    (D) *admit*〔əd'mɪt〕v. 承認

12. (**C**) 克莉絲汀任職於<u>委員會</u>，負責規劃該國鄉村地區的商業發展。
    (A) diploma〔dɪ'plomə〕n. 畢業證書；文憑
    (B) merchant〔'mɝtʃənt〕n. 商人
    (C) *commission*〔kən'mɪʃən〕n. 委員會
    (D) attendance〔'ətɛndəns〕n. 出席
    serve〔sɝv〕v. 服務；任職　　regulate〔'rɛgjə,let〕v. 管理
    commercial〔kə'mɝʃəl〕adj. 商業的　　rural〔'rurəl〕adj. 鄉村的

13. (**D**) 提摩西請求<u>允許</u>離開房間。
    (A) pulsation〔pʌl'seʃən〕n. 脈搏；脈動
    (B) impression〔ɪm'prɛʃən〕n. 印象
    (C) complication〔,kɑmplə'keʃən〕n. 複雜
    (D) *permission*〔pə'mɪʃən〕n. 許可

14. (**C**) 單親父母較可能對子女<u>寬容</u>。
    (A) explicable〔'ɛksplɪkəbḷ〕adj. 可解釋的
    (B) assignable〔ə'saɪnəbḷ〕adj. 可指派的
    (C) *permissive*〔pə'mɪsɪv〕adj. 寬容的
    (D) extensive〔ɪk'stɛnsɪv〕adj. 廣泛的

15. (**A**) 埃薩克被拒絕給予大學<u>入學許可</u>。
    (A) *admission*〔əd'mɪʃən〕n. 入學許可 < to >
    (B) pretension〔prɪ'tɛnʃən〕n. 假裝
    (C) expulsion〔ɪk'spʌlʃən〕n. 驅逐；逐出
    (D) supposition〔,sʌpə'zɪʃən〕n. 推測；假設
    deny〔dɪ'naɪ〕v. 否認；不給予

請連中文一起背，背至一分鐘內，終生不忘。

1

emit	發射
omit	省略
submit	屈服
commit	委託
transmit	傳送
intermit	中斷
permit	允許
admit	承認
remit	匯款

2

emission	發射
emitter	發射器
emissary	特使
omission	省略
omissive	疏忽的
omissible	可省略的

submission	屈服
submissive	屈服的
submitter	屈服者

3

commission	委員會
commissioner	委員
commitment	承諾
transmission	傳送
transmissive	傳送的
transmitter	傳播物
intermission	休息時間
intermittence	間歇性
intermittent	間歇的

字根 mit

4

permission	許可
permissive	許可的
permittance	許可
admission	准許進入
admissive	准許進入的
admittance	入場

5

remission	減輕
remissive	寬恕的
remittance	匯款
remitter	匯款人
remittee	受款人
remittent	時好時壞的

6

missile	飛彈
mission	任務
missionary	傳教士
message	訊息
messenger	信差
dismiss	解散
dismissal	解散
demise	死亡
demission	辭職

字根 mit

Group 19 字根 *spire*

目標： ① 先將47個字放入短期記憶。
② 加快速度至39秒之內，成為長期記憶。

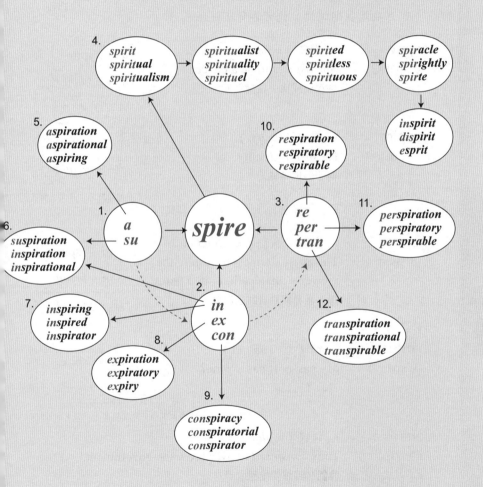

4.
spirit
spiritual
spiritualism

spiritualist
spirituality
spirituel

spirited
spiritless
spirituous

spiracle
spirightly
spirte

inspirit
dispirit
esprit

5.
aspiration
aspirational
aspiring

10.
respiration
respiratory
respirable

1.
a
su

spire

3.
re
per
tran

11.
perspiration
perspiratory
perspirable

6.
suspiration
inspiration
inspirational

2.
in
ex
con

12.
transpiration
transpirational
transpirable

7.
inspiring
inspired
inspirator

8.
expiration
expiratory
expiry

9.
conspiracy
conspiratorial
conspirator

1. 字根 *spire* 核心單字

字根 spire 表 breathe「呼吸」之意，核心單字共 8 個字，可分成 2 個、3 個、3 個一組來背，背熟至 5 秒之內，可成爲長期記憶，就可再背下一組。

aspire
〔ə'spaɪr〕

v. 渴望（= *desire*）
She *aspires* to be a dancer.
她渴望成爲一位舞者。

a ＋ spire
｜　　　｜
to ＋ *breathe*

對～吐氣，即是「渴望」

suspire
〔sə'spaɪr〕

v. 嘆息（= *sigh*）
He *suspired* sadly.
他悲傷地嘆氣。

su ＋ spire
｜　　　｜
under ＋ *breathe*

在心底難過地呼吸，即是「嘆息」

inspire[4]
〔ɪn'spaɪr〕

v. 激勵；激發（= *stimulate*）
The artist attempts to *inspire* the viewer's imagination. 這位藝術家想要激發觀賞者的想像力。

in ＋ spire
｜　　　｜
in ＋ *breathe*

吐氣進去，就是爲大家打氣，表示「激勵」

字根 spire

expire[6]
〔ɪk'spaɪr〕

v. 到期（= *run out*）
My passport has *expired*.
我的護照到期了。

ex ＋ spire
｜　　　｜
out ＋ *breathe*

吐出最後一口氣就結束了，引申爲「到期」

conspire
〔kən'spaɪr〕

v. 共謀（= *plot*）
They *conspired* to overthrow the government.
他們共謀想要推翻政府。

con ＋ spire
｜　　　｜
together ＋ *breathe*

壞人一鼻孔出氣，即是「共謀」

respire
〔 rɪˈspaɪr 〕

v. 呼吸（= *breathe*）
The patient continues to *respire* under his own power.
這位病人持續用自己的力量呼吸。

re	+	spire
again	+	breathe

一再呼吸，即是「呼吸」

perspire
〔 pɚˈspaɪr 〕

v. 流汗（= *sweat*）
The athlete began to *perspire*.
那位運動員開始流汗了。

per	+	spire
through	+	breathe

透過皮膚呼吸，即是「流汗」

transpire
〔 trænˈspaɪr 〕

v. 蒸發（= *evaporate*）；發生（= *happen*）
Plants *transpire* if placed in direct sunlight.
植物如果直接在陽光下照射，水份就會蒸發。

tran	+	spire
A→B	+	breathe

植物將水份由葉片吐到大氣中，即是「蒸發」，引申為事情「發生」，為人所知。

【背誦祕訣】

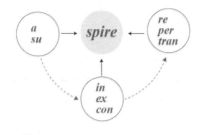

aspire
suspire
第一組記「渴望」、「嘆息」。

inspire
exprire
conspire
第二組是 in「裡」，ex「外」，con「一起」。

respire
perspire
transpire
第三組是 respire「呼吸」，perspire「流汗（透過皮膚呼吸）」，transpire「蒸發（植物葉片呼吸）」。spire 前各有 2 個、3 個、4 個字母，很好記。

字根 spire

2. *spirit-spiritual-spiritualism*

這一組有 15 個字，都是 spirit 的衍生字，要 9 個、
3 個、3 個，分組背，背熟至 8 秒之內，變成直覺。

spirit[2]
(ˈspɪrɪt)

n. 精神；靈魂（= *soul*）；烈酒
He's with us in *spirit*. 他精神與我們同在。

```
spir    + it
 |        |
breathe + n.    呼吸是供給每一個「靈魂」的生命來源
```

spiritual[4]
(ˈspɪrɪtʃuəl)

adj. 精神的；心靈的（= *immaterial*）
Aaron consulted a priest for
spiritual guidance.
艾倫向一位神父求助心靈指導。

```
spirit + ual
  |       |
 精神   + adj.
```

spiritualism
(ˈspɪrɪtʃuəlˌɪzəm)

n. 招魂說（= *spiritism*）
She believes in *spiritualism*. 她相信招魂說。
* ism 表示一種「學說」或「主義」

spiritualist
(ˈspɪrɪtʃuəlɪst)

n. 靈媒
The *spiritualist* claims to communicate with the
dead. 那位靈媒宣稱能跟死者溝通。
* ist 表示其學說或主義的「信仰者」

spirituality
(ˌspɪrɪtʃuˈælətɪ)

n. 靈性（= *otherworldliness*）
The book explores the subjects
of *spirituality* and the
supernatural. 這本書探討靈
性和超自然方面的主題。

```
spiritual + ity
   |         |
 心靈的    + n.
```
注意重音在 ity 前一音節上

spirituel
(ˌspɪrɪtʃuˈɛl)

adj. 高雅的（= *refined*）；活潑的
His friends described her as *spirituel*.
他的朋友們都形容她很高雅。
* 重音在最後一音節，來自法文。

spirited[2]
（'spɪrɪtɪd）

adj. 有精神的（= *energetic*）；熱烈的（= *heated*）
The proposal was met with *spirited* opposition.
這項提議遭到了激烈的反對。

spiritless
（'spɪrɪtləs）

adj. 無精打采的（= *without energy*）
We found her performance to be *spiritless*.
我們覺得她的表演很沉悶。
* spirited 跟 spiritless 爲反義字，要一起記。

spirituous
（'spɪrɪtʃʊəs）

adj. 含酒精的（= *alcoholic*）
He was told to avoid *spirituous* beverages.
他被告知要避開含酒精的飲料。

spirit + uous	
| |	酒精在過去被稱爲生命之水，
烈酒　 *adj.*	喝酒以後就會表現得 spirited。

spiracle
（'spaɪrəkḷ）

n. 【昆蟲】呼吸孔；【鯨魚】噴水孔
（= *breathing opening*）
The whale shot a jet of air and water
from its *spiracle*.
這隻鯨魚從牠的噴水孔中噴出一道水柱及空氣。

spiracle

spir + acle	
| |	呼吸的通道
breathe + *n.*	

sprightly
（'spraɪtlɪ）

adj. 有活力的（= *energetic*）
Grandma is very *sprightly* for an 85-year-old woman.
就一個八十五歲的女人來說，祖母是很有活力的。
* 注意是 sprightly 形容詞，不是副詞

sprite
（spraɪt）

n. 小精靈（= *fairy*）
In her dream, she was visited by a *sprite*.
在她的夢裡，有一個小精靈來拜訪她。

sprite

字根 spire

inspirit
〔ɪnˈspɪrɪt〕

v. 鼓舞 (= *inspire*)
The coach's locker room speech failed to *inspirit* the team.
教練在更衣室裡說的話，無法激勵這支隊伍。

in + spirit
│ │
into + 精神

注入精神

dispirit
〔dɪˈspɪrɪt〕

v. 使沮喪 (= *discourage*)
We didn't let the rain *dispirit* our celebration.
我們沒有讓雨破壞我們慶祝的心情。

di + spirit
│ │
away + 精神

使精神喪失

esprit
〔ɛˈspri〕

n. 精神 (= *spirit*)
The soldier's *esprit* de corps was damaged by the defeat.
軍人的團隊精神因為被打敗而受損。

* esprit de corps〔ɛˈspri dəˈkɔr〕團隊精神，此字來自法文。

字根 spire

【背誦祕訣】

第二組可分三部分記憶

spirit
spiritual
spiritualism

spiracle
sprightly
sprite

inspirit
dispirit
esprit

spiritualist
spirituality
spirituel

這三個字，母音為 /aɪ/。注意後兩字 spir 變成 spri。

這三個字以 spirit 為字根結尾。

spirited
spiritless
spirituous

這九個字以 spirit 為字根開頭。

3. aspiration-aspirational-aspiring

這一組有6個字，分成兩部份。第一部份是 aspire 的衍生字，第二部份是 suspire 和 inspire 的衍生字，背熟至 3 秒之內，就變成直覺。

aspiration
〔͵æspə'reʃən〕

n. 抱負（= *ambition*）
Josie's parents encouraged her artistic *aspirations*.
喬西的父母鼓勵她對藝術的抱負。
* 注意字首 a 母音唸 /æ/

aspirational
〔͵æspə'reʃənl̩〕

adj. 有抱負的（= *aspiring*）
He is an *aspirational* young man, eager to move to a higher social status.
他是一位有抱負的年輕人，很渴望能獲得更高的社會地位。

aspiring
〔ə'spaɪrɪŋ〕

adj. 有抱負的（= *ambitious*）
Aspiring people have great ambitions and desire to be successful.
有抱負的人都懷有野心，並且渴望成功。

suspiration
〔͵sʌspə'reʃən〕

n. 嘆息（= *sigh*）
She ended the sentence with a loud *suspiration*.
她說完話就大聲地嘆了一口氣。
* suspire 只有一個衍生字。

inspiration[4]
〔͵ɪnspə'reʃən〕

n. 靈感；激勵（= *encouragement*）
Rudy was an *inspiration* to us all.
魯蒂是鼓舞我們所有人的力量。

inspirational
〔͵ɪnspə'reʃənl̩〕

adj. 啓發靈感的；鼓舞人心的（= *inspiring*）
The book is an *inspirational* story about overcoming obstacles.
這是一本有關克服阻礙的勵志故事書。

inspiration	+	al
靈感	+	*adj.*

字根 spire

4. *inspiring-inspired-inspirator*

這一組有 9 個字，分成三部份。第一部份是 inspire
的衍生字，第二部份是 expire 的衍生字，第三部份是
conspire 的衍生字，背熟至 5 秒之內，變成直覺。

inspiring[4] 〔 ɪn'spaɪrɪŋ 〕	*adj.* 激勵人心的（ = *encouraging* ）；啓發靈感的 Your courage is *inspiring*. 你的勇氣能激勵人心。　*ing 表主動
inspired[4] 〔 ɪn'spaɪrd 〕	*adj.* 極好的（ = *brilliant* ） The gifted student gave an *inspired* performance and won a round of applause. 那位才華出眾的學生演出精湛，贏得全場的掌聲。 * p.p. 表被動（被啓發而來，所以是「極好的」。）
inspirator 〔'ɪnspə,retɚ 〕	*n.* 激勵者（ = *one who inspires others* ） The coach is a capable *inspirator*. 那位教練很會激勵人心。

```
inspir + ator
  |       |
 激勵   +  人
```

字根 spire

expiration[6] 〔,ɛkspə'reʃən 〕	*n.* 到期（ = *expiry* ） What is the *expiration* date of your credit card? 你的信用卡何時到期？ * expiration date = expiry date（到期日）
expiratory 〔 ɪk'spaɪrə,torɪ 〕	*adj.* 吐氣的 The medication will interfere with your *expiratory* ability. 這藥物會阻礙你的呼氣能力。
expiry 〔 ɪk'spaɪrɪ 〕	*n.* 到期（ = *expiration* ）；滅亡 I wouldn't drink that milk; it is way past its *expiry* date. 我才不喝那個牛奶；它早就已經過期了。

conspiracy[6]
〔 kən'spɪrəsɪ 〕

n. 陰謀（= *plot*）
He admitted to being involved in a *conspiracy* to assassinate the President.
他承認有捲入刺殺總統的陰謀。

conspir + acy
    | |
共謀　 + 　*n.*　　注意沒有 conspiration 這個字。

conspiratorial
〔 kən,spɪrə'torɪəl 〕

adj. 陰謀的（= *relating to a conspiracy*）
"Here he comes," Helen said in a *conspiratorial* tone. 「他走過來了，」海倫用有什麼陰謀似的語調這麼說。

conspirator
〔 kən'spɪrətɚ 〕

n. 陰謀者（= *plotter*）
The *conspirators* were given long prison sentences.
那些陰謀者被判處長期監禁。

【背誦祕訣】

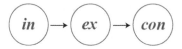

$in \rightarrow ex \rightarrow con$

紅字爲重音，注意發音：

inspiring	/aɪ/	重音在字根 spir 上，i 唸 /aɪ/
inspired	/aɪ/	
inspirator	/ɪ/	重音不在字根 spir 上，i 唸 /ə/

expiration	/e/	第二、三字重音在字根 pir 上，
expiratory	/aɪ/	i 唸 /aɪ/
expiry	/aɪ/	

conspiracy	/ɪ/	不管重音是不是在字根 spir 上，
conspiratorial	/o/	i 都唸 /ɪ/
conspirator	/ɪ/	

字根 spire

5. *respiration-respiratory-respirable*

這一組有 9 個字，分成三部份，第一部份是 respire 的衍生字，第二部份是 perspire 的衍生字，第三部份是 transpire 的衍生字，背熟至 5 秒之內，變成直覺。

respiration
〔͵rɛspə'reʃən 〕

n. 呼吸（ = *breathing* ）
The patient is unable to breathe without artificial *respiration*.
這位病人沒有做人工呼吸，就無法呼吸。
* artificial respiration　人工呼吸

respiratory
〔 rɪ'spaɪrə͵torɪ 〕

adj. 呼吸的
SARS is an abbreviation for severe acute *respiratory* syndrome.
SARS 是「嚴重急性呼吸道症候群」的縮寫。

respirable
〔'rɛspərəb̩l 〕

adj. 適合呼吸的（ = *fit for breathing* ）
The trapped miners were running out of *respirable* air. 那位受困的礦工快用完可呼吸的空氣了。

perspiration
〔͵pɝspə'reʃən 〕

n. 汗水（ = *sweat* ）
His T-shirt was soaked with *perspiration*.
汗水濕透了他的 T 恤。

perspiratory
〔 pɚ'spaɪrə͵torɪ 〕

adj. 排汗的（ = *relating to perspiration* ）
She suffers from overactive *perspiratory* glands.
她受汗腺過份發達所苦。

* expiratory-respiratory-perspiratory 這三個字重音都在字根上，以 atory 結尾的形容詞一起記。

perspirable
〔 pɚ'spaɪrəb̩l 〕

adj. 可排汗的（ = *emitting perspiration* ）
These shoes are made of *perspirable* leather.
這些鞋子是由可排汗的皮革所製成。

字根 spire

transpiration
〔ˌtrænspəˈreʃən 〕

n. 蒸發（ = *the process of passing water through the surface of a plant's leaves* ）
Some plants return oxygen to the atmosphere by the process of *transpiration*.
有些植物藉由蒸發的過程，把氧氣重新排到大氣中。

transpirational
〔ˌtrænspəˈreʃənḷ 〕

adj. 蒸發的
Nutrients are brought to the soil's surface by *transpirational* pull.
養分藉由蒸發作用被帶到土壤的表面。

transpirable
〔 trænˈspaɪrəbḷ 〕

adj. 可蒸發的（ = *capable of being transpired* ）
The plant serves a *transpirable* function.
這棵植物會行蒸發作用。

【背誦祕訣】

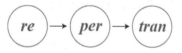

最後一組最好記，都是先 ation 結尾的名詞，再來是 atory 或 ational 結尾的形容詞，最後是 able 結尾的形容詞。

respiration	*n.*
respiratory	*adj.*
respirable	*adj.*

perspiration	*n.*
perspiratory	*adj.*
perspirable	*adj.*

transpiration	*n.*
transpirational	*adj.*
transpirable	*adj.*

字根 spire

Exercise : Choose the correct answer.

1. Most people ＿＿＿＿ to be wealthy.
   (A) impose　　　　　　(B) attend
   (C) aspire　　　　　　(D) pulse

2. These paintings ＿＿＿＿ the imagination.
   (A) compose　　　　　(B) deserve
   (C) inspire　　　　　　(D) assign

3. ＿＿＿＿ refers to an immaterial reality, or an inner path which enables a person to discover the essence of existence.
   (A) Imposition　　　　(B) Simplicity
   (C) Spirituality　　　　(D) Attention

4. On the ＿＿＿＿ of the mayor's term of the office, the citizens will hold a farewell for him.
   (A) signal　　　　　　(B) expiry
   (C) deposit　　　　　　(D) posture

5. ＿＿＿＿ musicians are welcome to enter the talent contest.
   (A) Depressing　　　　(B) Aspiring
   (C) Preservative　　　　(D) Subservient

6. ＿＿＿＿ rate in plants will increase when subjected to higher light intensities and slow when there is no light.
   (A) Disposition　　　　(B) Transpiration
   (C) Exposition　　　　(D) Multiplication

7. The candidates engaged in a ＿＿＿＿ debate.
   (A) suppliant　　　　　(B) spirited
   (C) simpleton　　　　　(D) consignable

字根 spire

8. Behind his back, they ridiculed Cody's _____ of stardom.
   (A) conservations
   (B) aspirations
   (C) interposals
   (D) triplications

9. It was the most _____ movie I have ever seen.
   (A) inspiring
   (B) observing
   (C) compressing
   (D) opposing

10. The contract will _____ at midnight.
    (A) expire
    (B) comply
    (C) design
    (D) pressurize

11. There is a _____ of silence about police brutality.
    (A) potentiality
    (B) tendency
    (C) conspiracy
    (D) multiplicity

12. The sun has been the subject of and the _____ for countless works of art.
    (A) reservation
    (B) inspiration
    (C) pretension
    (D) proposition

13. The terrorists _____ to hijack an airplane.
    (A) repressed
    (B) applied
    (C) signalized
    (D) conspired

14. He is on a _____ quest to find inner peace.
    (A) spiritless
    (B) spirituous
    (C) respiratory
    (D) spiritual

15. The _____ was visible on the tennis player's brow.
    (A) perspiration
    (B) reposition
    (C) suspiration
    (D) designation

字根 spire

字彙測驗詳解

1. (**C**) 大部分的人都渴望變有錢。
   - (A) impose〔ɪm'poz〕v. 強加
   - (B) attend〔ə'tɛnd〕v. 參加
   - (C) *aspire*〔ə'spaɪr〕v. 渴望
   - (D) pulse〔pʌls〕v. 脈動

   wealthy〔'wɛlθɪ〕adj. 富有的

2. (**C**) 這些畫能激發想像力。
   - (A) compose〔kəm'poz〕v. 組成;作(曲)
   - (B) deserve〔dɪ'zɝv〕v. 應得
   - (C) *inspire*〔ɪn'spaɪr〕v. 激勵;激發
   - (D) assign〔ə'saɪn〕v. 指派

   painting

3. (**C**) 靈性指的是一種心靈上的真實性,也可說是讓個人去發掘存在本質的一條內心道路。
   - (A) imposition〔ˌɪmpə'zɪʃən〕n. 稅;負擔
   - (B) simplicity〔sɪm'plɪsətɪ〕n. 簡單;單純
   - (C) *spirituality*〔ˌspɪrɪtʃu'ælətɪ〕n. 靈性
   - (D) attention〔ə'tɛnʃən〕n. 注意(力)

   refer to 是指　immaterial〔ˌɪmə'tɪrɪəl〕adj. 心靈的;非物質的
   path〔pæθ〕n. 道路　essence〔'ɛsn̩s〕n. 本質

4. (**B**) 市長任期屆滿時,市民將會為他舉辦送別會。
   - (A) signal〔'sɪgn̩l〕n. 信號
   - (B) *expiry*〔ɪk'spaɪrɪ〕n. 到期;屆滿
   - (C) deposit〔dɪ'pazɪt〕n. 存款;押金
   - (D) posture〔'pastʃɚ〕n. 姿勢

5. (**B**) 有抱負的音樂家都歡迎來參加才藝比賽。
   - (A) depressing〔dɪ'prɛsɪŋ〕adj. 令人沮喪的
   - (B) *aspiring*〔ə'spaɪrɪŋ〕adj. 有抱負的
   - (C) preservative〔prɪ'zɝvətɪv〕adj. 防腐的　n. 防腐劑
   - (D) subservient〔səb'sɝvɪənt〕adj. 卑屈的;有貢獻的

6. (**B**) 植物在較強烈的日照下，<u>蒸發</u>率會增加，而沒有日照時就會減緩。

(A) disposition 〔͵dɪspə'zɪʃən 〕 *n.* 性情；氣質

(B) *transpiration* 〔͵trænspə'reʃən 〕 *n.* 蒸發

(C) exposition 〔͵ɛkspə'zɪʃən 〕 *n.* 展覽會

(D) multiplication 〔͵mʌltəplə'keʃən 〕 *n.* 乘法

transpiration

rate 〔 ret 〕 *n.* 比率　　subject 〔 səb'dʒɛkt 〕 *v.* 使遭受；使暴露於
intensity 〔 ɪn'tɛnsətɪ 〕 *n.* 強度

7. (**B**) 這些候選人參加了一場<u>激烈的</u>辯論。

(A) suppliant 〔'sʌpliənt 〕 *adj.* 懇求的　*n.* 懇求者

(B) *spirited* 〔'spɪrɪtɪd 〕 *adj.* 有精神的；激烈的

(C) simpleton 〔'sɪmpḷtən 〕 *n.* 笨蛋

(D) consignable 〔 kən'saɪnəbḷ 〕 *adj.* 可委託的

candidate 〔'kændə͵det 〕 *n.* 候選人　　*engage in* 參加；參與
debate 〔 dɪ'bet 〕 *n.* 辯論

8. (**B**) 他們在寇弟的背後，嘲笑他想成為明星的<u>抱負</u>。

(A) conservation 〔͵kansɚ'veʃən 〕 *n.* 保存；節省

(B) *aspiration* 〔͵æspə'reʃən 〕 *n.* 抱負；渴望

(C) interposal 〔͵ɪntɚ'pozḷ 〕 *n.* 介入；干涉；妨害

(D) triplication 〔͵trɪplə'keʃən 〕 *n.* 三倍

ridicule 〔'rɪdɪ͵kjul 〕 *v.* 嘲笑　　stardom 〔'stardəm 〕 *n.* 明星的地位

9. (**A**) 這是我看過最<u>激勵人心的</u>一部電影。

(A) *inspiring* 〔 ɪn'spaɪrɪŋ 〕 *adj.* 激勵人心的；啓發靈感的

(B) observing 〔 əb'zɝvɪŋ 〕 *adj.* 注意的；觀察力敏銳的

(C) compress 〔 kəm'prɛs 〕 *v.* 壓縮

(D) oppose 〔 ə'poz 〕 *v.* 反對

10. (**A**) 合約在午夜時就會<u>到期</u>。

(A) *expire* 〔 ɪk'spaɪr 〕 *v.* 到期

(B) comply 〔 kəm'plaɪ 〕 *v.* 遵從　(C) design 〔 dɪ'zaɪn 〕 *v.* 設計

(D) pressurize 〔'prɛʃə͵raɪz 〕 *v.* 迫使；逼迫

contract 〔'kantrækt 〕 *n.* 合約

11. (**C**) 關於警方的暴行，有一種保持緘默的<u>協定</u>。
    (A) potentiality〔pə,tɛnʃɪ'ælətɪ〕*n.* 潛力；可能性
    (B) tendency〔'tɛndənsɪ〕*n.* 傾向
    (C) *conspiracy*〔kən'spɪrəsɪ〕*n.* 陰謀；共謀
    conspiracy of silence （對非法行爲的）保持緘默的協定
    (D) multiplicity〔,mʌltə'plɪsətɪ〕*n.* 衆多
    brutality〔bru'tælətɪ〕*n.* 暴行；野蠻

12. (**B**) 太陽一直以來都是無數藝術作品的主題，也是<u>靈感</u>的來源。
    (A) reservation〔,rɛzə˞'veʃən〕*n.* 預訂
    (B) *inspiration*〔,ɪnspə'reʃən〕*n.* 靈感；激勵
    (C) pretension〔prɪ'tɛnʃən〕*n.* 假裝；自負
    (D) proposition〔,prɑpə'zɪʃən〕*n.* 提議；論點
    countless〔'kauntlɪs〕*adj.* 無數的   *work of art* 藝術品

13. (**D**) 恐怖份子<u>共謀</u>要劫機。
    (A) repress〔rɪ'prɛs〕*v.* 鎭壓；抑制
    (B) apply〔ə'plaɪ〕*v.* 申請；應用
    (C) signalize〔'sɪgnə,laɪz〕*v.* 使顯著   terrorist
    (D) *conspire*〔kən'spaɪr〕*v.* 共謀
    terrorist〔'tɛrərɪst〕*n.* 恐怖份子   hijack〔'haɪ,dʒæk〕*v.* 劫持

14. (**D**) 他正進行一趟尋求內心平靜的<u>心靈</u>之旅。
    (A) spiritless〔'spɪrɪtləs〕*adj.* 無精打采的
    (B) spirituous〔'spɪrɪtʃuəs〕*adj.* 含酒精的
    (C) respiratory〔rɪ'spaɪrə,torɪ〕*adj.* 呼吸的
    (D) *spiritual*〔'spɪrɪtʃuəl〕*adj.* 精神上的；心靈的
    quest〔kwɛst〕*n.* 尋求；探索

15. (**A**) 在這位網球選手的額頭上看得到<u>汗水</u>。
    (A) *perspiration*〔,pɝspə'reʃən〕*n.* 流汗；汗
    (B) reposition〔,ripə'zɪʃən〕*n.* 放回；儲藏
    (C) suspiration〔,sʌspə'reʃən〕*n.* 歎息
    (D) designation〔,dɛzɪg'neʃən〕*n.* 指定；任命
    visible〔'vɪzəbl̩〕*adj.* 看得見的 brow〔brau〕*n.* 額頭（= *forehead*）

字根 spire

請連中文一起背,背至一分鐘內,終生不忘。

1

aspire	渴望
suspire	嘆息
inspire	激勵
expire	到期
conspire	共謀
respire	呼吸
perspire	流汗
transpire	蒸發

2

spirit	精神
spiritual	精神的
spiritualism	招魂說
spiritualist	靈媒
spirituality	靈性
spirituel	高雅的
spirited	有精神的
spiritless	無精打采的
spirituous	含酒精的

spiracle	呼吸孔
sprightly	有活力的
sprite	小精靈
inspirit	鼓舞
dispirit	使沮喪
esprit	精神

3

aspiration	抱負
aspirational	有抱負的
aspiring	有抱負的
suspiration	嘆息
inspiration	靈感
inspirational	啟發靈感的

字根 spire

4

inspiring	激勵人心的
inspired	極好的
inspirator	激勵者
expiration	到期
expiratory	吐氣的
expiry	到期
conspiracy	陰謀
conspiratorial	陰謀的
conspirator	陰謀者

5

respiration	呼吸
respiratory	呼吸的
respirable	適合呼吸的
perspiration	汗水
perspiratory	排汗的
perspirable	可排汗的
transpiration	蒸發
transpirational	蒸發的
transpirable	可蒸發的

字根 spire

【劉毅老師的話】

　　這種背單字的方法，如果全班一起背，速度更快。兩個同學在一起，你背一遍，我背一遍，效果奇佳。

Group 20 字根 *cede, ceed*

目標： ① 先將53個字放入短期記憶。
② 加快速度至45秒之內，成為長期記憶。

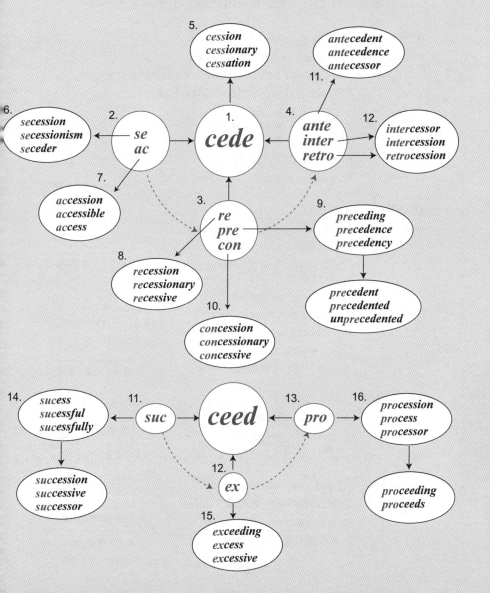

1. 字根 *cede* ; *ceed* 核心單字

這9個字，3個一組一起背，可先背6個再背3個，
背熟至5秒之內，可成為長期記憶，才可再背下一組。

cede
〔 sid 〕

v. 放棄（= *yield*）
cede 這個字根的意思是 go ; yield「走；讓步」
The dictator agreed to *cede* power by next month.
那位獨裁者同意在下個月前放棄他的權力。

secede
〔 si'sid 〕

v. 脫離（= *break away*）
The state of Texas is threatening to *secede* from the union.
德州威脅要脫離聯邦。

```
se   + cede
 |       |
away +  go
```
走開離去，即是「脫離」

accede
〔 æk'sid 〕

v. 同意（= *assent*）
It is unclear if she will *accede* to our demands.
不確定她是否會同意我們的要求。

```
ac + cede
 |     |
to +  go
```
向～走去，即是「同意」

recede
〔 rɪ'sid 〕

v. 後退（= *retreat*）
It will be a few days before the flood waters *recede*.
還要幾天洪水才會退去。

```
re   + cede
 |       |
back +  go
```
向後走，即是「後退」

precede[6]
〔 prɪ'sid 〕

v. 在…之前（= *go before*）
A short advertisement will *precede* the program.
一段短短的廣告將在節目之前播出。

```
pre    + cede
 |         |
before +  go
```
走在前面，即是「在…之前」

concede[6]
〔 kən'sid 〕

v. 承認（= *admit*）
The candidate *conceded* defeat to his opponent.
那位候選人承認輸給對手。

```
con      + cede
 |           |
together +  go
```
一起走，即是「勉強承認」

antecede
〔͵æntə'sid〕

v. 在…之前（= *forego*）

Stone tools *antecede* all forms of metal machinery.
石器比各種金屬機器早出現。

```
ante  + cede
 |        |
before +  go        走在前面，即是「在…之前」
```

intercede
〔͵ɪntə'sid〕

v. 調停（= *interpose*）

I do not wish to *intercede* in your family's dispute.
我不想要為你們的家庭糾紛調停。

```
inter  + cede
  |        |
between +  go       走在兩者之間，即是「調停」
```

retrocede
〔͵rɛtro'sid〕

v. 歸還（= *return*）

The land was *retroceded* to Virginia by an act of
Congress. 國會通過法案，將那塊土地歸還給維吉尼亞州。

```
retro    + cede
  |          |
backward +  go      向後走，即是「歸還」
```

【背誦祕訣】

　　這九個字，就是字根 cede 的核心單字，
想到 cede，腦中就要浮現這個圖像。

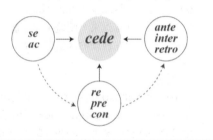

字根 cede, ceed

2. cession-cessionary-cessation

這一組是由 cede-secede-accede 衍生出來的單字，一共有 9 個字，三個一組一起背，背熟至 5 秒之內，變成直覺。

cession
〔'sɛʃən 〕

n. 讓與 (= *relinquishment*)
Israel agreed to the *cession* of the West Bank to Palestine. 以色列同意將約旦河西岸讓與巴勒斯坦。

cessionary
〔'sɛʃən‚ɛrɪ 〕

n. 受讓人
The *cessionary* took possession of the disputed property. 那位受讓人得到那爭議性財產的所有權。

cessation
〔 sɛ'seʃən 〕

n. 停止 (= *termination*)
Respiratory arrest is the *cessation* of breathing.
呼吸停滯是一種呼吸停止的現象。
* cess 是 cede 的變體，一樣表示 go; yield。

secession
〔 sɪ'sɛʃən 〕

n. 脫離 (= *breakaway*)
Many world leaders supported the Ukraine's *secession* from the Soviet Union.
許多國家領導者支持烏克蘭脫離蘇聯。

secessionism
〔 sɪ'sɛʃən‚ɪzəm 〕

n. 脫離主義
Secessionism has been a recurring feature of Western Australia's political landscape since 1829.
自從一八二九年以來，脫離主義這個特色一直浮現在西澳的政治景況中。

> secession + ism
> 　｜　　　｜
> 　脫離　　+主義
>
> 脫離的主義，即是
> 「脫離主義」

seceder
〔 sɪ'sidɚ 〕

n. 脫離者
Through Sebastian's efforts, a large number of *seceders* were brought back into the fold.
由於賽巴斯汀的努力，許多脫離者都重回組織了。

accession
〔 æk'sɛʃən 〕

n. 就任（ = *taking over* ）
Tomorrow is the 50th anniversary of the King's *accession* to the throne.
明天就是國王即位的五十週年紀念。

accessible[6]
〔 æk'sɛsəbḷ 〕

adj. 可取得的（ = *available* ）
Our goal is to make the program *accessible* to everyone.
我們的目標，是讓每個人都有辦法取得這個程式。

access[4]
〔'æksɛs 〕

n. 接近或使用權（ = *right of entry* ; *right to use* ）
She was denied *access* to the party.
她不能進去那個派對。

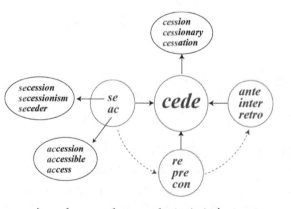

【背誦祕訣】

由 cede-accede-secede 衍生出來的 9 個字，除了 seceder 之外，全部都是以變體 cess 爲字根，三個一組，每一組的第一個字結尾都是 cession，唸起來很順。

字根 cede, ceed

3. *recession-recessionary-recessive*

這一組是由 recede-precede-concede（後—前—
一起）衍生出來的 12 個單字，三個一組一起背，可先
背 6 個，再背 6 個，背至 7 秒內，終生不忘。

字根
cede,
ceed

recession[6] 〔 rɪ'sɛʃən 〕	*n.* 不景氣（ = *depression* ） The economic *recession* has caused sales to decline. 經濟不景氣已經造成營業額的下滑。
recessionary 〔 rɪ'sɛʃən͵ɛrɪ 〕	*adj.* 衰退的（ = *declining* ） The market has taken a *recessionary* turn. 市場開始衰退。
recessive 〔 rɪ'sɛsɪv 〕	*adj.* 隱性的（ = *latent* ） Wilbur carries a *recessive* gene that blocks his ability to taste or smell. 偉博體內有一種隱性基因，會阻斷他的味覺或嗅覺。
preceding 〔 prɪ'sidɪŋ 〕	*adj.* 先前的（ = *foregoing* ） The tough new laws are the result of *preceding* events. 這些嚴峻的新法令源自於先前的事件。
precedence 〔 prɪ'sidn̩s 〕	*n.* 領先；優先權（ = *priority* ） She has to learn that her wishes do not take *precedence* over other people's needs. 她必須了解，自己的願望不一定優先於別人的需求。
precedency 〔 'prɛsɪdənsɪ 〕	*n.* 領先；優先權（ = *precedence* ） The two inventors argued over the *precedency* of their similar ideas. 那兩個發明家想法類似，為了誰先誰後而爭辯。

precedent[6]
（'prɛsədənt）

n. 先例（ = *example* ）
The trial could set an important *precedent* for similar cases.
這場審判能為類似的案件立下先例。

precedented
（'prɛsə‚dɛntɪd）

adj. 有先例的（ = *having a precedent* ）
The recent oil spill could cause more environmental damage than ever *precedented* in the past.
最近的漏油事件可能造成前所未有的環境傷害。

unprecedented
（ ʌn'prɛsə‚dɛntɪd ）

adj. 空前的（ = *having no precedent* ）
This is an *unprecedented* achievement.
這是空前的成就。

concession[6]
（ kən'sɛʃən ）

n. 讓步（ = *yielding* ）
The firm will be forced to make *concessions* if it wants to avoid a strike.
若要避免罷工，公司不得不做出讓步。

con	+ cess	+ ion	
|	|	|	
together	+ *yield*	+ *n.*	一起讓步，即是「讓步」

concessionary
（ kən'sɛʃən‚ɛrɪ ）

adj. 讓步的（ = *concessive* ）
The leader refused to agree to any *concessionary* measures. 領導者拒絕同意任何讓步的措施。

concessive
（ kən'sɛsɪv ）

adj. 讓步的（ = *concessionary* ）
We strongly objected to the *concessive* nature of their proposal.
我們堅決反對這項提議中妥協的成分。

4. *antecedent-antecedence-antecessor*

這一組是由 antecede-intercede-retrocede（前—
中—後）衍生出來的 6 個單字，背至 3 秒內，才不會忘。

antecedent
〔͵æntə'sidn̩t〕

n. 祖先（= *ancestor*）
Frank is an Englishman with
Irish *antecedents*. 法蘭克是
個有愛爾蘭祖先的英國人。

ante	+ ced	+ ent
before	+ go	+ 人

走在前面的人，即是「祖先」

antecedence
〔͵æntə'sidn̩s〕

n. 優先（= *anteriority*）；在前
Your argument has no *antecedence* in this matter.
你的論點在這件事情上面毫不居先。

antecessor
〔͵æntə'sɛsə〕

n. 先行者（= *precursor*）；前往
The winner gave a respectful tribute to his *antecessors*.
那個贏家對他的前輩們表示敬意。

intercessor
〔͵ɪntə'sɛsə〕

n. 調停者（= *go-between*）
The *intercessor* tried to
resolve the dispute.
調停者試圖解決這場爭論。

inter	+ cess	+ or
between	+ go	+ 人

走進兩者中間的人，即是「調停者」

intercession
〔͵ɪntə'sɛʃən〕

n. 調停（= *interposition*）
Many severely ill patients have claimed to be cured
by divine *intercession*.
很多重病患者宣稱是因為神的介入而痊癒。

retrocession
〔͵rɛtro'sɛʃən〕

n. 歸還（= *return*）
Many feared the *retrocession* of Hong Kong to
China would lead to financial ruin.
很多人害怕香港回歸中國大陸將造成財政崩潰。

5. succeed-exceed-proceed

這一組單字來自於字根 ceed 的三個核心單字。
共 17 個字，背熟至 10 秒內，成為長期記憶。

succeed[2]
(sək'sid)

v. 成功；繼承 (= *inherit*)
Prince Charles will one day *succeed* Queen Elizabeth to the throne.
查爾斯王子將來有一天會繼承伊莉莎白女王的王位。

suc	+	ceed
under	+	go

走在～下面，即是「繼承」

exceed[5]
(ɪk'sid)

v. 超越 (= *surpass*)
Our profits have *exceeded* expectations.
我們的利潤已經超過預期。

ex	+	ceed
out	+	go

越過～向外走去，即是「超越」

proceed[4]
(prə'sid)

v. 前進；繼續 (= *continue*)
We will now *proceed* with the meeting.
現在我們要繼續進行會議。

pro	+	ceed
forward	+	go

往前走去，即是「繼續進行」

success[2]
(sək'sɛs)

n. 成功 (= *achievement*)
Phil attributes his *success* to hard work and determination. 菲爾將他的成功歸因於努力與決心。

successful[2]
(sək'sɛsfəl)

adj. 成功的 (= *prosperous*)
Mary is a *successful* lawyer. 瑪莉是一位成功的律師。

successfully
(sək'sɛsfəlɪ)

adv. 成功地 (= *fruitfully*)
Our mission was completed *successfully*.
我們的任務成功地完成。

字根 cede, ceed

* succeed 的衍生字，先背三個「成功」相關字；再背三個「繼承」相關字。

succession[6]
〔 sək'sɛʃən 〕

n. 繼承（ = *inheritance* ）；連續（ = *sequence* ）
A *succession* of droughts led to the famine.
連續的乾旱造成饑荒。

successive[6]
〔 sək'sɛsɪv 〕

adj. 連續的（ = *consecutive* ）
Cameron won the contest for the third *successive* year.
卡麥隆連續第三年贏得比賽。

successor[6]
〔 sək'sɛsə 〕

n. 繼承人（ = *inheritor* ）；後繼者
He set many examples for his *successors* to follow.
他立下許多榜樣供後繼者學習。

exceeding[5]
〔 ɪk'sidɪŋ 〕

adj. 過度的（ = *excessive* ）
His *exceeding* politeness could not hide his anger.
他那過度的禮貌並不能掩藏他的憤怒。

excess[5]
〔 ɪk'sɛs 〕

n. 過度（ = *intemperance* ）
He started drinking to *excess* after the divorce.
離婚後他開始飲酒過度。

excessive[6]
〔 ɪk'sɛsɪv 〕

adj. 過度的（ = *exceeding* ）
I felt that the punishment was *excessive*.
我覺得這個懲罰太過度了。

字根 cede, ceed

───【 劉毅老師的話 】───

　　無論做什麼事情，都要找出最好的方
法，英文東學一點，西學一點，沒有成就感，
字根一組一組地背，背一組就一組，背多了
又不忘記，累積的力量不得了。

procession[5]
〔 prə'sɛʃən 〕

n. 行列（＝*parade*）
The funeral *procession* moved slowly through the streets. 送葬隊伍緩緩在街道前進。

process[3]
〔'prɑsɛs 〕

n. 過程（＝*procedure*）
v. 加工；處理（＝*handle*）
They hoped to find an answer by a *process* of elimination. 他們希望透過刪去的過程找出答案。

processor
〔'prɑsɛsɚ 〕

n. 處理器
My computer *processor* isn't working properly.
我電腦的處理器無法正常運作。

proceeding[4]
〔 prə'sidɪŋ 〕

n. 行動；活動（＝*event*）
The Mayor will open the *proceedings* at the City Hall tomorrow.
市長明天將在市政廳為這些活動揭開序幕。

proceeds
〔'prosidz 〕

n. pl. 收益（＝*profits*）
The *proceeds* of today's celebrity auction will be donated to charity.
這場名人拍賣會的收益將捐贈給慈善機構。
*這個字只有複數型。

* proceed 的衍生字，先背 cess 的三個；最後再背 ceed 的兩個。

────【劉毅老師的話】────

只要下定決心，鎖定目標，不怕失敗，
堅持到底，沒有什做不成功的事。

字根 cede, ceed

🖌 *Exercise* : Choose the correct answer. ✦

1. The warring nations agreed to a ＿＿＿＿＿ of hostilities.
   (A) conception
   (B) cessation
   (C) construction
   (D) competition

2. Bangladesh ＿＿＿＿＿ from Pakistan in 1971.
   (A) seeded
   (B) seethed
   (C) seemed
   (D) seceded

3. John was a teenager when his hairline began to ＿＿＿＿＿.
   (A) repress
   (B) reprimand
   (C) recede
   (D) receive

4. Sally refused to ＿＿＿＿＿ her mistakes.
   (A) concede
   (B) contrive
   (C) conceptualize
   (D) condition

5. The singer ＿＿＿＿＿ to requests for an encore performance.
   (A) accepted
   (B) availed
   (C) acceded
   (D) avowed

6. Most English adjectives ＿＿＿＿＿ the noun they modify.
   (A) prohibit
   (B) punctuate
   (C) prevail
   (D) precede

7. Political conflict in the region resulted in renewed calls for ＿＿＿＿＿ from the Union.
   (A) submission
   (B) secession
   (C) secretion
   (D) subrogation

8. Only high officials have ＿＿＿＿＿ to the president.
   (A) acceptance
   (B) absence
   (C) account
   (D) access

9. Many people start their own home-based businesses during a
   _____.
   (A) repetition　　　　　　(B) requisition
   (C) registration　　　　　(D) recession

10. The decision has been made, so there's no need for _____
    discussion.
    (A) exceptional　　　　　(B) expressible
    (C) exponential　　　　　(D) excessive

11. The events _____ World War II are closely tied to the rise
    of Fascism.
    (A) preparing　　　　　　(B) prevailing
    (C) presenting　　　　　(D) preceding

12. He was late for school three times in _____.
    (A) succession　　　　　(B) successive
    (C) success　　　　　　(D) successful

13. Young drivers have a tendency to _____ the speed limits.
    (A) exceed　　　　　　　(B) explain
    (C) except　　　　　　　(D) expose

14. Thanks to the Internet, more information is _____ than
    ever before.
    (A) accusable　　　　　　(B) acceptable
    (C) accessible　　　　　(D) accountable

15. Male baldness is believed to be caused by a _____ gene
    which is passed down from the maternal grandfather.
    (A) recessive　　　　　　(B) repetitive
    (C) reposition　　　　　(D) resignation

字根 cede, ceed

字彙測驗詳解

1. (**B**) 交戰的國家同意<u>停止</u>戰爭。
   - (A) conception〔kən'sɛpʃən〕*n.* 概念
   - (B) ***cessation***〔sɛ'seʃən〕*n.* 停止
   - (C) construction〔kən'strʌkʃən〕*n.* 建造
   - (D) competition〔ˌkɑmpə'tɪʃən〕*n.* 競爭
   - hostility〔hɑs'tɪlətɪ〕*n.* 敵意；(*pl.*)交戰

2. (**D**) 孟加拉於一九七一年<u>脫離</u>巴基斯坦。
   - (A) seed〔sid〕*v.* 播種
   - (B) seethe〔sið〕*v.* 煮沸
   - (C) seem〔sim〕*v.* 似乎
   - (D) ***secede***〔si'sid〕*v.* 脫離
   - Bangladesh〔ˌbæŋglə'dɛʃ〕*n.* 孟加拉
   - Pakistan〔ˌpækɪ'stæn〕*n.* 巴基斯坦

3. (**C**) 當約翰還是青少年時，髮際線就開始<u>後退</u>。
   - (A) repress〔rɪ'prɛs〕*v.* 鎮壓
   - (B) reprimand〔'rɛprəˌmænd〕*v.* 斥責
   - (C) ***recede***〔rɪ'sid〕*v.* 後退
   - (D) receive〔rɪ'siv〕*v.* 收到
   - hairline〔'hɛrˌlaɪn〕*n.* 髮際線

4. (**A**) 莎莉拒絕<u>承認</u>她的錯誤。
   - (A) ***concede***〔kən'sid〕*v.* 承認
   - (B) contrive〔kən'traɪv〕*v.* 圖謀
   - (C) conceptualize〔kən'sɛptʃuəlˌaɪz〕*v.* 概念化
   - (D) condition〔kən'dɪʃən〕*n.* 情況

5. (**C**) 那位歌手<u>同意</u>安可表演的請求。
   - (A) accept〔ək'sɛpt〕*v.* 接受
   - (B) avail〔ə'vel〕*v.* 有用
   - (C) ***accede***〔æk'sid〕*v.* 同意
   - (D) avow〔ə'vau〕*v.* 坦白承認
   - encore〔'ɑŋkor〕*n.* 安可；再一次的表演

6. (**D**) 大部分的英文形容詞會<u>在</u>它們所修飾的名詞<u>前面</u>。

    (A) prohibit〔proˈhɪbɪt〕*v.* 禁止

    (B) punctuate〔ˈpʌŋktʃʊˌet〕*v.* 給…加標點符號

    (C) prevail〔prɪˈvel〕*v.* 盛行

    (D) *precede*〔prɪˈsid〕*v.* 在…之前

    adjective〔ˈædʒɪktɪv〕*n.* 形容詞　　noun〔naʊn〕*n.* 名詞
    modify〔ˈmɑdəˌfaɪ〕*v.* 修飾

7. (**B**) 這個地區的政治衝突再度引起要<u>脫離</u>聯邦的聲浪。

    (A) submission〔sʌbˈmɪʃən〕*n.* 服從

    (B) *secession*〔sɪˈsɛʃən〕*n.* 脫離

    (C) secretion〔sɪˈkriʃən〕*n.* 隱藏

    (D) subrogation〔ˌsʌbrəˈgeʃən〕*n.* 取代

    renewed〔rɪˈnjud〕*adj.* 重新開始的　　Union〔ˈjunjən〕*n.* 聯邦

8. (**D**) 只有高級官員才能<u>接近</u>總統。

    (A) acceptance〔əkˈsɛptəns〕*n.* 接受

    (B) absence〔ˈæbsn̩s〕*n.* 缺席

    (C) account〔əˈkaʊnt〕*n.* 帳戶

    (D) *access*〔ˈæksɛs〕*n.* 接近或使用權

9. (**D**) 很多人在經濟<u>不景氣</u>期間開創自己的家庭事業。

    (A) repetition〔ˌrɛpɪˈtɪʃən〕*n.* 重複

    (B) requisition〔ˌrɛkwəˈzɪʃən〕*n.* 需要；徵購

    (C) registration〔ˌrɛdʒɪˈstreʃən〕*n.* 登記

    (D) *recession*〔rɪˈsɛʃən〕*n.* 不景氣

    home-based *adj.* 家庭的

10. (**D**) 已做了決定，所以不需要<u>過度的</u>討論。

    (A) exceptional〔ɪkˈsɛpʃənl̩〕*adj.* 例外的；異常的

    (B) expressible〔ɪkˈsprɛsəbl̩〕*adj.* 可表達的

    (C) exponential〔ˌɛkspoˈnɛnʃəl〕*adj.* 【數學】指數的

    (D) *excessive*〔ɪkˈsɛsɪv〕*adj.* 過度的

字根 cede, ceed

11. (**D**) 第二次世界大戰<u>之前</u>的這些事件，和法西斯主義的崛起有密切的關連。

    (A) prepare〔prɪˈpɛr〕v. 準備   (B) prevail〔prɪˈvel〕v. 盛行
    (C) present〔prɪˈzɛnt〕v. 呈現
    (D) *precede*〔prɪˈsid〕v. 在…之前
    be tied to 和～有關   rise〔raɪz〕n. 升起；發跡；發生
    Fascism〔ˈfæʃˌɪzəm〕n. 法西斯主義

12. (**A**) 他<u>連續</u>三次上學遲到。

    (A) *succession*〔səkˈsɛʃən〕n. 繼承；連續
    (B) successive〔səkˈsɛsɪv〕adj. 連續的
    (C) success〔səkˈsɛs〕n. 成功
    (D) successful〔səkˈsɛsfəl〕adj. 成功的

13. (**A**) 年輕的駕駛人會有<u>超越</u>速限的傾向。

    (A) *exceed*〔ɪkˈsid〕v. 超越
    (B) explain〔ɪkˈsplen〕v. 解釋
    (C) except〔ɪkˈsɛpt〕v. 除去
    (D) expose〔ɪkˈspoz〕v. 暴露

14. (**C**) 由於網際網路，<u>可取得的</u>資訊比以前多了。

    (A) accusable〔əˈkjuzəbḷ〕adj. 可指責的
    (B) acceptable〔əkˈsɛptəbḷ〕adj. 可接受的
    (C) *accessible*〔əkˈsɛsəbḷ〕adj. 可取得的
    (D) accountable〔əˈkauntəbḷ〕adj. 可說明的
    thanks to 由於   ***than ever before*** 比以前

15. (**A**) 一般相信，男性的禿頭是由外公遺傳下來的一個<u>隱性</u>基因造成的。

    (A) *recessive*〔rɪˈsɛsɪv〕adj. 隱性的
    (B) repetitive〔rɪˈpɛtɪtɪv〕adj. 重複的
    (C) reposition〔ˌripəˈzɪʃən〕n. 儲藏
    (D) resignation〔ˌrɛzɪgˈneʃən〕n. 辭職
    baldness〔ˈbɔldnɪs〕n. 禿頭   maternal〔məˈtɝnḷ〕adj. 母親的

字根 cede, ceed

請連中文一起背，背至65秒內，終生不忘。　★

1

cede	放棄
secede	脫離
accede	同意
recede	後退
precede	在…之前
concede	承認
antecede	在…之前
intercede	調停
retrocede	歸還

2

cession	讓與
cessionary	受讓人
cessation	停止
secession	脫離
secessionism	脫離主義
seceder	脫離者
accession	就任
accessible	可取得的
access	接近或使用權

3

recession	不景氣
recessionary	衰退的
recessive	隱性的
preceding	先前的
precedence	領先
precedency	領先
precedent	先例
precedented	有先例的
unprecedented	空前的
concession	讓步
concessionary	讓步的
concessive	讓步的

字根 cede, ceed

4

antecedent	祖先
antecedence	優先
antecessor	先行者
intercessor	調停者
intercession	調停
retrocession	歸還

5

succeed	成功
exceed	超越
proceed	前進

success	成功
successful	成功的
successfully	成功地
succession	繼承
successive	連續的
successor	繼承人

exceeding	過度的
excess	過度
excessive	過度的

procession	行列
process	過程
processor	處理器
proceeding	行動
proceeds	收益

字根 cede, ceed

【劉毅老師的話】

　　你的小孩如果太小，不要強迫他背。你可以面對著他練習背，你背不下來時，說不定他會提醒你。

INDEX・索引

※ 背完本書後，可利用索引來檢視背誦的效果。

INDEX・索引

INDEX · 索引

高三同學要如何準備「升大學考試」

　　考前該如何準備「學測」呢？「劉毅英文」的同學很簡單，只要熟讀每次的模考試題就行了。每一份試題都在7000字範圍內，就不必再背7000字了，從後面往前複習，越後面越重要，一定要把最後10份試題唸得滾瓜爛熟。根據以往的經驗，詞彙題絕對不會超出7000字範圍。每年題型變化不大，只要針對下面幾個大題準備即可。

準備「詞彙題」最佳資料：

背了再背，背到滾瓜爛熟，讓背單字變成樂趣。

考前不斷地做模擬試題就對了！

你做的題目愈多，分數就愈高。不要忘記，每次參加模考前，都要背單字、背自己所喜歡的作文。考壞不難過，勇往直前，必可得高分！

練習「模擬試題」，可參考「學習出版公司」最新出版的「7000字學測試題詳解」。我們試題的特色是：
①以「高中常用7000字」為範圍。 ②經過外籍專家多次校對，不會學錯。③每份試題都有詳細解答，對錯答案均有明確交待。

「克漏字」如何答題

第二大題綜合測驗（即「克漏字」），不是考句意，就是考簡單的文法。當四個選項都不相同時，就是考句意，就沒有文法的問題；當四個選項單字相同、字群排列不同時，就是考文法，此時就要注意到文法的分析，大多是考連接詞、分詞構句、時態等。「克漏字」是考生最弱的一環，你難，別人也難，只要考前利用這種答題技巧，勤加練習，就容易勝過別人。

準備「綜合測驗」（克漏字）可參考「學習出版公司」最新出版的「7000字克漏字詳解」。

本書特色：

1. 取材自大規模考試，英雄所見略同。
2. 不超出7000字範圍，不會做白工。
3. 每個句子都有文法分析。一目了然。
4. 對錯答案都有明確交待，列出生字，不用查字典。
5. 經過「劉毅英文」同學實際考過，效果極佳。

「文意選填」答題技巧

在做「文意選填」的時候，一定要冷靜。你要記住，一個空格一個答案，如果你不知道該選哪個才好，不妨先把詞性正確的選項挑出來，如介詞後面一定是名詞，選項裡面只有兩個名詞，再用刪去法，把不可能的選項刪掉。也要特別注意時間的掌控，已經用過的選項就劃掉，以免重複考慮，浪費時間。

準備「文意選填」，可參考「學習出版公司」最新出版的「7000字文意選填詳解」。

特色與「7000字克漏字詳解」相同，不超出7000字的範圍，有詳細解答。

「閱讀測驗」的答題祕訣

① 尋找關鍵字——整篇文章中，最重要就是第一句和最後一句，第一句稱為主題句，最後一句稱為結尾句。每段的第一句和最後一句，第二重要，是該段落的主題句和結尾句。從「主題句」和「結尾句」中，找出相同的關鍵字，就是文章的重點。因為美國人從小被訓練，寫作文要注重主題句，他們給學生一個題目後，要求主題句和結尾句都必須有關鍵字。

② 先看題目、劃線、找出答案、標題號——考試的時候，先把閱讀測驗題目瀏覽一遍，在文章中掃瞄和題幹中相同的關鍵字，把和題目相關的句子，用線畫起來，便可一目了然。通常一句話只會考一題，你畫了線以後，再標上題號，接下來，你找其他題目的答案，就會更快了。

③ 碰到難的單字不要害怕，往往在文章的其他地方，會出現同義字，因為寫文章的人不喜歡重覆，所以才會有難的單字。

④ 如果閱測內容已經知道，像時事等，你就可以直接做答了。

準備「閱讀測驗」，可參考「學習出版公司」最新出版的「7000字閱讀測驗詳解」，本書不超出7000字範圍，每個句子都有文法分析，對錯答案都有明確交待，單字註明級數，不需要再查字典。

「中翻英」如何準備

可參考劉毅老師的「英文翻譯句型講座實況DVD」，以及「文法句型180」和「翻譯句型800」。考前不停地練習中翻英，翻完之後，要給外籍老師改。翻譯題做得越多，越熟練。

「英文作文」怎樣寫才能得高分？

① 字體要寫整齊，最好是印刷體，工工整整，不要塗改。

② 文章不可離題，尤其是每段的第一句和最後一句，最好要有題目所說的關鍵字。

③ 不要全部用簡單句，句子最好要有各種變化，單句、複句、合句、形容詞片語、分詞構句等，混合使用。

④ 不要忘記多使用轉承語，像*at present*（現在），*generally speaking*（一般說來），*in other words*（換句話說），*in particular*（特別地），*all in all*（總而言之）等。

⑤ 拿到考題，最好先寫作文，很多同學考試時，作文來不及寫，吃虧很大。但是，如果看到作文題目不會寫，就先寫測驗題，這個時候，可將題目中作文可使用的單字、成語圈起來，寫作文時就有東西寫了。但千萬記住，絕對不可以抄考卷中的句子，一旦被發現，就會以零分計算。

⑥ 試卷有規定標題，就要寫標題。記住，每段一開始，要內縮5或7個字母。

⑦ 可多引用諺語或名言，並注意標點符號的使用。文章中有各種標點符號，會使文章變得更美。

⑧ 整體的美觀也很重要，段落的最後一行字數不能太少，也不能太多。段落的字數要平均分配，不能第一段只有一、兩句，第二段一大堆。第一段可以比第二段少一點。

準備「英文作文」，可參考「學習出版公司」出版的：